PROMISE OF PASSION

"God, you're gorgeous when you're angry," Hunter rasped, brushing a lock of hair from Sable's face and tucking it behind her ear. The gesture was so casual, so familiar, Sable's anger began to fade. She grasped it before it vanished.

"I still am! Or are you too thick-headed to see that?"

He knocked her hands away and she fell onto his chest, her face inches from his. Sable knew she was in trouble. For there was a sudden promise in his pewter gray eyes; the promise of sensual pleasure, a promise she'd enjoy whatever he had in mind, and the threat that she'd love it.

Suddenly his mouth was on hers, hot and hard, his tongue spearing between her parted lips and Sable was caught, passion's fury driving her hands into his hair to grip fistfuls, her knee drawing up of its own volition. Her mouth rolled back and forth over his, hungrily stealing his breath, her emotions devouring her. She wanted to hate him, give him a permanent reminder of it. Yet at the same time, unbridled excitement coursed through her and she understood the narrow bridge between rage and desire.

Amy J. Fetzer

Thunder
in the Heart

ZEBRA BOOKS
KENSINGTON PUBLISHING CORP.

ZEBRA BOOKS are published by

Kensington Publishing Corp.
475 Park Avenue South
New York, NY 10016

First Printing: April, 1994

Printed in the United States of America

To
My little bits of thunder

Nickolas Robert
and
Zackary Cain

Who stayed on the ground so Mom could soar

Acknowledgments

To
John Scognamiglio
my editor
Thanks for suffering through those 14-hour time delays,
harassing postcards, and my title quibbles with patience and
a terrific sense of humor.
Domo Arigato

Prologue

Tennessee, 1863
Behind Confederate lines

At the faint rustle, Hunter McCracken's head snapped up.

His hand instinctively moved to his gun as keen eyes scanned his surroundings, checking for disturbed growth, a flash of movement, a glimpse of the color gray. The sound of hooves echoed like the drums of death, and he leaped to his feet, vanishing into the dense forest. He ran, his lungs burning as he sucked in humid air, strong legs pulling him deeper into the vegetation. His life depended on his swiftness.

Booted feet darted agilely over rocks and bushes, silent as a deer's step, his long body shifting around thick trees. Branches slapped at his face and throat, leaving ugly welts and scratches behind. Sweat poured down his temples and was a river streaming between his shoulder blades. Hunter forced himself to keep moving.

Twilight was settling over the land when he paused to rest against a tree. The evening offered no relief from the heat, and his buckskins were like oilcloth, smothering in the dampness. Hunter ignored the discomfort, knowing the poorly tanned hide further disguised his presence. Exhausted, he withdrew a piece of jerked beef and bit it hungrily, washing it down with the stale water he hadn't had the chance to freshen or replace. He'd hoped to sleep tonight, but was too close to his objective. He would be there, if luck held, in five days.

Swiping the back of his hand across his mouth, he replaced the canteen, then glanced down, wiggling his toes. Damn if his boots weren't nearly worn through. His feet throbbed from blisters, and his nose told him he was in need of a thorough scrubbing. Sleeping in ditches, on soggy earth, and eating his own meager kills for the past weeks had grown tiresome. Fingering the packet lashed to his side, he pushed away from the tree, adjusting his weapons. If anyone were to see Hunter McCracken now, they would see a determined man, out to do his job or die trying. He hadn't taken two dozen steps before his blood turned cold.

No more than thirty yards into the forest he spotted the yellow glow of a small fire surrounded by the shadowed figures of several men. This must be the supply wagon, he recalled, moving silently, rapidly, searching for the guards and a way around them as he retraced his steps. He was sent to deliver confidential papers, nothing more, not to stop food and medical supplies to the wounded. Hunter didn't want to think of the men he'd killed to get this far.

Hunter moved slowly now, picking his way around the small group, his gaze catching the guards to his left. He felt his way in the dark, cautiously pushing aside a cluster of branches and ducking beneath, careful to release it slowly. He straightened and heard the click of a firing hammer an instant before the cool steel touched his throat.

"Well, looky what I done found." The voice was soft, a twangy drawl. A hardness flashed in Hunter's eyes as his hand moved slowly to the grip of his knife. He couldn't afford to alert the others. "Don't move, bluebelly."

Hunter's heart pounded in his throat, and he swallowed it back. Silently, he prayed for forgiveness. Like a spring uncoiling, Hunter twisted, jamming his hand between the hammer and pin as he sent his blade between the Confederate's ribs. He shoved it upward, jerking the man off his feet, hearing bone crack just as the steel pierced a rebel heart. Gently, Hunter laid the dead man on the ground and without looking at the soldier's face, withdrew his glade, wiping it across his thigh before resheathing it in his boot. Prying his hand loose from the jammed gun, Hunter methodically searched the man for papers, orders, food, and ammunition, pocketing what he found while watching for enemies. He turned to leave. The body's position on the slope caused it to slide, and in the moonlight Hunter saw the face—eyes open with shock, an unleashed scream of pain etched on parted lips, and to his great horror, the smooth, young jaw that had yet to grow whiskers.

Washington D.C.
Five days later

The strawberry roan skidded to a halt, kicking up dust and pebbles as its rider sawed back on the reins and slid smoothly from the saddle. He strode up the crescent shaped steps as if he owned the luxurious mansion. Uncaring of the mud he tracked on the plush carpet, the young officer didn't wait to be announced, just shouldered his way past the uniformed servant, striding toward the small cluster of people gathered near a lavishly set buffet. The commotion he made caused the party guests to gape with wide eyes, his formidable presence eliciting startled gasps from those of delicate constitution.

At the sight of the intruder, Colonel Richard Cavanaugh's features yanked taut and he was already meeting the man halfway, fairly dragging a young woman along with him when she refused to disengage his arm.

The captain halted, his gaze marking some distant point as

he snapped to attention, executed a perfect salute and remained so until it was returned. The room went silent.

Cavanaugh peered closer. "McCracken? Is that you, man?"

A ghost of a smile played across the soldier's lips; then it was gone. "Yes, sir. It is, sir."

"At ease, Captain." The colonel waved, his gaze taking in the changes since he'd last seen the man. "Good God, son, you look a damn sight!"

The slip of fluff dangling on the colonel's arm gasped dramatically, a hand fluttering to her throat. "Papa, please, your language! And I must insist you do this elsewhere. People are staring."

He ignored her.

"What the hell happened to you, son?"

"It's a long story, sir." McCracken's head moved a fraction. The soldiers' eyes met, locked for a split second, then the younger man's returned to stare straight ahead. In that flicker Cavanaugh saw his struggle, heard the screams, smelled the scent of blood, of burning flesh and acrid gunpowder. There was a tainted wildness in the young officer, an honorable man on the brink between his sanity and the insanity of the war.

The woman pouted at being ignored.

"One tale I'm certain I'd like to hear, son."

"If I remember correctly, sir, the Colonel will not give me leave until all has been accounted for."

Cavanaugh grinned, and McCracken held out a thick packet with a poorly bandaged hand.

"Oh, Papa, not tonight!" Indignantly, the colonel's daughter looked between the men and the leather envelope, watching her father accept it. "But it's my birthday!" she wailed in a sulky tone.

"It can't be helped, pumpkin," Cavanaugh replied unsympathetically as he broke the seal and removed the contents. He read.

The girl's accusing gaze sliced to the Captain, her disdain for him and his intrusion obvious. He looked positively barbaric, cloaked in knives, guns, and grime. Wrinkling her nose, she cuddled closer to her father.

"Make him go away, Papa. He's filthy."

McCracken's eyes darkened at the insult.

"Your manners, Sable," her father reminded without looking up.

"And he smells, too," she persisted.

"Sa-ble." She finally heeded his warning tone, snapping open her fan and flapping it vigorously.

Captain McCracken knew exactly what he looked like and didn't need a snotty little chit to remind him of it. Christ, every cut, scratch, crumb of dirt, and drop of sweat that clung to him stung and itched to the point that it took steel willpower not to race out the doors and dive into the nearest puddle. His mother would be mortified that he'd allowed himself to be seen in the company of ladies in such a disgrace, but propriety was the least of his worries. He'd ridden with the devil chomping at his rear since Tennessee. He was tired, starving, hadn't bathed or found the opportunity to shave since he couldn't remember. Yet more than anything, he feared he was about to crack from all he'd seen, all he'd done.

While the colonel read the dispatch, McCracken permitted his gaze to slip briefly over the man's daughter. She was scarcely a woman, really, her body and face still plump with the roundness of a childhood. Yet McCracken couldn't deny there was a great beauty in her that had yet to bloom. It would likely rot on the vine, he thought maliciously, with that nasty tongue of hers. Dressed in a very adult gown she'd no doubt coerced her father into purchasing, the woman-child had spoiled brat pasted on her from the petulant tilt of her chestnut red hair to the annoying tap of her satin-slippered toe. But for all her airs, she had yet to look him in the eye.

The colonel slipped the papers back in the hide envelope and lifted his gaze. McCracken continued to stare straight ahead, wrists crossed and braced at the base of his spine. Exhausted to the point of swaying slightly, the man still observed every rule of military protocol. Amazing, Cavanaugh thought. For the lad's appearance said he'd gone through a blood bath to get here. It also told him Captain McCracken hadn't changed much.

"Follow me, Captain. I need to study these further and write out a dispatch. Hungry?"

McCracken's stomach roared embarrassingly, but the man remained like a painting, frozen.

"Papa!" Sable said before they could depart. Her hands on her hips, her eyes flashed with irritation as they bounced off the dirty Captain.

"Oh, pardon me. Captain Hunter D. McCracken, my youngest daught—"

"That's not what I meant, and you know it!" She hadn't bothered to acknowledge the Captain's bow, mocking though it was. "He's ruining everything!" She lashed an arm at Hunter. "And this is my night!"

Richard Cavanaugh sighed, his gaze asking for sympathy as it briefly met McCracken's over her ribboned head. His shameless pampering of Sable and her sister, Lane, was showing, but he was simply not the man to deny them anything, not since their mother had died.

"I know this is your party, pumpkin," he said gently, taking her hands and placing a kiss there. "But men are dying and I must see to business."

He turned and left her standing alone.

"Dratted war," she pouted, stomping a slender foot, ruining the ladylike picture she presented. She watched her papa, uniformed in his finest, trailed in perfect cadence by that Captain what's-his-name. The sour look evaporated an instant later as a bevy of young soldiers swarmed around her, each eager to hold the Colonel's daughter in their arms for a dance.

Hunter followed the Colonel across the opulent room and

down the hall to his home office. Cavanaugh was right. Men were dying this night. His men.

Hunter felt immeasurably better as he finished off the plate of food and handed the tray to the waiting servant, snatching back the crystal tumbler of whiskey the Colonel had personally offered him. The change of clothes did his pride good. The Colonel's valet had pressed the uniform while he'd bathed and scraped off a good inch of stubble and grime. Hunter sipped his drink, settling his back against a stone column. He'd even danced once with Lane Cavanaugh. As far as Hunter was concerned, she was just an older version of her sister.

Distantly he heard a feminine giggle, a deep coaxing moan, and Hunter grinned, glad some man was feeling the softness of a woman this night.

"I'm leaving tomorrow. Don't do this to me," a masculine voice pleaded. She must have shaken her head for the man's disappointed groan was audible. Damn tease, Hunter thought, sipping his drink. "With respect for you, I must ask you to come back inside."

"Is that what you really want?" she cooed.

"You know I don't, Miss Cavanaugh."

Hunter stiffened, twisting around the pillar to see.

"Then why go?" Her fingers trailed down the man's arm.

"I do not . . . trust . . . myself," the trooper stammered, easing back on the stone bench.

Out of sympathy for the girl's father Hunter cleared his throat—loudly. The young corporal leaped to his feet, smoothing his hair, and even in the darkness Hunter saw the flush of his embarrassment. McCracken gestured curtly with his head.

Displeasure showed in her slight form as Sable rose, watching the trooper's hasty retreat. Her gaze immediately shifted to the porch, and she straightened her shoulders, snapped

13

open a lace fan and waved it slowly beneath her throat. Her hips swayed almost in exaggeration as she strolled closer. Hunter bit back the urge to snicker.

He bowed slightly. "My apologies for intruding on your entertainment again, Miss Cavanaugh."

Her flawless brow creased as she ascended the steps. "Again? Have we met, sir?" she asked, moving close enough for her skirts to brush his calves.

His smile was thin. "You said I was filthy and that I stank."

Recognition dawned and she inhaled sharply. "Oh, dear me!"

Hunter viewed her from beneath half-lidded eyes. "Would you have preferred I'd been your father, just then?" He inclined his head ever so slightly to where she'd been with the corporal.

"Oh, that—it was nothing," she sighed, fanning herself. "I simply needed something to do."

Heartless bitch, Hunter thought, with the sudden urge to crush her fan into dust.

"What you *need,* little girl, is to have those frilly skirts tossed up and your lacy rump paddled," he murmured into his glass, sipping, his gaze focused off in the distance.

"How dare you!" Her delicate hand came up to slap him, but never met its mark, her wrist caught between two long brown fingers. "Papa will have your commission for this!" she hissed.

A raven black brow lifted slowly. "Will he?" She twisted to be free, but his locked fingers may as well have been iron shackles. "You play with fire, Miss Cavanaugh," he snarled softly. "Teasing a man, giving him hope for a little tenderness to remember when he's about to go fight, to fight, I remind, so you're safe enough to celebrate your precious birthday."

"A gentleman would never do anything such as you're suggesting, Captain." Her voice quivered, and Hunter leaned a bit closer.

"Gentlemen respect *ladies,*" he enunciated pointedly, watch-

14

ing her fume. "What would you do, brat, if a man didn't respect you, your daddy, and you taunted his pride until—" Hunter yielded to impulse, something he never did. He yanked her close, giving Sable Cavanaugh her first feel of a man's body pressed solidly to her own. "He simply took."

"No! I didn't mean—oh please, let me go," she cried, and he stilled at the child-like plea. But it was those eyes that did him in. The quick leap of raw fear, wild, like a startled doe's. Lavender eyes. Imagine that. He'd only wanted to scare her, teach her she couldn't play games with grown men while she was still just a girl. But Christ, when she looked at him like that he actually thought of—with a smothered curse, he released her.

"Run, little girl, and stay very close to Papa until you grow up."

Chapter One

1868

It was late, and no one gave the shrouded woman a passing glance as she hustled down the street and vanished into the darkness of an alley. She hoped that all who had seen her would assume she was merely a servant returning home. Yet beneath the threadbare black cloak lay a Worth gown of blue watered silk trimmed in ecru lace and a slim throat draped in ropes of baroque pearls.

She rapped twice. The door immediately opened a crack, yellow light slicing a wedge in the black void. Pulling her skirts close, she stepped over the threshold and was sealed inside.

Upon seeing the hooded figure, three servants ceased their work, set down their utensils and quietly departed.

"Sabella," a male voice whispered, the Italian accent laced with affection. "It has begun, no?"

"*Sì*, Salvatore." Sable Cavanaugh pushed at the hood, allowing it to pool at her shoulders. "I am so sorry to disturb you at this hour." She began to pace nervously. "But she's having such a dreadful labor, and since I am of no constructive use at home—" She paused, her lips twisting wryly, eyes glistening with unshed tears. "Lane threw me out."

16

Salvatore Vaccarello frowned at the self-deprecating remark yet said nothing as he grasped her shoulders to take her cloak, then pushed her toward the long table. Tossing the garment over a chair, he turned away to prepare her a cup of espresso.

With a heavy sigh, Sable slid onto a stool and absently donned an apron. She began chopping, slicing, and brooding over the neat piles of vegetables. Salvatore returned to his seat on the opposite side, placing the cup before her. She smiled her thanks.

"She's changed so much, Salvatore. Why, I actually caught her folding laundry last week!" She shook her head at the thought. "The Lane Cavanaugh I knew would never dream of doing such menial chores." Sable took a dainty sip, savoring the stimulating coffee, then went back to slicing fresh green peppers. "I don't think she likes me very much anymore. We argue over the silliest things. And she constantly reminds me that I'm not much help—at anything."

"You do yourself an injustice, *cara mia*, speaking this way." Salvatore smiled to himself. She was not even aware that she had instinctively known how to prepare each vegetable by the order of the pile. It was something he'd been attempting to teach his assistants for months now.

"There's truth to what she says," Sable admitted grudgingly. She glanced up to catch his reaction but was entranced for a moment as his slim fingers wielded a knife around a chunk of veal. An artist, she thought, amazed, her gaze moving from the pile of meat to the bone scraped clean. "But I can stitch a sampler as well as she," Sable proclaimed in her own defense, yet didn't mention that every shirt she'd attempted appeared as if an octopus had sat for the fitting. "I can give a splendid party, order an army of servants, and dole out duties." *And I still have no knowledge how they do whatever it is they do,* she mused. *I live on the outside, just like Lane said.*

"And you are jealous that she is no longer as spoiled as you are?"

Her head snapped up, eyes narrowing imperceptibly. "What ever for?" She popped a slice of pepper in her mouth, knowing he'd be annoyed. "I like my life just the way it is."

His dark gaze slipped over her, black eyes teasing. "You are a lovely, desirable woman, Sabella. Any man would be pleased to have you as his parlor ornament."

She lifted her nose with an injured air, the remark hitting too close. "I should slap you for that, Signore Vaccarello."

"Then I shall consider myself fortunate that I am on your elite list of friends." He knew she was easily wounded and enjoyed toughening her thin skin. Standing, he carried the platter of meat to a counter near the stove. With his back to her, he breaded the veal, then slid it into the hot oil. He knew what she wanted—reassurance that it was acceptable to be so sedentary.

"What is it that you wish from me, my sweet? To—how do you say—gripe with you?"

"I don't gripe."

"You sulk, you pout, and . . ." Giving a little, he spared her a look over his shoulder. "You are a great help to me, Sabella."

"Oh, come now, Salvatore." She waved disgustedly at the vegetables. "I merely play in your kitchen." Her frown evaporated. "You are the chef." She paused. "And a magnificent one, too."

"You did not think so when first we met."

"Oh, drat! Must you always—" She shook her head ruefully, pearl hair pins shimmering. "Yes, I suppose you must." It was another reminder of how poorly she'd once behaved. "I shall never live that down."

He twisted, grinning at her, white teeth flashing against his olive complexion. "It is not every day an arrogant chef has his prize dish insulted by a—"

"I still say you added too much basil," she cut in before he could insult her as well.

"And I will always disagree."

18

"Stubborn Italian," she muttered and he chuckled to himself, removing the pan from the fire and returning to his seat at the table. That particular evening four years ago, she had delivered her criticism with such finesse he'd hardly felt the bite. Salvatore had invited her into his kitchen to observe the preparation of *osso bucco*—veal shanks—and their secret friendship had blossomed.

He frowned at her, pausing in garnishing the dish. "How did you escape your papa this time?"

Any trace of a smile vanished. "He's been closeted in his study since Lane went into labor. She's being so brave, no tears, no screams, no complaints. I believe that's exactly what Papa would like, so he can throw it back at her."

"Your papa, he is—"

"Angry, Salvatore. Ashamed, embarrassed."

A dark brow lifted. "Did anyone ever tell you that it is impolite to finish another's sentence?"

She covered a gasp with a delicate hand, looking apologetic. *"Mi dispeaci, Signore Vaccarello,"* she said, then stuck out her tongue. He threw his dark head back and laughed heartily, the rich sound singing through the deserted restaurant kitchen. Salvatore was a handsome man, slender, framed with the exotic look of his nationality. He could actually be called pretty, Sable supposed, the silver peppering at his temples giving him an aristocratic look.

When his annoying laughter finally died, he said, "You must consider your Papa's feelings, Sabella. He is a man of honor, and that his daughter is having a child out of wedlock is difficult to endure."

"But Lane *is* married."

"In her eyes and those of the child's father, but not your papa's."

She slid off the stool. "Isn't that what truly matters?" Then she paced a few steps, halting long enough to deliver her most irritated look. "Honestly, must we discuss this again?"

"*Sí*, little one. Your Papa blames himself for her predicament."

"As well he should!" she snapped indignantly, hands on her hips.

Salvatore sighed. Her vision was far too narrow. "Any man would assume ten armed men a sufficient number to protect his daughters. And what of your sister? Did she not do all so *you* could get away?"

Feeling guilty, Sable dropped her gaze, clasping her fidgeting hands. "Yes."

"Did he not search for months for her?"

She glanced up and groaned. He had that lecture look about him. "Of course he did. But she didn't want to come back."

"The thought of her wanting to stay with her kidnapper is unthinkable to him."

"Well," she began in small voice. "It's beyond me too, but it's all she talks about." She sniffed, head bowed dejectedly. "I missed her and worried about her so much, Salvatore, and now all she wants is to leave again."

"Sabella."

She looked up to see him rise, and as if he knew what she needed, he opened his arms. "Oh, Salvatore!" She flew to him. "She's so unhappy, and I don't want her to go away again and don't know what to do, and then there's Papa. He never smiles and never acknowledges the babe's existence."

He smiled over her head. Sabella always babbled when she was upset. "Lane wishes to be with the man she loves." He patted her back. "It is how it should be."

Sable shrugged delicately. "Perhaps. She's not the same woman, Salvatore. And I'm not sure I like it."

"That is not your choice."

She had no retort, and he knew she was feeling left out of something incredible that only the experience itself could fulfill.

After a moment, she leaned back, brushed away a tear,

then lightly kissed his cheek. "You're such a good friend, Signore Vaccarello."

"I am an old man who lives for your charming company."

She laughed softly, reaching past him to grab a slice of warm, crisp veal, deftly eluding his swatting hand. She snatched up the borrowed cloak as she moved to the door, bidding him good night over her shoulder. Regardless of what Lane had said, she needed Sable tonight.

"Push now, honey," Melanie coaxed softly. "You're doin' juzz fine, Missy Lane. Juzz fine."

"Oh mercy, Laney! I can see the baby's head!" Sable gasped over Melanie's shoulder as her sister fought to bring the child forth.

"For goodness sakes, Sable, calm down," Lane said breathlessly when the contraction eased. "And get out of Melanie's way."

Sable hastily stepped aside, poking her tongue out at the slim black housekeeper when Melanie dealt her a superior look.

"I'm trying. Honestly I am," she said contritely, moving to the side of the four-poster bed and falling to a chair. "I gather I haven't been much help?"

Lane smiled her big-sister-forgives-you smile. "Your being here is all I want, Sae." Lane grasped her sister's hand as another contraction twisted her distended body, her grip so fierce it nearly snapped the delicate bones.

"Ouch! Gracious, Laney!" The pain in her fingers was dismissed when Lane seemed to strain forever, grunting, bearing down. Sable bit her lip, her body curling, a sympathetic groan escaping her throat. Lane hadn't made a sound so far, but now, near the end, she let loose a roaring cry, not one of agony, but of triumph. An instant later a wiggling black-haired baby lay in Melanie's capable hands.

"Oh, he's beautiful!" Sable exclaimed, rather shocked that

he truly was. She'd always heard newborns looked like wrinkled prunes. But this baby was plump, round faced, and, well, simply adorable. Sable instantly fell in love with the tiny bundle.

Wrapping the freshly bathed infant in a soft fluffy blanket, Melanie laid the child in his aunt's arms, then swiftly went about making Lane clean and comfortable. Sable waited until Lane was ready to hold her son.

"He is beautiful, isn't he?" Lane murmured, dropping a kiss atop his dark head.

"You done good, Missy Lane," Melanie said proudly. "Real good."

Sable plopped onto the lavender Queen Anne chair, brushing a chestnut lock from her forehead, feeling as though she were the one who had given birth. A boy child. He had his father's hair, obviously, but Sable couldn't know for certain, having never met the man. But he'd have his mother's eyes. The newborn blue already bore the gray tint of Lane's.

"Oh, I wish his father were here," Lane said brokenly, clutching the baby closer. "He'd be so proud."

"Any man would be," Sable remarked enviously, reaching over to stroke a dark curl. "But if he were, be certain Papa would enjoy killing him."

Lane slumped onto the pillows and Sable instantly regretted her thoughtlessness.

"Oh Lane, I'm so sorry," she murmured.

Lane lifted a hand and Sable accepted it, allowing herself to be drawn down onto the bed. Lane brushed aside a fallen lock in a motherly fashion. Sable was so innocent, she thought, so sheltered. "It's all right, Sae. I'm fine. I'll get back to him somehow."

Sable gaped at her. "But you've just had a baby, for heaven's sakes!"

"A matter of nature," Lane replied with an indifferent shrug. "Just as my being with him again is a matter of time."

More and more Sable saw changes in her sister. Big changes that pushed them further apart, made them strangers.

"Papa will never allow it. Not after all he's been through to get you back."

A light came into Lane's eyes that Sable had come to recognize. "To hell with Papa and what he wants! This is my son, and it's my life! When will you see that because of Papa, we've turned out just like Mama?"

Sable stood abruptly. "It's not his fault, Lane. We've let him coddle us, and I, for one, prefer it."

"That's because you've never tired to go beyond it. You know nothing else."

Sable was about to say, "And you do?" but wisely kept her mouth shut. Lane did. She'd been loved by a man, been fought to the death for, swept away with her love for him and now, had given him a son, a future, while Sable sat around, adored by their father and stitching samplers. She wished Lane wasn't always right.

"Papa loves us, Laney."

"I know," she sighed. "But he also protects us to the point of suffocation."

"That's not true. We're allowed rides and parties an—"

"Oh, grow up!" Lane barked, making her flinch. "There is more to life than gowns and parties."

Sable folded her arms beneath her breasts. "I suppose now you'll recite how wonderful it is to run around half naked, eating nuts and berries."

"Miss Sable," Melanie interrupted when she saw the battle growing between siblings. "Maybe you best go sees where yo' Papa be keepin' hisself. Ought to be mighty curious 'bout his grandson," she stated, returning the conversation to the baby, the buffer.

The argument fizzled out of Sable when her eyes drifted to the child suckling at his mother's breast. Her nephew had his tiny fingers curled around her heart, and a tear crept into her eye. He had a right to know his father, just as Lane had the

23

same right to choose her own life. No matter how bizarre it seemed to Sable. Her gaze swept up to meet her sister's and the apology was relayed without words.

"I'll go fetch Papa."

The scream of pain echoed through the house, bleeding through the polished wood walls, seeping into the pores of Richard Cavanaugh's tall uniformed body. It left the seasoned soldier drained, and with one hand he grasped the desk edge to steady himself, with the other he brought a tumbler full of twenty-year-old sour mash to his lips, draining it without stopping. He trembled, rage and sympathy blending furiously within the colonel. He wanted to kill the son of a bitch who had done this to his daughter, shaming her, forcing her to deliver the man's bastard. He had yet to recover when he heard the cry of the child, and he was filled again with a strange mix of emotions. Was it a boy or girl? Was it healthy? Dear God, was Lane even alive?

Richard wanted the man's head on a platter.

A knock sounded and Richard snarled for whoever it was to get inside. Corporal Johansen brushed past the maid and snapped to attention, saluting sharply.

Tersely, Cavanaugh returned the salute, then barked, "Well!"

"At this time, sir, I've been unable—"

"Damn," Richard cursed, running his hand over the top of his gray head. "How difficult is it, in a city this size?" Johansen started to speak but was cut off again with, "All I want is a woman to take it away."

It, Johansen thought. *He refers to his grandbaby as an it.* This was not like the colonel. He was usually quite compassionate. Johansen respected Colonel Cavanaugh, admired him. The man was a war hero, instrumental in ending the Southern Rebellion, but the Brass Bear was going over the edge now. Sworn to secrecy, the young corporal prided himself in being taken into the colonel's confidence, but he was having doubts about his involvement now. Carl Johansen wanted to tell someone, wanted to stop this madness.

"Your orders, sir?"

Richard looked up, bleary-eyed and haggard. He sighed heavily, the past year showing on his tanned features. "Keep trying, Johansen," Cavanaugh whispered. The trooper nodded, saluted, then spun on his heels, yet before he reached the door he heard, "And thank you, son."

Richard stared at the tumbler, sloshed in more liquor, continued to examine the contents. He was doing the right thing. It was best for Lane. Hadn't he done his damndest to see her spared the ridicule, the gossip? Hadn't he left his post at Fort McPherson and brought the girls back here? Hadn't he seen every man who had witnessed her return and her loud demands to be sent back rapidly dispersed so talk would die? Christ, if the child were so much as seen she'd be ruined. Yes, it was best to bury matter, he tried to convince himself. She'd endured so much already. Caroline would agree if she were here. He stared at her portrait suspended over the mantle. No woman should suffer that kind of humiliation.

He was doing this for her.

Sable Cavanaugh plastered herself against the wall near the stairs when the door to her Papa's study flew open. She remained frozen until the trooper departed, unable to believe what she'd heard. *Oh, Papa! How can you do this? How can you look Lane in the face and tell her you're giving away her son?* A sudden thought hit Sable. He hadn't planned on doing that. He was going to abscond with the child and then tell her. Sable turned and fled up the stairs and into her sister's room. She slammed the door and fell back against it.

"What happened? What's the matter?" her sister demanded when she saw the horror on her face. Sable chewed her lip, unable to look at her. "Tell me!"

Her gaze flashed up. "Papa's going to give the baby away!" she blurted tactlessly.

"That beast!" Lane gasped, clutching the child so close he cried out at the poor treatment. She soothed him, patting him gently.

"Wha'cha gonna do, Missy Lane?" Melanie asked suddenly from the bedside.

"Oh, what can she do?" Sable cried, pushing away from the door and coming to the foot of the bed. "We can't defy him, Lane. He's our father."

Lane stroked her son's cheek, her voice calm, steady. "I have to get my son to his father."

"What!" Sable gawked, eyes wide. "Be serious, Lane. You can't travel for weeks!"

"Not me." There was a trace of a smile. "You."

Sable's eyes widened until they absorbed her face. Her gaze shot between her sister and the housekeeper. Hot panic swept over her. They looked too much like a garrison ready to wage war. "Impossible. Tell her it's impossible," she begged of Melanie. When the old woman's craggy brown features pulled into a smile, Sable put up her hands to stop the ludicrous thought. "I can not, will not, do it! No, no, no, no, no!" She shook her head for emphasis. "We'll just have to delay this until you can travel. That's all there is to it." Sable folded her arms beneath her breasts, nodding nervously, satisfied with her brilliant solution. "I'll be more than willing to aid you then."

"But that will be weeks. Can't you see what he's capable of now?"

But I'm not capable, Sable thought wildly, *not of taking this child halfway across the country. I'm not.* She'd been privately schooled in the northeast, and her most recent adventure to the west last spring proved to be an utter disaster, the baby the result. She'd never traveled alone, never been without female companionship, or at least a military escort or two. She didn't know anything about caring for a child, especially one so

26

young. Her charity work consisted of delivering food and medicines and leaving their application to more experienced hands. She examined her fingers—slim, smooth. Useless.

Sable lifted her head, a tear trickling down a rosy cheek. "I can't, Lane. I wish I could, but I simply can't."

Lane's gaze dug into her sister's. "You owe me, Sable."

Drat her and those telling eyes, Sable thought.

In one fleeting moment during that afternoon ride last spring outside Fort McPherson, Lane had proven her love for her sister. The Sioux attack was swift and heated and while Sable was in a hysterical panic, Lane shoved her toward the only horse left standing while she grabbed up a fallen soldier's gun to protect her retreat. But she was out of bullets and a warrior, painted, savage, and determined, swooped down, struck Lane unconscious, then threw her over the neck of his horse. Whether Lane's tactics made a difference at the time remained a mystery, but she was kidnapped—while Sable fled to safety. *And she's suffered incredible heartache because of it,* Sable thought, *while my life has scarcely changed at all.*

Just then the door burst open, banging against the opposite wall. Richard Cavanaugh filled the doorway, the top three brass buttons of his uniform opened, a glass of whiskey wobbling in loose fingers. He looked wildly about the room, his watery gaze seeking out the babe. Sable moved protectively closer to the bed. She'd never seen her father like this, unkempt, unshaven, besotted. She glanced fearfully between her sister and her sire.

"Come to see your grandson, Papa?"

Sable was amazed at her sister's composure.

A boy, he thought, and for a brief moment pride made him stand a touch straighter. Then he saw the jet black hair, and his rage returned like a clap of thunder. He lashed an arm toward the infant. "That—that—" God, he couldn't even say it, "is not my grandchild."

Lane flinched, tears wet her eyes, but she refused to let him

27

see how much that hurt. "He's my flesh and blood, Papa. That makes him—"

"The devil's spawn," he snarled, taking a step inside, unable to break his gaze from the child.

"Papa!" Sable cried, horrified, clutching his arm when he continued to bear down on mother and child. "Stop this! Lane has been through enough!"

He looked down at her. "I know she has, pumpkin." Sable wanted to slap him for smiling. "And I'm going to see that she doesn't suffer again." Sable recoiled; the determination in his expression stunned her. He spun about, leaving them to stare at the empty doorway.

Something new and strange rose up in Sable Cavanaugh just then, making her chin lift and her elegantly clad shoulders pull back. From that moment, everyone in the room knew the pampered debutante would deliver her nephew to his father—the Sioux war chief, Black Wolf.

Chapter Two

"You want me to do what?!" Laughter rang with the question throughout the smoke-filled saloon. "What horse choo fall off 'a, lady?" Another burst of deep chuckles.

Sable's lips pulled into a thin line and her eyes narrowed. This was the same reaction she'd had in every establishment ventured into since dawn.

"I apologize." She leaned a bit closer. "Perhaps you're deaf, sir?" The burly man's humor instantly died. "I do believe I enunciated clearly. I said—" she raised her voice a fraction—"I wish to contract your services to guide me to the Dakotas."

The man gave her a sideways glare. "I ain't deaf, an' I ain't gonna do it!" He ran a beefy hand over his bearded face. "Damnation, ma'am. Ain't no man around here with a lick 'a sense gonna take a white woman, 'specially one lookin' like you, to them savages!"

This was an obstacle Sable hadn't considered when she left home weeks ago. Getting away had been her only concern; keeping her nephew fed, adequately clothed, and safe was her priority now. "I'll pay you handsomely," she persisted.

"It ain't enough!" He turned his back on her and drained the shot of whiskey.

Sable grasped his arm. "You must help me."

He looked down at her hand, pale and delicate and soft as

a kitten's underside, contrasting so sharply with his dirty sleeve. He considered her and her proposition. "Why you want go to those murderin' bastards?"

Sable's cheeks colored at the vulgarity and she snatched back her hand, resisting the urge to run somewhere and wash. "That is my business."

"It be mine, if'n I'm takin' ya."

Her face brightened. "You will?"

"Nope."

Sable smothered the urge to slap him for getting her hopes up, even for the brief moment. She glanced at the men surrounding her. No one was accepting her offer. In fact, as in the other five taverns, they were leering at her as if she were lying on a silver platter with an apple in her mouth.

"Then I thank you for your time, sir, and bid you good evening."

She grasped her skirts, lifting them a touch, unaware of how many libidos she sent humming with the frilly display, and turned to leave, only to find her path barred by several rather odorous males. Gracious! Did no one bathe in this town, she wondered, lifting a perfumed hanky to her nose.

"Please, allow me passage," she said softly, the panic rising in her voice.

"I'll take yah, darlin'," a thin man leered. "If'n payment's a night 'neath them lacy skirts."

Sable gasped at the insult. Men chuckled as they moved closer.

Frightened, she looked down at the floor, wrapping her ermine stole tightly. "Please! I beg you."

"Let the lady pass, boys," a rough masculine voice said from somewhere beyond the circle.

The group reluctantly parted, yet Sable couldn't tell from where the quiet command had come. She looked around to offer her thanks, but could see only a man's boots propped on a table, buckskinned legs disappearing into the darkened corner, and one of those painted trollops rubbing her bare foot along its length. Sable knew her face was as red as the harlot's lip rouge, and when no one came forward, she welcomed her good fortune and made a hasty exit, head bowed and lacy petticoats rustling.

The tinkling of a piano drew the revelry back to its normal din as the patrons sought out livelier companionship than the lady in green brocade.

In a far corner Hunter McCracken gulped a slug of whiskey straight from the bottle, then slowly swiped the back of his hand across his lips, unable to take his eyes from the elegant woman's rapidly vanishing profile. He didn't know what she was doing in here, and he didn't care. But he already knew she was a damned idiot to walk into this place dressed so lavishly. Ought to consider herself lucky to get out untouched. That delicate creature was about as out of place here as a whore like Molly would be at a charity picnic. He chuckled at the image, drawing a startled look from more than one person. Only his eyes shifted as the lady's skirts disappeared beneath the batwing doors, then he dismissed her from his mind, drawing the whore onto his lap. His calloused hands slid beneath the folds of her skirt, finding her warm and soft and willing to please. He'd been in the hills too damn long this time. He'd make Molly here, a rich woman by morning. Tired, but rich.

Sable grasped the wood post outside the saloon to catch her breath, her heart hammering like a train engine. Lane had simply chosen the wrong person for this adventure. She glanced back over her shoulder into the saloon and noticed two rough-looking men leering at her from the doorway. She spun away, dainty heeled boots clicking as she moved swiftly down the wood walk toward her hotel, hoping she didn't draw any more attention to herself. How many vulgar little towns have I been in? How many times have I been treated so crudely? She entered the hotel lobby and tiredly mounted the stairs, finding the proprietor's wife on the top landing.

"What are you doing out here?" she demanded sharply, quickly ascending the stairs. "Where's my baby?!"

Etta Clarkson's grin was smug as she looked down her bulbous nose at Sable. "The little savage is back there." She gestured with her head down the hallway. Sable didn't hear the remark because she was already running down the corridor pulling out her key. Jerking open the door, she fearfully scanned the room for the baby. In the faint light of the hall lamp, she saw him, snuggled in the center of the bed. She sagged against the frame with relief. Assuring herself he was unharmed, she closed the door and chased after the sitter.

"I paid you good coin not to leave him!" Sable snapped, closing on the woman's heels. "What kind of creature are you to leave a newborn alone?"

"I ain't wet nursing no half-breed bastard." Sable sucked in breath, eyes round. "Left that little detail out, din'cha, honey?" Missus Clarkson shoved her chubby face into Sable's. Fat tub of pig lard, Sable thought maliciously as the woman folded her arms around her rotund middle. "And my man ain't gonna like it neither, so you best pack your bags and git!"

Sable lifted her chin, rage blending with the urge to see if this bovine madam would pop if she stuck her with a hat pin. "You needn't bother. I shall leave within the hour." She gulped, gathering courage in anger. "And be certain I'll spread far and wide the news of the—of the—the unlaundered sheets and maggot-laced menu of this establishment!"

Missus Clarkson's head yanked back indignantly. Sable spun about and marched to her room, truly surprised at her own boldness. She waited until she'd closed the door before allowing herself to cry.

It was the same everywhere she went, she agonized, covering her face with her hands and releasing her misery. On the train trip she'd paid for a private berth but was forced to sleep in the immigrant coach, with a hundred other bodies of varied sizes and scents, when word leaked of the child's parentage. Refused room after room, meal after meal, in four separate towns, it was becoming increasingly difficult to find someone trustworthy enough to care for her nephew while she looked for a guide. She had not one prospect. Dropping her head, she let the tears pour freely. *I am no closer to Black Wolf than Lane was in Washington.*

To make matters worse, she'd fled one town outside Fort Leavenworth when she saw a cavalry officer who looked familiar. Sable never doubted for an instant that Papa would come searching for her and Little Hawk.

The boy stirred, cooing softly, and Sable pushed away from the door, wiping her cheeks. Lighting a lamp, she began to pack. It was routine now. She still didn't know what to do once she found a guide. Where would they sleep tonight? And what of milk for the baby? And clean clothing? Changing diapers had been a new experience, and she abhorred the task each time. All babies do is mess and eat, she decided. Little Hawk fussed, and she stopped, sitting gently on the bed.

"Are you hungry, little man?" She rubbed his bare belly. "Is that tummy empty, or are you just up for some polite conversation?" He gurgled, making bubbles, his eyes wide and bright with wonder, tiny arms and legs wiggling. Sable smiled, wrapping the blanket more securely against the cold, then laying down beside him.

She'd assumed the identity of his mother, hoping to avoid crude prying questions, yet when it came to the Indians, white people lost all proper manners. She'd been treated deplorably since she left home. Yet all she had to do was remember that Lane would be on the receiving end of the ridicule, the shoves off the walk, the stares, whispers, and pointing fingers, and Sable gathered the will to go on. She nuzzled the baby's soft coppery skin, cuddling him close.

Lane had entrusted her with the most precious thing in her life, and Sable was determined not to let her sister down.

Two days later Sable was ready to give up. With the baby lashed to her body in a makeshift sling fashioned from a crocheted shawl, she struggled with the heavy steamer trunk, dragging it down the walk and pulling it into an alley. She plopped down on the top with a deflated sigh, then adjusted the baby to a more comfortable position. She was tired, cold, hungry, smelly from sour milk and Little Hawk's urine. Her traveling suit, which was once a lovely navy wool, now hung limply from her shoulders, a tattered, dusty mess. Why, last night she actually slept in an ox cart! Her back ached from that and carrying Little Hawk, but she didn't dare trust another person with his care. Once Missus Clarkson had opened her blabby mouth, word traveled fast, and Sable was denied a room even in the seediest hotel, not to mention a seat in this town's poorest restaurant. Her money had not made a wit of difference. As far as anyone was concerned, she was a woman with an Indian lover. That stung more than a hundred male prides at once. She fingered the list of names, then in a fit, tore the paper to shreds and watched the wind take it out to the street.

Never in her life had she been treated like this. Not once in her twenty years did she have to ask for the simplest of things, and *never* had a bath and clean sheets been more on her mind. She was tempted several times to inform the blackhearts of exactly who she was, but wisely refrained. She wasn't far enough away yet, and that bit of news would send Papa and his cavalry here before dawn. Sable brushed a lock back and attempted to make her coiffure more presentable when a door abruptly opened. She turned her head in time to be hit square in the face with a tub full of dirty water. The baby whimpered, startled, and absently she patted him as she sat on the trunk, dripping wet.

Chapter Three

"Uh-oh." The slender boy gulped, then hollered, "Momma!" over his shoulder. He looked back at the lady. "Momma! Come quick!"

Wiping her hands on a soiled apron, a tall, sturdy red-haired woman of about forty came up behind him, peering over her son's head at the sopping sight. "Land sakes, Eli!" She rushed around him. "What have you done?"

"I didn't see her, I swear," he defended, trotting at her heels.

She rounded on the boy, making him jump back to avoid crashing into her. "You better not swear! Now git inside an' git me a blanket." The fourteen-year-old obeyed instantly, and Phoebe Benson turned back, kneeling before the woman. "Are you all right, Miss?"

Hunched over, Sable shuddered, her lip quivering. She wanted her sister. She wanted to be in her own room, safe and warm, and mostly she wanted her papa to be the kind, considerate man he once was and come get her, hold her, and tell her he would make it all better again. But that wasn't going to happen. It was like a slow squall. Short choking sounds came first, then a second or two of stilted squeals when she tried to hold back the tears. Then it burst, the storm of hopelessness crashing into pitiful wails, her weary shoulders shaking with the force.

35

Little Hawk cried in unison.

"Lord, a baby, too!" Phoebe whispered, pulling the woman off the trunk and ushering her toward the door. "Come on, Miss. It's all right now. Don't cry."

Sable couldn't speak, the tears were coming too fast. She allowed the woman to help her inside.

Phoebe gently maneuvered her into a chair.

"Eli, the blanket!" Red-haired Eli flew around the doorway, and his mother snatched the quilt, wrapping it around the woman. She knelt down, checking the girl for injuries as she said, "Git me a basket, Eli, another blanket, and some sheets and towels, the good ones."

"What for?"

Without looking up she said, "She's got a baby tied to her."

Eli's dark eyes widened, and he raced to do as she bid. "And git your brothers in here!" she called after him, brushing a dripping lock from the woman's face. Her costly garments didn't escape Phoebe's notice. "It's okay, honey. You're gonna be fine." Sable cried harder, and Phoebe's heart went out to the pitiful thing. "Let me take the baby," she said gently over the sobbing, trying to extract the screaming child from its mother.

"No!" Sable cried, clutching Little Hawk tighter, her eyes wild.

"All right. I won't touch him. I promise." Phoebe understood fear. "Why don't you tell me your name?"

"Sable," she wailed. "Sable Cav—" She stopped midsentence, her gaze flying to the woman's face.

Phoebe ignored it. "I'm Phoebe Benson, Sable."

Sable sniffled juicily, working a hand out of the quilt and offering it. "I'm pleased to make your acquaintance, madame."

Phoebe stared at the delicate hand, shocked for a second, then shook it gently. Tucking the blanket, she asked, "How did you end up in my alley?"

Sable peered into the kindly face, seeing the first measure of sympathy since she'd left Washington. The past weeks flooded back, and what was left of her composure disinte-grated, a river of tears spilling down her cheeks, soaking her further.

"Oh, it's been simply awful. Papa was so hateful, and Lane needed me. I told her I couldn't do it. But she wouldn't listen. I tried, honestly I did." She beseeched Phoebe to believe her. "And the baby, he's been so good, and I love him, but I don't know what I'm doing, and if it's the right thing, and then the train passengers were so ug-ly to me." Her lip quivered. "They actually spat at me! I need a guide, so I went into those awful saloons. They all thought I was touched in the head. *I* think I'm touched in the head. Then that foul Missus Clark-son left him alone. Alone! Can you imagine it! She's a gossip, you know, and—and now no one will rent me a room." Sable caught her breath, swallowed, and plunged on. "We slept in a c-cart last night. Outside! I'm tired, I feel so dirty, and Little Hawk's hungry and—" Her body jerked as she broke again. "I can't even do something so simple as find him some food. I'm useless." She shook her head. "Totally useless."

Phoebe wrapped her arms around the girl, comforting her while trying to make some sense of the rush of prattle. Then she recalled the talk from dinner that evening. This was the woman with the half-breed infant.

"You aren't useless, Sable. Just ill-equipped. You've man-aged this far. You're alive, and the babe's fine." She patted her gently and felt the tension crumble in the slender shoul-ders.

"Oh, what am I going to do?" Sable muttered, savoring the motherly hug.

Just then three boys came into the kitchen, and over Sa-ble's head, Phoebe motioned them into silence. "First we're going to get you and that baby warm and dry." She gestured with her head for Eli to stoke the dying fire in the hearth. "That all right with you?" Sable nodded childishly.

Phoebe straightened and went to the stove, pouring a cup of coffee from the pot on the back plate. She started to turn away, then stirred in a spoonful of sugar and a spurt of milk before she held it out to Sable.

"Drink up," Phoebe ordered.

Sable pushed back the quilt and accepted the cup, wrapping her hands around it for warmth. She blew, then sipped, and continued until the cup was drained, then handed it back with her thanks. Looking down at Little Hawk, she untied the shawl and brought him to her shoulder.

"Oh, goodness. He's soaked." She began unwrapping her nephew, forgetting that she was in even worse shape.

Phoebe smiled. "Eli, bring in the trunk and anything else you find that looks like it belongs to Miss Sable."

Sable's head snapped up at the words, and for the first time she noticed the three boys of various coloring and sizes. They stood back, staring curiously, except for Eli. He was already hefting her belongings inside. Eli set the smallest bag on the table. Sable stood and immediately went about removing the baby's wet garments, accepting the fresh towel with a smile from the youngest of the three. She vigorously rubbed Little Hawk, warming his tiny feet between her hands and drying his hair. He fussed and squirmed at the treatment, but Sable didn't cease. He'd catch cold if she didn't get his skin warm, and she'd be the only one to blame.

"Cal, you and Daniel start filling kettles and add more wood to the stove," Phoebe ordered over her shoulder as she disappeared into a small room near the back door. The boys scampered in two directions. She returned a moment later, dragging a copper tub into the room and setting it before the fire. Eli placed the basket on the table, cushioning the bottom with a blanket just as Sable had the baby clothed and dry. Little Hawk cried.

"He's hungry," Sable said guiltily.

"So feed him," Phoebe replied, then saw Sable flush, her gaze on the wood floor.

Seeing the kettles were on, Phoebe sent the boys from the kitchen. "You want a little privacy?"

"No, it's not that." Sable chewed her lip, wondering if she should trust Phoebe, then decided she had no choice. "I'm not his mother."

Phoebe sucked in her breath, then eyed her suspiciously. "Then just exactly what are you to him?"

"His aunt."

"Honey, I think you've got some explaining to do." Phoebe gestured to the chair as she refilled Sable's cup, then prepared one for herself. "Cal," she called as she seated herself. "Fetch some milk, please."

"Aw, Mom," both women heard just before a door slammed somewhere.

Sable spilled out her heart to Phoebe Benson, and the woman managed to piece together the real story from all that nonsense before.

"Well, looks like you've got you're work cut out for you."

"But I can't do it! Isn't that plain to you? It certainly is to me." Sable sighed heavily. "I suppose I'll just have to go home."

"Your sister's depending on you, and whether he knows it or not, so's that baby and his papa."

Sable dropped her gaze, fingering the cup handle. Mrs. Benson was right. But no one had ever depended on her for much of anything before this. She still didn't believe she was up to the monumental task. In the lengthening silence Sable's imagination heard Lane's soft weeping, visualized her resolute stares out the window, waiting for the man she loved, praying he hadn't abandoned her completely. And the hope she'd all but lost until the day her son was born.

It could have easily been me.

But it wasn't. I didn't suffer, Sable reminded herself and speculated what kind of sister she was when, after months of worrying over her Lane's fate, she'd returned to Washington, to her former life of parties and suitors and friends while Lane was sequestered behind Papa's lies and locked doors with only heartache for company. How can I do less than this one task for my own flesh and blood? But how? It was hundreds of miles to Red Cloud's people and if events thus far were telling, Sable knew she'd fail.

Her thoughts were interrupted when Cal entered, lugging a bucket over to the sink, Eli behind him. Without being asked, Eli filled the tub. Cal stood by fidgeting, and his mother shooed the black-haired boy out, ordering no one to enter the kitchen until called.

"Get yourself out of those wet things, Sable," Phoebe told her while she took a bowl from the cupboard and a clean rag from a hook. She poured milk into the bowl, dipped the rag, then went over to the baby. She put the rag in his mouth, and the child sucked hungrily. Phoebe noticed Sable was still dressed, her gaze glued to where Cal had disappeared through the doorway.

"You're wondering 'bout my boys?"

Sable flushed, shook her head, embarrassed at being caught gawking and quickly worked the buttons of her jacket, peeling off the sodden material.

"It's all right. You see, your sister and I are about the same in some ways." Phoebe lifted the child from the basket, then sat down, dipping the rag in the milk. She fed the baby while she talked. "I was married, and Eli was just this size," she nodded to Little Hawk, "when the wagon train we were with was attacked by Cheyenne. My David was killed and Eli and I were taken captive."

"My word!" Sable's skirt plunked to the floor, her imagination running wild with memories; of painted faces and shrill war cries, spilling blood, and arrows thunking into the chests of young soldiers whose only crime was wanting to escort the Colonel's daughters on their daily ride.

"Sable, honey, you all right? You look a might pale."

"Lane was first taken by a horrible man, Phoebe," she said fumbling with the petticoat laces. "He beat her, starved her, treated her no better than an animal." She met the older woman's gaze. "My sister's husband challenged him for her, in a fight to the death."

"He must have loved her a great deal."

Sable shook her head. "He hadn't so much as spoken a word to her. I never understood that." She shrugged, stepping out of the wet petticoat. "Lane did, and that's all that matters, I suppose."

"Well, I didn't have it quite that bad. Indians are fascinated by red hair." She smiled faintly. "Blue Feather, that's Cal's father, was good to me, but the tribe didn't like me givin' their chief the son he'd wanted. See, he already had a wife." Sable's eyes widened at that. "It isn't uncommon," Phoebe explained. "She couldn't have any children, so when I became pregnant, he made me his first wife."

Clad in corset, chemise, and torn stockings, Sable searched her bags for her precious perfumed soap, listening intently, wondering if Black Wolf had had a wife before Lane, how his tribe felt about her sister, and Black Wolf for killing one of his own to protect her? Dropping the bar into the tub, she silently questioned if the tribe, or perhaps even his father, would reject Little Hawk.

"Blue Feather died, and my life was miserable," Phoebe said, her expression growing wistful. "God knows I loved him, just like I loved my David." Suddenly she shook herself. "Anyhow, I was allowed to leave with my boys, but after a time I regretted it."

Sable frowned, pausing in her attempt to undress beneath a quilt. "Surely civilization is better?"

"Can't say it is." *She's gonna have to get over that shyness,* Phoebe thought, tamping down the urge to roll her eyes. It was a long way to the Dakotas. "I was treated much worse than you've been, Sable. I'm not lookin' for pity, mind you. But I didn't do anythin' wrong. I met Daniel's father when I was workin'." She looked down at the babe in her arms. Sable didn't need to know she'd been a whore to feed her kids. "He was decent, married me, and gave me a home." She gestured to the house as a whole, then looked back to Sable. "He died three years ago."

41

"I'm sorry for your losses, Mrs. Benson." Sable envied the woman's strength. "But how have you managed since then?" With the quilt wrapped loosely, Sable stepped into the tub. Holding it above the water, she let it drop to the floor as she sank into the steaming water.

"Call me Phoebe, please. I take in boarders to make ends meet."

Sable paused in soaping her hair, looking above herself as if she could see through the wood, and Phoebe laughed softly, making her face appear immeasurably younger.

"Trust me, it's a big house." She stood and placed the sleeping child in the basket, then went to the stove, adding cool water to the boiling pot to rinse the girl's hair. When she turned back, kettle in hand, Sable's head was bowed and her hands folded primly. "Sable?"

The younger woman looked up. "I was thanking God that Eli dumped water on me."

Phoebe grinned. "Bet that shocked the good Lord down to his sandals."

"Perhaps." Sable smiled. "But I can't thank you enough, Phoebe, for taking me in like this. I don't know what I'd be doing if you hadn't."

"My pleasure, darlin', and I like having you here." She poured the water over Sable's head. "It's been a long time since I had a woman to chat with."

Sable's eyes rounded as she wrung out her hair and swiftly wrapped it in a towel. "Surely you have women friends?"

Phoebe's expression was indulgent. "In this town—in any town, Sable—I'm considered filth because I've been with an Indian. They don't understand how proud they are or that they have strict morals and honor and laws."

Scrubbing her arm, Sable glanced up, speculative. "You really admire them, don't you?"

"You have to. We've been takin' their land for years, and they still keep fighting."

"With my papa and his garrison," she added wryly, attacking her legs.

"He can't help that. It's his job."

"Yes, but by heavens! That does not excuse what Papa tried to do to his own flesh and blood!" She smashed a fist into the surface, then blushed, covering her mouth when the fountain of water landed on the floor. "Forgive me, Phoebe."

Phoebe waved, tossing a towel over the puddle, seeing Sable's true innocence, and God forgive her, her weakness. Imagine that, feeling guilty over showing your temper, Phoebe puzzled, wondering how the stifled woman had gotten this far alone. "Ever stop to think there was another reason your papa wanted Little Hawk gone?"

Sable tilted her head. "That's what Salvatore said." At the questioning look, she explained her acquaintance with the chef.

Phoebe's eyes widened in surprise. "You've got more gumption than I thought, meeting him secretly like that."

Every inch of Sable's exposed skin pinkened furiously at the implication. "Oh, no, it's not like that! Why, Salvatore is old enough to be my father!"

"Don't get your corsets in a tangle, honey." Phoebe waved from her seat. "I understand. What else did he tell you?"

"He said to trust no one, not even my heart. But then, he's never met you."

Phoebe's smile melted when her gaze darted to the basket. "How 'bout you tell me exactly who's that baby's papa?" She gestured with her chin.

"He's Sioux. A war chief, Lane claims." Phoebe felt herself go cold. "And his name is Black Wolf."

Phoebe muttered a curse, launching out of the straight-backed chair. She stood near the hearth, staring into the blaze. This was an entirely new situation.

"What is it?" Sable could see the fear in the older woman's face. "Why should his father matter?" At the continued silence, she pleaded, "Phoebe, please, you're scaring me!" then gripped the tub rim.

Phoebe lifted her head. "Black Wolf is feared, Sable, by white men and red. He's legendary, for the coup he's counted, the scalps he's taken, and that his face has never actually been seen by a *living* white man. Story tells he's a ghost, disappearin' like smoke."

Sable pooh-poohed the idea of a mystical apparition, accepting the offered towel and climbing out of the tub. Lane couldn't possibly have fallen in love with such a horrible creature.

"The army's been after him for years," Phoebe continued. "Hell, I even recall talk of his bravery and courage when I was with Blue Feather, and Black Wolf was just a boy then!"

"What does this mean? To Little Hawk?"

"That baby is just what the army's been lookin' for, bait to lure Black Wolf into a trap."

Sable looked horrified. "But he doesn't know the child exists!"

Phoebe grasped her shoulders. "And no one had better," she warned. " 'Cause there's a passel of folks that'd take pleasure in killin' his son."

Panicked, Sable went to Little Hawk, checking him as if harm could have come merely with the words spoken. The infant yawned adorably, then his eyes opened, staring trustingly up at his aunt. I'm the only person he has now, she realized, looking at things from a new perspective. His perspective. There was no place safer for the newborn child than in his father's arms. Her determination to put him there sent her bare shoulders back. Lifting her chin in as close as she'd ever come to a defiant manner, she said, "I promised, no, I *vowed* to get him to his father."

"Ain't a soul alive crazy enough to guide you."

"Surely there must be one man unafraid of this warrior?" Phoebe's wrinkled features stretched taut. "You do know. Tell me, please!" Sable begged, gripping her arm.

"God forgive me, Sable, he's just as ruthless as Black Wolf."

Chapter Four

Resting his forearms on the bar, Hunter McCracken stared into the golden liquor, his fifth or sixth—he didn't know or care. He lifted his head and was assaulted by his own reflection in the silver glass suspended on the opposite wall. *God, is that really me?* he debated silently, raking his fingers through his shoulder-length hair. He hadn't shaved since last fall, and the dark beard was matted, reaching several inches below his chin. His looks were repulsive. The only people it didn't seem to offend were the other occupants of the saloon and the whore with whom he'd spent the last evening. Hunter lifted the glass to his lips, but his hand stopped midway to its thirsty goal.

In the mirror he saw a small figure standing behind him. His gaze shot between the reflection and the portly bartender making his way closer to him, his rag moving in a constant slow, circular motion across the scarred wood bar.

"Been standin' there goin' on five minutes," the bartender snickered, implying that Hunter was too drunk to have noticed. Shark cold eyes assessed the bartender before the cheap whiskey finished its path. Fearful, the bartender stepped back, putting up his hands. "Hell, Mister Hunt, she's been askin' for you all over town."

Hunter gestured for a refill as he turned, settling back against the bar and folding his arms, taking in the Indian woman's appearance from head to toe.

She was shrouded almost like a nun, he decided, snatching up the whiskey and draining it. Her bowed head and small shoulders were draped with a tattered brown shawl that reached past her waist, and her hands were tucked beneath its heavy folds. Her buckskin skirt—which had seen better days—grazed the dusty floor. The shawl was drawn across her face just below her eyes and tossed over her shoulder and what little hair he could see was jet black. She neither looked at him nor moved, but her presence had gained the attention of everyone in the saloon, and they slowly gathered around her. Hunter glared a few interlopers back, giving himself breathing room.

"What do you want?" he said after a moment; he could have sworn she flinched.

She answered in the harsh guttural tones of the Cheyenne.

"No," he said when she'd finished, then turned back to the bar. He was in no mood for this.

"Looks like she ain't got the message," Nate Barlow chuckled, assuming the same position to Hunter's right.

Hunter looked up at the woman's reflection. "I said no!" And when she didn't move, he repeated it in sign language.

"What's the squaw want?" Barlow asked.

"Not that it's any of your damn business," Hunter spared him a glance, "but she wants me to take her to the Sioux."

Barlow rubbed his chin whiskers, his smile sly. "Dakotas, huh?" He shrugged. "So do it."

A muscle worked in Hunter's jaw.

"Go on, Hunt, take her back to her own kind," Nate goaded.

Hunter stared into his new drink. "Anyone ever tell you, you talk too much, Barlow?"

Barlow didn't heed the warning. "Hell, the red bitch oughta be good for a few tussles along the way fer your troubles." That brought a round of laughter.

Hunter's hand shot out, grasping Nate's shirt and yanking the man close. A woman was a woman, no matter what the

46

race, and he wondered why he just didn't do the world a favor and kill the bastard. McCracken was drunk, and the shots he'd just downed made him meaner, and everyone in the saloon knew it.

"I pay," she interrupted in Cheyenne.

Hunter's gaze darted to the squaw's reflection, then back to Nate. With little effort he thrust the man away, forcing Nate to grab the bar to avoid falling on his skinny rump. Hunter turned fully, leaned back and rested his elbows on the bar, then crossed a booted foot over his ankle. Christ, she was just a little thing.

Sable was petrified, scared to death that someone would notice how badly she was shaking and see through the farce. She'd caught a glimpse of this Hunt person in the looking glass before she obediently lowered her gaze. He was a disgusting pile of filth, and Sable decided if forced to spend weeks with this odious bear of a man, she would keep a sizeable distance. He was nothing but grimy buckskins and hair. Black hair on his head, his face, and, Lord even a dusting on the skin exposed between his shirt laces.

She took a deep breath, keeping her head down, and from beneath the shawl, lifted out a worn leather sack. She and Phoebe had planned every move, every word of this transaction, and aside from the near brawl, it was going as hoped. Sable hated lying; had never been good at it, anyway. This deception went against everything she'd been taught. Then she thought of her nephew, his sweet cherub face, and the price he'd suffer if she didn't get him away, and soon.

"I pay," she repeated in Cheyenne, the harsh words she'd practiced for a week stumbling uneasily off her tongue.

Hunter eyed the sack swinging from her gloved fingers. No matter how much she had, it wasn't enough to force him to keep company when he didn't want it.

"My price is two thousand," he said with a thin smile, knowing she couldn't begin to meet it.

Soft murmurs of translation floated around them with

bursts of snickers over the outrageous sum. The room gradually quieted.

"Agreed."

Hunter's eyes widened, and he straightened abruptly. He reached for the bag, but she snatched it back, and he watched along with everyone else as she dipped her hand inside and withdrew gleaming yellow nuggets.

"Christ, looky there!" he vaguely heard, his eyes snapping sharply between the gold and its owner as she deposited the handful in her skirt pocket.

Furious, Sable spoke in English. "Half now, half when I arrive." She paused, adding meaningfully, "Unharmed."

Hunter found himself backed into a corner, and he damn well didn't like being maneuvered into it by this conniving little witch. Damn! Where the hell did a squaw get all that gold anyway?

Angrily, Sable tossed the bag in his direction and was surprised the drunken lout managed to catch it. Then she remembered Phoebe's parting words, and removed her worn leather glove and extended her hand, her gaze bravely venturing as far as his furry chest.

"Your word."

Hunter gnashed his teeth. Ignoring the ribald comments, he grasped her hand. The contact was biting, like the clash of sabers, vibrating to his bones. "I give my word."

Her gaze flew to his, and his eyes widened a fraction. Lavender eyes. She had lavender eyes. A half breed. For one breathless moment they stared, and Hunter felt as if he'd been kicked in the gut. Then she dropped her gaze, jerking her hand free. She spun about, took a step, then halted.

"Near the cottonwood, by the church, sunrise," she said in Cheyenne, then made a hasty retreat, cradling her tingling hand against her stomach.

Hunter shoved the gold in his pocket as his booted feet rapidly followed her path out of the saloon. The wood planks groaned as he met the steps, his head snapping back and forth, pewter eyes searching the poorly-lit streets. He could find no trace of the woman.

Sable gathered up her skirts and ran, her heart thumping wildly. She darted into the alley, flattening back against the wall to catch her breath. He felt it. She knew he did. "My heavens," she whispered, pressing a hand to her chest. Never have I known such, such, mercy me, I don't know what that was!

She rapped urgently on the door and was immediately let inside.

"Lord, you were gone so long I didn't know what to think!" exclaimed Phoebe.

"How is Little Hawk?" Sable asked breathlessly, falling into a chair. Finding him safe, she said, "It was frightening and degrading and—this Hunt person is a big man with a great deal of hair, Phoebe."

"I told you that."

Sable graciously accepted the cup of coffee she was offered. "But you didn't tell me he would be besotted, mean, and that this trip would cost me two thousand dollars."

Phoebe dropped into a chair. "Why, that—that—"

"I know." Sable waved airily, taking a sip. "My upbringing forbids me to call him what I truly desire."

Always the lady, Phoebe thought, then leaned forward, smiling. "It worked, Sable. By heavens!" She thumped the table. "It actually worked!"

Sable shook her head warily. "I'm not so certain. He's an intelligent man, and—and," she stumbled, guiltily dropping her gaze. "I looked him in the eye."

"I warned you, girl. Those eyes were the only thing we couldn't disguise."

"And I spoke in English," she added dejectedly.

"Oh, Sable," Phoebe scolded.

Her gaze flew upward. "But he gave his word before witnesses."

Phoebe's softly wrinkled face split into a triumphant smile, and she relaxed. "Well, if I know anything about Hunt, it's that he'll keep his word."

Phoebe didn't mention that if he gave it to kill you, he'd keep that, too.

Beneath the cottonwood Sable stood beside her small sorrel, securing a shawl across her face as she watched the sun break the horizon and light the brisk morning with a dewy pink glow. It was certainly a lovely sight, she decided, never having been up this early to witness one. Patting her mouth to cover a yawn, she checked her horse and other supplies and saw that the baby was dry and comfortable. Then she inspected everything again. Including herself. As to her own appearance, it was the same as last night; her hair was covered with black boot polish, for the town was without hair pigment of any kind, and the skin of her hands, face, throat, and a touch beyond her shoulders was dyed a pale red-brown with diluted iodine. It would take time to wear off, but she needed those days, or perhaps weeks, to continue deceiving that Hunt person, until they were far enough away that he couldn't take her back. She dreaded that moment, having already witnessed a sample of the man's temper.

Nervously she tightened the hide lacings of the cradle board Eli had fashioned for Little Hawk. Everything had to look authentic, at least for a while. The week's worth of schooling from Phoebe was imbedded in her brain; the letter Lane had given her was tucked away with an envelope she was not to open until face to face with the child's father. That scared her even more than seeing Mr. Hunt again, but she forced it from her mind. Black Wolf was weeks away.

"You ready?"

A little cry escaped her and she spun about. The air wouldn't move fast enough into her lungs as she stumbled back, crashing into her horse. She pressed a hand to her throat. Surely this was not the same man from last night? Please don't let it be, she prayed, swallowing hard. Sable, considered herself an excellent judge of men's looks, having been in their constant company most of her life, decided—much to her annoyance—that this was a very handsome man.

"I know you speak English." There was a warning in his tone.

Sable blinked, licking her lips. "You?"

"Yeah, it's me." He didn't like looking into the eyes that had haunted him since last night.

Sable groaned inwardly. He'd bathed. The scraggly moustache and beard were clean and neatly trimmed close to his face. Even with red-rimmed eyes and dark smudges beneath, his chiseled good looks showed through, and she scarcely noticed that his tanned features were sharp and creased in a deep scowl. He looked cozy, she thought idly, his dark head nestled in the snowy lamb fleece lining of his broad jacket collar. He stood a bit too close for her comfort, smelling of mint and spice, his weight resting arrogantly on one denimed leg. His saddle bags were slung casually over one broad shoulder, the reins of his mount threaded loosely in one hand. Why hadn't she noticed last night how shiny and black his hair was, or that it tumbled adorably over one eye? Gray eyes. Hard, mean, gray eyes. That's what snapped her out of her reverie. He didn't want to be here, she reminded herself, and turned away to mount the horse. She shrieked when his hands clamped on her waist and lifted her unceremoniously into the saddle. *How dare he touch me without permission!* she thought peevishly, shoving her skirts down over her stockinged legs.

Hunter heard an unfamiliar sound, and his head jerked back and forth, a hand going to his gun.

"What the hell is that crap?" He lashed a hand toward the goat and pack mule. Damn, it hurt to move that much.

Sable couldn't stop the heat from rising in her face at his curse, yet managed to lift her chin a notch and stare straight

51

ahead. "We have a bargain. What I take with me is not your concern."

"It is if you plan to get there before next year!" he bellowed, then groaned, his head pounding as his own voice vibrated back at him.

Little Hawk cried out, and Sable lifted his cradle board, blowing in his face. She hated doing that, but Lane had insisted. An Indian child did not cry unless hungry or hurt—the sound would alert their enemies and endanger the rest of the tribe.

"A baby! You want to take a God-damned baby to the Sioux?" Hunter ran a hand through his still damp hair. This couldn't be happening.

"Is there a problem?" Mercy, he looked ready to pop!

"Hell, yeah! It's damn savage country, lady! Tough enough on a man let alone a—!" He waved in the general direction of the child.

"You gave me you word, Mister Hunt. Take me, take my son."

Sable heard a low growl and glanced about herself, trying to discover its source. Her eyes widened measurably when she realized it radiated from him. He was half bear or cougar or something as vile, she decided, and feared he would go back to their deal until he abruptly mounted his horse and nudged it with his heels.

"Let's go!" he barked, jamming his Stetson on his head. "We're losing God-damned daylight!"

Sable flushed, making a mental note to speak to him about his constant taking of the Lord's name—when, and if, they were ever on friendlier terms, she cautioned, watching his rigid back. Highly unlikely, she thought sensibly, resecuring Little Hawk to the saddle. Mister Hunt was a mean, uncouth, foul-mouthed, two-fisted drunk. Despite his infinite list of shortcomings, Sable smiled. She'd gotten her way.

Hunter glanced back over his shoulder. Her baby, huh? So, Violet Eyes was a momma. Christ, he must have been pickled last night to have given his word on this!

Chapter Five

All he could hear was the slow plod of the animals' hooves, an occasional clip-clop against stone. Hunter thanked God for the blessed silence of the forest, because the seventh cavalry was marching through his skull. The cadence of agony was too perfect not to be. Trying not to move his head too much, he slipped the canteen from the pommel, unscrewed the cap, and drank cautiously in an attempt to ease the sticky lint taste in his mouth. The softly muttered vow never to drink again was a puff of frost in the morning air as he shifted in the saddle, tugged the collar of his jacket up over his cold ears, and twisted a look behind him.

Violet Eyes held the child tucked close to her body, her head bowed, and he could scarcely make out the tune of a lullaby. In the other hand she loosely held the reins. Lucky for her, he thought, that the animals followed so easily, for she wasn't paying the slightest attention to their direction. She hadn't spoken since they'd begun their journey, and that pleased him immensely. He didn't care for chattering women, Cheyenne half-breed or otherwise. Why the hell wasn't she with the baby's father, anyhow? How'd she get separated from the tribe in the first place? An Indian man wouldn't let his son and woman out of his sight, especially to be among white men. Not if he cared.

Why should he even give a damn? He didn't need this aggravation. Hunter only had to remind himself that the little witch maneuvered him into taking her, and he became more incensed. He'd given his word, and as much as he hated being in the company of anyone, he'd deliver the female to whatever tribe he could get close enough to and leave it at that. He was being paid well enough for his troubles. This venture included guiding and protecting her, not talking to her. His gaze slipped over her once more, then returned to the unmarked path ahead as she tossed the shawl over the child and fidgeted beneath it. He supposed she was feeding the boy, and he edged up a little further to give her some privacy.

As the space between horses widened, Sable was grateful that he had even a small amount of manners. She grabbed the chance to feed the baby in private, needing to keep up the pretense. This wasn't an easy task, she realized—the horse's rocking gate nearly unbalanced her as she slipped the milk-filled animal bladder into the baby's mouth. From within the warmth of her fur-lined coat Little Hawk made ravenous smacking sounds, and she smiled down at the sleepy-eyed boy as he suckled his dinner. The crude nurser belonged to Phoebe when her own body had refused to produce milk for her second child because she'd been near starvation herself. The bladder had a hide casing stitched over it to protect it from puncture, and the ugly brown rubber nipple had only the slightest peak. Sufficient, she thought. Glass was out of the question in the wilderness.

She returned her gaze to Mister Hunt's straight back. He hadn't said anything to her, except to occasionally bark a command to keep up or to curse. Perhaps when they stopped for a break and he ate something, she would find him in a more pleasing mood. Sable dreaded to think he was *always* such a foul-natured creature.

They hadn't traveled more than a half mile when Little Hawk began fussing and squirming, and Sable realized the bladder was filled with more air than liquid. Drat, she thought, easing back on the reins and watching Mister Hunt disappear around a bend in the trail. With his present disposition, he was to sure to be angry over this delay.

Hunter was downing a slug of water when he spared a look behind him and found himself suddenly alone. Damn! They'd been at it for only one day and already she'd gotten herself lost! Didn't she realize anyone could come upon them—at any time? Annoyed that he was so hung-over he hadn't noticed her departure and that it was a serious inconvenience to look for her, he quickly backtracked.

Branches slapped at his shoulders and legs, his heart pounding unreasonably fast as he retraced their path, his mind seeing her and the child mutilated by attack. Slackening his pace before he missed her entirely, he caught a glimpse of movement in the brush and he withdrew his pistol, prepared for anything. *Except this*, he thought, reining up sharply. Violet Eyes was squatting, milking the goat, her face screwed up in a grimace, her aim far from the small tin pail beneath the goat. It was a simple enough task, especially for an Indian woman. Thinking on her incompetence made his head throb.

"Why the hell didn't you call out?" he barked, and Sable let out a shriek, falling back on her rump and spilling what little milk she'd managed to contain.

"I did." She didn't look up.

"Well, I sure as hell didn't hear you!"

"Do tell," she muttered to herself, climbing back into position and dusting off her hands. She didn't want him around, certain he'd notice how inept she was at the task, and focused her attention on the floppy udder of the goat, trying once again to remember Eli's lessons on milking. After a deep breath, she gathered the courage to touch the beast and wrapped her fingers around the pliant teat, squeezing as she tugged. *This*, she thought, *is positively disgusting.*

Determined not to fail under his watchful eye, she managed to get enough milk in the pail, then stood and turned her back on him while she filled the bladder, pretending to drink the warm, sweet liquid.

Hunter frowned at her back. "Why are——?" He stopped before he asked something ridiculous and regarded her thoughtfully as she replaced the pail in a burlap sack tethered to the mule. When she simply stood beside the animal, he snapped impatiently, "Well! Put a fire under it, woman! We're wasting time!"

Her lips pulled into a thin line. Put a fire under it, indeed! Unable to speak of her distress to a man, she walked onto the path. The intoxicating scent of her perfume hadn't escaped him, and it seemed now that every breath he inhaled was filled with it. It gave him pause; aside from the fact that Indian women never wore it, the delicate scent was laced with the distinct odor of boot polish. After years in the army, there were some things a soldier didn't forget. Giving his J.B. a four-finger pinch, he adjusted the battered hat lower on his forehead, feeling he was being made to look the fool.

"We'll camp here," he said, without looking at her.

Sable slid wearily from her horse, taking in the small clearing near a brook. She pressed her forehead to the warm saddle, too exhausted to care where they were. Her trembling legs ached horribly, and she was certain she was bruised in the most delicate of areas. She'd never sat in a saddle more than an hour or so before this and still didn't know how she managed to keep up with his swift pace. Resisting the urge to thoroughly rub her sore bottom, she removed a satchel from the horse and set up her own little camp near a fallen log. Then she unlaced Little Hawk from his cradle board and went about making him comfortable and warm on a blanket before she saw to her own needs.

Hunter tossed down the stack of wood. "Bed closer to the fire," he ordered, as she walked between her animals and the child. She paused briefly and shook her head, then continued with her work. "It'll be damned cold tonight." No answer. He shrugged and bent down to build the fire.

Sable decided to ignore Mr. Hunt for as long as she could. He was bullish, mean, swore far too often, and hadn't a kind word to say since they'd met. In no mood to endure any more of his loathsome company, she filled the growl in her stomach with a dry biscuit she'd packed. Then she washed, curled up beside the baby, and immediately fell asleep.

Hunter stared at the fire, warming his hands on the tin mug of coffee. It felt good to be back in the wild. Going into civilization had its merits, like whores and decent food, but other than that, it wasn't worth much. He'd seen enough killing in the bar alone to last another year or so. No, he corrected, forever. The baby whimpered, and he darted a look at Violet Eyes, seeing her hand automatically pat his blanketed bottom. So, she wasn't sleeping as soundly as she appeared.

"Coffee's hot," he said softly.

No answer. He shrugged. Suits me fine, he decided, setting the cup aside and fishing in his saddlebags for tobacco and papers. Smoothly he rolled a cigarette, sliding it between his lips before picking up a glowing timber and touching it to the tip. He drew deeply, exhaling in a tired rush. He had to admit Violet Eyes cared well for her baby, better than for her animals. What a sight they must be, especially with that damn goat. He still couldn't believe he had agreed to this. But a deal was a deal. Adjusting his hat over his eyes and slipping his finger around the trigger of the gun lying across his stomach, Hunter took a last drag on his smoke before tossing it in the fire and settling back against his saddle. He didn't sleep, not much anyway. Hadn't since '63.

Little Hawk stirred beside Sable, and she woke slowly, pulling him onto her chest and kissing his dark head.

"Good morning, Little Hawk. Sleep well?" she whispered. He cooed back, making bubbles, and she laughed softly, sitting up.

"You're paying me to protect and guide you, not to do your damned work!" Sable's head jerked to the side where Mr. Hunt was tightening the cinch of his saddle, his back to her. "It's God-damn cruel to leave a beast saddled and thirsty!" He faced her, words catching in his throat. The shawl no longer covered her face, and her hair had come unpinned, the waist length mass a wild swirl about her shoulders. Light eyes wide with fright stared back at him while she protectively clutched the baby beneath her chin. Jesus! She was beautiful! How hadn't he noticed before now? The heavy coat gaped open, drawing Hunter's unwilling gaze to the tantalizing curves of her shirt-covered bosom, the full, ripe swells stirring him.

Aw hell, not her!

His anger seemed to spread and burn through him, and he looked like a dark dragon spitting fire as he stomped across the clearing. Sable leaped to her feet and yanked the shawl over her head.

"Listen up, woman! You—!"

"I-I'm sorry about the animals, M-Mister Hunt," she interrupted, staring at the dirt. "I was quite tired and simply forgot. Thank you very much for seeing to them for me."

The wind went out of Hunter's sails at her shaky reply and his tense body relaxed. She was so shy, her voice smoky-soft. When was the last time he was near someone so demure? That reminder sent a spurt of renewed anger through him.

"Don't let it happen again," he growled, then turned away.

Sable sighed deeply, trying to collect herself. So much for her pleasant morning, she thought, taking care of the necessities, then packing the animals. While Hunt kicked dirt over the glowing embers, she milked the goat, making sure she had enough for most of the day. Heaven forbid she would need to stop for something as trivial as food and water, she brooded,

58

annoyed at her bungling around such a disagreeable man. He'd been raised with wolves, she thought maliciously, struggling to lift the saddle. Suddenly it was ripped from her hands, and in a matter of seconds, cinched and repacked.

"Thank you, Mister Hunt." He didn't bother to look at her, offering only a primal grunt as he turned away.

Mr. Hunt was already gathering wood when Sable managed to climb from the saddle at dusk. She was angry. He hadn't bothered to tell her they were stopping—again. He had simply dismounted and gone about his work as if she weren't there. He had no consideration for her or the baby. She'd managed to keep up, changing the child while they rode, but now she had hours of work to do, and it was unfamiliar work: laundering clothes and managing to bathe Little Hawk in anything less than frigid water. She swiped at her forehead, making a face at the grime on her hand. She couldn't stand it another moment. Her scalp itched from the boot polish, and she was all too aware of the pungent odor that radiated from her person. She needed a bath and fantasized about a long relaxing soak. She was knocked out of the dream by the smell of Little Hawk's urine when she removed the bundle of soiled diapers.

Hunter looked over his horse's back at Violet Eyes, and a small semblance of a smile etched his lips. She held a tied clump of cloth out with two fingers as if it would contaminate her, her sour face turned away. She walked to the outskirts of their camp and dropped it, then scurried back to the horses. A hand on one hip, she shook her finger at the tiny wiggling bundle lying on the ground, and he could hear her softly scold the baby in a jovial manner. She gathered up and lifted the babe high, nuzzled his belly, then hugged him close. The sight gave him a strange feeling, pleasing him in a way he'd never experienced before. The smile evaporated. Indian children didn't wear diapers. Clean moss was usually placed

59

around the baby inside the cradleboard for absorption. Hunter found himself watching this woman more closely.

Mr. Hunt already had the fire in a comforting blaze when Sable managed to remove enough satchels and bags to reach the saddle. Uncinching it, she tugged and pulled. Her arms quivered with the weight, and she stumbled back, then defeatedly let it drop to the ground in a puff of dust. She stared at the chunk of tooled leather, her shoulders drooping pathetically. Her hands and arms hurt, her back throbbed, and she wanted nothing more than to curl up near the warm fire and sleep—endlessly—and hope that when she woke it would be in her own soft bed.

With the baby strapped to her back she slowly urged the goat, mule, and horse toward the stream, then returned to the camp to gather the items needed. Her bath would be freezing, but the baby's would be warm. After making several trips to the stream, filling her water supply and the pail, she set the bucket on the hot rocks surrounding the blaze, trying to ignore the gray eyes that followed her every move. He was done with his work, she thought peevishly. He had only himself to worry over.

Sable was not in a courteous mood when she walked downstream, far enough that Mr. Hunt would not see her at her bath. She laid the fresh clothing, soap, and towel on the bank, then dropped to the ground to unlace her boots. The earth was cold and hard beneath her, but the crisp scent of grass and pine trees was far more pleasant than her own fragrance. Propping the baby in his cradleboard against a rock and bundling him with a blanket, Sable stood, gathering the courage to remove her coat. Her skin prickled with goose flesh as she slipped it off. The blouse was made of coarse, sturdy fabric, not what she was used to, and the material irritated delicate skin that had only been touched by silk and the finest batiste. On the other hand, the skirt was as soft as butter, she thought, unfastening the buckskin and letting it drop. She unbuttoned her blouse, and it followed the same path. Pulling the pins from her hair, she let the sticky tresses shroud her bare shoulders and her fingers shook with cold as she plucked at the laces of her petticoats.

Hunter moved silently through the woods, following the stream. "She should have told me where she was going. One minute she was there and then the next—" He froze like a statue when he spied her, lacy petticoats pooled around trim ankles. She stepped out of them, tossing the white fluff aside, then bent over to remove her garters and roll down her stockings. Hunter swallowed thickly, the sight of shapely bare calves stirring him into silence. This was very ungentlemanly, he thought with a lecherous grin, his gaze raking over the rounded bottom so sweetly displayed. With ungodly speed his body answered the lush sight, and he silenced a groan.

A twig snapped. Sable gasped, snatching up her petticoats to cover herself as she spun about.

"How dare you! Go away this instant!"

Hunter moved around the tree and leaned back against it, folding his arms across his chest.

"Go, please!" Holding the petticoats up at her throat, Sable gathered her soiled clothing as further protection against the eyes that kept roaming over her. She'd seen that look once too often, and it scared her. How long had he been there? Mortified beyond reason, she crouched on the ground, certain her pale feet were now out of sight.

"How can I see to your safety, lady, if you wander off without telling me?"

"I didn't wander off, Mr. Hunt. I needed privacy!" She flushed even redder. How could he just stand there, the brute, looking at her like that? Had he no manners at all? "Please, might we discuss this at another time!"

"Sure."

"Well?" she nearly shrieked when he didn't move.

"Go ahead, have your bath. I'll be right here."

Sable ground her teeth, striving to remember she was a lady, and ladies didn't scream with rage, even at thick-headed buffoons like this one.

"Mr. Hunt," she began in a less than patient voice, "I am paying you to protect me, not to view my personal hygiene."

A jet black brow arched as he smoothed his moustache with a thumb and forefinger. Damn if her speech didn't become more refined every time she spoke. It was an extremely long moment before he said, "When someone pays me to protect them, I do my job."

"Then do it with your back turned from beyond the trees. Please, I'm freezing!"

He looked her up and down, a slow cold appraisal that made her shiver. Without a word he withdrew his gun and moved back into the thicket.

Sable strained to see if he was still lurking about and considered getting dressed again, but her itchy scalp stopped her. With a swiftness she wasn't known for, she stripped off the corset, chemise, and pantalettes, then, wrapped in a blanket, tiptoed to the water's edge. She stared at the dark water with obvious distaste. She'd never taken a cold bath before, much less in a river with a nosey man so close by.

"No use delaying the inevitable," she told herself, her body shaking with cold, the cake of soap clutched tightly in her hand. After glancing about to see if she was indeed alone, she dropped the blanket and ran, diving into the water.

Oh, blessed mother! Ice cold! She burst through the surface and quickly rubbed the soap over her body, scrubbing until her skin glowed. Her hair was a different matter however, for without warm water to make a sufficient lather, it took three soapings to get the polish out. Oddly, she enjoyed the refreshing sensation of the brisk water that seemed to rejuvenate her tired, sore limbs—for about the first fifteen seconds. Her legs were already numb and the bone jarring shivers made it difficult to remain standing. Though the baby was in sight and unharmed, she decided not to stretch her privacy further and paused briefly to check whether that uncouth Mr. Hunt had returned before she hurriedly emerged from the water, twisting her hair. Her hands trembled as she dried herself, then hastily donned her clothing. The canvas corset was difficult to lace, but she savored the extra warmth.

To her utter annoyance, Mr. Hunt had assumed the same position against a tree as he had on previous occasions, looking predatory and still stroking that infernal moustache as she neared the camp. She stopped, tugging the heavy shawl across her face. His eyes touched and dipped over her body, the look sending strange flashes of heat through Sable before they slowly rose to meet hers. Silver eyes mocked her, and for the first time she saw him smile. No, that was definitely a leer, she corrected, flushing crimson, itching to bean the hairy beast with a rock. Head bowed, she raced past him, Little Hawk snuggled close. *I positively loathe that man!*

Chapter Six

Hunter didn't like it. Not one damn bit. A suspicious man by nature, he preferred facts, clear cut, laid out, a plan to follow, an objective to achieve. But Violet Eyes, she was, well, odd, he decided as she practically sprinted past him and huddled near the fire like a kicked puppy.

One minute she threatened to burst into tears, so submissive it irritated him, and the next he could see the faint spark of rebellion in her eyes, yet it never flamed, snuffed out like a pinched candle. She wore a constant blush, and he'd swear she was a pack rat. Every time they stopped she pulled more and more luxuries out of those satchels. Nothing about her fit.

What enraged him further was his attraction to her. Purely physical, he decided. Had to be. They'd hardly spoken at all. She intrigued him—the sound of her voice, like a husky whisper lovers shared beneath cool sheets. It sent a stampede of desire racing through him. He didn't want it. He didn't want to need anything. But those eyes, pale, round, lavender, prodded a memory he just couldn't grasp. He studied her more closely, his gaze plucking away the layers to find the woman beneath, and Sable felt it and clutched her coat more securely against the cold.

He made her nervous, for she realized, when she'd discovered him standing so close while she bathed, exactly what she'd brought upon herself. She was alone—with a man—in the wilderness. Why, he'd seen her practically naked just moments ago! Heat burned her cheeks at the very thought of her vulnerability. For she would be defenseless if he should want to use her body. She hadn't thought of convention, of how many proprieties she was breaking just by being in his presence, unchaperoned. It was Little Hawk she'd been most concerned about, and she still was.

What had he seen, the cad, before she'd discovered him lurking in the woods? I'm not doing a very good job of deceiving him, she confessed silently, then sucked in her breath when she glanced at her chilled hands. With all the washing, the dye was wearing off more rapidly than she'd anticipated. She worried her lower lip, glancing covertly in his direction. Had he noticed? Oh Lord, had he seen the definite mark on her shoulders? No, she was certain her hair had covered that much, and hoped the darkness further aided her secret. He was suspicious—of what, she wasn't certain—and tensed when he walked past her toward his gear, those gray eyes following her moves.

Hunter removed a tobacco pouch and papers from his saddle bags, then settled himself beyond the fire from her, rolling a smoke. She was bathing the boy, oblivious to him, her hands working swiftly with practiced ease as she rinsed, dried, and dressed him. Immediately she slipped on gloves and moved back, that hideous shawl draped over them, shrouding the pair in secrecy. Even though he couldn't see it, he knew her hair was sopping wet. Going to catch a cold, he thought, lighting the cigarette, and he wasn't about to play nursemaid to her if she did. She shivered so violently the shawl slipped off her head, and he leaned forward to toss another gnarled branch onto the fire, insisting he was doing it for the boy. He stirred the flames to a high blaze, and she met his gaze for an instant. What the hell did he do now, he wondered, reading the animosity in those dark eyes.

Annoyed that he looked so warm and cozy on the other side of the fire, Sable rubbed her hands vigorously over her face, brushing aside the cobwebs of exhaustion. She fed Little Hawk then bedded him down for the night. Forcing herself to gather up the soiled garments, she moved listlessly to the river and performed the loathsome chore. With wet hair and hands, the icy night air bit into her skin, and she grit her teeth against the bone-raking shivers. *I can't put this disgusting mess on my hair again,* she despaired, looking at the small tin in her palm.

"It was crying."

She jerked around to see Hunt holding Little Hawk out by the lacings of his cradle board, the infant dangling like a Christmas ornament from a tree limb. Without thinking, she dropped the tin and leaped to her feet, grabbing the child and putting him to her shoulder. He burped loudly, instantly quieting.

"You want to tell me what the hell this is all about?" He held out the tin of boot polish.

Her gaze snapped up. "No."

He took a step. She retreated. Then his hand snaked out, yanking the shawl from her head. Sable gasped, jerking free the hair he'd managed to catch in the process.

"Explain yourself, lady," he rasped.

"Wh-what is it-t you wish to kn-know?" She clenched her teeth to stop the clicking.

"Your hair's brown," he spat.

"So?"

"It was black this morning." Impatience punctured his tone.

"Very as-astute, M-m-mr. Hunt."

"Well, so you do have a tongue." He hooked his thumbs in his waist band, hips forward, the stance intentionally vulgar. "And here I thought you were the shy, retiring Cheyenne."

"And now?"

His lips curled in a sneer. "You're a lying bitch, and I want to know why."

Sable's hand cracked against his cheek with such force his

66

head whipped to one side. Slowly he turned his head, eyes glacial, then like a flash of lightning he grabbed her shoulders, jerking her off the ground and up in his face.

"Don't ever do that again." The words were slow, threatening. "Damn it! Look at me when I talk to you." He shook her roughly, and her gaze flew up to meet him.

"Don't call me names, Mr. H-H-Hun-t-t."

His grip tightened. "Why the damned boot polish?"

"Y-You're hurting me!" Sable was losing her grip on the child. "Please, I'll drop the baby!"

Instantly Hunter set her to her feet and realized she was shivering uncontrollably. With a smothered curse, he scooped up the wash and roughly propelled her toward the camp. When they entered the clearing, he pushed her down near the fire.

"Dry that mess before you get sick," he snarled, then left her.

"Heaven forbid," she muttered to herself, taking out her comb. She hovered near the crackling blaze.

Hunter threw another log on the fire, glaring intermittently at Violet Eyes' back. Hell, he didn't even know her real name! Dipping out a handful of beans from a sack, he tied them in a thin cloth, then dropped it into a coffee pot, setting it over the fire. What else was she hiding?

"I don't like being made to look the idiot, lady," he said while fishing in his pack.

"No one makes you *look* the idiot, Mister Hunt. You manage that rather well on your own."

"What!" he roared, spinning around.

Sable slapped a hand over her mouth, gauging his temper to near explosion. Dropping her gaze, she fidgeted with her comb. Oh, why did she let her mouth run away like that? Little Hawk's life was at stake!

"I apologize, Mister Hunt," she mumbled weakly.

"Dammit, woman! Quit apologizing and start answering some questions!"

Sable dealt him her most chastising glare, rising up on her knees, hands on her hips. "Mister Hunt! Must everything you utter be so thoroughly saturated with profanity?"

Hunter blinked. "Is that all you have to say?" he bellowed. He took a step toward her, pale eyes glowing murderously from within the darkness of his features.

She swallowed nervously, dropping back on her calves. "We—we have a bargain, Mr. Hunt." Sable envisioned her whole plan crumbling into dust and gathered up every smattering of courage she possessed. "You needn't worry yourself over the details, because I will *not* reveal them. I don't care in the least for you, and I'm very aware it's reciprocated. Shall we simply leave it at that and remember that *I* am *your* employer?"

His chiseled lips twisted in a cruel smile. "Is that so?"

"Certainly. The thousand in gold you accepted says so."

"Not anymore." The sack landed near her knees. "Consider this arrangement terminated, lady."

She stared at the worn leather bag, hot panic sweeping over her. "You gave me your word, Mr. Hunt." Her gaze snapped up at his vile curse, his gray eyes piercing her thin veneer of courage. He was leaning back against his saddle, the base of a whiskey bottle resting on one bent knee, his face turned away. She'd stung his pride. And she counted on it getting her to Black Wolf.

"A word given on deception means nothing, lady."

Why, the thick headed, narrow-minded clod! "Are you saying if my hair was black, my eyes dark, it would make a difference?" She held her breath.

Hunter cursed the logic of the female mind. How had she twisted it around so he sounded like a bigot?

"Well?" she pestered.

Silence.

"Mister H—"

"No, dammit!" Hunter glared at her as he raised the bottle

68

to his lips. The liquid glugged and his Adam's apple bobbed as he drained nearly a third of it.

"Really, Mister Hunt, how are you to protect me and my son if you are besotted with spirits?"

An ebony brow shot up as he drew his sleeve across his mouth. Spirits, was it? She looked awful prissy right now, and damned adorable.

"Do I tell you how to mother?" he shot back.

"That's hardly the point, now is it? Aside from the fact that you haven't the facilities to care for a child, nor yourself for that matter, as—as stewed as you are. You haven't the good sense God gave a—a tea cup! What if we were attacked? Why, I'd be shocked if you could manage to stand on—" She clamped her mouth shut, not caring in the least for the way those flint gray eyes peeled away the layers of her clothing with unparalleled ease. She turned away from him, ignoring the sharp tingle spreading rapidly up her body and busied herself with the chore of drying her hair. How could he do that with just a look?

"You gots a sassy mouff fer a squaw." *God, I'm drunk,* he thought, annoyed that she'd clammed up. "Go on, darlin'. Let's hear it." When she remained silent Hunter chuckled, a low, lecherous sound that would have struck fear in the toughest of women. A smirk tugged at his lips when she cringed.

I'm a witless ninny, Sable thought, afraid she'd held too much stock in the man's word of honor. It was best not to provoke such a crude sort in any possible manner, or she could find herself in a far worse situation. What that actually entailed, Sable didn't know, but doubted anything he inspired could be considered entertaining.

The woman had a little snap, but no teeth, Hunter decided, taking a slug of liquor, enjoying the sight of the smooth curtain of hair as she dragged a comb through the mass. It wasn't brown, he realized hazily, but a dark chestnut red.

Mahogany. Yeah, that was it. The color of rich, polished wood.

Sable twisted her hair into a tight bun, securing it snugly at the back of her head before she rose and hung her damp clothing on a nearby bush, careful not to allow Mr. Hunt even the teeniest glimpse of her lacy underthings. No telling what would set the beast off, she thought, quickly settling down beside Little Hawk and tossing a blanket over them both.

"Good night, Mister Hunt," he heard after a while.

"What's your name, lady?" The words slurred into one.

Sable remained silent, hoping he'd simply pass out.

He thought her asleep and took another drink, wishing she'd left her hair down. "G'night, Violet Eyes."

Hunter never saw the soft smile that curved Sable's lips. Perhaps there was hope for him yet, she thought as she drifted into the arms of sleep.

Sable woke with a start. Dawn was scarcely turning the sky a deep purple, and something was very wrong. No one was barking at her to *put a fire under it.* She sat up, her head whipping back and forth as she searched the camp.

Mr. Hunt was gone.

Quick alarm swept through Sable. The pig! The unforgivable beast! He'd gone and done it. He'd left her alone in the wilderness! A hysterical turmoil such as she'd never experienced welled up inside her, making her tremble. What would she do? How would she get back? Good God! She didn't even know where she was! Tears pricked her eyes as she called out for him.

No answer.

Shocked that he'd actually abandoned her, Sable reprimanded herself for her exceedingly poor judgement—again. Before falling asleep she'd been almost certain she had convinced him to continue with their bargain. How would she survive? She told herself it was useless, that tears accomplished nothing, but they came just the same, like the gush of a hot spring. Covering her face with her hands, she sobbed quietly, wishing the absolute worst on the man.

She was scared to death, imagining all sorts of horrid creatures lurking beyond the tree line, all waiting to have her for breakfast. Her nerves tingled. Her breath came in quick pants, syncopated with her wildly beating heart as she thought of the fate he'd left her to.

Toweling his hair dry, Hunter strode into the camp and stopped short. Violet Eyes was on her knees, her face in her hands. At least she's up, he thought, moving closer, leaves crunching beneath his boots. She looked up, and he heard the air race into her lungs, saw wide-eyed horror painted across her face. God, she was pale.

He slid to his knees before her, grasping her arms and she screamed, struggling against his hold.

"What is it? A snake bite?" She clawed at his face and bare chest like a wild cat. "Did you see something?" he demanded, then realized she didn't recognize him. "Violet Eyes! It's me, woman!" He shook her so hard her head snapped back and forth. "It's me!"

Sable blinked. It took several seconds for the face to register, then she sagged with relief, dropping her head forward, weeping with relief.

"Are you hurt?"

She shook her head.

"Then why the hell are you crying?"

She flinched at his razor tone. "After last night, I thought . . . you left me!"

He cursed under his breath. "Whatever gave you that idea?"

"You gave me back the gold and said our agreement was over, and—and when I woke you were gone. I called out, but

71

you didn't answer." She drew in a ragged breath and rushed on. "It was so dark, and I thought you were an Indian, which is reasonable since your hair's so long and you're wearing those fringed things." She waved in the direction of his trousers and choked on a sob. "I thought you left me out here!"

"Well, I didn't," he snapped, releasing her sharply. "And if you'd bothered to look around before you flew off the damn handle, you'd have seen that I was still here!" He was yelling at her now.

Sable glanced to the side and felt like a complete idiot when she saw his horse grazing just past a cluster of trees, saddled yet still in the same place as last night.

"Oh," she said stupidly, then lifted her gaze to meet his.

Dimwitted or not, she had eyes a man could get lost in, he thought, watching her momentary shame fade, replaced a second later with a dark indigo spark that grabbed at his gut.

"Don't ever do that again!!" She punched his chest with every word. "It was cruel!"

"Jesus, woman! I only went to take a bath. Ouch!" He rubbed his chest and failed to dodge another stinging blow. "Now will you cut that out?"

"No. I'm upset." She punched him some more, like a scrappy pup against a great bear. "I was scared out of my mind!"

"What did you want, lady?" he said on a laugh. "An invitation to watch?"

She gasped, horrified he'd suggest such a thing. "How dare you! You—you filthy uncouth drunk!" This time she aimed for his face. Her small fist caught his jaw in just the right angle to make his aching head reel with pain.

"Why, you little—!" He grabbed her hands, pinning them behind her as he slammed her against the hard wall of his chest. "I've had just about enough of your damn complaints and name callin', lady, an—"

"Release me this instant!" she demanded, squirming feebly against the abrupt contact with his body. He tightened his

72

grip and Sable winced at the pain, fear stilling her movements as his free hand moved roughly up her back, burying itself in the twist of hair, dislodging pins. Would he beat her?

Hunter heard her soft gasp of surprise, saw her flinch, but couldn't stop himself as he pulled on the cloud of silk, jerking her head back.

"Release me," came in frightened whisper.

"Shut up." Final, bitter, his breathing labored as he fought the incredible heat, brushfire quick and spreading. Who was she to do this to him? He'd warned himself about this idiotic attraction to her, that he was simply infatuated by the mystery that surrounded the woman. Hell, being near her forced his pickled brain to work overtime, but touching her—hell, nothing before equaled this.

Damn her!

Yet it was that trembling lower lip, plump and invitingly wet and those deep violet eyes staring back at him with unmistakable fear and confusion that did him in. He'd never hurt her, but he *had* to taste her. Desire, cold and emotionless preyed on her innocence, thieving past the once honorable man and overtaking his control. Even as his mind screamed he had no right, no right to touch, he knew he would.

"No, Mister Hunt. Don't do this!" she hissed, jerking her head back as his face neared. "Please, don't."

He wasn't listening, suddenly obsessed with feeling those lush lips beneath his own. His mouth made a hard slash across hers, swallowing her protests and forcing her lips apart. The faint scent of wild flowers filled his already light head as her hair tumbled down her back in a claret wave, coating his bare arm. Her body, womanly, supple, and still warm from sleep, wreaked total havoc on the desire he couldn't rein in, unleashing his passion. She jerked against him as his tongue pushed between her lips, but he brushed aside the absurd notion that the experience was new to her. She tasted winesweet and ripe, and he ached for more.

And he took it—his lips and tongue demanding the precious nectar within the warm forbidden haven.

Good. Damn good.

Shock jolted through Sable as his tongue swept inside her mouth. Had anyone described this to her she'd have been repulsed, but . . . his tongue, his lips rolling over hers—he tasted like danger and rage and want, and she didn't dare move a muscle. She'd no idea why a man who yelled at her constantly even *wanted* to kiss her, but he was, quite thoroughly. She should push him away. Yes. She should fight harder. Fight at all, she thought, suddenly conscious of his wide chest, bare and damp and the luxurious feel of her thinly cloaked bosom pressed to his cool skin. Her breasts ripened, swelling to fill any space left, catching Sable between utter mortification at her body's response and this new exquisite pleasure ripping down to her toes.

Was this desire? Passion? Her sister spoke of it, how uncontrollable it was, how wonderful it felt. This scared her. This was more real than anything Sable had experienced before. Who would have thought such a beastly man could make her feel so incredibly wicked, so wonderful?

It was simply not fair.

Hunter released her hands and they fell bonelessly to her sides. She swayed. And he waited, waited for her to join the kiss when he could feel her need blossoming, waited for her to touch him. Please, he thought. Touch me. Just this once.

Her senses tripping over each other, she grabbed onto him for stability, her hands clamping to the flesh of his ribs, the skin tight and smooth, and absently she felt a jagged scar beneath her fingertips. Naked. He was half naked! Oh dear! This was wanton, shamefully improper, she reminded herself. But her hands played ignorant, sliding around his waist and climbing up his muscled back. He made a growling sound of approval that vibrated against her breasts and he pulled her tighter against this iron hard body.

He was dangerous. He could continue to take whatever he

wanted and she'd have no defense. She was supposed to be married—a mother, for heaven's sake! But Sable couldn't be bothered with that just now, not with all the wildly pelting sensations screaming for her attention. Curiously, hesitantly, she stroked the ropey muscles of his back, naked and cool beneath her palms and heard his moan of pure masculine pleasure. She'd never dared touch a man like this; the opportunity had never arisen before now. It gave her an unquenchable thirst, a power, and she yielded to it, her mouth suddenly hot with demand.

Hunter's legs buckled when every inch of her softened against him, and he fell back on his calves, pulling her between his thighs, his large hands guiding her hips closer to his heat. Muscled arms wound around her slim body, trapping her, and he paused briefly, staring into violet-blue eyes, then wordlessly took her mouth again, the sudden longing to have more than just her lips beneath him pushing him past the point of rational thought and racing down a trail of sudden disaster.

He deepened his kiss.

She answered, opening her mouth wide.

God.

He was on fire.

Sable felt his hand move roughly, possessively, over her hip, her waist, heat gathering with his touch as it moved upward to mold over the sensitive peak of her breast. She tore her mouth away, pushing sharply at his chest.

"No more!" she uttered on a quick gasp, her skin burning, scared at what he'd do next, ashamed that she'd allowed him this much.

Hunter stared at her, dragging the air into his lungs. He felt like he'd been ridden hard and put away wet. He was spent, exhausted, but still wanted more. When her fingertips grazed her bruised lips and she gaped at him with undisguised wonder, he puzzled further over the woman in his arms. Damn, if she didn't look incredibly young and innocent right now.

"You put your tongue in my mouth." Half accusing half surprised, a flaming blush sweeping down her face before the words were completely out.

"Want to put yours in mine?"

"Certainly not!" She shoved at his chest, leaning out of his reach. "Mister Hunt. This has gone far enough!"

"Not for me," he murmured silkily, refusing to release her, nibbling anything he could reach.

She shoved again, twisting away. "Please—Mis-ter Hunt!"

He caught her close, his smile lopsided, roguish, and Sable's heart did a quick flip-flop. "You can quit calling me *Mister Hunt*, darlin'. I think we've gone past that."

"No, we most definitely have not!" Shame swept her in thick wretched waves. What must he think of her after such a display? "And it's not proper for me to call you anything except—"

"The name's Hunter," he husked, bending to nibble at her lobe.

"I'm terribly happy for you," she gritted, turning her head so his lips caught the spot beyond her ear as she tried to peel off his hands. "Mister Hunter, will you please release me?"

He didn't. "Call me Hunt, Hunter, even McCracken, but please, darlin', leave off the mister."

She stiffened in his arms, her head turning slowly toward him.

"Would you repeat that, please?" she asked quietly.

He sighed, not noticing how her eyes had narrowed. "My name is McCracken. Hunter D. McCracken."

It hit him like a kick in the stomach. A moment ago he'd held a soft, wiggling, desirable woman. Now he held a chunk of the frozen North—cool, motionless, violet eyes suddenly gone pale as twilight. But it was the hatred in those eyes, the pure fury directed solely at him that made his arms lower slowly to his sides.

Christ, what a morning!

Chapter Seven

So, Sable thought bitterly, this is what's become of the in-famous Captain McCracken, her father's prized soldier, the army's most decorated fighting man. Oh, of all the people, why did it have to be *him?* For years the humiliation and con-descension she'd suffered at his hands haunted her, reminders of her deplorable behavior and that her feminine charms were of little defense against a determined man. And he was, if the last moments were any proof.

And he'd done it again, blast him, made her feel stupid and weak and helpless—and afraid—then snatched opportunity in her fear, fulfilling the threat he'd promised five years ago.

I've acted like a shameless harlot, she thought, climbing to her feet, utterly disgusted with herself.

"Why are you looking at me like that?" he asked, grabbing her hand before she could move away. Those eyes said she'd gladly carve him up for breakfast. She glared down at him, then his touch, but he dismissed the silent command. "You liked that as much as I did."

Shame brightened dyed skin, yet Sable refused to give him any more weapons. "I've no difference to the matter, Mister McCracken."

"Liar," he said, unfolding to his full height like a threat. "You felt the fire." He tugged on her hand, his voice softening to a husky whisper, weakening her. "You came alive in my arms, Violet Eyes. We both know it."

She dared not admit it. "I simply chose not to fight, Mister McCracken," she said tightly, throwing water on his flaming arrogance, her childhood memories shadowing the gentleness in his eyes. "It would have done little good, since you possess the greater strength."

Her accusation slammed him in the gut. Then like whiskey to an open wound the baby stirred, the innocent gurgle shattering any fantasy he harbored, bringing reality back like a gun blast. His features pulled taut, his gaze shooting to the boy as she yanked her hand free and spun away.

She was married. A mother. And in a million years he wouldn't be good enough for her, even if she was willing.

What the hell was she supposed to do when he practically attacked her? Christ, did he need another reason to see that he still wasn't fit for pleasant company? He railed against himself, his steps measured as he went to his horse, her malicious ring of metal pots and kettles vibrating in his aching head.

Touching her opened a door he'd no intention of walking through again. She wouldn't stick around if she knew the ugliness inside him anyway, so why bother? He forced the words to repeat in his brain as he shoved his arms into a fresh shirt, never feeling more crude or boorish or exposed than at that moment. Stuffing his shirttails into his trousers, he glanced over his shoulder, but she ignored him, sipping her tea, nibbling daintily on some bread, all the while collecting her belongings and seeing to the child. It was a homey, comforting sight, and he cursed her for reminding him of what he was . . . what he could never have.

Donning his sheepskin jacket, he moved toward the blaze. His foot landed on the pouch. Bending to retrieve it, he hefted the sack once, glancing in her direction before jamming it in his pocket.

"We leave in ten minutes," he said too loudly for his own ears.

She nodded but made no reply, yet it was a full hour later before she was in the saddle, still refusing to look him in the eye, staring straight ahead as if the sight of him would make her sick. At least she wasn't complaining any more, he thought, regaining some of his usual meanness as he donned his stetson.

He mounted up, instantly regretting the quick motion as his brain sloshed to one side of his skull. He moaned, rubbed his throbbing temple and she made a sympathetic sound. His gaze flew to hers and in that instant they both remembered the kiss, the fire and heat when they touched. The taste of her still lingered on his lips, battling with the shame he saw in her eyes. His body won, his groin thickening with blood, giving new meaning to a hard ride in the saddle.

Damn, this was going to be a long trip.

As they plodded the unmarked trail, Sable didn't try to understand exactly how she angered and enticed Hunter McCracken in the span of a few moments. (Even with her little experience, men had never made any sense.) Instead she tired to fill the boredom with details about her guide. What she recalled wouldn't crest a thimble's rim, but she'd snooped and eavesdropped on enough of Papa's conversations to ascertain that Hunter McCracken had been a Union spy, instrumental in bringing an end to the war though he'd gained the fury of several generals for refusing to commandeer medical wagons headed to the enemy. A commendable act, she thought, considering his sour disposition.

Did Papa know his favored officer had become a scruffy mountain man, and a disagreeable one at that? She recalled a time when her father received a dispatch concerning the man who now protected her life, but what she could remember now was the deathly pale expression on her father's face and how heavily he drank that evening. Though her father never spoke of it, Sable suspected the young captain had spent time in a Confederate prison. Hunter McCracken disappeared without a trace soon after, and at the time she was thankful, the memory of their encounter still fresh in her young mind.

She glanced around, bone-chipping wind biting into her cheeks as she snuggled her nephew deep within her coat. Had he come *here* then? Why? The iron gray sky met the rugged flat terrain, its bleakness randomly broken with a sprinkle of bare trees crimped by winter's touch, and bolders, jagged, dark, like angry scepters cursing the heavens. The trail strewn with abandoned wagons and furniture spoke of hardships and loneliness, and the thought of even *wanting* to live out here depressed her. Her gaze returned sharply to her guide. What, in God's name, had made a man with such a promising career forsake his family and civilization for so many years?

Hunter hadn't heard a peep out of her all day and glanced over his shoulder to make certain she was still behind him. He frowned at the intense way she was looking at him, then returned his gaze to the trail. He could feel her eyes boring into the back of his neck and had the uncontrollable urge to yank up his collar to protect the sensitive area. Infernal woman was going to give him nothing but problems. He just knew it.

"He's expecting you, sir." The trooper pushed the door open and stood back, allowing Colonel Richard Cavanaugh to pass.

"Bring the colonel some coffee, son," the man standing behind the desk ordered, his face marked with concern.

"Yes, General." The trooper closed the door as the general came around the side of his deck, offering his hand.

"My God, Rick, you look like hell."

"Don't feel much beyond that, to tell the truth," Cavanaugh replied, shaking his hand, then closing his other over it. "I need a favor, Jim."

General Curtis gestured to the high-backed leather chair, noticing the bleakness in his old friend's eyes. What more could the man endure, he wondered as he lifted a carved box from his desk and flipped the lid, offering a cigar.

Richard's lips curved slightly. "Havanah?" He plucked one out, searching his pocket for his snipper as the general produced one that was scratched, dented, and very plain. Richard recognized it from years before, and suddenly felt more at ease about what he needed to ask of Jim. Matches struck and a moment later pale smoke swirled between the old friends like a worn gray blanket, comfortable and familiar.

"I need a transfer, Jimmy."

Jim's bushy silver brows shot up. "After all we did to get you an assignment in Washington?"

"Circumstances have made it impossible for me to remain here."

The general frowned. "That sounds like a dispatch, Rick. You know nothing will go beyond these walls," he waved at the elaborately decorated office. "Nothing ever has."

Raw agony flashed across Richard's features and Jim stamped out the cigar. "God almighty, Rick, what's happened? Are the girls all right?" The trooper knocked, entered and without a word set up the service, prepared the general's coffee the way he preferred and left.

"No, they're not all right. Nothing's right, damn it!" Richard lurched out of the chair and strode to the window, staring at the glossy black carriages and finely dressed people strolling past. "Sable's disappeared," he blurted.

General Curtis settled against the desk. "You're certain my goddaughter isn't throwing a tantrum over some minor indiscretion?"

"No. She's left the city this time." Jim Curtis was the only official privy to the facts about Lane's capture. Cavanaugh had been able to keep things quiet solely due to Jim's help and influence. Something nudged his arm, and he looked down to see Jim held out a shot of sour mash. "Lane gave birth to that bastard's child." He tossed back the aged whiskey in one gulp.

Jim's eyes widened over the news and he choked on a sip. "Good God, man, I'm already old—don't shave off any more years!"

"Sable took the baby and disappeared."

"Why would she do that?"

Richard glanced at his friend. "I can only assume she overheard my plans."

The general set the glass down with a thump, his spine stiffening. "And those were?"

"To give the little savage away. What else?"

"What else? For the love of God, Rick, that's your grandchild you're talking about. Your *daughter's* son."

Richard ignored that. "I tried to keep it all quiet. The house in Maryland, no visitors. And thanks again for your help."

"Don't think I'd have offered if I'd known your plans," Curtis shot back bitterly.

Richard glared. "Do you know how I feel? It's Caroline all over again. To have my daughter give life to that man's child? His band killed half her escort! Good men lost just to save her! And now she claims her undying love for the son of a bitch!"

Jim knew that Caroline's death had left him deeply scarred. "Where's Lane now?" he asked.

Jim's tone calmed the storm churning his insides. "At home, under guard, and spitting nails, but smug that Sable managed to elude my protection."

"Any idea where Sable went?"

"Black Wolf's camp. Were else could she go?"

"Sable?" His eyes widened. "You can't be serious! Why, she's just a baby. A pampered little innocent without—"

"A lick of sense beyond her own little world," Richard finished. "I know. I wanted to keep it that way, for all the good it did. Don't you see why I have to go after her? She's without escort, chaperon, maid—nothing. She won't survive, Jim, and with an infant to care for." Richard mashed a hand over his face. "Hell, I doubt Sable could manage to properly dress herself."

It was a long moment before Jim spoke. "Do you know where she is—exactly?"

Richard shook his head. "Atlanta, last telegraph."

"Well, at least she won't get much farther. She wouldn't be senseless enough to try going north alone, and there isn't a white man alive who'd take a woman like Sable to the Sioux."

"Not and want to live long," Richard added angrily. He'd been trying to console himself for the past weeks with that. But the less often he heard from his detectives, the worse he felt.

"You can have leave to go looking. I might be able to swing a transfer, but don't count on it."

"Thanks, Jim." Richard offered a weak smile, shaking Jim's hand. "To think I nearly got kicked out of the army for decking my superior twenty years ago," Richard said. Jim rubbed his nose, which was still crooked from the right cross Rick had dealt. A friendship forged on a fistfight, he thought, then turned to his desk to sign the necessary papers.

Any reasonable amount of Sable's sympathy or curiosity concerning Hunter McCracken vanished the instant he came to an abrupt halt and went about tending to his own business. She maliciously hoped he was vomiting up what little he'd eaten today, unreasonably annoyed he hadn't acknowledged her presence once. Simply avoid him, she warned herself, for speaking so often had already revealed far too much of her upbringing to him. Another heinous blunder, she thought dejectedly as she dragged the saddle from her horse. It took her nearly an hour to unpack the mule and by then Little Hawk was fussing for his supper. She stopped, fed and changed the child, then went back to work. It was routine now, and she ought to be used to it, but the tasks still took a toll on her meager strength.

She gathered twigs and rocks to build a fire, unceremoniously dumping the pile at his feet, then turned away, ignoring the peculiar look he gave her. She recalled that Phoebe said Indian women made the camp, cooked, and did darn near everything while the men hunted. Well, since he wasn't hunting he could start the fire, she decided peevishly. She led the animals to the thin stream, then washed diapers, tended to her personal needs, and fetched fresh water. Her work was only half done. She had yet to rub down her mount or the poor mule or check their hooves for stones or—oh, she didn't want to think about all that just yet.

Furious at the universe in general, Hunter pulled a small sack of beans and a tin pot from his packs, dumping it on the ground where she was kneeling. She looked up, her eyes wary.

"Fix some coffee," he growled, then went to his packs, retrieved a bow and quiver of arrows and without a word, started for the woods, knowing her eyes were on his every move. *Let the scared little witch stew for a bit.*

Sable stared at the items as if she'd never seen them before. Coffee? She hadn't the vaguest idea how to brew coffee! What now? She chewed her lip nervously. Well, it couldn't be *that* hard, she thought, and a few moments later set the prepared pot over the largest rocks, satisfied she'd done as just as he had in the days before. She'd show him.

The rich aroma of coffee warmed the air, warning Sable of just how long he'd been gone. Noting this time his horse was still hobbled close, Sable saw through his motives to scare her. She hadn't completed the thought when he strode into the camp and dropped a pair of dead, bloody rabbits at her feet. Sable recoiled from the sight of the soft fluffy animals with gaping holes in their little throats.

"Dear heavens! Get those away!" She waved at the creatures, fighting down the bile rising to her throat.

"Skin, clean, and spit 'em if you want supper, lady," he snarled, then strode off into the woods again. Sable's gaze cautiously moved to the dead animals. She stared sadly at the bunnies. Oh, how could he? Well, she didn't need to eat them, and simply could not do as he'd asked. Remove their skins? The very idea! She had a mind to give the little darlings a proper burial, but that would only send him into a tirade. *That* she didn't need. With her head turned away and wearing her gloves, she picked up the rabbits and deposited them on his side of the fire.

If he wanted to eat them, then he could clean them.

When the odor of cooking meat didn't reach his nostrils as he approached, Hunter knew she hadn't prepared his dinner.

He stopped opposite her, hands on his hips, his features sharp with annoyance.

"You got a problem with work, lady?"

Remember, Sable, you are a lady.

"Well?"

She looked up. "I do not feel the need to eat those poor creatures, Mr. McCracken, and it was cruel of you to kill them unnecessarily. We both have plenty of food."

"Woman, do you think I like killing?" Her look said as much and it rankled him. "We have to eat off the land when we can and save the rations for when there isn't any game to be had. And believe me, there won't be."

"That remains to be seen, Mr. McCracken. I refuse to touch those poor bunnies."

"Poor *bunnies?* Jesus! You act like they had feelings or names or something." He stared at her for a strained moment, a muscle working in his jaw. "What kind of Indian woman are you that you won't do a simple task?" His eyes narrowed, his voice gone ominously soft. "Or is it that you can't?" Her features stretched taut as the truth hit home. So that was it, he realized. Well, another little tidbit about the lady, and Hunter fell back on the idea that she was raised in a convent. "Well, here's your first lesson, honey."

To Sable's horror he grabbed the rabbits and knelt beside her. First he gripped the bunny's neck, twisted, ripping off the head and tossing it aside, then slit the belly and gutted the animal, spilling the bloody innards on the ground beside her. Sable thought she would vomit but refused to disgrace herself before a man who desperately wanted to see her do it. He caught the edges of its skin and yanked viciously, separating the fur from the rabbit in one mighty tug, and then, for extra torture to her delicate sensibilities, he chopped off the tiny furry feet. Swiftly he repeated the process with the second and in a moment had them spitted over the fire.

He stood. "Any questions?" he mocked.

Her face was pale, her eyes wide as they shifted from the debris to the rabbits. Slowly she lifted her gaze. Then her color returned and those lovely violet eyes narrowed.

"I suppose you derived a great deal of pleasure out of that little display, didn't you, Mister McCracken?" Her voice dripped contempt.

He arched a brow. Her perfect articulation hadn't escaped him. "It was simple enough. You can do it next time." He turned away.

"I don't think so."

He stopped, facing her. "No? Then you starve and so does that baby." He nodded to the boy.

Little Hawk only required milk, but he didn't need to know that. "What do you care if we starve?"

"I don't."

Her expression turned sour. "Now, why doesn't that surprise me?"

"Look lady, I didn't want to bring you out here! You knew that from—"

She put up a hand. "Spare me the soliloquy, Mister McCracken. I know exactly how you feel about me and our agreement." She stood on shaky legs, hands on her hips. "Rest assured, I'll be certain to die in a prone position so you can simply light a fire to me and be done with it. Heaven forbid my death should inconvenience you any further." Her gaze caught on the bloody debris at her feet. "And clean up your mess, Mister McCracken. I'm nobody's servant." She

86

snatched up a cloth to rub down her animals and walked away. "And Mister McCracken?" she called out in a sing-song voice, still walking.

"What!" he spat back over his shoulder.

"Your bunnies are burning."

Hunter whirled about. "Shit!" He grabbed up a cloth and lifted the charring animals from the fire, patting out the flames. He glared in her direction, her soft giggle grating down his spine. She'd done it again—made him feel like a cad, and a mean, spiteful one at that. He fell back on his rear, replacing the rabbits in a less flammable position, cursing the woman with violet eyes.

He was munching on a chunk of meat when she returned, leading her horse, mule, and goat back from the creek. He watched with half-closed eyes as she tied the animals up for the night, then milked the goat. She looked exhausted, and he felt a small twinge of sympathy when she tiredly gathered up soiled diapers and set off toward the banks. He shifted his position so he could keep his eye on her through the tree-line, his loaded gun beside him. Hunter chomped into the meat, his stomach revolting at the poorly cooked animal, and he resolutely tossed the remains into the hole he'd dug, then snatched up a tin cup. At least the coffee was ready, he thought as Violet Eyes came into view. She quickly decorated the area with drying diapers, then returned to the fire, bending over and warming her hands. He ignored her as he poured himself a cup, then settled back. Sable watched as he blew on the liquid, then took a huge sip. His eyes grew suddenly round.

"Ahhh!" He spat the coffee aside. "Jesus Christ, what the hell did you do to this?" He pointed to the pot.

Sable straightened abruptly. "You wanted coffee. I made coffee."

He climbed to his knees and lifted the pot from the fire. "You made tar, woman." He flipped back the lid. "Shit!"

"Mister McCracken, please! Your language!"

He glared up at her. "Lady, you didn't even put the beans

87

in a cloth, not to mention that you used enough for ten pots!" His voice grew louder with every word. "Can't you do anything right?" He rose to his feet, glowering down at her like a spitting dragon. "You can't skin or cook, can't manage your animals, can't keep up the damn pace, and you can't even make a decent pot of coffee! What the hell good are you!"

Sable swallowed the lump in her throat, her eyes widening to keep back the tears. "I'm two thousand dollars in your pocket good, Hunter McCracken. That's how *good* I am."

"Well, if this is what I've got to put up with," he kicked the pot aside, "it sure as hell isn't enough!" he snarled and saw her expression vanish. With stiff shoulders, she turned her back and moved to her private area. Hunter stomped over to the animal remains, kicking dirt into the hole, then went to his belongings and dropped down onto his bedroll. After a curse-filled minute, he found his bottle of whiskey, took a swig and nearly puked in his lap when it hit his stomach. He didn't look in her direction, but stilled when he heard her soft sob. Aw, hell!

The tears fell quietly. He's right, blast him! What good am I? I can scarcely take care of myself and the baby! Who could blame him for being furious? I am a burden to him, and every time I opened my mouth he was reminded of his unwanted bargain. Feeling dejected and useless, Sable swallowed repeatedly in an effort not to blubber out loud. Searching her satchel for a hanky, she wiped her running nose as Little Hawk Suckled at the milk bladder. He was her only joy. For the remainder of the evening, she immersed herself in the baby, letting him wiggle within the warm blankets. She played with his toes, nuzzled his soft belly, and held him close, showering him with the only thing she was easily capable of—love.

Chapter Eight

Hunter glanced back over his shoulder and the smug smile slid from his face. Damn if she wasn't right behind him, astride like a soldier, straight in a brisk lope. That was another thing about her that didn't fit, aside from her eloquent speech. Hell, she was just too delicate and frail in her mannerisms to have been raised in the wild. And even if she was raised in a convent or by missionaries or perhaps by her white parent, in the white world, she'd at least have sense enough to cook. But the woman was just plain ignorant about common things.

You can sure be nasty when the mood strikes you, McCracken, he railed silently, recalling the ugly things he'd said to her. It put a hole in his heart to see those puffy red-rimmed eyes the next morning. Since that crap about the rabbits, Violet Eyes hadn't said a word to him, hadn't looked his way nor acknowledged his presence. And to gnaw on him further, every morning she was packed and ready to leave, sipping tea, waiting for *him* to waken. It galled him to no end, for every time he looked at her, with that heavy shawl shrouding her features, his memory intensified, burning into his brain the feel of her soft skin and supple curves pressed to his body, scorching the sweet taste of her mouth on his lips, again and again.

It had felt damn good to hold her, he remembered, regardless of her less than willing response. How the hell was he supposed to get the intimate image out of his head when her body spoke of endless passion between the sheets—even when she did something as simple as walk across the damn camp!

Another man's woman.

Forbidden fruit.

His body clenched at the reminder of what he'd done. She belonged to another. That it was an Indian made no difference to Hunter. She'd had his child, lain with him, let *him* love that ripe body.

Yet she responded to my kiss.

But he couldn't forget that something else turned her further away. She knew something. His short laugh was without humor. He didn't know squat about her.

Not that it mattered.

He sawed back on the reins and turned toward her, watching as she halted just as sharply. His gaze sketched over her once, then moved beyond her to the open terrain.

He squinted, removed a pair of field glasses from his saddle bags, held them to his eyes for a brief moment, then without putting them away, reined around.

"That way!" He nodded and took off toward the tree line. They rode out in the open for nearly a mile before he found a spot to enter the thicket. He kept up the pace, branches slapping at his face and arms as they moved. She was right there, he marveled, the babe strapped to her body, the heavy coat bound around them both. He stopped, slid from the saddle and pulled her and the animals behind him.

"Stay put," he ordered, then took off in a run, vanishing into the dense woods before she could comment.

Sable climbed down and slumped back against the horse, trying to catch her breath. She was going to die—simply sag to the ground right there and perish. How could he do this to her? No break in five days! Why, they'd passed Fort Kearney without so much as a cursory glance! She would simply have to give in and ask him to slow down, she decided, if anything because the baby was ill from such a violent ride and she longed for better food and a decent night's sleep. Her staples were still plentiful, but their nutritional variety was definitely suspect.

Pushing away from the horse, she unstrapped the baby, laid him gently on the ground, then stretched briefly before she took the opportunity to relieve herself in private. She milked the goat, noting that Arabelle looked rather haggard too, the poor thing. After giving her animals some water and a handful of oats, she quickly refilled the bladder and tucked it away. Sable yawned, her eyes canning the area for the captain with the thought just now occurring to her that he had been rather eager to leave her alone.

Hunter moved cautiously up the gentle slope, eyes keen as he peered from behind a cluster of branches. With a measured click, his thumb drew back the pistol hammer. Silently he slid to the ground, stretching his body across the chilled earth. His eyes moved rapidly across the terrain beyond the brush, but he could see nothing now. He'd had a feeling they were being followed, though he wasn't certain until just a few moments ago. The cloud of dust just scarcely dissipating had confirmed it. He waited, impatient for some tiny movement, a distant sound, a hoofbeat on cold ground. His heart thudded a slow beat, his senses tuned to his surroundings; the smell of the dry winter grass, the scent of the cool breeze, its whisper brushing over the leaves. Tension made his shoulders hunch and he forced himself to relax.

This was too much like old times, except this wasn't Confederate land. After another thorough look, he slid back and climbed to his feet. He didn't ease the pistol hammer down nor did he stop searching the brush for the intruder as he moved.

He'd taken them out into the open for just this reason, to force whoever was following to show themselves. Hunter knew this country well. He'd lived and traveled through Indian territory undisturbed for years, most tribes knowing by word of mouth that he bothered no one and trapped only what he needed. But the knowledge wasn't so widespread that it would save his neck if he trespassed on sacred lands. *Sacred lands,* he scoffed. That was before the government wanted it, he thought with a grimace, and all Indians either dead or *contained*.

They'd have to go south, then north around Pawnee lands, as he'd usually done, but what if anyone got a decent look at Violet Eyes? He'd end up fighting some horny bastard who'd think she was a prize of the wilderness. Hell! He'd known this trip was a stupid idea from the beginning and would have been a helluva lot safer and shorter if they'd gone upriver on a steamer. But she had refused, and Hunter sensed she was hiding more than her identity. The less people that saw her, the better.

Hunter dismissed the questions rolling around in his brain and continued to search the area. No telling if their *friend* had gotten ahead of them somehow. When he returned to where he'd left her, she was mounted up and waiting. It set his nerves on end.

"We have a visitor," he growled, holstering his gun. He grabbed his rifle and checked the load.

She gasped, eyes wide as her head snapped back and forth around her. "Where? Who is it?"

"I don't know." His brows drew together. "Could this be one of your people?"

"No!" she shot back a bit too quickly.

He slid the rifle into its scabbard, then mounted up and moved beside her. "You sure?"

Sable lifted her chin. "Of course, I'm certain."

He shrugged. "Just askin', lady. Our uninvited guest is either stupid or he wants us to know he's near." Her defiant act crumbled and Hunter saw raw fear in her eyes. She clutched the baby close, staring intently at the infant before she lifted her gaze.

"You won't let them take us, will you, Mister McCracken?"

His expression soured. "That's a helluva question to ask!"

"Well," she swallowed. "You've made your feelings abundantly clear about how we've inconvenienced you, and that burden would be eliminated if this intruder were to ta—"

"Christ, woman! What kind of man do you take me for? Don't answer that," he added quickly when her brow arched and her mouth opened. "Regardless of your impressions, I'm not a man to leave a woman and child helpless to whatever's out there!" He grabbed the reins from her hand, pulling her into the forest with him.

He continued at a swift pace, and Sable wondered how she managed to stay in the saddle with the branches whipping at her face and shoulders. Her cheeks stung, and the warmth of blood trickled down her skin. She wouldn't utter a word, a cry, nothing. He was concentrating. His head turned constantly and after a mile, he paused, dismounted, vanished into the woods, then came back moments later, breathless and sweaty, mounting up and continuing without so much as a word. He repeated the process three more times before he stopped, slid from the saddle and began clearing a small area.

"No fire," he said when she started gathering wood. Before she could protest, he added, "No noise. Keep your voice low, and camp over there." He pointed to an area where brambles and vines had formed a cave of sorts in the wild under brush.

Sable looked to the hiding place, then to him. "Will—will he try to come here? Tonight?" She couldn't bring herself to say attack.

"That's what I'm hoping." He flipped the cinch strap and yanked off the saddle, dropping it to the ground.

"You would provoke this person?"

"Look, lady," he said tiredly, working a cloth over his horse's coat. "He's following *us*. I'd call that provocation enough. We'll just wait to see what he's gonna do."

"You mean to kill him, don't you?"

He turned to face her, his voice surprisingly calm considering she assumed the worst of him. "No. Not if I can convince him to hightail it out of here. Now, do whatever you got to do and be quick about it. I'll take care of the animals."

"Thank you, Mister McCracken," she said softly, and Hunter wasn't sure if her gratitude was for the animals or the explanation.

Cold, tired, and frightened, Sable's nerves jangled like a charm bracelet. Tucked beneath the canopy of vegetation, surrounded by bushes and packs and animals she rocked Little Hawk, beating down the urge to hum. Mr. McCracken was less than a yard away, out in the open, a small campfire glowing near his feet, giving no more light than a candle. His gun lay against his stomach, fingers curled loosely around the stock and trigger as he reclined on his side, propped on one elbow, facing her. Awfully relaxed for such a dangerous situation, she thought and could only assume this daring on his part was to draw the intruder toward him. What then? Would he shoot this person? What if there's more than one? The possibility that he could be wounded in the process disturbed her, and though uncertain of whether it was for her safety or his, she grasped comfort in that he was alert and focused on their surroundings.

He glanced sharply in her direction and her breath caught, feeling the intensity of his gaze despite the chilled darkness. Did he remember their kiss like she did, with a clarity that left her breathless and aching? No, highly unlikely. He had probably brushed the entire event aside as his due. She tried to push it out of her mind, stacking everything she disliked about the man, which was considerable, against the delicious warmth he had provoked in her with just his kiss. Did other people kiss like that? With every inch of their body and half their soul?

He bent his knee, and she flinched.

"Relax, will you?" he whispered out of the side of his mouth. "You're coiled up tighter than a clock."

"One wonders why," she muttered dryly, and his lips curved into a faint smile.

"Why don't you try to get some sleep?"

"You can't be serious?" she hissed. "When some cut-throat is about to-to-cut our throats?"

Hunter snorted, trying to hold back his laughter. "Nothing may happen tonight," he managed to get out.

Her eyes narrowed. "Oh, this is a fine time to inform me of that!"

"Take it easy, lady. I said, nothing may happen, didn't say for—"

A wrenching scream tore through the silence, and her eyes widened until they absorbed her face.

"Guess the traps worked," he said with a quick grin, then leaped to his feet, dousing the fire before he vanished into the darkness.

Sable shivered. Traps. The thought of someone caught in a pair of rusty steel jaws made her stomach roll. She patted the baby's bottom, absently rocking, waiting, her mind forming gruesome images, then shoving them away.

"You can come out now, lady." The voice cut sharply into the silence, startling her into palpitations. My word, he could have at least given a warning noise or something!

Cautiously, she peered from her hiding place. All she could see in the darkness was a rather broad shadow looming over her. She strained for a better look, then it separated into two. Sable stood, clutching Little Hawk close.

Hunter struck a match, holding it to the other's face. "Remember him?"

She squinted. "The man in the saloon?"

"Hey, she talks English real good," the intruder said.

Hunter slid a glance at Sable. "Yeah, amazin', ain't it?" he said, then dropped the dying match. She heard shuffling, the distinct *thwack* of fist meeting flesh, then the crush of leaves before she saw the quick spark of another match. The rapidly growing flame revealed Mr. McCracken, squatting, adding dry brush to the new fire. Nate Barlow was a few feet away, flat on his back, unconscious.

She peered down at the man. His boot was mangled and she suspected that the dark stain coloring the ground was his blood. I'm going to be ill, she thought, swallowing repeatedly and focusing her attention on her guide.

"Wha—what did he want?"

"You."

She inhaled sharply. "Me? What on earth for?"

He looked up, his gaze moving freely over her shrouded body. He'd like to show her exactly what for. "The same thing that got you that baby, lady, and Barlow didn't care much if you *weren't* consenting."

"Oh, dear Lord." Sable dropped numbly into a boulder. Barlow had come all this way to rape her? The thought was unbelievable! She rubbed her forehead, her fingers trembling. Her knowledge sorely lacking in details, Sable could only imagine that prior to a baby coming out, something had to go in to plant the seed. Something belonging to a man. Lane had tried to expound in detail the *act*, but Sable wouldn't allow her to get any further than a man climbing on top of her. The very idea! A sweaty, heavy, groaning—she quickly redirected her thoughts, rising and coming to stand beside her guide.

"Are you certain it was me he was after? Could he perhaps have had another reason?" Sable was considering that Barlow may have discovered Little Hawk's parentage and had taken it upon himself to steal the baby for ransom.

Hunter frowned. She was going to choke that kid the way she was squeezing him. "You mean a grudge with me?"

She shrugged, eyeing her boots.

"Nope," he answered flatly.

She looked up. "You're positive?"

"Yup." He toyed with a twig.

"But you made a fool of that man in a rather populated drinking establishment, Mister McCracken."

"He was a fool already."

"But you know him . . ."

The twig snapped in his grip and he tossed it into the fire, his shoulders hunched as he stood and moved the three paces to his horse, retrieving supplies. She followed. "Look, lady, I've seen Barlow maybe twice in the past three years." Few people knew Hunter was alive and he preferred it that way. "No, it isn't me he wanted."

"But—"

He rounded on her, making her stumble back.

"That jackass wanted to kill me just to have you. He would have taken you, your gold, anything useful, left that baby to be eaten by wolves, and raped you until he was tired or bored or you were dead!" He was shouting, inches from her face. "Is that God damn clear enough?"

Sable blinked, wide eyed. No one yelled at her as much as this man. "Th—thank you, Mister McCracken."

"What the hell for?"

"For my life, and Little Hawk's."

Hunter forced himself to relax. God, she was so pretty and vulnerable, why did he always feel the need to pound his words into her? "I was saving my own skin, too."

"That's all well and good, but thank—"

"Forget it." He turned and walked away.

Chapter Nine

Sable felt a small measure of admiration for McCracken as she bent to settle the baby near the warmth of the fire. Regardless of the resentment he harbored for her, he'd predicted the man's every move without knowing who he was. Amazing. His training, it seemed, hadn't been lost over the years. Sable realized now he would do anything to protect her and chided herself for doubting his capabilities. But how would he react when he discovered it was Black Wolf's tribe that she wished to visit. If these shouting fits of his were any indication, she dreaded the moment.

She watched as he disappeared into the dark, then returned immediately leading an unfamiliar horse. He removed the weapons, ammunition, and food, but left the water. Then with a strength that surprised her, he agilely tossed the unconscious man across the saddle, tied his hands and feet to the girth, and led the animal away from their camp.

"Excuse me?" She waved as if hailing a hansom, then chased after him. "Ah—excuse me?" His stride was quick, his silhouette blending into the darkness like ink on ink, and she skidded to a stop at the edge of light, cowardice keeping her from venturing further. A instant later she heard the slap dealt to the horse's rump, the thunder of hooves still sounding as he returned.

He halted sharply in front of her. "What the hell's the

matter now?" She looked ready to box his ears or something.

"Was tying him up like that absolutely necessary?" She lashed an arm toward the black nowhere of wilderness beyond the trees.

Hunter cursed under his breath, dragging his hat from his head and running his fingers through his hair. The woman was going to drive him clean up a tree.

"I suppose you think I ought to have just sent him on his merry way—weapons and all?" Before she could comment, he continued, "He'd hightail it right back here! Did you think about the fact that the bastard traveled for over a damn week just to get to you?" When she looked at the ground, he barked, "Well?" and she flinched.

"No, I admit I hadn't considered—"

"That's right! You didn't consider a damn thing! Look, lady, you paid me to protect and guide, and I gave my word that I will." He jammed on his hat. "Stop questioning every God damn thing I do and leave the thinking to me. It's clear *you* don't have the sense God gave a damned cow pie!"

He stood before her, glaring at the top of her head.

"It isn't necessary to insult me every time we converse, Mister McCracken."

Hearing the fractured catch in her voice, his shoulders sagged. What did you expect, McCracken? For her to throw herself into your arms and thank you for insulting her—again? His mother would be ashamed of her eldest son. Hell, Father would consider that tirade worth a thrashing behind the wood shed. Hunter knew exactly why he was angry, and it wasn't her damn quizzing.

Years back he'd shoveled his emotions into a fathomless grave, yet each day, each moment he was near her, spoke to her, she unearthed a bleeding fistful of twisted sensation and tortured memory, holding it in front of his face for inspection, proving how completely he'd disintegrated.

He'd have to watch it. This poor excuse for an Indian

99

woman had no idea of how dangerous it was to dig where she wasn't wanted.

Not that she knew she was.

Instantly drawn from his dark thoughts as she slowly lifted her head, Hunter could only marvel at the storm gathering in those violet eyes. He expected a flood any second.

"Mister McCracken. I've had just about enough of you and your crude remarks about my character." He blinked, stunned by the cool fury in her words, the rosy flush of her cheeks. "I admit I haven't traveled the country such as you, but Mama taught me that it was disgraceful behavior to constantly hurl insults and demean a person." She drew in a huge breath, reveling in the release of pent-up anger. "And I don't need you—mighty lord of the forest—to tell me how inept I am!" How she could look down her nose at him from her slight height, he didn't know. "Heaven knows you must have been raised in a pig sty, with the utter filth that spills from your lips on an hourly basis. Why, I should think an entire cake of lye would never be enough to scrub out that gutter you consider a mouth! One wonders—"

The words died on her lips when he did the last thing she ever expected.

Hunter smiled, an honest-to-God smile. She'd finally let the cork pop, and it was spectacular! Though she didn't see his humor, if he was reading that glare correctly. He immediately studied the toes of his boots, his shoulders shaking suspiciously as he rubbed the bridge of his nose with thumb and forefinger.

She peered close. "Mister McCracken?"

That did it. He busted loose, the rich peal of his laughter rumbling in the small clearing.

"Oh, fine! That's just fine!" Sable stomped off in a huff, but he caught her arm as she passed. He failed miserably to control his mirth as she jerked and tugged, but her surprising strength caused Hunter to stumble backward, his boot heel catching on an exposed root. He landed flat on his back, his grip on her arm sending her sprawling across his legs in a most unladylike manner, her skirts hiked up beyond her knees. Knocked breathless, she stared into his grinning face for a second, then immediately tried to scramble off, but his arms quickly encircled her, locking her to him.

"Release me this instant!" she demanded.

His smile broadened, a flash of white teeth against his dark beard. "Feel better now that you said those things to me, instead of just thinking them?"

"Immeasurably," she said with feeling as she struggled to disentangle herself. "And I guarantee, sir, what I *truly* think of you is not at all flattering." Beastly man, she thought, how could he make pleasant conversation when he was holding her captive?

"Figures. Want to know what I think?"

She slapped her hands on his chest, flattening her palms, and ground out, "I do not!" as she tried shoving herself off. He grunted at the sharp press of her hips to his. Jesus, she was gong to feel what her squirming did to him any minute.

"Aren't you the least bit curious?" Hunter never met a woman who wasn't.

"No!" she shouted, her cheeks bright.

"God, you're gorgeous when you're angry," he rasped, brushing a lock of hair from her face and tucking it behind her ear. The gesture was so casual, so familiar, Sable's anger began to fade. She grasped it before it vanished.

"I still am! Or are you too thick-headed to see that?"

He knocked her hands away and she fell onto his chest, her face inches from his. Sable knew she was in trouble, for there was a sudden promise in his gray eyes; the promise of sensual pleasure, a promise she'd enjoy whatever he had in mind, and the threat that she'd love it. She couldn't. She was supposed to be a married woman, for heaven's sake, a mother! Yet in the flash of an instant his vicious words vibrated in her head, melding with the exquisite image of his tongue in her mouth, his body growing against hers, and she was torn between scratching his eyes out and kissing him.

"God almighty," he growled, searching her features. "If you could see what I see ..." He frowned, staring at her more intently.

Suddenly his mouth was on hers, hot and hard, his tongue spearing between her parted lips and Sable was caught, passion's fury driving her hands into his hair to grip fistfuls, her knee drawing up of its own volition. Her mouth rolled back and forth over his, hungrily stealing his breath, her emotions devouring her. She wanted to hate him, give him a permanent reminder of it. Yet at the same time, unbridled excitement coarsed through her and she understood the narrow bridge between rage and desire.

His and hers.

He made her feel like a woman.

He held control of *her* world, of Little Hawk's.

He could still take her back to her father.

Her fears made her defenseless. Blast him!

Tearing her mouth away, his lips a fraction from hers, Sable breathed the only weapon she had left, "I'm certain you're aware I cannot fight you, Mr. McCracken, so if you must continue assaulting a *married woman*, then proceed quickly."

His lungs laboring for air, Hunter went still as granite, reining sharply on the lust bursting through his body. "Are you a prisoner?" he demanded in a rough voice. "Look at me, damn it!"

Her gaze met his and the upward flick of his eyes drew her attention to the ground surrounding his head. His hands were out to the side, and Sable gasped when he wiggled his fingers, punctuating the fact that he wasn't touching her—hadn't been touching her—at all.

"You could have had your freedom," he said caustically, his tone cutting with the truth. "You just didn't want it."

She scrambled off him and to her feet, her armor of rage

suddenly stripped bare. *"You—you* assaulted *me,"* she flung rightously, ashamed of her behavior.

Hunter was slower to stand, the bulge between his thighs prominent. He didn't care, even when her gaze dropped to it. She couldn't dump the blame on him this time, not entirely. And the little witch needed to see her own desire for what it was: just as uncontrollable as his.

He scooped up his hat, positioning it on his head with great care. "Now, how d'you figure that?"

"Perhaps you have another description for dragging me to the ground, then refusing to let me go?" Her contemptuous expression said he was nothing better than pig fodder. "Or is succumbing to your advances whenever *you* decide I need a—a good mauling some part of the bargain I wasn't aware of?"

Hunter tensed at the accusation, drawing on steel will power as he thoughtfully stroked his beard. "No, can't say it was."

Sable resisted the urge to kick him in the shin. "Then I assume this is another facet of your character I must continue to be on guard against?"

He folded his arms over his chest, staring down at her from beneath the brim of his stetson. "It isn't my *character* I'd be questioning, woman." His smile was thin, sadistic. "You were showing off a good portion of *yours*—without any trouble."

Her palm itched to slap that smug look off his face. "Don't flatter yourself, Mister McCracken," she sneered in an ugly voice. "I retaliated the only way I could, since so far this evening you have referred to me as nothing short of the contents of a chamber pot, laughed in my face, then attempted the—the—" she waved at the ground—"molestation of my person. I am not yours, Mister McCracken. In fact, other than proving yourself capable of protecting Little Hawk and myself, I find nothing in you that even remotely resembles the qualities of a gentleman. You, sir, are rude, crude, and socially unacceptable, and the last man with whom I would ever willingly associate!"

He leaned down in her face, arching a brow. "What were you saying about disgraceful behavior and hurling insults?" She blanched, then her lips pulled into a tight thin line. "You made your point, lady," he said before they went at it again, "And so did I."

"I suppose that makes us even."

His face lacking emotion, he hooked his thumbs in his waistband, hips at a rude slant. "Not hardly."

Sable sent him a dismissing glare, checked the baby, grabbed her wash, and without a backward glance marched off toward the creek.

Hunter watched her retreat, then kicked at the dirt. Damn woman! Nothing would make them even, regardless of this insult-for-insult game they played. More than his vulgar past separated them. She was married! Hunter shouldered the blame for most of this battle, but being the only one partic- ipating in that kiss wasn't part of it. *Jesus, McCracken, didn't take you long to forget your own advice, now did it?* Sullenly, he hunkered down near the fire.

"I see nothing in you that even remotely resembles the qualities of a gentleman," he mimicked at the crackling blaze. A gentleman. Another part of himself burned to ashes. What did it matter? He was never leaving this wilderness, would never be fit for anyone's company. Hadn't he tried to tell her that? Hell, he'd proven it often enough lately. He rubbed his hands vigorously over his face, his emotions thrashing like a labyrinth—no way in and too twisted to find their way out. God, if she ever knew, ever witnessed . . .

He wanted and couldn't have.

Existed, yet never lived.

Felt and swiftly crushed the sensation, for allowing any- thing to emerge brought his memories. And he didn't want to face them, to relive is failures and die a little bit more.

Taking a couple of deep breaths, he drew his hands down.

His gaze fell on the boy. Handsome kid. Helluva head of hair, he thought. How did she meet the boy's father? Who was he? Did she love him? Hunter didn't want to confront the man, afraid he'd do something ridiculously chivalrous like fight for her when he did. Hell, she was just a female. Nothing special so far.

He leaned over and rewrapped the blanket where the boy's plump little legs had kicked it free, a stab of envy for the babe's sire burning through his chest. A son. What he wouldn't give to be worthy of being someone's father. He wasn't. Hunter realized that years ago.

No kid would want a coward for a Pa.

Chapter Ten

Sable hesitated at the edge of light and braced her hand on a winter-stripped boxelder, letting embarrassment and guilt sweep her. Well, Sable, you and your mouth have done it again, chiseled the man down to his knee boots. Papa once said her tongue could be sharper than his calvary sabre, and the past few moment were testimony that society's restrictions hadn't curtailed its cut.

Her. behavior was deplorable, and since she was lying to him in every respect, by what right did she judge! Looking back over her shoulder, she saw him cover Little Hawk from the cold and she contemplated making amends, then resolutely sank to the wet ground.

Sable discovered some unsettling facts about herself.

She lusted.

And she liked it.

But it isn't the same for him, she protested, attempting to ease her guilt. She was new at this and he had likely touched *hundreds* of women. Touched? Sable nearly laughed out loud. Hunter McCracken didn't just touch, he mastered.

Uncertain as to which upset her more—that her knowledge of the male anatomy was not as lacking as she first imagined or that she wanted to explore the possibilities—her cheeks flamed as she recalled the strong outline of his masculinity. *The part that goes in,* she thought back, and blushed cherry red.

Only in her mind could she admit her excitement over this part of him that seemed to openly acknowledge his desires and that her kiss had brought forth such a bold declaration. There was untapped power in passion, she decided, and he wanted hers, for the *act*.

That much she had the good sense to ascertain correctly. She wanted to kick herself for not allowing her sister to elaborate beyond what the signs of her purity signified. It was the mention of blood and pain that made Sable put a halt the discussion, yet she realized now, if just a little, why Lane spoke of participating in what could only be considered a ritual of sheer agony with such a dreamy expression. Lust, she decided, had a tendency to overshadow one's reasonable thought process. What good was her virtue, anyway? When she returned, provided she survived this horrendous trip, no proper suitor would call, not once it was known she'd traveled with a man, alone, for months, unchaperoned. You're being disgustingly practical, she thought. Perhaps that's why Hunter was always advancing on her. Perhaps he thought she was like one of those painted ladies Phoebe had mentioned? Her recent behavior could certainly lead him to that conclusion.

She sighed, telling herself to be practical. This verbal battle would serve no purpose other than to make this trip harder. They still had so far to go, and they had to trust each other, at least start to—sometime.

Deciding to think about it later, she slapped a hand over the pile of soiled laundry and struggled to her feet, the bulky coat annoyingly cumbersome. Straightening, she pivoted toward the river and slammed smack into an Indian. She let loose a blood-curdling scream, and he merely smiled. She screamed again and his smile broadened to a toothy grin. Sable stumbled backward, then took off in a run, only to collide with Hunter.

"Indian!" she gasped between breaths, gripping his lapels. "There!" She pointed her shaking arm in the general direction.

Hunter pulled his gun from the holster and shoved her behind him. "Get the baby."

Sable immediately went to Little Hawk, lifting him in her arms as the savage strolled nearer to the campfire. He halted at the rim of light and smiled. Hunter relaxed visibly and holstered his gun. What was he thinking? Sable's eyes rounded as he quickly stepped forward and spoke to the men in a tongue that sounded remotely like what Phoebe had taught her. Then to shock her further, they shook hands! For land's sake! Sable slumped to the ground and quickly draped the shawl over her hair and face, concealing all but her eyes. She trembled. What now, she wondered as she changed the baby and drew him inside the warmth of her coat, allowing him to suckle at the milk bladder.

The savage wasn't as tall as Hunter but his shoulders were as wide, the buckskin laced tight across his chest, his shiny black hair hanging well past his shoulders, center parted and drawn into wide ornamental bands. His wrists were adorned with hammered silver cuffs, and even from the distance, Sable could see he was quite handsome, his features rugged, strong. There was an almost aristocratic quality in his bearing.

Hunter gestured for Swift Arrow to come closer to the fire but when they turned into the camp, Hunter stopped short, his expression startled. How in the hell would he explain her? He glanced at Swift Arrow, whose gaze was riveted on the woman.

"You have been busy since our last visit, my friend?" Amusement danced in the Cheyenne's eyes.

Hunter grunted, non committal, his mind racing for an explanation. *But why should I,* he thought. *She's Cheyenne—let her do it.*

Sable didn't care for the smug look on McCracken's face when he poured coffee into two tin mugs, handing one to the Indian. Hunter settled on the ground beside her, close, an almost possessive gesture as the savage hunkered down opposite them both, his fringed trousers fitting like a second skin to his legs. Sable dropped her gaze to Little Hawk, yet she could feel both men staring openly, especially the Indian.

"What do you call your woman?"

There was silence, and it forced Sable to look up.

She darted a glance at Hunter.

"He asked you a question."

"I don't—I didn't understand him."

"Now how's that? He's Cheyenne."

She wilted at the subtle challenge. "I know very little," Sable confessed to her lap. How did she get out of this one?

Hunter smirked. "Interesting," he muttered, relaxing back, taking a sip of the warm brew before answering in the soft guttural tones of the Cheyenne. "I call her Lady. Don't know her real name."

Swift Arrow grinned. "It's not like you, Standing Cougar, to be in the company of women and not know all there is."

Hunter chuckled and Sable stared at him with wide eyes. How could he laugh after the fight they'd just had? Wasn't he upset? Evidently not, she mused, ignoring how handsome a smile made him look.

"If she is not your responsibility, then why do you travel with her and," the savage peered closer, "a child?" He looked expectantly over the rim of his mug. Hunter cleared his throat uncomfortably. "She's paid me to guide her north."

Swift Arrow choked on a mouthful of coffee, spewing an amber shower into the air. Droplets hissed as they hit the fire, sending a geysers of steam into the cool night. Sable could only gape as the savage fell back on his rump, laughing deeply.

"A woman paying *you?*" he rasped over his chuckling. "This is rich."

"Shut up, Swift Arrow," Hunter gritted, "before I bash your face in."

The Indian grinned, a flash of straight white teeth. "Like you tried in Shenandoah?"

Hunter responded with a cold glare, then gulped his coffee.

Sable's gaze shift between the two men. She hated not being able to understand and her eyes said as much when she turned them on McCracken.

"She has fire, Cougar. Whose child does she suckle, if not yours?" Swift Arrow enjoyed taunting what appeared to be a sensitive subject.

I wish it was mine. The thought flashed through his brain, without warning, unheeded, and his gaze hardened. "She keeps that to herself." Among other things.

A soft smile danced across Swift Arrow's lips and he stared at the woman until she hesitantly looked up. He'd observed them from the other side of the stream for a moment before he'd approached, watching her expression shift and change as she looked at Hunter through the tree line. Yet now in her eyes he could see her fear, her unease. Beautiful pale eyes, he thought, then wondered how Hunter could be so stupid as to not see she was a white flower, disguised as an Indian woman. Swift Arrow knew the women of the People and this one was definitely not of the blood. Should he tell his friend? Or did he already know?

"You guide her to the Sioux?" Hunter nodded and Swift Arrow's expression turned grave. "Let us hope it is not to Black Wolf, my friend."

The cup paused half way to his lips. "Why?"

"He has become a bitter angry man in the past seasons." Swift Arrow said, finally turning his attention to Hunter. "He raids on anyone who dares near his domain."

"That doesn't sound like him. He's been so sedate, lately. Letting the legend cover his tracks."

"The attacks have become brutal." Swift Arrow's tone showed his contempt, then added hesitantly, "The cavalry has not been spared, either."

Hunter cursed softly, flinging the coffee into the blaze. The steaming cloud made Sable flinch, then frown at her guide as she laid Little Hawk within a bundle of blankets.

"Why the hell's he doing that now?" Hunter leapt to his

110

feet and paced. "Damn him! I know it's rough for his people but he promised to keep it simply for food and supplies!" He was speaking in English and hadn't realized.

Swift Arrow remained calm, casually sipping his coffee, then pouring more before he answered. "It is said his heart is crushed," he answered in Cheyenne.

"That's horse shit!"

"Mister McCracken!" Sable blurted without thinking and the men looked at her as if she'd suddenly appeared.

"Ah—ha! The lady speaks," Swift Arrow said in perfect English and she gaped at him as he stood and walked over to her, then went down on one knee like a knight begging favor. He grasped her hand. "Since Hunter is his usual cloddish self, not offering an introduction, allow me. I am Christopher Swift."

"Christopher?" she squeaked as he brushed a kiss to the back of her hand.

Swift Arrow grinned into her bewildered face, and Sable felt its warmth down to her chilled toes. Slowly he released her fingers. "Your guide and I are old friends. Schooled together in New England."

Her gaze flitted briefly to Hunter. "But—I thought you were an Indian."

"I am. Well, half really." He settled down opposite her, ignoring Hunter, who was still fuming. "In the white world I am Christopher Swift. Here," he gestured to the forest, "I am Swift Arrow."

Sable inhaled sharply, searching his features. Swift Arrow. What a regal name. Hadn't she noticed a difference in him before?

"My mother was English."

"Yeah, yeah, nobility or something snooty and your father a war chief. What's your God damn horse anyway, Chris—or is it Swift Arrow today?"

"Mister McCracken!" Sable blasted. "Must you always be so rude?"

Hunter sent her a level look, his eyes dark and smoky with sudden jealousy. Did he have to sit so close to her, oggle her like that? She doesn't want me touching her, but she lets a God damn stranger fawn all over her, kissing her hand and— *Christ!* Hunter thought, *I need to get away!*

"It is beyond the stream, north of the ridge," Swift Arrow said without taking his gaze from Sable. "I am capable of retriev—"

"Forget it. Consider it a host's duty." Gun in hand, Hunter stormed off. Sable watched him until he disappeared into the brush, then sighed, dropping her gaze and fingering the tattered ends of her shawl. She flinched when Swift Arrow reached up and drew the fabric away from her face, her attempt to stop him fading under his suddenly chilling stare. She imagined him bare chested, his sculptured face painted for a raid, his muscular form clad in a breechcloth and moccasins, a feathered war lance primed to throw. Was that the life waiting for Little Hawk?

"What do you hide from him?"

"I'm not hiding a thing."

His look warned her not to try that with him. "You are not of the people, Young lady." Lavender eyes, he thought, how intriguing.

Sable was afraid, scared he'd tell Hunter and all her efforts would be for nothing. She looked down at Little Hawk sleeping peacefully, then back to the handsome half-breed.

"Who I am is not your concern, Mr. Swift Arrow. I have an arrangement with Mister McCracken and I plan to hold him to it—" her chin went up—"regardless of what you believe."

"Then you won't mind if I tell him your skin is painted, with what? Iodine?"

Her eyes rounded, nearly absorbing her oval face and she fought him when he grasped her hand, his once gentle touch turning to iron as he twisted her wrist so he could see the underside. He shoved the sleeve of her coat up to her elbow. "You should do it again. It's fading."

"It's the washing—oh, drat!" She batted his hands away and slipped on her gloves, then folded her arms over her middle. "Go away, Mr. Swift Arrow."

"We are not in a drawing room, miss, where you can dismiss me and run to your rooms. You are in my domain."

Sable ignored the veiled dig. "Oh, really?" She arched a tapered brow. "Is that a Harvard accent I detect?"

"Very astute. Miss—?"

Sable harumphed, snubbing the air and it was all Swift Arrow could do not to laugh. She was a prize, he thought, frightened until threatened, then she showed a hidden fire. He wondered if she expressed that excitement in bed? Or was she all woman-soft and tender, recalling the love she couldn't disguise when she looked at the baby. He studied the infant.

"Whose child?"

"Mine."

Now he did laugh. "And Hunter believes that rubbish?"

"Believes what rubbish?"

Sable jolted, twisting to see Hunter lead a horse into the clearing. He stopped.

"What?" he demanded. They looked too damn cozy for his liking.

Sable turned a pleading look on Swift Arrow, beseeching him not to reveal his discovery. Swift Arrow took her hand in his and gave it a quick squeeze, then in a smooth motion, came to his feet.

"I know your mother, Hunter, and she would be appalled that you've eavesdropped on a private conversation."

Sable relaxed, offering a generous smile of thanks to the Indian. Hunter glared at the two, his scowl black and menacing when Swift Arrow sent her a roguish wink, leaving her blushing demurely as he strode to his mount.

"Oh, you dastardly man!" she suddenly cried, setting the baby aside and scrambling to her feet. Every inch of her small

113

form radiated quick anger as she marched over to them. "That—that," she pointed to the mount. "That horse belongs to the man in the saloon. See the blood?"

"Now who's on the lady's bad side?" Hunter muttered resolutely, his lips twitching as he flipped the reins in the air and moved away.

Swift Arrow shrugged. "My mount went lame," and I needed another." He dragged the saddle from the beast.

"But what of er, ah—"

"Barlow," Hunter supplied, pleased she was mad at someone else besides him.

Swift Arrow dropped the saddle on the ground at his feet and in a sincere tone said, "I cut his throat, chopped him into little pieces and ate him for supper."

Sable staggered back and Hunter was there, catching her as she fell into a dead faint.

"Chris, you jackass!" Hunter rasped.

"Good God, Hunt! She doesn't honestly believe that!"

"Apparently." Hunter swept her up in his arms and carried her to her bed roll, laying her gently on the blankets. "Get some water, damn you!" God, she was so pale and still, her eyes closed. He rubbed her wrists and her lids fluttered. She blinked.

Sable stared up at Hunter, his features crinkled deep with concern. His gray eyes were smoky soft and tender as they studied her. The look made her breath catch. This was a side she didn't think he possessed, and she wondered what other attributes he kept hidden.

"Welcome back, Violet Eyes." His voice was husky and she felt its affect in a heated rush that shot straight to the core of her.

She glanced around; suddenly realizing she was on the ground. "I didn't—did I?"

"Yup. Fainted dead away," he answered flatly, then chuckled.

Sable covered her face with her hands. "Ohhh, no!" How

humiliating, she thought, dropping her hands and attempting to sit up.

Hunter slid his arm beneath her back, giving help she really didn't need. His touch was firm, his face so close, and she had the urge to caress his bearded jaw. He smiled, faint and tremulous. He isn't sure what to do, she thought, marveling at his unease.

She looked beyond him to see Swift Arrow holding out a tin cup. He nudged Hunter and he took it, offering it to Sable, pushing her to drink it all. She set it aside and turned her attention to the Indian, her expression piqued.

"Tell her." Hunter's voice was tight and he still hadn't removed himself from his close position there on his knees.

"The horse's owner is walking back to . . ." he shrugged, "wherever."

Sable climbed to her feet, forcing Hunter to move back and do the same.

"That was very cruel, Mister Swift Arrow."

"And you are very gullible, Miss—?" His grin was devilish, teasing.

Hunter tensed as he waited for her to give her name.

Violet eyes narrowed sharply as she looked from one man to the other. I'm a spineless ninny, she thought, embarrassed at having shown another weakness to these men. She would be on her guard from now on, for Swift Arrow knew her secret.

"Lady will do just fine, thank you, gentlemen." Her lips scarcely moved when she added,"And I use the term loosely," then brushed past them both, her head held high. Ignoring their soft chuckles, she went to her packs and flipped open the leather satchel. "Is it expecting too much to ask either of you to do the manly thing and hunt?" She spared them a withering glance.

"Allow me the honor." Swift Arrow bowed low, then retrieved a bow and quiver of arrows from his trappings and took off into the woods.

"You haven't eaten today, have you?" Hunter asked. Sable

vaguely acknowledged McCracken's question, her mind on her hunger. She would not allow herself to become so vulnerable again, her fainting resulting more from lack of sustenance than the cannibalistic images. This was the end of it! She wouldn't give them the advantage simply because they were men. She'd pull her own share and do it without complaining. Brave words, she thought as she went to the fire and poured herself a cup of coffee, sampling it, allowing the hot brew to fill her empty stomach before she placed a kettle of water on the heated rocks.

She was raised to be protected and nurtured, to run a home, not a forest camp. Sable understood what Lane tried to tell her. Papa had coddled them and her uselessness showed in full blown proof to Hunter and Swift Arrow, her lifestyle serving no purpose when she was forced to do for herself. Now it was a test of wills between her and this barbaric country. Sable was realistic enough to know it would take everything in her just to make it to Black Wolf and give him his son. Pain lanced her heart, so sharp she rubbed the spot over her breast as she looked at her sleeping nephew. Could she simply hand over this precious bundle to a stranger?

When his offer to make a hoist to suspend the pot over the fire didn't gain a response Hunter continued to whittle branches, watching her ignore him and go from packs to pot. She knelt close to the campfire, a broad leather case on her lap. Inside were several smaller pouches and bottles securely tied to the leather. She dipped two fingers into the pouches, then sprinkled dark powders into the simmering water. From another she dropped in tiny dried leaves. Hunter could smell the simmering herbs already. By God, the little minx could actually cook! he realized as she jerked closed the pouches and replaced them neatly in the case, then headed for her packs again. With a frown creasing her delicate forehead, she appeared to be moving on instinct, unaware of what she was doing as she returned with a small knife, a thin broad block of wood, a long-handled ladle, a couple of potatoes, onions,

116

and a carrot. Where the hell did she keep that stuff, he wondered, surprised the food wasn't rotten. Hunter almost voiced his thoughts but knew if he did it would break the spell, and he was entranced as she pared and diced like an experienced cook, slanting her cuts, making the most of her stores, then gently plopping the vegetables into the hot water.

She was burying her peelings when Swift Arrow strode into the camp and dropped two hares beside her.

Hunter couldn't suppress a snicker, and Sable's gaze sliced to him, then to Swift Arrow.

Now the truth hits, Hunter thought, his grin blaring annoyingly as he walked over to her, bending to pick up the hares and skin them himself. Swift Arrow, remembering she was not an Indian squaw, made to do the same. But Sable grabbed the poor creatures before either man, took up her knife and came to her feet, heading toward the stream with a determined step.

Hunter shook his head, staring at her retreating back, properly stunned.

"The woman looked as if she'd thoroughly enjoy skinning me instead of those rabbits," Swift Arrow said.

"To her they're bunnies."

When Swift Arrow frowned Hunter quickly relayed their last episode concerning rabbits. "A week ago she would have puked at the sight. Hell! For all I know she could be saying prayers over their graves."

"She is concerned for the life of her attacker, and now mere hares. A woman with a kind heard, my friend."

Hunter heard the implication.

"That sleeping little bundle is proof she's got a man, Chris." His tone warned but Swift Arrow didn't take offense. He'd witnessed the blistering looks Hunter sent the woman when she wasn't aware, and wondered if he should tell his friend what he had discovered, then decided to keep his silent promise to the lady. Yeah, let the man suffer a bit longer. Hunter needed a little confusion in his life. What little of it there was.

Chapter Eleven

Sable knelt near the stream bank and stared at the fluffy brown rabbits. She couldn't do it. She simply could not! Oh, she should have allowed Mr. McCracken to do this horrible task. In his eyes she was an absolute catastrophe at everything she said or did, anyway.

The notion sent her chin up a notch.

She didn't want to be a failure, a useless *parlor ornament* for some man's home. *No man will ever have you,* Sable reminded herself, *not after this adventure.* Certainly her father couldn't keep this incident quiet like he had Lane's capture, and Sable wondered if Lane realized how much she'd given up for her.

The metallic scent of blood stirred her back to her task. McCracken's voice filtered to her through the forest, his tone clear and deep. He'd just love the opportunity to come over here and offer another *demonstration* and that knowledge pushed her to complete the task, no matter how vile she thought it was.

Well, just think of it as one of Salvatore's plump capons, she told herself, and picked up the knife. Clenching her lower lip between her teeth, Sable lifted her arm; it hovered above her head for a moment before she brought the blade down on a pair of the bunny's feet. Her stomach roiled violently and with three more quick strikes, she lopped off the paws of both creatures.

118

Tears blurred her vision as she repeated the process exactly as McCracken had so callously shown her; slitting the belly and spilling the organs on the ground. Her mouth watered, bitterness taunting her as if it were Hunter's goading voice. She trembled as she held a downy ear in each fist. Closing her eyes, Sable yanked. Nothing. Her throat constricted. She wasn't strong enough and had to make a slit between the ears before she ripped the hide from the tiny body, her skin creeping at the tearing sound as she was forced to tug until the last of it snapped off. Blood splattered her face, blouse, and coat. Swallowing repeatedly, she knew she still had the second hare to dress, and she did it, quickly, clumsily, her breathing fast and loud by the time she was finished.

The rank smell of the animal's bowel was more than she could endure, and she twisted away, retching uncontrollably until she nearly choked on the sharp, heaving punches of air. Sable swiped her mouth with the back of her wrist, smearing blood across her lips and cheek. She stared at her bloody hands, appearing black in the darkness, then slowly rose and staggered to the stream. Dropping to her knees in the shallow creek, uncaring of the icy wet soaking her boots and skirts, she splashed water on her face, then rubbed vigorously, before cupping the clear liquid to her lips. She drank, soothing her burning throat.

Hands clamped heavily onto her shoulders and a short shriek escaped her before she twisted to look behind. McCracken.

"You all right?" In the dark all she could see was the gleam of white teeth. Why, the insensitive brute was laughing at her!

Sable elbowed him sharply aside, struggling to stand in the sodden skirts and when he made to help, she hissed. "Don't you dare touch me!"

Sloshing to the bank, Sable tripped on the heavy fabric and her humiliation reached the ultimate summit when she fell on her face in the cold mud. *Do not cry. Do not!*

Felled like a dead tree, Hunter thought, rubbing his moustache

119

with a thumb and forefinger, effectively daming back a laugh as he walked out of the stream. Extraordinarily pleased she skinned the rabbits, Hunter never doubted the entire act was meant to vindicate herself from his earlier lesson. He reached down to assist her out of the mud, but she was already groping for the game and pulling herself to her feet again.

"Don't!" she snarled, traipsing back to the stream to rinse the rabbits.

Hunter held back his temper. "I was only trying to help."

Suddenly she was up in his face. "Well, I don't need it!" She lost her footing, found balance, shoved hair and mud and blood from her face and nearly stabbed herself with the heavy knife as she said, 'And I am not so stupid, Mister McCracken," her tone bit like the chink of metal, "to not know when you're making light of my distress. You do it rather well, and *far too often!*" The last she shouted up at him, growing an inch with each word, before she turned away.

"Hell, it isn't like you provoke the hell out of me," he said following her up the incline. He loved it when her fur was up.

"Simply *existing* provokes you, Mister McCracken," she returned, pausing briefly to deliver her most sarcastic glare. "And any gentlemanly efforts on your part are forever suspect."

Couldn't he be the least bit considerate of what it took to skin those poor rabbits? No, he believes I'm an Indian woman, she recalled with a rueful twist of her lips, *and expects such things from me.* Sable couldn't honestly blame him for *her* outrage, certain she had the man utterly confused. My my, she savored, settling beside the fire with a watery squish. What a comforting thought.

Hunter halted close to the fire and dropped to the ground, removing his boots and pouring out the water. "I never claimed to be damn gentleman."

Her gaze flashed up, her gloved hands freezing in the task of chopping meat. "Obviously." She slapped tiny body parts into the bubbling liquid with vengeance.

Swift Arrow chuckled and Hunter's gray eyes threatened a

beating, then honed in on Violet Eyes as he wrung out his socks.

"You need to get out of those wet things," he said, propping his boots near the blaze to dry, "or you'll catch cold."

"My, *what* a revelation," she muttered dryly, clanking the lid and wondering why she couldn't remember cutting up vegetables and adding spices.

A stretch of silence and then, "I believe it's your volley," Swift Arrow said to Hunter.

"Shut up, Chris, and I said—"

"The entire Nebraska territory heard you, Mr. McCracken." She didn't have another coat, all her blankets were needed for the baby and that was that, she thought, pulling on her gloves.

Suddenly he was beside her, hoistering her to her feet. "Do it, or I will."

"Has anyone told you you're a insufferable bully, Mister McCracken?" she asked, jerking from his grasp.

"Hundreds, every day," he said flatly. "Off with it." When she didn't comply he made to do it for her, but Sable retreated out of his reach, stripped the coat off and rolled it in a ball. His expression promised retaliation for what she had in mind. She smiled thinly and threw it at him.

Swift Arrow's laugh was more of a snicker as Hunter dragged the coat from his head, watching her retreat to the safety of her baby's care before he spread it across the packs to dry.

"Damn woman." He sank to the ground, propping his forearms on bent knees and staring at the dirt.

"I like her. She's got spice."

"She's got no sense and too much sass and I liked her better when she was petrified of me."

"You really are a bully, Hunter," Swift Arrow said gravely.

Hunter glanced up. "If I'm not she's going to do something that'll get herself killed."

He tried to maintain a reasonable surveillance of their surroundings, but for nearly a half an hour she went from her gear, to the baby, the goat, and even checked her horse, then draped herself in a woolen shawl, poured water into a pail and placed it by the fire, stirred the stew, replaced the lid, washed her face and hands—at least he thought she did; she had her back to him then. But her puttering was grinding on his last nerve and he was about to tell her so when she started off toward the woods with a bundle in her arms. Hunter scrambled to his feet.

"Hey! Wait!" he yelled. She didn't and he went after her, stubbing his toe. He limped across the uneven ground. "Damn it, lady!" He grabbed her arm and spun her around to face him. "You can't leave the camp."

"And why not?"

For an instant he debated whether or not to tell her what he suspected, then decided to. "This is wild country. Anybody could be beyond those trees."

Her smile was tolerant, as if indulging the village idiot. "In case it's escaped your attention, Mister McCracken, I am still soaked to the bone."

His gaze dropped to the blood-stained blouse, lingering a bit too long at the open vee at her throat. "I've noticed," he finally answered.

She jerked her arm free, pulling the shawl snugly. "Then how do you propose I change if I don't leave the camp?"

"Dress here." His lips twisted in a insolent grin. "We won't look."

Her cheeks burned with shame. "Do try to be realistic, Mister McCracken."

Hunter's lips thinned. "You either do it here or stay wet. Got that?" He stormed back to the fire, ignoring the sticks and rocks poking his bare feet. She had to be the most contrary individual in all of Nebraska territory: taking her coat so she wouldn't catch cold, yet refusing her the opportunity to change.

Sable glared holes into his back and hoped he felt every

single one. Such a crude, despicable man, she thought, water making a puddle around her feet. She could swear he enjoyed putting her in these embarrassing predicaments!

Swift Arrow glanced between the two and sighed, then stood and went to his own gear. Without a word, he strung a blanket between two trees, then bowed regally. "Madame, your dressing chamber," he said without a hint of humor, though these two were the best entertainment he'd witnessed in weeks.

Sable smiled her thanks, and was about to slip behind the partition when the baby cried. She dropped her garments and immediately went to him.

"You're going to spend all night making me look like an ass, aren't you?" Hunter muttered out of the side of his mouth, watching her.

The Indian grinned. "You don't need my assistance." A growl rumbled in Hunter's chest and Swift Arrow moved closer to the fire. "Why do you make things so difficult?" he said in a low voice. "Has it been that long since you've enjoyed the company of a lady?"

"Lady? Yeah, right."

Swift Arrow stared at him, daring him to deny what was so obvious to himself.

Hunter's shoulders rose and fell in a gesture of indifference, yet his gaze drifted to the baby, then back to the dancing flames. He could hear the thick liquid pop and bubble inside the kettle. The lid jiggled, pouring the delicious aroma of stew into the air. His mouth watered, a hungry knot twisting his stomach as he leaned back against a rotting stump. He dipped his fingers into his shirt pocket and withdrew a pouch and papers, smoothly rolled a cigarette, then tossing the fixings to Swift Arrow. Hunter slid the smoke between his lips, then touched a glowing timber to the tip. Years, he thought inhaling deeply. Years since he'd been with a woman that didn't stink of cheap liquor or the last man she'd slept with. Years since he'd spent this much time with any one individual. *I live too much on the edge to be sane,* he thought, drawing in a lung full of smoke and exhaling slowly. He didn't care if he died tomorrow, and on several lonely, very hellish nights he had considered taking it out of God's hands. But he wouldn't, and he knew he was half crazy and stupid to be near a beautiful creature like Violet Eyes. He took three deep drags, then snubbed out the cigarette. She and that little boy had suddenly become his only reason for sticking it out a little longer.

He looked in her direction, a smile shadowing his lips when she lifted the baby in her arms and kissed the top of his head. She spoke to him softly, her face radiating her love for the child as she wrapped him in blankets and furs and settled him for the night. The tender sight made the air go out of his lungs.

She stood and gathered her clothes, shivering so violently her hair tumbled free of the neat bun. In a smooth motion Hunter came to her, lightly touching her arm before she could disappear behind the blanket.

She glanced warily from his touch to his face.

"You're freezing."

"I'm fine. I'll manage." Her clicking teeth chopped her words.

Hunter sighed. Her I-don't-need-your-help attitude was going to kill her. He raised his hands and she stumbled back. Hunter stopped halfway through taking off his fleece-lined jacket, eyeing her sudden fear. Christ! That was one way to smash his lust all to hell. Removing the sheepskin coat, he wrapped it around her shoulders, waiting patiently as she slipped her arms into the sleeves.

"But *you'll* freeze." Sable snuggled into the coat, his body heat clinging to the lining, easing her chill.

God. When she looked at him like that, like she honestly cared what he was thinking, he had to battle the urge to drag her to the ground and into his arms.

"I've got a duster and a pelt or two in my pack." He tugged the collar up around her neck, the gesture bringing her closer to his tall frame, the back of his knuckles grazing the smooth curve of her jaw. An incredible warmth scorched her there.

"Thank you," she whispered. There was something about being so close to a man who wore no stockings or shoes that was unbelievably intimate.

"Your welcome, ma'am." His thumb brushed her chin, and heat stole up her cheeks. Sable backstepped, and he lowered his arms, shoving his hands into his pockets.

"Is that ready?" He inclined his head toward the stew pot and she nodded. "Good. The smell is driving me crazy."

Her skin flushed, the compliment warming her numb toes. "You ought to serve yourselves before it burns," she said. Unconsciously she nuzzled the pristine fleece of his jacket.

Their eyes locked and Hunter absorbed the sparkling color, her delicately arched brows and pert nose before his gaze lowered briefly to her lips, cherry ripe and glistening. Temptation. His conscience screamed to crush the thoughts, while a lonely ache deep inside urged him to take her in his arms and unleash the banked indigo fire he saw in her eyes. And let it burn him, sear him with the heat and the life of her.

And maybe discover if he was still capable of loving—real loving.

God.

He didn't care.

"Look," he blurted out, then paused, gathering his thoughts and directing them. "We have a long way to go and we can't keep up this battle when our lives might depend on at least trusting each other." Hunter felt her relax as surely as if he wore her skin and offered, "I'm sorry about what I said . . . earlier."

Sable sent him a skeptical glance. "I suppose I would be remiss if I did not offer an apology, too," she said in a tired voice.

"Jeez, don't strain yourself."

"Well, you haven't exactly been a martyr to trust." Her words suggested he keep his hands and lips to himself.

"And you, madame, have not been very truthful." His mocking tone made her concede before he probed into her lies.

"You're suggesting a truce, then?" She studied the ground.

"If that's what you want to call it, yeah."

"Should we set terms?"

He should be furious at that, but couldn't muster the energy, not when she was trying to be so damn reasonable. "Been that bad, has it, Violet Eyes?"

Her gaze flew to his. The way he said that name, as if it belonged only on his lips, made her heart thump, a river of blood gushing through her body. Suddenly she was smoldering like the blaze beside them.

"To be honest, it's not anything like I expected," she said in a throaty voice, breathless.

He frowned, not harsh, but with more curiosity. "Are you saying you haven't traveled like this before?"

Hunter waited for her to answer, and Sable recognized the eagerness in his eyes. She didn't relish that being this close to him made her fling caution aside, and she was instantly annoyed that she didn't have some witty retort handy.

"When I sort the matter out, Mister McCracken, I shall be certain to inform you," she said and moved behind the partition.

Hunter stared at the air, then shook his head and went back to his place by the fire. Just for moment there, it had been good and easy between them. He hadn't mistaken the sudden flush to her cheeks and how she'd lowered her guard. What on earth was the woman hiding that made her so damn defensive?

"I gather your peace offering didn't work?" Swift Arrow said, grinning.

"It wasn't a peace offering," Hunter hissed softly, then ladled the stew onto tin plates, handing one to Swift Arrow.

126

"Has it been this way since you began this journey?"

Hunter's gaze sliced to the side. "What way?"

"Good God, Hunter, I can dice the air with the tension between you two." He waved, then forked a carrot. "And it's more than just a difference of opinion."

"So what? I got a right to be sore. The little vixen conned me into taking her."

"You mean she got the better of your drunken senses."

Ignoring that, Hunter shoved a spoonful of food into his mouth as Swift Arrow leaned back against the saddle, his smile smug and patient. Hunter's spoon paused halfway to his lips and he sighed, dropping the utensil onto the plate.

"Yeah. She did."

"Amazing that one so delicate could take you down a peg."

Hunter actually smiled. "If that woman grinds me down any further I'll be crawling in the dirt."

"You know she's white!" Swift Arrow realized.

Hunter glanced to the side. "I might be slow, Chris, but I'm not stupid."

"That proves you're still vulnerable, and it sits in your belly like rancid meat." Swift Arrow's grin said he enjoyed enlightening Hunter to this. "You'd like nothing more than to have the upper hand with her, but you can't, because she treats you like the man you are."

"And that is?"

"Cold, rude, mean, insensitive," he said without malice.

The barbs glanced off Hunter's thick hide. He knew who and what he was. "It's been a long time since we last saw each other, Chris," he said after a spell. "And a woman like her shouldn't be out in a place like this, with a kid . . . especially with me." It was a warning, or perhaps a plea to get her away before something happened.

"The lady seems to be holding her own." Swift Arrow studied his friend, then asked quietly, "Are you ever going to leave here?" He gestured to the wild.

"And go where? Home?" He shook his head. "I can't, not like this."

"But we all need a goal, a future plan. You have to put those times behind you."

"Don't you think I've tried!" he hissed softly, his face darkening to a mask of haunted shame and guilt. *"Those times* were lives, Chris. Living, breathing human beings dead because I . . . failed."

Swift Arrow cursed his goading. Who was he to judge what Hunter should feel and for how long? He just wished Hunter could imagine the possibility of a life beyond his self-imposed seclusion. Perhaps it was asking too much after what he'd experienced.

"I'm sorry, Hunt."

"Don't mention it." And he meant it.

Vigorously, he rubbed his face, his palms brushing over the trimmed beard and moustache. The last thing Hunter needed was to contemplate a future.

"Oh, Lord help me!" Swift Arrow whispered, and Hunter glanced to his side, then followed his gaze. His features yanked taut.

Violet Eyes was undressing, the wet garments dropping to the ground in a heap beneath the thin Indian blanket. Unfortunately for her the glow of the fire gave off a silhouette of her shape with amazing clarity. Hunter swallowed thickly, his gaze raking over the shadowed curve of her spine, the points of her breasts, and her slim, shapely legs.

"Turn your back, Chris." Swift Arrow's brows rose at the sharp command. "She isn't on display for you—or me," he added in a rock-tight voice.

Hunter didn't want any man looking at her, especially when she didn't know it and slanted a maming glare at his friend. The Indian sighed and with boyish reluctance, shifted his back to her. Hunter stole a lingering look, savoring the vision, then did the same. He closed his eyes, the outline of her naked figure burning across his brain. Damn, damn, damn!

After moment Hunter returned his attention to the spot where she'd disappeared behind the partition.

"Give her some privacy. She'll be along in moment," Swift Arrow assured. "Don't worry."

"I'm not worried," Hunter snapped and Swift Arrow chuckled softly. Yet Hunter continued to watch, eating his stew without tasting it, impatient for her to materialize. His frown deepened. Seconds ticked by. There was no movement beyond the blanket. No silhouette either, he thought grimly. Tossing the plate aside, he climbed to his feet and headed for the treeline, gun in hand.

He'd throttle her for scaring him like this. Hell, she'd been gone nearly ten minutes already. Surely that was long enough to take care of anything. The deeper he went into the woods, the angrier he became. He didn't give a shit if he embarrassed the chit, he was going to blister her cute little bottom for this!

Working himself into a splendid fury, Hunter forgot years of training and thrashed through the brush like a raging bull. Silver slivers of moonlight dappled the foliage in his path. He almost didn't see the pale lump until he was nearly standing on it.

There on the ground at his feet was his sheepskin jacket, fresh blood staining the white fleece collar.

Chapter Twelve

Hunter was frantic. Indians had her. Three hours before daylight he'd found unshod horse tracks and hoped he was on the right trail, for he was exhausted, going on pure adrenalin to catch up. They were heading homeward, to safety, and Hunter was acutely aware they'd be expecting him once they camped. Why they didn't just come and get him and Swift Arrow when they were stupid enough to relax their guard he wasn't sure, but Violet Eyes was paying for his mistake.

Now, tromping deep into Indian lands, Hunter was tense and scared out of his mind. Silently, he could admit that. It felt better not to lie to himself anymore. The warriors were reputed for their daring and bravery, and they had a nasty way of torturing a body that kept a captive alive for days. Hunter knew that from firsthand experience. He wanted to get her before they had a chance to stop for play time.

Most white men had the good sense not to trespass on Indian lands. Hunter claimed to not have any good sense left and if they hurt her, he vowed not to let a single one live. He'd kill her himself if she was too far gone.

He shoved the thought aside. They hadn't time to do much. But how long did it take to rape and beat a woman? *God, you're callous, McCracken. No. Realistic.* He prayed, God how he prayed, the Pawnee didn't have her. But that wouldn't be realistic either. This was their territory. Hunter assumed the absolute worst and it made him sick inside.

It didn't pay to hope anymore.

Reining gently back, he slid from his mount and grasped his rifle as he lightly tossed the reins over a branch. Toeing off his boots and socks, he jammed them under the saddle blanket before he crouched and worked is way deeper into the brush. Thirty yards away, he judged. Good.

He couldn't see her, but knew she was there, knew they hadn't dumped her some where along the trail. One mount he'd tracked bore its weight more to one side, the erratic hoof depressions like a calling card. Two riders, one horse. Hunter grinned, thin and sinister. Like old times. Circling the camp, he moved in from the west. Surprise, surprise.

There were five that he could see, perhaps a sixth keeping guard. Two were armed with revolvers. Damn. He wasn't counting on that. Hunter inched closer, each barefoot step patient and measured and absolutely soundless, Years of training coming into play. He forced his breathing to slow and quiet. Carefully he pulled back thin branches, cautiously releasing them after he stepped over a small boulder. The cool season made the woods sparser and him more visible. He'd have to ride hell-bent for leather to get her out of here—if she was alive. His blood thrummed in his ears, his senses so keen and sharp it was nearly painful.

He lowered himself to the ground as he brought the rifle forward from the shoulder harness. Slipping his hand inside his shirt, he withdrew the scope, threading it into position without looking. Level on the hard earth, Hunter adjusted his elbows and sighted. His hands shook and he jerked back, taking a deep breath before sighting again.

His darkest nightmare focused in the magnifier.

Pawnee.

A raiding party, from the look of the spoils. Like a slam to his chest memories flooded; of grueling pain and blistering heat, of painted faces and men—his men—screaming for a swift merciful God who ignored their cries. His skin prickled, and he grit his teeth until his jaw ached as he battled grisly phantoms. With the back of his hand he swiped at the perspiration on his upper lip. It gave him a second to smash it all down between the weakened cracks in his mind and regain his concentration.

He studied the small group. Drunk, a plus. Where was she? Had he been wrong? Had they killed her somewhere on the trail and he'd missed it? His pulse thundered in his ears. He could have sworn he sensed—Hunter swerved the barrel to the left. Violet Eyes. The wild thumping in his chest eased a fraction. Alive, set slightly apart from the others, her back to him, her arms tied behind her and stretched around a narrow tree. She was working at her bonds.

Good girl.

Hunter shifted. He could pick off two real quick, he thought, using his scope to follow movement. Hunter lowered the rifle slightly, his brows drawn tight.

Violet Eyes wasn't their only captive.

Sable was miserable, frightened, and on the verge of a hysterical scream that would last an hour. She shivered, and with no coat every tremor intensified the splitting pain banging around in her head. Her toes felt frozen inside her wet boots, and she was certain her arms would pop from the sockets any second. The wound had stopped bleeding, she deduced, for the warm wetness no longer trickled down her neck and back. A fine mess, she thought dejectedly, drawing up her knees to ease the pressure on her arms. Discreetly she shifted her hands up and down, scraping the hide bonds against the rough bark. She watched her captors through blurry eyes.

The braves squatted around a smokeless fire, close enough that she could the smell rancid grease smeared over their skin. They passed a bottle of whiskey and some dark mass she assumed was food between themselves while casting killing glares at her. Hours ago she'd roused to her body smacking against the withers of a bony horse, yet any discomfort rapidly churned to near building rage when she managed a decent look at their clothing. Most of them wore pieces of calvary uniforms, hats, jackets, officer trousers. Fairly clean ones at that. The red-haired scalp anchored to one warrior's waist hadn't escaped her attention either. Sable never thought she could hate this much.

She wouldn't allow herself to dwell on exactly what these men wanted with her. The blond calvary trooper was explanation enough. Suspended from a rope slung over a low branch, the man hung from his wrists, his head slumped forward between upstretched arms, his knees scarcely grazing the ground. He wore no boots and his chest was stripped bare. Sable suppressed a moan of sympathy. His exposed skin was a series of jagged, bleeding slices, and oozing black burns.

One Indian suddenly hopped to his feet and Sable watched with a repugnant fascination as he picked up a flaming piece of kindling and raked it across the trooper's skin from waist to shoulder. She drew in her breath sharply. The man flinched, reared back and came to his full height for a brief instant to tower over the savage. He didn't utter a sound. Sable admired his bravery, however useless. Then the trooper's right knee shot up, catching the Indian in the stomach. As soon as he made contact he passed out, slumping against his ties. The Indian, still buckled over, stuck him hard across the face. An officer, she realized, the satin leg strip shining in the dark. Dread plummeted through her. Her turn would come next.

I'm terrified, Lord. Help us. Please, somebody, help us.

Her mind raced, desperately clinging to reason as vividly gruesome images danced across her terrified mind. She didn't know if the Indians attacked the camp after they'd taken her or simply spirited her quietly away. But the gouging doubt that Mr. McCracken or Swift Arrow were injured or perhaps dead because of her stupidity kept her from truly accepting the possibility of any rescue. Realistically, she couldn't count on anyone but herself.

She had to escape. Little Hawk needed her and the thought of her nephew left to the wolves made Sable scrape the hide ties against the bark with renewed vigor. The tightly laced strips cut into her wrists, blood dripping into her curled palms.

She cringed back against the tree when one of the Indians leaped to his feet, a slim pole clenched in his fist as he strode toward her. He stopped not two feet from her and spoke. She could do no more than tremble and stare. Like the others, his face was painted with broad red slashes across his forehead and cheeks, his head shaved but for a slim stiff column of hair running from crown to nape. Piercing his ear were several feathered rings and beneath the blue calvary coat she could see smeared yellow war paint. He was bare but for the coat and breechcloth. Thumping his chest proudly, he gestured to his friends, the officer, then her. Their laughter was cruel and biting, then suddenly he threw back his head and let loose a shrill yelp as he thrust a war lance into the ground between her legs. She choked back the scream flooding her throat. Her stomach revolted and she slumped to the side, vomiting on the ground, the rope tugging at her throat. The savage shouted at her. She didn't care. Her heart mourned the men who'd died such horrible deaths. Had she ever met any of them? Were they Papa's troops? Oh God, what if those soldiers were sent to find her? The savage shouted again. Sable didn't look, spitting dryly. An instant later his fingertips dug into her jaw, jerking her head around, forcing her to meet cold black eyes. Liquored breath punctured the air between them. A tight dry moan caught in her throat when her gaze darted to the scalps.

My fault. It's all my fault.

Chapter Thirteen

Her skin actually crawled, moving with a cool prickle up her back, creeping across her scalp and tightening her features. There was a venomous gleam in his black eyes, a twisted pleasure at inflicting pain.

"Lame Bear!" He thumped his chest. "Slave." He poked hers.

Slave indeed, Sable thought, trying not to show her shock. It was likely the only English word he could speak. And not very well, she added maliciously, attempting to be courageous.

Lame Bear slid his hand downward from her jaw to her throat, his fingers circling, tightening slowly until her world tilted sharply and her a thickness pounded behind her eyes.

He's proving his power to me.

An instant before her vision went black he let her go and she slumped forward, gasping for air, tears scorching her eyes as she waited for them to focus. Cautiously her gaze crept across the ground, then lifted slowly upward to the cavalry officer. As if sensing her eyes on him he turned his head—ever so slightly as to not attract the attention of the others—and their eyes locked. Despite his wounds, Sable saw fierce strength in those eyes and she clung to it as the Pawnee's hand mashed over her breast, gripping the soft flesh with bruising force. She winced, throwing her head back and biting her lower lip. Blood pooled in her mouth. Shame swept

135

her. He'd taunted her like this since she'd regained consciousness.

His fist tightened. When she didn't cry out, he let go, the rope sliding tautly through his hands as he straightened. She'd forgotten about the leash. He jerked it, pulling it high, and Sable's neck stretched to accommodate it, her ears burning where the scratchy rope dug into her tender flesh. His chuckle was dark with sinister warning as he tugged her like an disobedient dog, bringing her bottom off the ground and nearly sucking her arms from their sockets. Sheer stubbornness crushed down her tormented scream.

He didn't like it and back-handed her across the face, reeling agony blistering her chafed skin. He struck her again, raised his hand for a third blow, then grunted something, abruptly released the rope and turned away, staggering the few steps to his comrades. Sable fell forward, nauseating pain sprinting through her body. Salty tears spilled down her throbbing cheeks to drip off her chin, the soft splats like a ticking clock as she waited, endlessly it seemed, for her violent spasms to subside. Through a curtain of tangled hair Sable stole a glance at her captors, her eyes glittering with a gemstone hardness as she scraped the bonds against the bark—again.

Hunter clamped a hand over the Pawnee's mouth as he slammed him sharply back against his chest. Instantly he gave the man's neck a quick jerk to the right, the splintering of bone a ringing crack in the otherwise soundless night. Without a glance, he laid the body on the ground, crouched, circling the area for other guards. Finding none, he made his way closer to the camp site. With his long-barreled rifle Hunter knew he could maintain a reasonably safe distance and still get off a shot or two before the direction of fire was located. It was small comfort.

A faint sound, like a snapping twig, made him freeze. Using his rifle scope, he squinted, sighting between the branches to see the drunken Pawnee deliver a blow to her face. Rage tore through him and Hunter ground his teeth nearly to powder, desperately struggling not to lose control and riddle the place with bullets. Not yet. But the Indian raised his hand again. Do it, he threatened, his finger pulsing on the trigger, and it'll be your last act on this earth. The temptation to shoot was nearly irresistible, but he refrained when the bastard simply walked away. His gaze shifted back to Violet Eyes. She was slumped to one side, passed out, making it difficult, but not impossible, to get her out. Right now, he was simply thankful that she hadn't unleashed that mouth on the Pawnee. She'd pay worse for back-talk.

His gaze stopped on the man hanging from his wrists. Poor bastard. Had to give him credit for fighting. Maybe he could get him out alive, too. Maybe. But one against five were lousy odds. He watched, listened, his brain ignoring the snatches of the Pawnee's conversation, his senses honed in on the woman. The woman, lady, Violet Eyes. Hell if he wasn't going to demand her real name after this. She was closer into the rim of camp light than he'd first thought. Damn. He'd planned to simply sneak up, cut the ties and drag her out of there, but he couldn't afford so much movement without being seen.

And he didn't think it was wise to attempt getting a revolver to Violet Eyes, even if he could. The woman was a menace with a coffee pot, and God would never forgive him if he gave her a loaded weapon. Daylight was coming. Now or never, he thought, slipping around the curve of a tree and taking aim.

Sable winced, nearly climbing backward up the tree at the deafening cracks. One Indian arched, his chest exploding in a rain of chunked flesh and blood as he fell back, flying a little before he hit the ground. Before they could react, a second

Pawnee's head jerked sharply; he tripped sideways and fell. Half his skull was missing.

The three remaining Pawnee scattered, shooting toward the east between her and the trooper. Gunfire spat, streaks of red-white light spiriting out of the pistol barrels. She flinched with each report, stemming back a scream. The officer roused, on instinct to protect himself, she thought, curling away from the battle. My God! Who was it? More Indians?

Flattening himself against the rough bark, Hunter yanked back the breech loader, thumbed in another cartridge and shot the lever forward. Go ahead boys, keep using up that ammo. Just as he swung around the trunk he heard a bullet's airy path whine past his head. Sounded like an arrow, he thought briefly before bright stars splattered behind his eyes. Pain detonated in his skull. Shit, that's one or the bad guys. Hunter stumbled forward to the ground with a meaty *thunk,* and he fought to stay conscious. Damn.

Sable heard the empty panicked click of the Indian's revolver, then silence. White smoke drifted on the gentle breeze like a phantom's cloak. Indistinguishable figures moved stealthily within the powdery mist, harsh guttural shouts dicing the quiet, and she gasped as one Indian dragged a lifeless body by the hair into the clearing, dumping him before her. She couldn't see his face, but immediately recognized the clothes of her guide. Oh, God, was he dead?

The Pawnee dropped the rifle on the ground, then tossed Hunter's holster aside. He bent to search for more weapons. In one smooth motion Hunter grabbed the rifle and rolled over on his back as he cocked the loader and squeezed off his last round. The Indian straightened with the force of the blash, howling and clutching his shoulder. He stared in disbelief at the blood fountaining between his fingers, his arm useless at his side. Somewhere to his right the repeat of a spent revolver made Hunter flinch. Jesus!

Swaying, the wounded savage took aim at Hunter's head, then suddenly lurched forward, nearly stepping on his prey. Hunter came to his knees, turning the rifle stock out and bashing the Pawnee's legs. The Indian buckled. The primed pistol discharged into the air as Hunter scrambled to his feet, catching sight of the trooper's leg lowering to the ground as he dove in the direction of Violet Eyes.

Withdrawing his knife from his boot, he sawed once before she rasped, "Help *him!*" A third Indian advanced on the trooper, his tomahawk raised. Bare feet his only defense, the officer kept the Indian at bay for no more than a precious second.

It was enough.

Hunter spun on his knees and threw his knife through the air, sinking it into a Pawnee throat. Three dead, a fourth wounded. One alive.

With no more ammunition, Lame Bear hurled the gun into the trees as he lunged at McCracken, butting his head into his side and tumbling to the ground on top of him.

The two men grappled in the dirt, rolling over each other, across the fire and smashing into a tree. Blood streamed from Hunter's temple, blurring his sight. Lame Bear swung with accuracy, fists crashing into Hunter's face and ribs. Hunter retaliated, his wounds lessening the force behind each blow. It gave the Pawnee a chance to unsheath his knife, the silver winking like a death song before he stabbed at Hunter's throat.

Hunter blocked, but not before the razor point sliced open his cheek. Ramming his knee into the Indian's side, Hunter caught Lame Bare's wrist before a second swipe did more damage, his muscles straining to stay the blade from something vital. *Can't keep this up.*

Then the wounded Pawnee staggered to his horse.

Sable's panic escalated. He'll bring more, she knew, yanking furiously at her bonds, her shoulders screaming in protest when the ties snapped. She fell forward, then immediately darted toward Hunter's holster lying in the dirt a few feet away. Before she reached it the tether abruptly yanked her back, her breath blunted raw. No time to try the knots, Sable slid to the ground and extended her arm, fingers clawing the dirt as she stretched her body to its limits to grasp the gun. She strained. Just a little . . . a little more.

A keening war cry made Sable glance up.

The horseman rode toward the struggling pair, his feathered lance aimed to where Lame Bear half straddled Hunter, his knee pinning Hunter's arm to the ground. It had come down to a test of strength; one to kill, the other to survive. And the Pawnee had the use of both hands. Veins bulged and throbbed in Hunter's neck, his shoulders vibrating with his efforts to stay alive. His sight wobbled as the rider came into view, the horse's sharp hooves pawing the hard ground. The knife touched his throat.

Then he saw Violet Eyes.

Sable's fingers wrapped around the pistol butt, and immediately she hastened to her knees, shoving her hair out of her face and extending her arms. Doubled thumbs pulled back the hammer. She felt a moment of indecision. Which one first? She fired. The weapons bucked and Hunter's attacker fell backward onto the fire. Instantly she swerved to the left, smooth and precise, the barrel following the approaching rider. She drew back the hammer and squeezed the trigger. The savage tumbled sideways off his horse, but not before he managed to thrust the lance into something solid.

All movement ceased but for the vibrating wood staff.

The pungent curl of sulfurous smoke wafted, stinging her nostrils. She blinked repeatedly, poised to shoot again. Her fingers were numb, her breathing labored and thick. Hunter was flat on his back, lifeless. Dropping the gun, she struggled in her heavy skirts to get to him, stumbling once before the leash angrily wrenched her freedom. Pathetically her hands shifted between the stake firmly entrenched in the ground and the strip around her throat. Her eyes were riveted on Hunter.

"Mister McCracken?" A agonizing pause, then, "Answer me!" Tears wet her parched voice. She couldn't see him breathe. Her panic swelled. "Huun-ter!" she screamed.

Hunter turned his head slowly, blinking.

"Those God-damn sons of bitches!"

So relieved he was alive, Sable forgave him for swearing and withered to the ground in a heap.

Hunter tried to roll over but couldn't. Glancing to his side, his eyes widened a fraction before he removed the lance from his shirt sleeve and inspected the damage. A new draft, he thought, then shifted cautiously to his hands and knees. He came to her, pausing once to pull his blade from the dead man's throat.

"Oh, Lord." Acid bile rose in her throat, her eyes riveted to the bloody blade as Hunter cut her loose.

She crumbled a little more. He pushed a finger beneath her chin, tilting her head back. Hesitantly, she lifted her gaze. He looked awful. Blood trickled down the side of his head into his ear; his cheek lay painfully open, bleeding down his throat and staining his shirt; his jaw and lips swelled, blowing his features out of proportion. He looked wonderful.

"You came," she whispered dryly.

"Yeah. I did." She'd doubted him, and Hunter could have kicked himself for allowing her to suffer with that misguided thought.

"I, ah, I didn't know you could shoot," he said, clenching his fists, craving assurance that she was whole.

Her fingers trembled as she primly brushed tangled hair from her face in a habitual gesture to smooth it. "It seems that you continuously underestimate my abilities, Mr. McCracken."

He smiled, misshapen and bloody. "Thank heaven for my mistakes."

It was his way of expressing gratitude. They'd saved each

other. She glanced at the carnage surrounding them and swayed, reaching out, and Hunter immediately swept her into his arms, pressing her warmly to his chest. God, he never imagined touching anyone would feel this satisfying.

Sable buried her face in the curve of his shoulder, her shoulder jerking with her effort to keep back the tears.

"Ohhh! I don't think—I've ever been so frightened. They wouldn't give me any food or water and . . . and I didn't know what happened to you or Swift Arrow or Little Hawk. And I'm so cold. And I tried to be brave. I really tried. But they tied me like a dog. Did you see?"

"I saw." He wanted to kill again because of it.

"He hit me. No one's ever hit me before."

"It's over, Violet Eyes," he whispered, pressing a kiss to the top of her head. "You're safe, now."

His gentle smoothing hands on her back crushed her restraint, and Sable wept quietly, slipping her arms around his waist.

Bruised, bloodied, and beaten, Hunter thought at that moment he could tackle the Pawnee all over again. Nah, stupid idea, he corrected, tightening his embrace even though his ribs burned like fire. She was a shivering bundle of ice.

Sable tilted her head back and sniffled. Their eyes met, and Sable read the concern buried beneath that dark frown.

"I'm fine, now," she whispered. "But you." She tugged her sleeve over her fist and blotted the blood at his temple. He winced and she drew back, but he grasped her hand, turning his face into her cold palm and pressing it to his lips. Sable shuddered raggedly. So very warm, she thought, letting him draw her closer. Suddenly his mouth was on hers, blistering her lips with a thick grinding kiss. It was heart wrenching and passionate and unbelievably torrid. And Sable melted into it, allowing him to mold and shape her lips with his, over and over. I want this, she admitted as liquid lightening coarsed through her weakened limbs, warming her. Oh, how I need this.

142

"I hate to break up this tender reunion, folks." At the first words, they separated and turned. "But all that racket you made is bound to alert some relatives." The calvary officer straightened, dignified and military as if garbed in full dress uniform. He bowed to Sable. "Ma'am," he said, then attempted to loosen his bonds with his teeth.

He couldn't. "Would you mind?" he asked kindly of Hunter.

"I thought you were damn near dead," Hunter said, standing, then helping her to her feet.

"She didn't." Through a swollen eye, the officer winked at Sable.

"Then why the hell didn't you try to get free?" Hunter blasted, then wished he hadn't. A roaring thunder bounced inside his head and he cursed, touching the graze at his temple.

"With those odds?" The officer held out his wrists for Hunter to cut. "A little tough, don't you think? Besides, when they brought her I knew someone would eventually come."

"Is that a fact?" Scowling, Hunter slid the blade between the ties and with a quick jerk, he was free.

"Sure." The man kept his eyes on Sable as he gently peeled away the bloody strips. "A fetching creature like her is never alone—not for long, anyway."

Great, Hunter thought. *Another stag sniffing after her skirts.*

Chapter Fourteen

The warm blood oozed from dead men's wounds, steaming the air as Hunter examined the damage he'd done to his rifle. Repairable, he thought, then searched for anything useful. He tossed a shirt he'd found in the stolen packs to the trooper.

"You have a name?"

"Noah Kirkwood, sir." Hunter eyed the leg stripe. "Lieutenant," he corrected, gingerly pushing his arms into the sleeves.

Hunter scooped up his hat and extended his hand. "McCracken, Hunter."

As they shook hands, Noah's eyes clouded briefly, then cleared and widened. "Rumor has it you're dead, Captain."

"It's just mister now, Kirkwood. I've been released and," Hunter smirked, "you know what rumors and five cents will get you."

Grinning, Noah inclined his head to the woman. "Who's the lady, sir?"

Hunter's eyes narrowed. "If you're fit enough to be so damn nosy, son, then why don't you just see if there's a horse nearby, so we can get the hell out of here."

As if given a direct order, Noah strode unsteadily into the woods, armed with only a knife as Hunter gave a soft high-pitched whistle. A moment later his palomino trotted on the fringes of the clearing, stopping when he scented blood. The beast dipped his great head, snorting dual blasts of frosty steam as he pawed the hard dirt. Hunter offered a comforting pat and soft words of praise for remaining hidden, then he put on his boots.

Sable observed the goings-on with a detached manner, not really believing she was safe and unharmed and Hunter was close enough to touch. Or that she'd taken two lives so easily. She swallowed the urge to retch. God forgive me, she hoped, averting her face from the dead men as she walked on shaky legs toward her guide. He heard her approach and twisted sharply, a freshly loaded revolver in his hand. She gasped, back-stepping quickly, then tottered. Hunter shoved his gun into the holster and reached out, gathering her in his arms before she met the ground.

"Can you stand now?" he asked after a moment. Breathing rapidly, she nodded, but gripped the saddle for support as he eased her to her feet. He offered her water from his canteen. "Swish a bit in your mouth for a second, then spit it out before you drink more," he warned, assuming she hadn't had anything in her stomach since the morning before.

Sable obeyed, briefly slacked her thirst, then handed back the canteen. When he offered more, she shook her head. "There was no indication whether we will find water soon, Mister McCracken. I don't see the sense in being greedy when it isn't necessary."

He smiled, a little proud of this proper white woman. He rummaged in his pack and pressed a chunk of dried beef into her palm. Sable bit into it, famished, then with the meat clenched between her teeth she bent to lift her skirt. She glanced at him, eyeing his keen interest with a fair amount of censure as she tore a strip from her petticoats and straightened primly.

"You're bleeding everywhere," she said at his puzzled look, then pressed a cloth to his cheek. "Hold it firmly," she instructed, then tore another strip. "Please, stoop down, Mister McCracken. I cannot reach you."

145

Hunter obliged her and she carefully wrapped his head in the lacy white cloth, though the bleeding had stopped. He put up with her ministrations, considering the view was lush and full and damn near shoved in his face. *I've got nowhere else to look,* he convinced himself and availed his hungry gaze to the firm breasts hidden beneath the dirty broadcloth. He clenched his fist, unconsciously pounding his thigh to keep from filling his itchy palm. *Your lust, McCracken, is a dangerous thing.*

"That will have to do for now, I suppose," she said and he stood, still holding the cloth to his cheek.

"Thanks."

Sable smiled, checking his bandage. It was the first time he'd ever said that, or expressed any gratitude at all.

Eyes locked and they stared, sinking into the other's gaze, the longing to be held and reassured and comforted weaving a heavy mist between them. Yet neither moved to assuage it, neither uttered the thoughts tripping through their minds. They simply listened—to ragged breaths, the pulse of troubled hearts, honored vows and necessary lies denying their desire's freedom.

Noah towed a horse into the clearing, hanging onto the bridle for support. The couple stood close, looking so sweet he took mischievous pleasure in startling them.

"There was only one willing to be still long enough to catch."

Hunter stepped back, breaking the spell, his eyes darting to the U.S. Cavalry brand on the horse's rump. "Anything in those packs, Kirkwood?"

Noah pulled his gaze from the woman. "Ah, yes, sir, three, four days ration, ammunition for this," he bent and scooped up the spent pistol, "and," he added with flourish, "a few essentials." He grinned. "It's mine, sir."

"Insolent whelp," Hunter muttered, then gave the area a cursory look before he inspected his packs and swung up onto his saddle. He held his hand out to Violet Eyes, offering a lead up.

146

Sable glanced up at the dead Pawnee, then beseechingly up at Hunter.

"Don't even ask," he warned, recognizing that "shouldn't-we-do-something" look. "Not for murderers."

Her expression darkened. "You're right, of course," she said, slipping her foot in the stirrup and taking his hand. A brisk cry escaped her as he pulled her onto his lap. Hunter pushed up her sleeve, cursing vilely at the striped cuts and dried blood.

"Please, Mister McCracken, your language." She yanked her hand back.

"You're going to hear a lot more than cussing, woman."

"Spare me, please."

"Why didn't you tell me about that mess?" Roughly, he wrapped her in a blanket, noticing the welts on her throat before he reined around.

"They're minor compared to yours and the lieutenant's." She twisted and Hunter bit back a moan when her soft bottom settled atop his groin. Scrutinizing his features she asked, "Are you certain you're strong enough for this ride?"

"Don't have much choice, now do we?" His voice was unintentionally sharp as he dug his heels in the horse's sides. Sable grasped the pommel to keep from sliding off and turned her attention to the land ahead, riding stiff and unyielding. The constant rub of their bodies in time with the horse's brisk gate was enough to make her blush cherry-red.

"You can rest against me, Violet Eyes," he whispered close to her ear. "I won't bite."

"Oh, but you do, Mr. McCracken. Quite frequently."

Hunter felt like a heel. Her voice was strained and raspy and he hadn't even bothered to ask what happened *before* he got to her. Not one complaint, either. In fact, she'd been more concerned for him than anyone. He dropped into the pits of hell as a horrifying thought occurred to him.

"Violet Eyes?

She looked back over her shoulder.

147

"Did they . . . um . . . ?" he stammered, and Sable was cut to the heart at his uneasiness. It was so unlike him to be at a loss.

She shifted cautiously. "Did they what?"

He glanced away, then met her gaze. "Force you?" He nearly choked on the question, suppressed rage darkening his voice.

She briefly touched his jaw. "No." His features relaxed. "You found me in time."

"Not soon enough."

He blamed himself and Sable wisely clarified, "This wasn't your fault. My modesty is the culprit. I wandered off for more privacy."

"I thought as much."

They'd traveled at least three miles before she allowed herself to relax against him, and Hunter shifted, giving her no other option than to quit fighting exhaustion and to use him as a pillow. He absorbed every yielding curve pushing against his sore chest and lap.

Loosely holding the reins, Hunter brushed the tangled hair from her face. "What's your name, little girl?" he whispered into her dreams.

"Sable," she yawned, wiggling a bit.

Sable. That figured. What else could she be named for but a luxurious Russian fur.

Throbbing with pain from his beating, Hunter wasn't going to ponder anything beyond the soft, filthy woman in his arms. Except, perhaps, that she hadn't once asked about her baby. He briefly studied her features, then focused his eyes on the terrain ahead.

Sable, honey, you've got more secrets than me.

"You want to talk?" Hunter said as Noah trotted up beside him. Hunter gave the man credit. Despite his wounds he was alert, constantly searching the area.

148

Noah nudged his hat back and squinted at the sun before he spoke. "Not much to tell, sir. We were on patrol and they came at us from all sides, attacked and vanished. At least thirty-five, near as I could tell. It was over in less than ten minutes. Cates, he is—was—my sergeant. He killed five before he went down."

Hunter noted the affection in his voice, the pain.

"How come they spared you?"

Noah sent Hunter a threatening look. "You think I'm a coward?"

"Nope. Surviving is all anyone can do, Kirkwood. I've been there."

"I know, I heard about it at Fort Kearney." Noah sighed, his eyes scanning the terrain. McCracken was a legend within the military, one every young officer tried to match or better. "I was clubbed first," he pointed to the egg-sized lump on his forehead. "And when I woke, well, you saw my accommodations. The more I fought, the more they liked it, and the more they tortured me." He suppressed a shiver, recalling the clear threat of castration. "I knew if I was going to get out alive I had to get them to leave me alone for a spell. So," he shrugged, "I bored them to death."

Hunter frowned, then his lips curved slightly. "No fight, no fun, huh?"

"Yes, sir."

"What were you doing on patrol way out here?"

"I'm afraid that's confidential, sir."

Hunter understood better than anyone about military secrets. He looked to the sky, then down at Sable. Sable. God, it was going to take some getting use to her real name and the questions that went with it.

"Your wife, sir?"

"No." The tone told Noah he'd hit a brick wall.

"She's a brave lady."

"Yup."

Noah grinned even though it hurt like the devil. Where she

was concerned the wall was fortified better than a garrison. "You heading West, sir?" Safe enough subject.

"North."

"After all that mess!" He inclined his head behind him.

"I've got a job to do, Lieutenant, just as you have one to report back to your regiment."

Kirkwood was silent for a long moment. "God, I hate the thought of telling those men's families what happened," he hissed in an anguished voice.

"Then don't."

Noah's head snapped to the side, his tone caustic. "I beg your pardon?"

"Look, Noah, those men are gone." Hunter sounded incredibly tired. "No amount of gory detail is going to bring them back. Families don't need to be haunted with the nightmares of their sons and husbands getting their scalps lifted or their bodies mutilated. Dead is dead. Inform your superiors and leave it at that."

That's experience talking, Noah realized and fell into his own thoughts.

Hunter glanced down to see Sable staring at him, questioning eyes sketching his features. His expression molded to a cold oblique mask and he returned attention to their surroundings, but Sable ignored the icy dismissal and snuggled her arms around his waist, waiting for the tension to melt from him. It wasn't long. He hurts so deeply, she thought, and hides it; the raw pain she saw in his eyes drifting with her into sleep.

Chapter Fifteen

Sable roused slowly, headachy and stiff but surprisingly well rested. Lifting her eyes, she stared into Hunter's smiling face.

"Mornin', Violet Eyes." His voice, husky and unspeakably intimate sent a sensual tingling across her skin and she absorbed it, enjoyed it. "Make a decent bed, don't I?"

Sable flushed at the sensual implication in his tone and jerked upright, his mocking chuckle vibrating down his body and back up hers.

"I apologize," she rushed to say, studying her lap. "It was just that I was so very cold and I hadn't any rest and you were so warm, and—"

He bent his lips to her ear and rasped, "I was only teasing."

She stole a sharp glance. "But you're wounded."

"I've had worse."

She remembered the first time he kissed her and the jagged scar she felt on his ribs. "I know."

Darkness settled over his features. "No. You don't," he cut back, aloof and distant when a moment ago he looked ready to kiss her. *It haunts him, this secret pain.* Sable scolded herself for failing to recognize how deeply it ran. Not that she imagined this hard-bitten man *ever* allowing it to surface, but it made him vulnerable, human, and dangerous. And this desolate country likely intensifies it, she thought, studying the trail

151

strewn with weatherbeaten furniture, cracked barrels of china, and oxen carcasses. Past lives discarded for new adventures.

It was past noon before they found a campsite both Hunter and Noah could agree gave adequate protection from attack. Her guide, she discovered, knew every creek and stream in the territory and she counted her good fortune, for both men were exhausted and in far too much pain to continue. They hated to admit they were weakened, even to themselves, and Sable knew they'd sooner perish than admit it to her.

Sable slid from the saddle and turned to Hunter as he followed suit, his lips pressed to a bloodless white, the only indication that he was in pain.

Hunter gripped the saddle, waiting for his head to stop spinning.

She touched his sleeve. "Come sit in the shade."

He jerked free. "I can manage."

Infernal male pride, she thought. "Mister McCracken. At this point I really don't care if you can. You will be of no use to me if you stumble and lacerate your head further. Now, lean on me this very instant!" she ordered indignantly and practically forced him to comply.

Hunter's grin nearly split open his cheek as she *helped* him walk. Feisty lass, his father would say.

"Didn't anyone ever tell you it isn't safe to antagonize a wounded bear?"

Her gaze shot to his and pleasure lit her eyes. He was teasing her again. "Even bears bow to a gentle hand, Mr. McCracken."

The arm around her shoulder gave a little squeeze before he settled beneath the shade. She knelt down with him, concern wrinkling her brow as she eased off his battered hat and unwrapped the stained bandage. Gently she brushed back the blood-caked hair for a closer inspection of the graze at his temple.

"Are you dizzy?"

"A little."

"Does it throb or hurt constantly?"

"Throbs," he said with feeling and she drew back sharply, fearing she'd hurt him. "All over." His brows wiggled. "Wanna check?"

"Oh honestly!" she huffed, but couldn't help but laugh. Wretched man. If he could even *think* such lurid things he wasn't that bad off. Tossing his hat on his lap, she left him and went to Noah. He was removing his packs.

"Lieutenant?" He turned, swayed, and she reached out, but he straightened sharply. "If you don't have any objection I will see to your wounds."

He plucked at his shirt. "They aren't too bad."

"I'll be the judge," she informed him, then indicated the spot beside Hunter. "Sit."

"Yes, ma'am." He tipped his hat and obeyed.

Sable didn't doubt infection would set in if she didn't work quickly. As for Hunter, well, he was going to be unmanned when she informed him he would have to rid himself of that hideous beard. She removed the remaining packs and blankets, mentally taking stock of their provisions, and after asking how long it might be before they would be able to obtain more, she portioned out the food as fair and adequately as she could. After gathering dry wood, she started a small fire, of course, under the supervision of the men and in the area they'd designated to be the best spot. She ignored their remarks after that and did as she pleased.

She was in charge, Hunter thought, efficient and with a purpose. And he was damn glad she could manage when pushed because he honestly couldn't stay upright another second. His eyes rounded when she unsaddled his horse, and he and Noah lurched forward to help when the weight threatened to tumble her backward into the fire. But she straightened in time, depositing the saddle near the blaze in a puff of dust. She repeated the measure with Noah's before rubbing down both mounts, then hobbling the animals close. Incredible.

Within a few minutes she managed to have both men braced against their saddles and resting comfortably near the fire. Settled between them, she encouraged them to eat chunks of stale brown bread and dried beef while she sharpened a knife. A small pan of fresh water, a full canteen, whiskey, bandages, and food were distributed before her knees.

Testing the edge of the blade, she asked, "Who's first?"

"Him," they said in unison, pointing at the other.

She smiled, eyeing each in turn, then decided Noah needed tending first.

"Remove your shirt, please, Lieutenant." Her voice caught, cheeks flushing at such a request.

"Yes ma'am," he grinned, then added, "Call me Noah, ma'am."

"That's impossible, sir." Her nose tipped the air. "It wouldn't be proper."

Noah lifted a brow, regarding her, then Hunter. Hunter shrugged, instantly regretting it when pain drove up his side. He grunted and she turned to him, lightly touching his chest.

"Oh, for heaven's sake, Mister McCracken, don't move around!"

In one glance he absorbed her tangled hair, her own cuts and bruises left unattended, and the faintest streaks he could see on her throat where she'd done a poor job of applying the dark red dye. A white woman—a very properly raised one at that. He'd stake his life on it. How could he have been so blind not to see it until she was lying on top of him—spitting mad?

"Are—are you certain you'll be all right for a moment more?" For a fraction of a breath she was drowing in those intense gray eyes.

"Yes, ma'am." Her expression mirrored his every ache and pain and his heart tripped. *Quit dreaming, McCracken. She's simply being charitable and you don't have the right to be thinking any different.*

"I'm afraid this will hurt," Sable told the officer, her dismissal confirming his thoughts.

Noah looked from her to the knife and back. "What are you planning?"

She took a deep breath. "I must cauterize the knife cuts, for I've no salve and they are too shallow and broad to stitch closed." She sounded apologetic.

He glanced down at his chest. "I understand, ma'am."

Sable thrust the blade into the embers, then cleansed the less serious wounds on his forehead, wrists, and arms. Over a dozen thin criss-cross slices and blistering burns marred his chest. It was the burns she concerned herself with first. Common sense and sheer necessity directed her movements.

Noah's breath hissed out through clenched teeth as she probed the wounds for particles, punctured and drained blisters, then rinsed them clean. Her touch was incredibly gentle, the icy water she trickled a relief to his burns, yet every inch of his torso danced like loose nerve endings. His lips went pastey gray as she poured whiskey over the gashes, fresh blood and alcohol dribbling on the ground. He said nothing.

Sable lifted the glowing knife from the fire, feeling the heat through the pair of Hunter's gloves she now wore.

"Re-ready?" Sable hated the crack in her voice. It certainly didn't bespeak confidence. He answered by turning his face away.

"Want me to do it?" Hunter offered softly. She shook her head vigorously, afraid her nerve would shatter if she so much as looked his way. Gathering the tattered remnants of her courage, she pressed the flat of the blade to the wound in a quick smooth stroke. Noah flinched, grunting deep in his throat. His skin sizzled. Her eyes misted with tears, and she caught her lower lip between her teeth, fighting a sympathic cry. He'd been through so much already, and she hated inflicting more pain on him. Hunter handed her the necessary items without being asked, and though working swiftly and carefully, Sable was as relieved as he when she said, "It's done, Lieutenant."

Noah released a brisk rush of air before he looked at her. Sable sniffled back fresh tears. His tanned skin was ashen, dotted with a thin sheen of perspiration despite the cold. Hunter handed him the bottle of whiskey and Sable sent her guide an annoyed look as Noah quaffed a huge swallow, then another and still another. She took the bottle and corked it, then wrapped his chest in clean white strips from her petticoats and helped him into one of his own reasonably fresh shirts. He passed out the instant she fastened the last button.

She shot Hunter a panicked frown.

"Just cover him up. It's best he's out. That couldn't have been easy."

"I'll have to watch for fever." Hunter noticed she chewed her lower lip when she was deep in thought. "Isn't there an herb we can brew to ease the pain?"

The corner of his lips quirked. "The whiskey'll blunt his senses enough for now, but yes, there is. Hound's tongue or Solomon's seal. I'll look for some later."

"No, you won't. You'll tell me what it looks like and you will stay right there. You're next, Mr. McCracken."

"That sounds like a threat."

"Pretend it is," she said. "Take off your shirt, please."

He gave her a swollen leer. "I never thought you'd ask."

Heat swept her body. "Please refrain from such suggestive comments, Mister McCracken," she said tartly. "You need to have your ribs looked at, if not bound." She twisted away to search the packs.

"I'm all right, 'cept for this." He smudged his cheek and crusty blood came away on his fingertips. She placed a worn leather pouch between them and Hunter immediately recognized his shaving kit.

"What are you planning, Violet Eyes?" He tossed the shirt aside and leaned gingerly back against the saddle, trying to look unaffected as she stropped the straight razor.

156

"Dirt, dust, to say the least of the hair, and Lord knows what else living in that beard will certainly cause infection." Warming water, laying out implements—Sable focused on anything but that gloriously carved marble chest. "The beard must be removed. It's unsanitary."

"I'm not shaving," he sulked, folding his arms. "I'll live."

A sly shadow curved her lips, the razor winking in the sun light as she inspected the edge. "Afraid I'll cut your throat?"

"Hell, yes!" He suddenly recalled all the unkind things he'd said to her.

"I'm rather good at this." Her eyes glittered with suppressed humor as she swirled the brush in the tin cup. "I used to shave my father."

"And who might he be, Sable?"

Her pulse skipped, violet eyes clashing with his. "H-how did you know my name?" came in a airless rush.

"I asked, while you were half asleep." He felt rotten when the color drained from her face and added, "That's *all* I asked."

"Oh." A squeak like a frightened squirrel as she dipped the thread-bare cloth into the hot water. Her hands trembled and she hoped he didn't notice.

He did. "Odd name for an Indian, don't you think?" Who was she hiding from with this disguise?

"You're acquainted with a great number of Indian women?" She wrung out the rag.

"Yup, lots," he lied.

Jealousy reared, unwarranted but real, and she snarled murderously, slapping the saturated towel over his face. Steam rose in the cool air and she heard him chuckle, "Intimately, too," from behind the rag.

Beastly, beastly man, she thought, shaking her head ruefully. She repeated the process twice, denying him the opportunity to make another graceless comment before she lathered his jaw.

"I can do this myself, you know." *But rather you did.*

157

She met his gaze, her hand pausing, then moving slower as she swirled the brush across his chin. "Mister McCracken? Ah, I, ah—" Sable swallowed tightly, her voice a strained whisper. "I beg you not to reveal my name to Lieutenant Kirkwood."

"Why the hell not?" What could a cavalry officer do with knowing her first name? It wasn't *that* uncommon. Unless, he thought as she dropped the horse hair brush into the cup and stared at her chapped hands, it offered clues to something other than her identity.

"Promise me, please." The Union Pacific railroad and Fort McPherson were too close to risk discovery, and no matter how often she considered that Kirkwood's patrol might have been dispatched to locate her and Little Hawk, the slightest chance of recognition was a dangerous gamble. "It's such a small request."

He ducked close. "Give me an explanation first."

His warm coaxing tone surrounded her like thick steam, and she crumbled a little. Sable longed to confide in him, but with Hunter McCracken's devotion to the Army, his loyalties were suspect. The Army wanted Black Wolf's head, and she—well, Swift Arrow—had his son. If Hunter knew who she was, would he keep Little Hawk's location from her and abandon her at the nearest fort? Her feelings didn't matter. The baby, think of his safety.

"I cannot."

Uncontrollable hurt surged through his veins. She still didn't trust him.

"Then forget it, *Sable.*"

"Shhh!" She darted a glance at the sleeping lieutenant, then she pleaded in a frightened hiss, "Promise me! Now!"

Hunter glanced down at the tiny hand clamped with a death grip on his bare arm, then back to those tormented eyes. Hunter knew better than anyone that fear pushed a body into madness, but Jesus, she was absolutely terrified! What in God's name was so threatening? For one absurd moment he actually thought she was wanted for kidnapping, then discarded it. She was taking the boy—who was definitely Indian—to the Dakotas, not away. Was she staying? Visiting? Was her husband white and the child the result of rape by a warrior? The crushing thought made him burn with rage. But one thought stuck out in his mind: she never mentioned her husband, his name, nor gave any indication that she cared for him. Nor had she asked about her son. But she *had* to be married; no single white female with a lick of proper upbringing would bargain to go to the Dakotas.

A bargain. Nothing more.

That reminder ground viciously down his spine and he leaned forward, making her flinch. "You owe me for this, too, Sable," he whispered caustically, "And be certain—" he looked her over once, swift and lusty, "I will collect."

"I never doubted otherwise," she bit back, distraught that he might know more than he was admitting.

The air cracked between them. The fire popped, shooting ashes and sparks.

He'd agreed. Sable drew a ragged breath, withering with relief.

"Give me that," he growled, palm out for the razor. "Christ, the way you're shaking I'll be cut to shreds in seconds."

"Perhaps it will whittle down your contrary moods to just one," she said archly, and he gave her a thorough perusal, then flashed her a grin.

Sable groaned as her thoughts shifted to Little Hawk. Her precious nephew. His health, his food! The moment she saw Hunter in the Pawnee camp she knew Swift Arrow was caring for a newborn babe! My lord, a man with an infant! Was he capable? Would her nephew suffer for her mistakes? Heaven save us, would he reveal her ruse of feeding the boy from the bladder? And where were Swift Arrow and Little Hawk now? When would they meet again? She didn't dare ask, not with Kirkwood within hearing distance.

It wasn't until Hunter scolded her for drooping the mirror that she turned to look at him.

My heavens! He was scraping the last layer, revealing the man she'd met five years ago. This was the striking calvary officer who had risked his life for a stack of papers and bullied his way into her birthday party. This was the dashing rake the ladies had swooned over, the same man who had scared her to death with his bold embrace and callous words to a spoiled, selfish young girl.

"Why are you looking at me like that?"

She blinked. "You—you look so different."

He toweled away the excess shave soap. "That good or bad?"

Both, she thought, splendid to look at, bad for wilting equilibrium. "Inconsequential," she finally managed, waving airily and striving to sound unimpressed at the drastic change. She took small satisfaction that he looked disappointed as she rinsed and dabbed the cut on his cheek with a cool rag to bring down the swelling. Inconsequential indeed! Without the heavy dark beard and moustache his jaw was smooth and chiseled, the sensual carve of his mouth capturing her attention and threatening her breathing.

Double drat.

Plucking a long strand of hair from his head with more force than necessary, she dipped it and a needle in whiskey before threading the two.

"Where did you learn that?"

My sister, she was about to say, but snapped, "Don't talk," and scooted closer. Sable made to brace her arm on his chest, then drew back, shifting the hovering position of her hands at least twice in indecision as to where to properly place them.

"Best way would be facing me," he said.

"Yes, I suppose so," she mumbled distractedly, then without giving his suggestion much thought, swung her leg over his thigh, straddling his lap. Instantly she saw the gravity of her mistake and started to move off. He gripped her waist with both hands.

"You're here now. Just get on with it before I bleed to death."

Her expression withered, sympathy blossoming, and Sable knew she must set aside both her animosity and social dictates to help him. She stared at the cut, raw and bleeding again from the shave. It actually throbbed. She was going to be deathly ill. Think of it as an embroidery sampler, she told herself and pricked his skin. He didn't even flinch, his eyes following her every movement as Sable sealed the wound, taking tiny careful stitches. Sable wanted to cry for that brave pride. The pain must be incredible, she thought, feeling his hands tighten on her waist.

Hunter understood torture better than any warm blooded man at that moment. He tried to concentrate on his wound, making a show of being in pain. It hurt all right, but it was so hot and throbbing he couldn't feel the needle pierce his skin. But he did feel her. He had brought this on himself, of course. Yet regardless of the stern admonitions he continued to give himself, every warning crumbled to dust the instant she was near. And now he had a beautiful woman sitting on his lap—the best position possible, he silently agreed, for attack—his lusty instincts took over. He clamped his hands on her thighs, squeezing, taking a bit of skirt with him.

"Don't move, Mister McCracken." Sable was wise to his games, even if he was in pain. "I just might slip and *poke* you in the eye."

His gaze flashed up and he knew he'd been caught. He didn't care. And her glare said she knew it.

Her thighs gripped his as she concentrated on her stitches, the warm core of her rubbing against his groin, sending his imagination reeling down a luscious path, dreaming of the silken limbs wrapped around his hips, his hands sliding over soft pliant flesh to bury himself deep inside her. He smashed the urge to push her on her back and experience his heart's dark desires.

Then her breasts brushed his bare chest, life springing from her and he grit his teeth. Cushiony soft. The ripening points drilled into his bare skin, and oh Jesus—he had to see. His gaze drifted lower. *Don't torture yourself, Hunter, ain't worth it.* He looked. The cloth-covered swells were nubbed and plumping. It nearly did him in.

Sable bent close to clip the hair thread with her teeth and she froze for a instance, her lips pressed to his cheek, eyes locked with his.

"Done." She drew back.

"Hey, what's this?" He lightly caught her chin and with his thumb, rubbed the wetness on her cheek. "Why?"

"No matter what harsh words constantly pass between us, Mister McCracken," her tone said she was tired of it, "I truly did not wish to hurt you further." He harbored enough scars.

"It's all right. Probably looks worse than it is."

Her lips quivered pitifully. "But you received those wounds because my carelessness."

"You're forgiven."

He hadn't taken his hand from her chin and the feathery touch suspended her resistance, urging her, tempting her. "Mister McCracken," she whispered in feeble protest. "Please don't." But she wanted him to kiss her.

"Forgive *me*, Sable. Forgive me for not protecting you." A haunted plea, clawing with the hunger for forgiveness—in himself.

She recognized it. And gave it. "Oh, Hunter. We're alive. That's all that matters."

His name on her lips was like a bolt to his heart, his own aching to taste that sweetly banked energy she kept tamped and hidden. He crushed her mouth beneath his. Demand erupted, the heat making him tremble as he held her to his chest, uncaring of the ripping pain the motion caused. She yielded to him instantly, her appetite swelling. His mouth moved back and forth across hers, all warm velvety flesh, moist and hot and grinding, his tongue slipping between her lips and plundering the dark secrets within.

His kiss devoured her.

She offered a wordless moan, her arms reaching around his neck, fingers groping into his hair. Her hips tilted, rubbing shamelessly against the bulge growing between his thighs. Excitement destroyed any thought of proper behavior.

His hand slid down her chest, resting hesitantly just below her collar bone before slipping lower. He had to feel the rounded woman flesh, had to know if his imagination could be matched. He touched. God . . . The delectably soft mound filled his palm. And he stilled, waiting for the shove, the slap, and the viperous reprimand he richly deserved. But she didn't deny him; she curled even closer.

Steal it. Take it. It's all you'll ever have.

Crumbs.

Captured moments.

Borrowed tenderness pilfered with a jaded heart.

Chapter Sixteen

Rules were discarded, honor and secrets ignored as Hunter savored every morsel she relinquished to him, knowing she would never—ever—be completely his, not if she knew his past. Hunter held back, unwilling to give way to the fathomless longing this fragile woman created, for he understood the extent of his slender control. It mixed too easily with bitter rage and loneliness—and touching her, kissing her, was like groping in the festering cracks that bulged with ugly humiliation. No good would come of this. But the past that for so long kept him from feeling too much, wanting anyone or anything so deeply, demanded its fill—and unwisely he stole another surge of her pure untainted desire.

The surrounding air was punctuated with swift-caught breaths and purrs of excitement, the lusty calls shifting to a smarting groan, a sting-laced wince, yet each softened briefly to recapture the path to pleasure and skirt the bruised flesh and tender wounds. Desire lost as they simultaneously jerked back with low moans of pain, and their eyes locked.

Sable soothed the back of her head.

Hunter rubbed his side.

Tastes and scents lingered, laboring lungs a reminder of the soul-draining thirst that soared at the slightest touch. The imprint of his hand on her breast left her skin warm, craving the feel of him, while Hunter suffered an intense regret that he alone would ever know.

Her lips twitched and he answered her with a lazy smile, his gaze drifting over her to where she straddled his thighs. Sable blushed to the roots of her hair, her features yanking taut as she scrambled off. He chuckled lowly, reaching out to keep her there, then caught his side, yielding to the pain.

She hovered over him. "Oh, for heaven's sake." His head came up, banging into her chin.

"Sorry." Sheepish, soft.

Sable sat back on her calves, rubbing her chin, humor bright in her violet eyes. "You're a mess."

"I wouldn't be throwing stones, if I were you."

Her nose tipped the air. "Another gallant comment?" she quipped, smoothing her hair. Her fingers tangled in the wild mass and he laughed lightly, the smile fading as he frowned at the blood on his fingertips. It wasn't his.

"Come here."

She didn't, gingerly feeling the back of her skull, then wincing.

"Sable."

"You promised!" she hissed, glancing at Noah, who still slept.

He didn't wait for her permission and turned her so he could examine the wound. The skin was broken—not deep, but swollen and hard. He soaked a cloth from her neat stack and dabbed. She flinched once, then held still as he cleansed the wound.

"Where did you get all this cloth?"

She ducked her head, looking at him through the curtain of hair. "My petticoats."

He arched a brow, inspecting her in one sweep, then bent close to her ear. "At this rate you'll be naked before nightfall."

She came upright, a telltale blush darkening her cheeks. "Must you say such things?"

"When you get this flustered?" He tossed aside the cloth. "Sure." Her blushes were the most untainted he'd seen in years. And he craved them.

Her gaze skipped over his face, darting to his mouth before she met those piercing gray eyes. "You shouldn't have kissed me like that, Mr. McCracken," she whispered, aware her masquerade as a married woman slipped with episodes like that, destroying her validity and peeling back layers she needed to hide.

"And how would you like to be kissed?" he couldn't help but ask, smiling crookedly.

Sable rolled her eyes, exasperated, and muttered, "You know very well what I mean."

A flash of raw pain and dark secrets colored his features, then vanished, so quick she almost missed it. His voice dropped to a hollow whisper. "Yeah, I do." Then forced a teasing grin as he said, "And I should be horse whipped."

Sable took several strips of cloth, knotting them for a length to bind his ribs. "Don't tempt me," she said, jerking the fabric tight. "Lift your arms," she ordered, leaning forward. "Slowly."

"Be gentle with me," he murmured against her hair and Sable wished he was short, plump, and covered with warts.

"Does it hurt to breathe?" She concentrated on wrapping the lean torso.

"No. Why?" Her cheek grazed his chest as she reached around his back. She had dirt in her hair.

"Well . . ." she adjusted the band beneath his arm and sat back, "I imagine it would if something vital were punctured."

"What a comforting thought."

"You should be thankful." Sable answered, tucking the edge. "That Pawnee gave you quite a beating."

"Don't sound so damn pleased, Sable." Her eyes flared.

"Sorry, it'll be tough not to call you that since it's been killing me not to know your real name. Have a last name?"

"No." She held out his shirt.

"Witch," he rasped softly, ignoring the clothes and grasping her hands. He inspected her wrists. "We need to take care of that."

"*I* will take care of it, thank you very much." She started to move away but he wouldn't let her.

"Mister McCrac—"

"Shhh. Don't say it. Don't." He pressed her palms to his chest, flattening them beneath his own when she resisted. "God, I'm beginning to despise my own name," he murmured, husky and intimate, remembering the honeyed richness of her lips on his own, the polite restraint she showed before succumbing to her own desire and accepting his. She looked from him to her hands and back, the fresh guileless spark in her eyes shinning so bright and trusting, Hunter wanted to crush it, to deny its existence, deny that she belonged to another and would never be free.

His hands slid up her arms, not stopping until he cupped the gentle curve of her jaw in his broad palms. He drew her closer, and closer still. A tiny sound worked in her throat, yet she didn't resist. Since that day in the saloon he discovered he'd risk any pain for the chance to just *be* with her. She soothed him, softened his rough edges, and as her lashes swept down, sealing away the indigo glitter that danced nightly across his mind, she coaxed him again into a civilized man.

His lips brushed hers, her breath parting them for him. His tongue made a low pass over her lower lip, and she inhaled sharply. He could feel her trembling, waiting, ripe with want. He pressed his mouth to hers, each stroke and caress of his lips a smothered burst of the savagery kept hidden and safe from ladies like her. And when he was alone again, raked with self-loathing, his sleep twisted with nightmares, he would cling to this memory. And feel good.

He tasted like danger, felt like capped wildness, his quivering restraint bleeding through the gentle assault, paralyzing her with excitement. Her senses vividly remembered, reacted, a sumptuous tingling rushing up the back of her thighs and she wantonly wished he'd touch her there.

Carnal lust burned between her legs. His hands slid down to grasp her shoulders, pulling her flush against his bare chest and Sable gave up to the sensations, scorching his mouth, naively imitating the only kiss she'd ever known. His. She stroked his chest, the skin cool and smooth beneath her fingertips as she unconsciously brushed his nipple. His arms encircled her, mashing her to the thick muscular wall of his chest and he exploded in a roaring flood of passion.

Sable dropped into madness, answering the power.

A horse nickered softly. The breeze kicked up.

His hands charged a wild ride over her body, possessing her breasts, waist, hips, and thighs in one desperate sweep. Her violent shudder passed into him like a hot current as he dragged her skirts upward, seeking bare thigh. *After this, she'll hate you easy enough.*

She pushed at his chest, reality crashing in. She'd be found out! His grip tightened briefly, and his tongue invaded her mouth, tearing into her senses, licking the outline just inside her lips in such a heady, erotic motion that Sable moaned.

"Do you kiss your husband like that, Violet Eyes?" he breathed heavily into her mouth, and would rather die than have to utter the words.

"Who?" she peeped, eyes still closed.

"Your husband. You remember him, don't you? Little Hawk's father?"

Sable blinked owlishly, yanked back from the delicious world he'd taken her as his words sank in. Her face flamed scarlet as she threw off his hands.

"You are a cad, Mister McCracken."

A black brow arched like a raven's wing. *Hurt her. Hurt her so she'll never yield to you again.*

"And you're cuckholding little bitch." His thin smile mocked her and he saw the wounds he inflicted.

She inhaled sharply and drew her arm back to slap him, then thought better of it. "It is not as if *you* gave me a choice, now did you?" Her lips scarcely moved, her violet eyes bright with anger and humiliation, and hurt. How could he talk to her like this? After all they'd been through, how could he be so mean?

"Go ahead, heap the blame on me." Hunter leaned forward, his face inches from hers, and it took everything he had not to give into the gut-wrenching need to kiss away those crystal tears. "But you liked it," he sneered caustically, his insolent gaze raking her. "And when you're lying in bed with your husband, your legs wrapped around him, you'll think of me."

"Why, you vile, self-seeking, sanctimonious lecher!" she hissed, itching to knock that smug smile off his face. "You disgust me." Her words bit into his flesh with the stinging lash of a whip as she stood, glaring down at him. He didn't bother to look at her. If he did, he'd come apart. "You have the morals of an alley cat, Hunter McCracken, and I beg you to remember that I am *not* a base-born feline."

She walked away.

And he let her.

Stay away from me, Sable. For your own good, keep the hate fresh. She'd opened a door he slammed shut nearly five years ago and managed to press a dainty foot on the crumbling threshold, those violet eyes unlocking the repulsive side of him. Too close. Too damn close to a man with no compunction than to take another's wife and do with her as *he* pleased.

Distance. He needed it. If anything, for the time to gather the scraps of his self-respect. Hunter knew it wouldn't last long. It wouldn't. God, it couldn't. A twisted perverted side of him wanted to feast his eyes on her, even if she looked back with loathing, because she softened him, scraped off the shame and stirred a cleansing thunder in his heart.

But he had no chance. A woman like her would never accept a man with a past as degrading as his. Even if she was free.

Even if he was good enough for her.

He'd always known that.

Hunter welcomed the loneliness like a worn, familiar cloak. It fit well.

He let it envelope him, keep him down where he was safe. Bruising despair yanked at his vitals, pelting him with flashes of cold stone and threats fulfilled, of lost hope and the begging, the terrified pleas for help.

God how he wished, he wished . . . Hunter rolled over and pressed his forehead to the saddle, thumping the tooled leather with a balled fist. He wished her innocence would rub off on him—and make him feel clean again.

Chapter Seventeen

You are a lady, well-bred and gently reared, she reminded herself, smothering a throat-searing cry. One who didn't scream or show childish fits of temper. One who rose above such petty squabbles. She shot a deadly glare in his direction, her trembling hands knotted into fists. But *he* made it so difficult to behave, drat him. Perhaps I'll just shoot the beast next time he tries something, she thought maliciously, bending to dip a scrap of cloth in the stream and soothe her blistered wrists.

Trudging listlessly away from the creek, Sable didn't realize she was sobbing, unaware he could hear her, and the heart-wrenching sound was tearing him in half, pounding him with regret. Leaning back against a tree and pulling the brambles and twigs from her hair, she finger-combed the waist-length tresses with impatient moves, but it did little good, stung horribly, and she finally gave up, sinking to the ground in a deflated heap.

Oh, Sable, what will you do?

He had every right to say those horrible things. He was disgusted with his attraction to a *married* woman, dishonored that he'd breeched the lines of propriety once too often and lashed out at his only target. And . . . it hurt. Oh, heaven help her, it shouldn't, but it did. It did! Searing tears burst again and she viciously swiped her cheeks with back of her hand, wondering if she made herself as unappealing as humanly possible

171

it would save her from this misery. Looking down at her torn, stained clothes, Sable didn't think she could worsen her appearance, and considered what caliber of women he regularly associated with to be attracted to a filthy, rather pungent female such as herself.

Oh, what difference would it make? All the man had to do was touch her and she became mush, the liquid fire of his kiss bursting through her tattered senses, making her crave his suppressed wildness, the fluid warmth of his hands on her body. Making her see who she was, a real woman in Hunter's arms, not the sister fulfilling a vow, not the masquerading Cheyenne squaw nor the colonel's daughter. But a female soul he awakened to the thrill of being a woman.

I'm not married! I'm not a mother! she longed to scream, hating the secrets shrouded beneath this hideous disguise, yet realized any declaration was not only ridiculously impulsive, but dangerous. She could reveal nothing of her nephew's heritage to a man whose loyalties she didn't trust. The baby's life depended on maintaining secrecy.

His tiny image filled her mind, innocent eyes gazing adoringly at her. Dirty tears dripped off her chin, loneliness yanking at her heart. Little Hawk. Oh, how she yearned to hold him, to feel his little plump body cuddled close to hers, warm and safe, and to know she mattered—that all this fresh heartache was worth it. Sable cursed her father's bigotry for forcing her to play out this pathetic farce.

But there was no turning back.

The woman who'd secretly left Washington in the brisk April night was gone, leaving behind the useless unproductive life she had thought was perfect but now was so lacking in worth and purpose she was mortified to think about it. Discard the past for new adventures, she thought, glancing at Hunter, then the lieutenant. He was still unconscious, and prayed that when he was feeling up to it, he'd head back to his regiment—alone. Back to Fort McPherson.

That was the last place Sable wanted to go.

172

"I can ride."

"You were weak as a puppy, son."

Noah straightened as best he could without tearing open his wounds and donned his hat and gauntlets. "I believe *look* is the operative word here, sir."

Hunter pushed his fingers into his hair and sighed. The lad was determined to go it alone. "Fine. But I'm riding in with you." Noah glanced at the woman. "Her, too." Hunter didn't sound enthusiastic about the idea. Last night's battle was still raw with regret.

"I'd appreciate the company, sir, but I can manage."

Hunter slapped his hat against his thigh and stared at the ground. "You're a lone survivor, Lieutenant. Corroboration might help."

Noah understood immediately. Hunter was going to speak for him should someone dispute his claim of the attack or his actions thereafter. With Captain McCracken's impeccable reputation no one would question his word. Noah admitted he was a little relieved. "Thank you, sir."

"You need, you ask," Hunter added, then turned away and went to his horse, grabbing the saddle off the ground, pain digging at his side as he dumped it on the steed's back.

Sable was near. His senses knew it without even looking.

"We're heading into Fort McPherson."

Sable gasped, stumbling back. "No!" His head snapped to the side. "No, we can't!"

Hunter's eyes narrowed down to mere slits. Can't or won't, he thought. If she was terrified at Noah discovering her name, now she looked as if she'd faint any second. "Kirkwood needs me. We're going." He jerked on the cinch.

"*I* need you!" she blurted. Hunter pinned her with a side glance, quick and thorough. She immediately avoided those intense gray eyes, gathered her nerve and spoke in a shaky voice. "I didn't pay you to turn back, Mister McCracken. We're continuing north."

He faced her fully, his hands on his hips. "All right. What the hell is it about McPherson that you're not saying? Not that you ever do about a damn thing that's meaningful, anyway."

She wasn't about to give him a morsel, not now. "I see no reason to retrace miles that took forever to forge. We are going north. I need to get my son!" Panic and anger tainted her tone.

He propped his arm on the saddle. "Well, finally thought of him, have you?"

Sable felt as if she'd just been kicked in the teeth and was suddenly up in his face as much as her slight height would allow.

"You know nothing of what I think or feel, Mister McCracken. I've agonized over his welfare from the moment of my capture. Regardless of your judgment of me, I understand that Swift Arrow is caring for him. I can't help but worry whether my tiny helpless baby is warm and comforted and properly fed!" Tears made his image swim. "And if you were any kind of considerate human, *you* would have alleviated my fears instead of making advances." She poked his chest, her voice breaking. "Now, we are going to get my son!"

She spun away.

"You can, lady, but I'm not."

She stopped and whirled about, eyes wide as coins. "You—you'd actually leave me here?"

Hunter smelled fear and knew he had her. "Yup." He turned back to his horse, strapping on his blankets and saddle bags.

"I knew you couldn't be trusted."

His shoulders tensed and he slowly faced her. Sable met his escalating fury with her own.

"Even with the high price of your word, I suspected you'd break it."

174

He grabbed her arm, propelling her out of ear shot. Noah glanced in their direction, then discreetly moved away.

"My word has no price." His expression was black with suppressed rage.

"Really?" She jerked her arm free. "Then I believe you owe me a thousand dollars worth of gold, Mister McCracken." Her hand thrust into his line of vision.

He looked at her trembling blistered palm, then her pitifully determined face and knew if he returned the gold, which he didn't care about, he'd never see her again, regardless of whether she could find another guide. He couldn't do it. God, not yet. Even if she despised him for it.

"Who the hell you going to pay to get you out of here?" he forced himself to sneer, gesturing to the open terrain. "A couple of Pawnee?"

Her skin paled. "I-I'll go alone, if I must."

A nasty chuckle and, "You wouldn't make it one mile." *And I won't let you.*

"Perhaps." Discovering his loyalties truly weren't with her was a crushing blow, and she wanted him to suffer. "But can your pristine conscience bear it?"

He stepped close, his gaze a rude leer as it traveled over her body. "You ought to know by now," he pressed a coldness into his voice, "I don't have one."

Sable blanched, and Hunter opened his mouth to spar some more, then drew in a deep breath, disgusted that his past failing would push him to torment her like this. He didn't like what he was and Sable—just being Sable—showed him how low he'd sunk. Little by little, she gave him back his dignity, but memories and guilt threatened to take it away. He felt a duty to Kirkwood and the faceless men who'd died. It was the least he could do—this time.

When he spoke his voice was only a fraction calmer. "I'll get you to your baby and damn husband," he spat the last word. "But Swift Arrow might have gone to the fort for supplies." Another lie.

"I had plenty. And a goat for extra milk. I am not a fool, Mister McCracken, so don't expect me to believe a man like Swift Arrow needs to purchase anything to survive." She wiggled her fingers beneath his nose, not knowing what in heaven's name she'd do if he actually did hand it back. "My gold, please."

"That's *if* he was alone," he growled, jealous of her faith in Chris, his grab for the reins forcing her to step aside. He gave the camp site a quick once-over, then swung up onto the saddle, taxing his brain for a way, God forgive him, to break her spirit. His voice was harsh and cruel when he said, "This dangerous detour is your mess, Sable." Guilt swept her face and Hunter died a little inside. "And it'll be more than a week before we catch up to Chris. Now," he paused, "I can go on without supplies," his lips twisted in an arrogant smirk, "but you can't."

"Care to place a wager?" She folded her arms belligerently, ignoring the offered hand.

She'd do it, and in the space of a heartbeat Hunter saw reason. She'd risk anything for this faceless warrior, this man she never mentioned, never claimed to love. And when she was with her husband, could she ignore the desire they shared since the beginning and turn into the warrior's arms? The thought of it drove a spike of loneliness into his heart, and Hunter leaned down, nearly nose to nose with her and used the only weapon he had left. "You don't have a choice, lady. Swift Arrow has the boy, and *I* know where he is."

Sable itched to scratch his eyes out and clutched her skirts to keep from slapping him. He was her only hope of finding Little Hawk and then, Black Wolf. Her only hope, and he held her nephew hostage to get his way. Tears blurred her vision as she jammed her foot into the stirrup, grasped his arm and swung up behind him.

"You're a vicious barbaric man, Mister Hunter McCracken, and I positively loathe you."

"I figured as much." He clicked his tongue and kneed the horse forward.

Noah mounted up, riding a few feet behind them, silent, watchful.

"I will not set foot inside that fort," she hissed, determined to protect herself and her identity.

He glanced back over his shoulder, studying her with hard emotionless eyes. Bravely she met his steely gaze and lifted her chin, a gesture, he knew, that indicated her recently acquired stubborn streak was on the rise.

"Suit yourself, lady." He shrugged, facing front.

"I usually do, *McCracken*. I usually do."

Chapter Eighteen

An explosion blasted through her dreams.

The deadly splatter from the gun barrel shot out like a red dagger, penetrating the warrior's chest, renting it open to the bone. Blood spilled, dark, then a bright chilling red. The crack repeated, ringing in her head, over and over. Hands bit into her shoulders, shaking her, then came the soft rumble of a familiar voice. Sable sucked in the brisk air of the wilderness before she opened her eyes. Hunter's concerned face came into focus.

"Sable?" he whispered. "Are you with me, darlin'?" She latched on to him, burying her face in the crook of his neck. "It's all right. You had a nightmare, a loud one."

Her tears soaked his shirt collar.

"Oh, God. I killed them," came a tortured whisper. "I did!"

Hunter knew it wasn't uncommon for a person to come to grips with the realization long after it was over. It had happened to him more often than he needed to stay sane.

"God forgive me," she sobbed. "I've murdered!"

Instantly Hunter pried her arms from around his neck and gripped her shoulders. "No. You *defended* your life. And mine and Noah's and if you hadn't we'd all be dead and then where would Little Hawk be?" He shook her, hard. "Where, Sable?"

He waited for his words to penetrate past the fog and knew he'd succeeded when she sniffled, then wilted like a hothouse flower. He gathered her close, pressed her head against his chest, and she cried harder, the woeful sound clawing at his gut.

"It was either them or us, Sable." He rocked her, rubbing his hands up and down her spine. "Them or us."

Sable shuddered raggedly, grateful for his strength as grisly images fought their way back into her mind. Guilt swelled and she squeezed her eyes shut, gripping his waist. Thickly muscled arms tightened, his cheek pressing to the top of her head. The rhythmic surge of his hands slowed and she felt his lips against her hair. Nestled beneath his chin, she slowly tilted her head back, yet in the darkness she could scarcely make out his features. But she knew them, every contour, the clean line of his jaw, the cynical twist of his lips, and those fanthomless gray eyes, and even in the faint light she sensed the desire building there.

His face neared hers, and anticipation blasted her, crackling like a bolt of pure energy. She could feel the heat of him. His tongue made a sensuous stroke across her lower lip and Sable whimpered. She ached to respond, her body begged her to, but his cruel words from before rose up to taut her, reopening fresh wounds in her heart. And they still bled. Abruptly she reared back, then disentangled herself from his arms and pulled the blanket over her shoulders.

"Thank you. Good night," she muttered, then settled down in the still warm spot on the ground, turning away.

Hunter stared at her shrouded back, breathing deeply, and instantly knew the why of that brisk dismissal. Still stinging, eh? Well, so what, he thought snidely, climbing to his feet, the heaviness between his thighs making him groan. He could care less if the deceitful creature stayed awake all damn night. Yet, even as he tried to convince himself of that, he remained near, listening to her breathe, hoping she'd turn toward him again. That was the closest they'd been in four days, and it was the longest ninety-six hours he'd ever spent. Jesus, he thought, mashing a hand over his face, whiskers rasping. How could she be so close, and he still miss her? He moved away and considered starting another fight just so she'd have to talk to him, then wished he could simply change the past, his pathetic life, their uneasy alliance. *Go back to bed. Forget it. Forget what she does to you with only a glance of those soft eyes.* He settled down beneath the blankets.

Hell. He'd only heard her cry out because his own demons had come back to haunt.

Noah Kirkwood stole a glance to his left, observing the woman from beneath the brim of his hat. She rode on the rump of the palomino, behind McCracken, stoic and silent and if read her correctly, damned angry. For the past five days she hadn't spoken nor bothered to look either man in the eye expect while she checked or changed their bandages. Her own wounds, ones he could see, were showing her lack of proper attention. He didn't mention it, somehow doubting she'd appreciate anything he had to say. Her jaw and lip still bore the bruises from the Pawnee's abuse, though they were fading to a sickly greenish-yellow.

She was a mess. Hell, they all were, and he dreaded the commotion their presence would bring once they reached the fort. Noah felt pretty good considering the meager amounts of food and water. That was another odd thing about the woman. Noah never actually saw her eat or drink her share.

The surrounding territory increased in familiarity, and he curtailed the urge to race toward the structure he knew was beyond the winding trail of covered wagons snaking across their path.

McPherson, small but strategic, situated on the confluence of the North and South Platte river where the Indians once forded the waters in search of game. The fort's presence put a halt to that, but not the area's growth. Sweet Mary, it had flourished in the weeks he was on patrol! Even Jack Morrow's ranch, Junction House, stretched nearly to the fort's front door. Profit for progress, Noah smirked. Yet the military presence of two companies of U.S. Volunteers and two more companies of U.S. Calvary could be felt.

And seen.

Safety, a bath, a doctor, and some decent chow. And sleep. That's all Noah really wanted, rest without nightmares. They all had them, even the woman Captain McCracken called Violet Eyes. Noah heard her cries again last night. He made noises then, hoping the knowledge that *protection* was nearby would ease her fears. She wouldn't accept a comforting shoulder, beyond the return to reality, and soon drifted back to a dreamless sleep. He envied that, for he remained awake with a gun lying across his chest. McCracken, too.

"It's like this until late summer," Noah said, and she turned her face from it.

What was familiar about her? Something in her eyes? The tilt of her head when she spoke? Or was it her regal walk, as if she were garbed in a lavish gown and jewels. He shook his head, stealing another look at her before concentrating on the terrain. Impossible. Indian woman, half-breed, maybe schooled by whites; that was his conclusion and he liked it just fine. No need to ponder over questions neither would answer, even if she did look terrified enough to swoon.

Sable panicked. Look at all the people! An endless stream of canvas-capped wagons rocked in ruts left by previous travelers, bouncing over the flat terrain. Oxen labored under the load as women walked and children gathered dead wood and fetched water, running to catch up with their rolling homes. The crack of a bullwhip pierced the air, blending with shouts of warning and encouragement as Hunter's horse cut through the chaos. And there were soldiers—walking, riding, threading between the wagons, offering reassurance and a flirtatious smile as dark clouds swept away the sun. Sable turned her gaze to the river, the fort, and nervously clutched at Hunter's jacket for the next half mile.

Hunter shifted in the saddle, leaning back slightly. "Sure you don't want to ride in front?" he asked her without looking.

"No."

"You won't be able to stand once we reach the fort if you don't ride sidesaddle for a while."

"How considerate. Do try to remember I won't go in—"

"Through there," Noah spoke up, pointing to the shallow spot to ford the river. They quickened their pace down the slope, forcing Sable to grab onto Hunter or get bounced off the back. He's deliberately riding this fast, she thought, gasping for air as her bottom and thighs smashed against the horse's back. Together the horses launched into the icy Platte.

"Should have taken the offer."

"I will now," she groaned to his back, water splashing around her legs.

"Too late."

"Bastard," she mumbled.

"What's that? You swearing, Violet Eyes?"

He was grinning, she could feel it, and she thumped his back with her fist. He laughed, drawing a frown from Noah as they surged out of the river. Hunter tried to cover his grin, but she was talking to him again, and for the moment that was sheer pleasure.

"Mister McCracken!" She jerked on his coat, yet he still refused and rode in a brisk lope, even with Kirkwood, across the flat terrain and straight toward Fort McPherson.

Sable thought she'd be rent in half, then didn't care when they paused to look and be looked at by the sentries. She huddled beneath the blanket to hide her face. Tall planks uniformly surrounded the large fort, two hundred fifty yards square, and inside Sable knew the pattern of the enclosed town. That's what it was like to her. A dull, dirty, secluded, stifling town complete with a barracks, officers' quarters, quartermasters' quarters, the necessary blacksmith in the adobe barns, a small trading post, and the combination home and office of the commander.

Last year the commander had been her father.

At the bugle call Sable knew soldiers were flying down rough-hewned steps and into precise formation. Sable stared at the torn flat earth. Lane had been stolen from this very spot. To avoid scandal from spreading, Papa had dispersed as many men as he could who were involved in her sister's rescue. But if some had been reassigned? She couldn't risk it.

They were moving again.

"Please halt, Mr. McCracken!" The wind picked up around them, swirling dust and pebbles.

Hunter continued at a leisurely pace.

"Hunter, please." When she said his name he knew she was desperate but there wasn't a man alive that could make him relent and leave her beyond his protection.

"You can't stay outside," he said, tilting his head so she could hear and no one else. "Have some sense, woman—look at that."

He pointed to the clusters of dilapidated wagons and hastily erected tents, bearded traders and trappers selling their wares, weary families waiting to purchase fresh supplies, even a few Chinese laborers from the railroad near the Platte Valley. The stench of unwashed bodies and close living thickened the air. And the women, Sable saw, were attractive and voluptuous, parading in their undergarments, calling out to men as they passed their temporary canvas homes. Have they no pride, she wondered. She covertly peered at her guide. Silently pleased the soiled doves had no effect on him, Sable turned her attention to the hundreds of Indians camped beyond. Immediately she discarded the notion that Black Wolf could be among them, but considered if one of the Sioux here might take a message to him. And what would she say? *I've lost your son, he's with this half Cheyenne, and only God and my cantankerous guide know where and neither will tell me?*

183

He'd kill her for certain, sister-in-law or not.

Her anxiety increased as they approached the yawning fort entrance, knowing she must brave the night with the citizens beyond the timber wall or be trapped. Then to worsen her dilemma, it started to rain, a dampening drizzle she knew from experience would soon escalate. Swallowing back her uncertainty, she pulled the blanket over her head and wiggled to the edge of horse's rump, preparing to dismount whether he liked it or not.

Several people swarmed around Kirkwood's horse, suddenly recognizing him. Hunter's mount abruptly back-stepped to avoid trampling the crowd and the jolt sent Sable tumbling off and onto the spongy earth with a startled yelp. He twisted around to see her sprawled on the ground.

He grinned. "Happy now?" he asked.

"Positively delirious, can't you tell?" she muttered, struggling to her feet. Her wobbly legs gave out and she fell again, landing in the mud with a squishy plop. She glared murderously at him. He could at least dismount and offer her a hand hand up, she thought, but instead he spoke to a passing guard, then ambled his horse across the yard to a hitching post and slid from the saddle. Sable lumbered to her feet again, forcing herself to be patient with her stretched muscles. Her stance was improperly wide and she remained still for a moment, balancing, waiting for the tightness to relax. She glanced at Hunter. He smiled unabashedly, the rat, then disappeared into a cedar log building. Sable turned away, heading back out.

Two troopers blocked her path. When she protested, they shook their heads: McCracken's orders.

Frightened and a prisoner, Sable chose not to draw more attention to herself and quickly yanked the blanket up across her face. She wanted to rail against his high-handedness, but her upbringing wouldn't allow such a liberty and she could do no more than wait alone in the rain. Very aware of her haggard appearance, Sable felt the stares of utter contempt like slaps to her melting dignity. Passersby actually stopped in the biting cold downpour to look at the only *Indian* inside the fort. She avoided eye contact and inspected her boots, waiting. *Hurry, Hunter, please get me out of here. Please.*

Colonel Maitland was about to give orders to dismiss the troops when he recognized the lieutenant dismounting near the gates. Impatient to hear the circumstances of his lone return, he left the shelter of the porch and strode down to the formation. Maitland inspected his officer from head to toe as he returned the salute, noticing the angry red slash visible on Kirkwood's throat.

"What the hell did you find out there?" he said in a tight voice, motioning the man close.

"May I suggest privacy for my report, sir?"

The colonel briefly glanced down the covered walk to the women grouped solemnly on the porch before his office. They were Army wives, and knew what this meant. Damn, an entire patrol!

"In thirty minutes. After you've changed and—" his gaze shifted to the man striding forward. "Who's that?"

"My rescuer, sir, Captain Hunter McCracken." There was a soft murmur of surprise and awe throughout the eavesdroppers as Hunter stopped and shook the colonel's hand.

"And the woman?" Maitland gestured to her with his chin.

"Gotta be his squaw whore, sir," someone snickered from the ranks, and both Noah and Hunter glared the chucklers into silence.

"If not for the *lady*, Colonel," Noah said loud enough, "we'd all be dead."

"I'll meet you in my quarters, gentlemen." Maitland studied the woman intensely, then twisted to address his sergeant-major. "Dismiss the men," he ordered and while retiring colors and evening protocol went on, Hunter strode over to Sable.

"Get out of the rain, for God's sake." He pulled her beneath the wood awning, blocking her small body from the colonel's keen observations.

"I want to leave here, Mr. McCracken."

"Too bad. We're staying til morning."

She half-heartedly stomped her foot. "Why have you forced this on me?"

"You going to tell me what's really going on?" he countered, but he already knew the reason. This place was a threat to her disguise.

"I need to get the baby, quickly. Can't you understand that?"

Not *my* baby, or *my* son, Hunter noticed, eyes shark hard. But *the* baby. "Oh, I understand all right."

Oblivious, she stole a glance at the slow walking people who'd taken a deep interest in their conversation. So did he, and lowered his voice.

"Ever hear of duty, Sable?"

Sable exhaled through clenched teeth. That's all she'd heard her entire life. Duty. Her father's excuse for neglect, resulting in smothering affections which left his daughters nothing more than pampered spineless little girls. It seemed Hunter used it to get his way, too.

"Fine. You know where my son is, which leaves me no choice but to remain with you."

"That's the idea," he said flatly. "Now, I have to go with Kirkwood. Give a list of supplies to Travis. He's harmless, runs the trading post," he added briskly when she frowned. "I rented us what qualifies as a room." He inclined his head to the two-story cedar hostelry as he pressed the cold key into her hand. "After you're finished, go there and stay put."

Sable stared at the key, to the structure that didn't exit a year ago, then to him. "Us?"

"Yeah." Here it comes, he thought.

"Mr. McCracken." She straightened regally, thrusting the

186

key at him. "I can't possibly share a—a room with you. It's highly—"

"Improper?" he cut in, leaning down.

"Why, of course it is!"

"Lady, this entire trip is as *improper,*" he smirked, "as it gets. It's either that room, or nothing. We've been sharing a whole territory for weeks now," he gestured to the wilderness, "so what the hell difference do four walls make?"

Her gaze went twilight cool. "Plenty, and you know it."

His sly look was an insult. "Don't flatter yourself, darlin'." He curled her fingers painfully around the key. "Right now you're the most unappealing creature I've ever laid eyes on."

Sable jerked free, flushing with embarrassment. "You're no grand catch yourself," she snapped, glancing him over.

Snappy little runt, he thought, his anger melting. "Yeah, yeah, and I'm disgusting, foul-mouthed and uncouth. Anything else?" He arched a brow and she stared beyond him, her lips pressed tight to hide her smile.

Why can't I stay angry with this man?

Her shoulders rose and fell in a sign of annoyance. "You seem to have covered it rather nicely."

"Do you mean we actually agree?"

He looked so comically stunned, a smile filtered out as she stared up into his handsome face.

"You're quite pleased with yourself for manipulating me into this, aren't you?"

"Yup," he grinned, and Sable's stomach tightened in anticipation.

"And you have absolutely no shame over holding me hostage?"

His gaze drifted over her once, seeing the luscious woman beneath the wet wool and mud. "Nope."

"Incorrigible wretch," she muttered just as a soldier bumped her, pushing her off the walk. Hunter moved forward to defend, but her touch on his arm stayed him. He met her

187

gaze and read her fear as she adjusted the shawl, cloaking all but her eyes.

She was safe enough for now. With her dyed skin and the prejudice against Indians, no one would bother to look for the white woman hidden beneath—even with her violet eyes. But she would be a target. He wished he could give her a gun, but that would bring the entire fort down on them, and he was pushing his luck with the colonel already. Hunter just wished she'd tell him the truth so he could be better armed against any trouble. That would come, though with the way he had treated her in the past days, it would be a long time getting here.

"You can handle anything, Violet Eyes." He hated leaving her, but had to speak with the colonel first. "You're a hell of a lot tougher than you think." His praise warmed her cold skin and she beamed. God, Hunter thought, to look at that smile the rest of his life . . . "Now, think you can manage our supplies for this splendid holiday?"

"Certainly." She spun about and sloshed determinedly to the trading post. Hunter watched for a moment. Interesting. She knew exactly where it was without being told.

Chapter Nineteen

Travis Moffet!

Dear God. Would he even remember her from a year ago, she agonized, forcing her feet to continue, aware that Hunter was watching. She'd been at the fort a scant two months before Lane was captured and hadn't frequented his establishment, unless bored or unable to ride. Sable hesitated on the threshold, then bowed her head and stepped inside. The trading post was warm, unusually so, yet she snugged the wet wool blanket securely across the lower half of her face.

All conversation ceased.

She didn't dare meet anyone's gaze and weaved her way around kegs, crates, stacks of blankets, iron kettles, and tables of ready-made clothing to the counter. Clenching her fists, she waited for the portly proprietor to finish with a customer and notice her. He had, along with everyone else.

"Can I help you?"

The familiar voice startled her. Sable cautiously lifted her gaze to meet a pair of blue eyes, sparkling with kindness. She relaxed slightly. He didn't recognize her.

"Mr. Hunter McCracken asked me to procure supplies," she said softly.

"Hunter's here?" Travis glanced beyond her, then back. "Heck, I thought he was dead."

"That seems to be the general consensus, sir."

Travis smiled, showing he was missing a few teeth. "What can I sell you today?" So, this was the reason for all the gossip. He looked her over briefly just as the soggy blanket drooped. Jealousy, Travis decided after the timely glimpse. Even he could see the beauty beneath the grime.

"I do believe we should make a list?" Sable said, the words muffled behind the wool.

Travis's eyes narrowed as he withdrew the pencil lodged behind his ear, then produced paper from beneath the counter. He wet the pencil tip and started to write.

"I'll do it."

His bushy gray brows rose in surprise. "Well, ah, sure." He slid the sheet across the counter, watching. A half-breed, and properly schooled, though most Indians weren't educated— least ways not by white men's standards. It was the eyes. He'd get why they seemed familiar. It'd just take a little brain work.

Sable wrote neatly, pausing to glance around herself should she see something that would benefit their trip. That's when she noticed the women clustered near shelves stocked with canned vegetables. Clad in pale billowy dresses and crisp bonnets, the women gawked at her, then like a hive of disturbed bees, they buzzed and whispered behind gloved hands. Sable suppressed an envious sigh over their simple gowns as the women rudely pointed and nodded, obviously agreeing on what they assumed Sable to be. Straightening her shoulders, Sable delivered a glare meant to freeze water, then focused her attention on the list.

Charitable Christian souls, she fumed. How ironic. She wasn't so naive not to realize she might have joined that ridiculing cluster a few years ago. The revelation humbled her, shamed her. Sable rubbed her itchy nose, frowning at the dirt on her hands. She sniffed, glanced around herself, then sniffed again. Utterly mortified that the odor came from her, she slid the list back to Travis and took a step back. He scanned it.

190

"Got all different kinds of this stuff, ma'am. Why don't you take a look around and tell me which you'll be wantin'?"

"You select."

"Travis, get that red bitch outa here!" a man voiced behind Sable. "Or I ain't buying a dern thing from you again!"

Sable gasped, frozen with embarrassment as Travis glanced up, his blue eyes frigid.

"Be a might hard, Carl, seeing as this is the only post fer a good hundred miles. Unlessin' you want to pay Morrow's prices?" A tense pause, then tersely, "Now git outa my store, an' don't come back till you find yer manners!"

As the retreating footsteps and mutterings faded behind her, Sable looked up.

Her appreciative smile warmed Travis and he wondered again at the familiarity of those eyes. "If I know Hunter, ma'am, he'll want sturdy and simple."

"Then you've grasped more than I, Mister Moffet."

Not really, he was tempted to admit, no one did, yet said, "Won't hurt to have a look."

She sighed, nodded. It appeared he would badger her until she capitulated.

"You didn't add clothes to this," he remarked and the bees buzzed.

"I know."

Sable scrutinized the floor boards, unwilling to ask Hunter McCracken for anything. It did little good anyway, and considering his attitude lately, the notion was relatively useless. She'd begged enough this trip.

Browsing cautiously, Sable ignored the customers as Travis disappeared through an open door beyond the counter. Inspecting blankets, she selected two, plain and dark, avoiding the Indian stripes and bright colors. Someone shoved her, hard, and customers chuckled as she stumbled against a pickle barrel, the wood rim cutting into her hip. Tart brine sloshed. Sable grit her teeth and straightened, letting the rudeness pass, then gathered tin cups, plates, flatware, and pots for two, and placed them on the counter, deciding cooking utensils would only add unnecessary weight. She held the blankets protectively close. The women, who appeared to be accomplishing nothing more than keeping dust off the floor, moved slowly out of her path, intensely surveying Sable.

"Have you ever seen such filth, Caroline?"

The conversation was meant to be heard, Sable realized.

"Why, yes—I do believe it was behind a horse, my dear." They giggled shrilly at that bit of wit. Children, Sable thought, cowardly avoiding eye contact.

"I tell you, she's his whore."

Sable flinched and looked elsewhere, fingering a beautiful deep green gown hung high from the rafters. She blinked repeatedly, refusing her accusers the satisfaction of a single tear.

"Oh, pooh! Now look. I wanted that dress and Travis'll just have to burn it now," another whined. Sable immediately let go, turned toward the counter and smacked into a thin blond youth.

"Put that stuff down!" he barked.

Sable stared. Who was this pimple-faced ruffian to order her about? She brushed past him and he grabbed her arm. "I said, put it back! You ain't stealin' nothin' in this store!"

Her brows drew tight. "I wasn't stealing." She plucked uselessly at his fingers.

Tightening his bony grip, his glare sharpened with contempt. "Show me yer money, Injun."

"I don't have any. I—"

He immediately tried to pry the blankets from her. "Then how you gonna pay, you dirty slut—with yer looks? Ain't worth a penny!"

He tugged roughly, and Sable let go. He went flying backwards, smashing against the barrel-braced counter. She stood there, stunned as he scrambled to his feet, his expression more pleased than it ought to be. Suddenly he lunged, grabbing her about the waist and mashing her flat against his thin body. Sable shoved him as his hands paraded over her hips and waist, groping beneath the wet wool. She fought like a caged cat and together they banged against crates and kegs, toppling goods and shattering glass.

No one spoke.

No one helped.

No one cared.

He arched her back over a wooden box, forcing her thighs flush with his. Out of the corner of her eye, Sable glimpsed several knives joined with leather and dangling from a hook. Her hand snaked out, grasping a bone handle; it whispered from the sheath, the silver tip instantly pressed beneath the youth's downy chin. Women shrieked. Her assailant sucked in a lungful of air, his eyes wide as coins.

Travis barreled out of the storeroom and screeched to a silent halt.

"I've already killed two men this week, brat," Sable said in a clear frosty voice, then arched a tapered brow. "Care to make it three?"

The young man's eyes shifted rapidly between the knife and her. He swallowed cautiously.

Rain softly pelted the wood roof like drumming fingers.

"Well?" She poked when he didn't answer immediately.

"Ah, no, no. No, ma'am." The boy's arms slid from around her and went up in the air as he back-stepped, tripping over his own feet.

"Clive, what did you do now, boy?" Travis demanded, impressed by the young woman's fortitude.

Clive cast a glance at his boss. "I—I thought she was stealin'."

"You turkey's patoot! Your job's to stock, not mess with my customers!"

Sable gestured with the knife for the youth to step aside and retrieved the blankets, placing them on the wood slab.

"Sorry, ma'am," he offered.

Sable inclined her head graciously. "I do believe you ought to reconsider the quality of your clientele, Mister Moffet."

She looked pointedly at the queen bees, then met the youth's gaze as she tossed the knife on the counter. "Frankly, I'm repulsed by what you allow to slither into your shop."

Sable departed in silence, her head high, and prayed no one noticed how badly she was shaking.

While Sable defended what remained of her dignity, Hunter sat comfortably in the colonel's private quarters, a healthy shot of sour mash clutched in his hand. Colonel Maitland was younger than most of his rank, about forty-five, Hunter assumed, and recently widowed, if he'd heard the gossip right. It was his long silver hair that gave him a worldly distinction men usually earned on a battle field. Hell, if the troopers had confidence in him, he'd let the former supply officer's lack of combat time slide.

Maitland tossed the reports on his desk, then leaned back in his chair, steepling his fingers. "I find no mention of how the woman came to be captured."

Hunter continued to eye the toe of his boot. "I fail to see where it matters," he replied. He still felt lousy about that, dropping his guard just to give her privacy. It had cost her too much.

"Perhaps not." Maitland shrugged, taking up his own glass. "But it could give us an idea of how far the Sioux have dared venture off the reservation."

Noah and Hunter exchanged frowns.

"I beg you pardon, but it was Pawnee, sir," Kirkwood confirmed. That's twice, Noah realized, the colonel had misspoken of the Sioux.

"I understand your conviction, gentlemen, yet you have no proof." He gestured with the glass. "No weapons, nothing with tribal markings."

"Don't you mean scalps, Maitland?" Hunter put in, draining the whiskey and coming to his feet.

"Yes, as a matter of fact," the colonel said, as if the two

survivors should produce the grisly remains on the end of a captured lance.

Hunter set his glass on the desk with more force than necessary. "Whose scalp you want, Colonel—your men's or the Pawnee?"

Maitland stood slowly. "Your attitude borders on insubordination, McCracken. I'd advise you to watch your tongue."

Hunter snorted. "I'm not in the Army anymore, Maitland, so you might as well forget the threats." He folded his arms over his chest and briefly considered the colonel before adding, "You're trying to blame Sioux for this massacre and you're looking for an excuse to send out another patrol. Why?"

Maitland's posture improved as he delivered a cutting glare. "I do not answer to you, McCracken—you answer to me."

"We all answer to God, *Colonel,*" Hunter's tone was innocent as a school boy's, "and when a man is trying to carve you up for his latest sacrifice, *sir,* you have tendency to remember what he looks like."

Bristling over McCracken's insolence, Maitland returned to his chair, his gaze on Noah. "You say this squaw shot two warriors?"

"Yes, sir. Damn good shot, too."

"What's her name and tribe?" The colonel picked up a pen, dipped it in the well, the tip poised over the paper. "I have to include her in my reports."

"Cheyenne," Hunter put in, then sent Noah a hard look, hoping the warning registered. He was suddenly unwilling to divulge any more information. "And you couldn't pronounce it, let alone write it."

"I asked the lieutenant," he stressed, still hovering over the report.

"Violet Eyes is the loose translation I believe, sir." Noah offered an apologetic he's-my-superior-and-*I'm*-in-the-Army look to Hunter.

"Did you meet the woman in Council Bluffs or St. Joe, McCracken?" Maitland asked without looking up.

"Neither," Hunter lied, his eyes narrowing sharply as the commander scribbled. What difference did that make? He'd mentioned nothing of their meeting, destination or status. For all Maitland knew Sable could be his wife. Schooling his features, Hunter turned away and moved to the far side of the office, stopping before the room's only window. He braced his shoulder against the sill, absently watching the rain splatter the muted glass.

Maitland set the pen aside and picked up his glass. He knew the former Union spy would relinquish only what he wanted you to know, but Maitland owed a favor and he'd yet to question the woman. "The only reason she's allowed inside, for the night," he stressed, "is because she entered with you two." He rolled the tumbler between his palms, staring at the liquid. "I want no trouble, McCracken." He quaffed the whiskey. "Is that understood?"

Hunter sighed. The man was full of himself and his power. "Look, Colonel, I'm tired, sore, filthy, and hungry." He finally looked at the officer. "And I'd just as soon be long gone," he strolled closer, "but I felt it my duty to accompany Kirkwood here—" Words faded when he noticed the lieutenant slumped in the chair. "Noah? You all right, pal?" Hunter shook him.

Noah roused, his face pale, perspiration dotting his brow and upper lip. "I apologize, sir," he slurred.

"You may be dismissed, Lieutenant."

Hunter glanced up sharply as he hoisted Noah off the chair. The colonel sounded annoyed that the poor man's suffering had interrupted his inquisition.

"Made it this far," Noah said, shrugging off Hunter's help. The motion made him dizzy and he lurched for the door knob, gripping it moment for support before jerking it open.

Hunter followed, intent on getting far away from Maitland and his questions.

"Who is the red bitch, McCracken, exactly?" Maitland demanded, leaving his chair and coming around the side of the desk. "Your concubine?"

Hunter froze, then looked slowly back over his shoulder. So, the tiger shows his stripes, Hunter thought, his eyes hardening to a glacial gray. "Let's get one thing straight, Colonel G.T. Maitland: the Cheyenne woman is under my protection. I work for *her*."

Hunter's gaze darted to the stained yellow ribbon dangling from Maitland's fingertips before he grabbed his hat off the rack and stepped over the threshold.

"We are not finished, McCracken!" Maitland called out heatedly. "You have not been dismissed!"

"So hang me," Hunter said, melting into the dark.

Chapter Twenty

Son of a bitch!

Hunter wanted to hit something, preferably Maitland's face. The man was bent on the Sioux and didn't have any solid reason to be so damn interested in Sable and where she'd come from. Hunter never doubted she was hiding, possibly hunted—and he was determined to get some answers even if he had to shake them out of the fool woman.

Chaffing at the confines and questions, Hunter's stride was hard and long as he moved down the boarded walk. Rain dribbled between the awning boards above his head, splashing on his shoulders. Damn! He knew he should have said she was his wife, but no, he was thinking of her damn *sensibilities*. Christ. It burned him that they thought her a whore.

A scream ripped through his thoughts and his head snapped up, eyes scanning the grounds. It was her, he just knew it. He kept moving, booted feet picking up pace when he saw a group clustered outside the post office. Drunks. Lusty laughter. And beneath the torch light he saw her being shoved from one soldier to another. They pawed her crudely, licked her face, kissed her, rough and vulgar. He gave her credit for a couple of well-placed elbows and feet, but she was still out-muscled.

Rage surged through his body. Shouldering his way between uniformed soldiers, Hunter shoved drunk men aside, satisfying his fists and punching one when he didn't move fast enough. He reached her and she shrank back against the wood wall, huddling beneath the blanket.

"Violet Eyes. I'm here," he said in Cheyenne, coaxing her into his grasp.

Sable immediately recognized his voice and sagged into his arms.

"Get lost before I report the lot of you," he threatened in a dangerous voice and the men quickly dispersed, dragging their fallen comrade. Hunter gathered her up and immediately strode toward the hostelry. "What the hell got into you?" he whispered hotly. "Couldn't you see they were drunk?"

Sable brushed back the wet wool and met his heated gaze. "You're blaming me for that?"

"You're the one dim-witted enough to waltz between a passel of drunks!"

Sable fumed. "Oh, yes, of course. I suppose it was rather stupid of me to believe I would be unharmed on a military installation with men assigned to protect." He caught her sarcasm and lost some of his anger.

"I don't know where you've been in the last ten years, woman, but Indians aren't exactly welcomed around here."

"Do tell." Oh, he simply wouldn't understand it never occurred to her that a soldier would accost her. She was Colonel Richard Cavanaugh's daughter. At the time she had been reminiscing and had forgotten about her disguise.

She was about to tell him she was perfectly capable of walking under her own power when he abruptly stopped. She heard his name called. He released her legs and slid her to her feet. Something was definitely wrong. She could feel the tension radiating from his body.

"Don't speak, not a word," he whispered, his eyes on the approaching commander. He had to maintain his lies. "Go to the room and don't let anyone stop you." He glanced down and saw her confusion. "Trust me, Violet Eyes." He thrust her from his side.

"McCracken!" the colonel bellowed. "I am still commander of this fort and you will remain until ordered otherwise."

Keeping her head submissively bowed, Sable race toward the hostelry, yet as she brushed past the colonel, he caught her arm. She froze, heart reeling.

"Take your hands off her," Hunter warned, advancing.

Maitland ignored him. "What's your name, miss?"

The colonel's voice was gentle, respectful, and Hunter's nerves danced, senses alert.

"Answer the question," Maitland demanded, and Hunter stepped between them, forcibly breaking the Colonel's hold.

"I told you, she doesn't understand."

Panicked, Sable seized the opportunity and walked briskly across the grounds toward the hostelry. One didn't toy with the commander's power.

The rain pounded her head and shoulders, muddied the red earth and she slipped twice, barely saving herself from a fall. She slopped up the steps, pausing to kick mud off her boots, though it only served to fling it on herself and her skirts. Exhausted, she stepped inside. The clerk looked up as did three men lounging near the door to the clerk's quarters. She ducked her head and moved toward the stair case. Immediately she found her path blocked.

"Injuns ain't allowed," a squat man snickered. Sable showed him the key. "Where'd you get that?" He snatched it from her before she could draw back.

"Took it whilst he was still sleepin', I figger," another man concluded loudly.

Sable didn't dare argue for fear she'd abuse the Cheyenne language and someone might contradict her, not after the trouble McCracken went through in deceiving the Colonel, protecting her. She tried to take the key back, but the clerk held it out of her reach, laughing nastily. And when she attempted to pass him to get to the staircase, he latched onto the blanket, his chunky grip tightening over her braids.

"I says Injuns ain't welcome." Sable's eyes watered, her scalp screaming taut against her skull as she twisted, trying to remove his hand. He dragged her the short distance to the door as Sable clawed at his hand, nails digging into his flesh. With a yelp of pain he released her, inspecting his cuts, and Sable delivered a swift kick to his shins, then spun away. His friends chuckled.

"Why, you little bitch," he hollered, giving her a satisfied shove into the street. Tripping on her skirts, Sable stumbled down the steps and fell face-down in the mud. Masculine laughter peeled around her, grating down her spine before it faded. The door slammed shut. For a moment she considered the advantages of remaining right there; this seemed the least humiliating spot thus far. Yet she forced herself to get up, the heavy mud-caked skirts hampering her moves. Rain ran in torrents over the ground. She swiped at her face and flicked her fingers, sending clumps of mud into the air, then lumbered into the alley and leaned back against the wall. Biting her lip to keep from blubbering like a child, Sable crumbled to the ground, wrapping her arms around her knees and hiding her face. Tears rolled down her cheek, clearing a path of grime. Water trickled down her back and she shivered uncontrollably.

She wanted to scream. She wanted to break glass. She wanted a hot bath and a warm bed and for this to be over. She wanted Little Hawk safe and Lane with Black Wolf, and herself, well, a convent in the south of Mexico looked most inviting right now.

Swift Arrow skirted the more populated areas to avoid the stir his appearance would cause. It was unusual to see a man alone with a child anyway, especially with the two horses, a mule, and a damn goat trailing him, even more than that his garments were distinctly Cheyenne. This was Sioux country and every one knew it, respected it. Black Wolf's domain, though the legendary warrior had never been seen by a living white man. Except Hunter.

With Little Hawk nestled close to his side, Swift Arrow lay on his stomach, the unlikely pair tucked deep in the brush-dotted hills. Through a battered pair of field glasses, he observed the dilapidated cabin. That shack was Hunter's thin grasp onto something solid, something real. Confinement was not one of his strong suits. And he simply wandered, angry, half wild with guilt, as if staying put would destroy the shell he'd built. Black Wolf had met his match when he'd attacked Hunter, and it wasn't until they were both near death that Hunter had found compassion and tended Black Wolf's wounds. The warrior repaid the debt with a Sioux name and a secret bond of friendship.

As Swift Arrow expected, the flat meadow's serenity was suddenly disturbed by the small patrol of dust-covered troopers, hooves trampling the clearing in perfect military formation.

"Well, now, what do you suppose they want here, little warrior? Hum?" Swift Arrow whispered to Little Hawk.

The babe gurgled, his usual response to any query.

"That's what I thought, too." They wanted Hunter, and the grizzly trapper dismounting beside the lead officer, gesturing first to the cabin, then beyond to the hill to the badlands, had obviously guided them.

"Someone ought to teach those greenhorns how to blend in out here. Want the job?"

A gurgle, bubbles, and a whisper.

"Me neither."

Damn you, Hunter, hurry the hell up, he thought, then briefly glanced at the boy, plucking a dry blade of grass from the child's hair, then smoothing the wispy strands from his eyes. Could he even see at this young age? He didn't mind caring for him; in fact, he'd become quite adept at the forced task. It was the constant influx of troopers in the area that bothered Swift Arrow. He deduced they were searching for Black Wolf's band, which wasn't a surprise, or perhaps even the woman and child. Likely both, he thought, knowing the Army's need for thoroughness. Especially when it came to white women in Indian territory.

Slipping back behind the rocks, he wondered if the woman called Violet Eyes was still alive. And who was she anyway? *That* was a mystery he wanted to answer. Reaching for Little Hawk, he loosened the cradleboard straps and settled him on his lap, absently stroking his downy hair. He wouldn't know what to do with the boy if she were dead, didn't know whose son he truly was, though he had an odd foreboding about that.

Yet Swift Arrow discovered two important things while caring for Little Hawk: he loved children, (though changing the boy's soiled moss was a task he'd hand over quickly to anyone who'd relieve him of it) and motherhood was a constant, tiring, thankless job. He gained a new respect for women, his own mother in particular.

He frowned at the blackened sky.

Tonight was the eve of the new moon, five days since the woman had vanished. And if Hunter or the woman didn't show, what would he do with this little Sioux life?

Mud sucked at Hunter's boots and rained streamed off the front brim of his hat in a steady crystal beam as he led his Palomino across the compound to the adobe barns. Consoling himself that in lying to the colonel he was protecting Sable and the identity she wanted to hide, Hunter couldn't ignore the coming explosion if he didn't confront her for some answers. Yanking up his collar, he hunched down into the warmth of his jacket, hoping she was at least enjoying the bath he'd ordered for her, and wishing he was soaking in hot water now. Maybe even share the tub with her. Hell, she'd pitch a fit over just the suggestion, he decided, chuckling softly and drawing the attention of the smithy.

Inside, the adobe barn was pitch black but for the welcoming flicker of a single lantern and bright embers glowing in a raised pit. The coals brightened as the man standing beside the stone circle hearth pumped bellows, his massive biceps jumping with the quick motions.

"Got an empty one?" Hunter asked, uncinching the girth.

"First two just cleaned," the smithy called pleasantly, then twisted away and turned back with a horseshoe clamped between iron tongs. He shoved it deep within the coals and looked up.

" 'Tis a bleedin' shame, treating the poor beast as such." The accented voice was faintly chastising.

"Couldn't be helped." Hunter dragged the saddle from the horse's back and tossed it over the short partition between the stalls.

"Lord kens I taught ye better."

Hunter spun about and pain detonated in his jaw as a meaty fist connected with the tender spot. The force of the blow lifted him off his feet and sent him flying backward into a fresh pile of hay. He lay sprawled like a discarded rag doll, dazed and hurting. His horse nickered softly, as if laughing, then kindly nudged him before he sank into a familiar darkness. Cautiously propping himself up on one elbow, Hunter shook his head to clear the ringing in his ears.

"What the hell was that for?" He worked his jaw, tonguing his mouth for loose teeth.

" 'Tis owin' you that, I am, fer yer sainted mother. Shame on you, a son not writin' but once in three years!"

Hunter peered up at the barrel-chested blacksmith. "You know my mother?" The face came into focus. "Sergeant-Major?" He lumbered to his feet, glad he'd made the decision not to retaliate—not after that mammoth punch!

"Aye! Who'd ye think it was?"

"Dugal Fraser?" Hunter briefly turned his head to spit blood. "Sergeant-Major Dugal Fraser?"

"Bleedin' hell," Dugal cursed under his breath, "Must have hit ye too hard." Shaking his head, he grabbed a rag off a peg and dunked it in a bucket of water. "I promised yer da one punch tae knock sense into you," he muttered, a beefy fist squeezing water, "But now yer blathering like the town dunce." He offered the cloth.

Hunter grinned, wincing when he pressed the cloth to his jaw, his eyes scanning his former subordinate and his parents' neighbor. From beneath the leather apron his brawny frame glistened with sweat despite the cool weather. Flame red hair, which had drawn enemy fire on more than one occasion, was overly long and though he sported a moustache now, he hadn't aged much in five years.

"How is my father?"

"You'd bleedin' well know if you ever picked up a pen!"

"Ah, leave off, Dugal." Hunter turned his back and used the rag to swipe down his horse. "I can't."

"Yer meanin' you willna'. No' one word. Yer mother is beside herself with worryin' fer ye."

Hunter's hand stilled, the jab of guilt hitting hard. "I'm not fit for her company—nor Father's."

"But ye are for the wee Indian lass?"

Hunter turned, frowning. "You saw her?"

"Aye, as likely the whole fort." Dugal moved to his forge and withdrew the glowing shoe, inspecting it for hammering. "Yer doin's are the freshest bit of gossip since Christmas." He jammed it back into the coals.

Hunter shucked his jacket, tossing it near the blaze to dry as Dugal bent over a small box, flipped the lid and withdrew a flask.

"Taos Lightning," Dugal grinned, waving the silver bottle. He gestured to the low stone wall surrounding the forge, settling his mighty frame on the thick barrier.

"Liquid poison," Hunter chuckled, dropping down beside him.

"How are ye, Hunter, really?" He drew a swig, then handed over the flask.

"Shitty."

Dugal scowled and smacked him playfully, the light tap nearly sending Hunter back over the wall.

Regaining his balance, Hunter took a swallow, coughing over the steady burn tearing down his throat. He'd forgotten how strong the stuff was on an empty stomach.

"I never thought to see you travelin' with a woman."

"Well, she isn't long on good sense."

Dugal frowned, smoothing his moustache with thumb and forefinger. " 'Tis a puir attitude you have."

"And it isn't getting better," Hunter said in a quiet voice. He stared at the monogrammed flask and took another long pull, swiping his lips with the back of his hand.

Dugal considered the man beside him. The last time he saw Hunter he was stumbling out of Libby Prison, heading straight into the wilderness. Dugal was about to say, *you can come back now, lad, you needn't feel guilty—I've seen the horror, the filthy conditions, and how some men chose to deal with it, too. It was war, and one so young shouldn't carry the responsibility for the actions of every man placed under his command. Least of all a whey-face lieutenant.* Yet no words passed.

Hunter didn't care for the intensity of Dugal's look just now. It burrowed under his skin like a thorn. "What's been going on since I last—why are you here anyway, Dugal?" He gestured to the blacksmith shop.

"Working for a wage, or has the notion escaped ye?" Dugal waved off the offered flask and went to the forge and drew out the tonged shoe as he lifted his hammer. He slammed the mallet, sparks flying like midnight stars, and Hunter was entranced with the sight, the steady ring chiming like church bells in his head.

Dugal shoved the shoe into a water bucket. It bubbled and

206

hissed as it cooled. "With the railroad, wagon trains, och, and this lad, Black Wolf makin' a reputation for hisself, the Army was wee bit short of men. I volunteered me services." He glanced up. "As a civilian."

"And with Maitland, you'll be short again."

"Aye." He nodded sagely. "The commander is a hard one, Hunter. Keep the lass close tae ye." Dugal gave the hammered shoe a disgusted look and tossed it and the tongs aside, giving up for the day. "Maitland lost his bride in a raid on a wagon train heading tae Laramie, and he has a blood vengeance burnin' in him."

"His wife? Will hunting down the Sioux bring her back?" Hunter bit sarcastically, wondering what the hell Maitland's interest in Sable played in this.

Dugal arched a fuzzy red brow. "Who's tae sae how far that kind of loss will take a mon, Capt'n." The dig wasn't lost on Hunter and he returned it with a black scowl. Dugal accepted the flask, drinking deeply as he leaned back against the support post. He glanced around, checking to be certain they were alone, then leaned closer. "I heard himself is looking for the bairn of one of Black Wolf's warriors."

"What!" Hunter straightened. "God damn it! What the hell for?"

" 'Tis disgusting, the language yer usin' of late, an ye bein' a Scotsman." Dugal looked appalled. "And tell me now, Hunter *Dalmahoy* McCracken—" Hunter winced—"how am I supposed to be privy to that! 'Tis mutterings of drunken scouts an' troopers I lent me ear tae. No' the colonel himself."

Hunter moved restlessly around the barn. Horses nickered and stomped. A baby. Christ, the match just struck the fuse.

Dugal frowned. *"Ochaiee,* what ails ye, son?" The man was burrowing a groove in his dirt floor.

Hunter faced him. "I got this from Pawnee." He pointed to his cheek. "But Maitland wishes it was Sioux. So much he *suggested* I change my report."

"Ochaiee, Hunter, din you know usin' his authority for re-

venge must be covered with piles of them official-looking papers you officers love so well?"

Hunter sent him an amused smirk, then studied a cut on his hand. "And what's your theory, Dugal?" Talking things over with his sergeant-major, his friend. It was like old times. This was a man Hunter trusted.

"The scuttle has it a lass was stolen during an attack last year, a real lady, ye ken me?"

Hunter nodded absently, rubbing his whiskered chin.

"The Army stole her back a few months later." Dugal chuckled. "Kicking and screamin', I gathered."

McCracken shot him a hard look. "One of Black Wolf's tribesmen?"

Dugal's massive shoulders rose and fell in a deep sigh. "I wasna here sae I canna say, and nary a soul'll admit to it, but 'tis believin' I am, that this wee lass birthed the warrior a babe. And the Army covets *that* child."

"For bait," Hunter murmured, fists clenched white, "to lure Black Wolf south."

"Och, 'tis guid tae know years in the wild havna' dulled yer wits." He doffed his leather apron and hung it on a peg. "They ken a warrior wouldna risk a battle over the woman, especially a white woman."

Hunter spun about, scowling like dark thunder as Dugal slipped into a shirt.

"But for the bairn . . . and if he be a boy-child?"

The explosion blew up in Hunter's face.

Not one Indian would launch an attack over a female.

One *white* woman.

With a half-breed child.

God.

Black Wolf would kill for a warrior's son.

The army would kill to keep him.

And Sable was the mother.

Chapter Twenty-one

Hunter smacked his fist into his palm so hard it sounded like a bone cracking. He kept his back to Dugal and closed his eyes, but the Scotsman recognized Hunter's reaction, and his accented voice whispered across the barn.

"Och, lad, 'tis treason if ye dinna give the gover'ment wha' they want."

"Believe me, Dugal, when I say I *don't have* what they want." He couldn't lie to his friend, nor involve him either. Not until Hunter knew what he was going to do. He grabbed his hat and jacket then snatched up his packs and strode to the barn doors. "Thanks for the drink, Dug. And tell my parents you saw me."

"Ye tell 'em! And have a care!" Dugal called to the empty doorway, then softer, "Och, fer yer life, lad, have a care."

He strode determinedly across the compound, his steps sending up fans of muddy water in his wake. Facts ticked off in his mind. She didn't want Noah to know her name, which meant he might recognize it. That meant she was deeply connected to the Army. Damn. And he no longer doubted that she'd been here before, not with the fit she threw over coming. She knew the risks if her identity were discovered. Her ridiculous disguise was easy enough to pull off, the braids and red skin simply catalysts to heap on already bitter images, but what if someone saw through it?

One factor stuck out in his mind—she lacked the experience months of captivity would have given her. She might have it now, and Hunter briefly marveled at how much she *had* changed, but she had been an infant to this life when they first met. Hell, the woman was too stuck on propriety, and minding her manners still, for this to all mesh and make some sense.

He mounted the steps of the hostelry and moved straight to the staircase, unaware of the sly grins dealt to his back from the men lounging near the entrance. Outside their room he hesitated, wondering what he'd say to her. Christ, he was on the verge of committing treason—for her. He'd already lied to the colonel. Hunter needed answers to save them from a stint in the brig.

His muscles bunched, creating an annoying sting in his shoulder before he realized she didn't know they suspected her to be this captured female. Which was worse for her? For them to believe she was a half-breed, or a white woman who preferred a Sioux to white men? The latter, he decided immediately, rubbing a hand over his face, whiskers rasping. Jesus, what a mess. He knocked. No answer. His hand closed over the knob and he twisted. Unlocked?

The door swung open.

The large copper tub sat near the hearth, the fire blazing, the bath water still steaming. A quick glance around the small room told him she wasn't inside. Damn! Flipping the lock, he tossed the packsin in a chair, shut the door and spun about, descending the stairs three at a time.

"Where is she?" he asked the clerk without preamble.

"I told yer whore an' now I'm tellin' you, Injuns ain't allowed," the clerk said, never looking up from his register.

Hunter grabbed the clerk by his shirt front, slamming him against the wall. "I won't ask twice." For emphasis he withdrew his pistol and pressed it to the man's temple when the clerk didn't answer immediately.

"Sh-she tried to git in an—an—!" Hunter drew the ham-

210

mer back, the image of her being dragged into a barracks magnifying his fury. "I took back the key an' showed her the door," he squealed in a rush, eyes wide with fear.

"I'll just bet you did." Hunter holstered the gun, his fierce expression sending panic through the little clerk. "If she's harmed, I'll be back—for you."

Letting him sag to the floor, Hunter strode out the door, his eyes scanning the rain-drenched grounds. Racing toward the barracks at the far end, horrible images assaulted his mind, and didn't cease when he found the dormitory silent. He backtracked to the hostelry, searching under carts, peering in windows and behind open doors. Nothing. His fear escalated. She couldn't leave, so was she hurt, unable to call out? He leaned into the trading post's only window, eyes scanning. Empty, locked tight. Damn. He was desperate, itching to rip into anything that had the misfortune to cross his path, and was on his way to ask Dugal for help when he passed before a narrow ally and head a faint scrap. He stopped abruptly, sliding in the muck and catching the porch support before he fell on his rump.

Stepping into the dark passage, he squinted into the shadows. "Violet Eyes?"

Her head snapped up and Hunter cursed, going down on one knee. His heart clenched at the pitiful sight; rain water dripped steadily off her chin and nose, her garments were soaked to the bone and she shivered violently. She'd been crying, too, yet those red-rimmed eyes refused to look in his direction. *This is my fault. I should never have insisted we come here, never have left her alone.*

"Come on, darlin'." He pulled her to her feet.

"Th-that man—he took the key." She shuddered hard. "I tried to get in but—"

"I know, Sable. Forget about it."

"I didn't want to cause any more trouble, not after—" She looked up, swiping the dripping water with the back of her hand, frowning. "Why did you insist I not talk?"

"I'll tell you, later, when we're alone."

The tone of his voice sent an uneasy sensation creeping up her spine with the numbing cold as Hunter ushered her toward the inn.

Sable halted, yanking free. "They won't let me in."

Nudging at the small of her back, he said, "Trust me, they will."

He heard her sigh as she wrapped the soaked blanket across her face, the drippy end slapping Hunter in the mouth. Lips twitching, he brushed the cloth away as she threw back her shoulders and marched regally up the steps, hanging onto the shreds of her dignity. He admired, following close. Her chin high, her posture stiff, she didn't so much as spare them a glance as she met the stairs and ascended, a queenly trail of sludge left in her wake. Hunter paused at the base of the steps to address the clerk.

"Hot water, food, and lots of it."

"I ain't feedin' no Injun," the clerk defied, adjusting his spectacles as he slapped the key in Hunter's open palm.

Hunter's smile was sinister, never reaching his eyes, the stitched cheek scar adding to the furious glare as he leaned down in the clerk's face and spoke precisely. "Then consider me a very hungry man with an *extremely* short temper." The clerk gulped thickly as Hunter turned away and climbed the steps. He found Sable outside the room.

"I don't have the key," she muttered lamely, hugging herself and puddling on the floor.

Hunter immediately opened the door and followed her inside. She wouldn't need one, any way. He intended to keep her sequestered here until they left in the morning. Hunter couldn't help but grin as he leaned back against the closed door. A captive audience, he thought, noticing her apprehension as she looked at the room's only bed. Before the night was over he was going to have some answers.

"Strip, Sable."

She whirled around, aghast. "I beg your pardon?"

"Strip and get into that tub." He removed his jacket, tossing it and his hat on a chair as he advanced on her. When she made no effort to undress he yanked off the wet blanket, dropping it on the floor. He reached for the buttons of her blouse.

Sable slapped his hands away. "What are you doing! Stop that!" She backed up, bumping into the tub.

"Get in before I put you in."

She lifted her chin a notch. "Not with you present."

His hands were at her waist, tugging at her belt. "You're wasting the heated water, lady, and you'll be sick if you don't get warm."

She covered his fingers with hers, raking her nails across his skin. He winced and stepped back, rubbing the scratches.

"Jesus, you're dangerous."

She'd been well-schooled today and her patience with men who thought they knew best withered and died. Sable pointed to the door. "Get out, Mr. Mccracken," she said, tired of being manhandled by anyone who had the slightest inclination—him included.

"It's *my* room, Sable," he growled, deftly hiding his grin. "You've got ten minutes. Make the most of it, 'cause I need a bath, too."

"You can't possibly mean that you're coming back?" she called as he stepped out the door. "While I bathe?"

He shut the door on her question.

Sable sighed heavily. Well, at least she managed to get him out before he saw the mark on her skin. Not wasting a moment, she unbound her hair and removed the muddy skirts. The bath was all she wanted now and Sable told herself she would deal with his deplorable behavior later, after she was clean. Never did she need a soak as much as she did now. Her numb fingers wasted precious minutes on the wet corset lacings, and she kept glancing between the door and the tub, anticipating his return. Finally free, she grabbed the cake of soap left on the small stool and gingerly stepped over the rim.

Heat seeped into her legs, and she moaned with pleasure. It had been such a long time since she'd indulged in this luxury. Folding down on her knees, she dunked her head, lathered her hair, rinsed off the first layer of grime, then repeated the process.

That's how Hunter found her: perched in the copper tub like a dirty lily, luxurious white soap bubbles crowning her head, slender arms massaging gently. Her waist-length hair clung wetly to her back, the ends drawing his attention to the smallness of her waist, the pale sheen of her skin and the gentle flare of her hips. When his lazy gaze focused on more than her ripe curves, it was the bruises he saw. Her lower back was scraped, finger-sized marks striped her upper arms, and he could easily see that the gentle curve of her buttocks bore the abuse of riding on the rump of his horse. Must hurt like hell, he thought, and admired her for not complaining once. How much more was she willing to suffer for this warrior? No—it was for the baby. Protecting the child had always been her primary concern.

Hunter kicked the door closed. "Least you'll smell better," he said and she yelped, dropping into the water like a stone.

Sable's face turned scarlet and she sank to her chin. "You have the manners of a barnyard swine, Mr. McCracken. Please leave!"

"Guess you won't want these then, huh?" He stood intentionally close, holding up the pitchers of hot steaming water. He grinned hugely.

Sable bit her lip, unable to believe she wasn't screaming for him to get out. But she needed that water to rinse her hair. "Set them there," she pointed to the stool, barely lifting so much as a finger out of the water.

"Yes, m'lady." He bowed. "Would her majesty prefer scented water, or—"

"I apologize." She didn't mean to be so rude but couldn't afford for him to see the dye mark on her arms.

Hunter scooped up her clothes, inspecting the bone and

214

canvas corset with a jaundice eye, then dropped it back onto the sodden pile.

"What *are* you doing?" she snapped when he jerked open the door and called out. A moment later he gave them as a greeting to the hostelry's only maid.

"Burn 'em," he instructed and shut the door.

"Mister McCracken!" Sable twisted around as he rummaged in his saddlebags. "And what am I supposed to wear now?"

"You aren't going anywhere, so this is enough." He tossed one of his own clean shirts on the bed, then moved to the fire, warming his backside.

"Are you just going to stand there?" she managed, gripping the soap, incredulous that the man had the audacity to remain. "Can't I at least have a little privacy?"

"Yes, no, and," he grinned, the smile diabolic with the days' growth of beard and the cut on his cheek. "Want me to wash your back?"

"I most certainly do not!" Sable fumed, squeezing the soap so hard it popped out of her hands, straight up into the air to land at his feet. Hunter's gaze shifted from the mushy cake to her, debating on whether or not he'd make her come and get it, but decided that would be pushing his luck. This shy little cat had claws. Picking it up, he tossed the bar into the water with a resounding plop. Sable gave him an exasperated look, then fished beneath the surface for the precious cake.

She had no notion of how incredibly enchanting she appeared, he thought, watching her rummage under the water, a job he'd thoroughly enjoy. Lavish bubbles slid from her hair down to her iodined shoulders, her movements nudging away the suds enough for him to see the pale plump swells of her breasts. Flawless. He wanted to caress the soft flesh, feel her squirm beneath him, all naked and wet and slick with scented foam. And to know only a few gallons of water separated him from that lush body made him burn with wanting. His trousers tightened across his hips, and he turned toward the hearth, bracing his forearm on the mantle and staring at the fire. He wanted her, so bad he could feel it up to his grinding teeth, and Hunter knew it was more than just gratification he sought. There was a purity about her that drew him, a clear river of strength and purpose he wished he possessed again.

It wasn't smart for him to want anything this much. It would only cause them both a lot of pain, himself especially. And he was putting his freedom on the line for what? A few chunks of gold? A tender moment?

He had to get out of here. She was married, a mother, on her way back to her husband, he reminded himself, but without either here to see, to block his thoughts, Hunter's private longing seeped past the shield of honor.

Sable's face dunked into the water as she finally captured the slippery bar. Reaching blindly for a towel, one magically appeared in her hand. She wiped the sting from her eyes and looked up, inhaling sharply when she found his face inches from hers, iron gray eyes holding her motionless.

His finger swirled in a mound of suds, then trailed very slowly up across her bare shoulder, the side of her throat, burning a path across her jaw to graze her lower lip. It trembled and she shuddered softly, goose flesh blooming where he touched.

"Careful, Violet Eyes," he rasped. "Don't scrub too hard." He straightened and moved swiftly to the door. "That red skin just might rub off."

Chapter Twenty-two

"Drat," Sable moaned, the sound muffled as she sank deeper into the bubbles. Double drat! Well. She shouldn't be surprised, really. The day she opened her mouth she lent credence to his suspicions. It would do no good to kick herself for her mistakes now, and though she did wonder exactly when he'd figured it out, her primary concern was that Hunter McCracken could be informing the authorities while she sat in a tub of sudsy water.

But he didn't seem angry and could have walked away the moment he unearthed her lie, she reasoned. In fact, he appeared rather amused. That consideration eased her apprehension, but she decided a hasty departure from her only luxury in weeks was best. Sable rinsed the soap from her hair and body then left the tub, rubbing her skin dry and toweling her hair.

Keeping an eye on the door.

After slipping into the white shirt, she rifled his saddlebags for a comb, marveling at her audacity to be so familiar with his things, then dragged the quilt from the bed. Wrapped warmly, she sat on the braided rug before the hearth and worked the knots from her hair.

Hunter entered the room unannounced, carrying a tray laden with a bottle of wine, glasses, sliced bread, cheese, cold beef, and the only apple to be had for miles. He stopped short. *That worn rag of a shirt looks like a damn negligee.* He crossed the room, wondering how long he could withstand this intimate setting before the urge to steal a kiss got the better of his good judgment.

Belowstairs he was ready to demand answers, maintaining the hard grind that kept his temper high, but now, recognizing her sluggish movements, reality slapped him in the face. For the past five days she'd doctored two men, scarcely eaten, slept even less, suffered assault, hours drenched to the bone, cold and hungry, and now he couldn't find one question that absolutely *needed* answering—tonight.

He set the tray beside her and uncorked the wine, catching the light flowery scent left by the perfumed soap he'd scrounged for her. Hunter clenched his teeth.

Torture, pure torture.

Sable combed her hair, covertly watching as he splashed dark red wine into a chipped goblet. "I'm relieved, you know," she admitted to her lap, her voice scarcely above a whisper.

"You weren't very good at it, Sable," he replied just as softly while he poured her a glass.

She glanced up, her smile devilish. "Well enough to fool you, Mister McCracken."

Hunter's gaze flew to hers. "If you don't mind, madam, I'd rather not be reminded of the idiot I've been." Ignoring her smug expression, he took the comb and pressed the glass into her hand, urging her to drink. "Besides, you stink as an Indian."

"My, how gallant of you to say," she quipped, saluting him with the glass before taking a large sip. She shivered at the bitter taste, then frowned at the labeless bottle.

"Not the lady's favorite?" He slugged back some wine, then settled onto the rug.

Her gaze collided with his and she could see the black flecks in his eyes, count his indecently long lashes, the stitches she'd made in his wounded cheek. Raven black hair tumbled over his brow in a thick wave and she clutched the goblet to keep from reaching out. Muddy, rain-soaked, and heavily whiskered, he was hardly the refined gentleman she was used to, but Hunter McCracken was more man than she'd ever encountered. His raw masculinity seemed to swallow her, bend her, and her eyes lowered to his lips, arched and smooth. The cadence of his breath lured, the sun-bronzed skin tempted, and she wanted him to kiss her, take her in his arms, press her back to the rug and *really* kiss her; one of those glorious smoldering kisses that always trapped her excitement and consumed her with a seeking eagerness for something more, more fulfilling, more ...

She stared accusingly at her goblet of wine.

This would never do. Not alone in a hotel room!

"I'd hardly know one vintage from another." She bowed her head, flustered by her thoughts. "I don't drink."

"And here I thought you didn't recognize the bouquet," he said, maintaining an easy smile when he wanted nothing more than to carry her to the bed and show her just what those telling looks did to a man.

"Why did you tell me not to talk?" she asked, and prayed she didn't look as foolish as she felt.

He set his glass aside, then stuffed a slice of bread with meat and cheese. "So the colonel will believe you can't speak English."

She blinked, then slowly smiled. "You didn't!"

"Yup." He took a bit, chewed, watching her intensely.

"And just how long do you think it will take him to confirm your lies with Mister Moffet or the lieutenant?"

He swallowed. "Til morning, I hope."

"You—*we* could be arrested!" she realized, gripping the goblet stem, then taking a huge gulp.

"Yeah, that's usually how it goes ... followed by a hanging." He ate some more.

"How can you be so casual about it?" She flicked a hand at the sandwich he was devouring.

He shrugged, swallowed. "It's what had to be done to protect you." He leaned closer. "That's why you're paying me, right?" He popped the last of his dinner into his mouth and dusted his fingertips.

But money doesn't really matter to Hunter. Sable nodded.

"And the point behind this monumental fib?" Handing him a napkin, she gestured to the crumbs left on his mouth and he smiled.

"Had to throw Maitland off the track." He swiped at his lips, giving her a measured look. "He was too damn interested in *you*, where *you* came from and where we're headed." Her features slackened and he pounced on the advantage. *"Now*—tell me what I'm up against."

She dropped her gaze, swirling her finger around the rim of her glass. Wine sang. The fire blazed, sounding like sheets snapping in the wind.

She'd like nothing better than to unburden herself and let him carry the weight of her secrets, but their presence in the fort was testimony to his divided loyalty. Sable couldn't risk discovery while *inside* the fort—not when he was the only one who knew where Little Hawk was. Keeping her identity from him was her last advantage. The colonel's daughter would never get out of this fort; a Cheyenne half-breed at least had a chance.

His voice, low and serious and perhaps a little hurt, broke the stretch of silence. "Can't you see I'm in this for the duration?" *Trust me,* he was asking.

Her shoulders drooped and she looked at him, dispirited. "You traded Little Hawk's safety by bringing me here. That puts me in a position not to trust you."

"Damn it, Sable!" Stung, he launched a frontal attack. "The Army wants the boy." The color drained from her face and even beneath the iodined skin she was deathly pale. Without mercy, he relayed what Dugal knew. "The colonel suspects you're the woman he wants."

She jerked away from him, focusing on the twisting flames.

"Are you?" he prodded, watching fear and indecision skate across her profile. After a strained moment, she nodded, and he released the air trapped in his lungs. That was something, at least. Undulating flames reflected off her skin, and Hunter recognized the quivering lower lip for what it was.

"How could he have told?" she rasped, torment cracking her voice. "After all the trouble he went through to keep everything secret?"

"Who, Sable?" he whispered into her pain.

"Papa," came in a bitter hiss.

Hunter's eyes flared. Her own father had betrayed her!

"I didn't believe he could hate his grandson so deeply." She covered her mouth with a trembling hand, her heart breaking for the little boy. *Oh, Laney, the agony you must be suffering now.* "The Judas! He wants Black Wolf dead more than he cares—"

Hunter let out a vicious curse and she looked at him sharply.

"Oh, this is just great," he ground out, shoving his fingers through his hair. "Shit! Black Wolf!"

"We have to leave." Sable could think only of Little Hawk and the spies in blue uniforms her father might have stationed across the territory. "Now. Tonight." She tried to stand but he wouldn't let her.

"The gates are closed and petitioning to open them will only raise more suspicion."

"But he needs me! Surely you can see his life is at stake now more than ever!" She struggled, but he held tight.

"He's safer with Swift Arrow."

She clutched his arms, desperately searching his eyes. "Where is he, Mr. McCracken?" A tear fell, cutting straight into his heart. "Please tell me at least that."

"I can't."

She punched him, hard. "Blast you!" Small fists pelted his arms and chest. "This is your fault, yours!" Then she punched him again and he captured her hands, binding them

221

to his chest. She fought. "Little Hawk would be safe with his father if not for your insipid duty!"

"I know, damn it!" He jerked her hands and she stilled, yet refused to look at him. "But if the authorities discover your ruse they'll keep you here," he said in a calm voice, "permanently." She glared at him through a curtain of hair. "You mustn't have anything to tell them."

Her teeth caught her lip as another drop trickled down her cheek, then another, and he made a pained sound, pulling her in his embrace, stroking the back of her head. She held onto his shirt sleeves in desperation and Hunter knew he'd just crushed the only thing keeping her head above water— The baby's safety. He squeezed his eyes shut as she cried, her forehead pressed to his chest, her shoulders jerking miserably. It was a quiet, mournful sound—of failure and regret.

"Easy now, darlin'," he whispered into her damp hair, rubbing her spine until she quieted. Hell, she was just a woman protecting her son! "I'll get you out, Sable." He nudged her chin up til she met his gaze and with the edge of the blanket he dried her tears. "I swear, I'll make it right."

Feeling protected and safe, she offered a weak smile. "It's not your abilities I doubt, Mister McCracken." She pushed out of his arms, yet the warmth of his touch clung to her body, tempting her to return. "It's the Army's determination I underestimated."

"Stooping low this time, huh?" Desperate to occupy his hands, he offered her a fresh glass of wine. "Eat something," he said disarmingly. "You'll feel better." He stood and pulled his shirt from his trousers.

Sable blinked owlishly, a crust of bread caught between her teeth. "What are you doing?" she managed around the bread.

"Getting naked." He tossed the shirt aside, then removed his holster, boots, and socks.

"Mr. McCracken!" she repeated as each item met the floor.

He unbuckled his belt. "I need a bath, Sable," he said patiently, his lips twitching with a grin. She looked so adorably indignant, he couldn't resist shocking her worries right out of her. His fingers hovered at the buttons of his pants. "Turn your back if you don't like the view."

Sable shifted abruptly, huffing at the nerve of the man, then heard his trousers drop to the floor. She couldn't help flinching. He was bare. Behind her, Hunter McCracken was stark naked! Mortified, she yanked the blanket higher. He chuckled and she knew he was toying with her as she heard a soft splash, then his deep rumbling sigh. He was in the tub. In the same water she'd just immersed her body—*oh mercy, Sable, don't think of it.* Vigorously she combed her hair, snatching a piece of cheese, stuffing it in her mouth and just as she swallowed that, shoved in more, concentrating on anything but the naked man merely inches behind her.

But her mind refused the diversion, conjuring all sorts of forbidden images; the cloth dragging over muscled arms, the soap lathering between his strong hands, smoothing across his chest, down the stomach she knew was as rigid as a washboard, and then lower. She fanned her hand beneath her chin, unreasonably hot.

"Hey, Sable?"

"Yes." Cautious, shaky.

"Want to wash my back?"

"I should think not!"

"Figured as much."

"Then why ask?"

"My back's dirty, and" he chuckled quietly, "one day I'm going to ask and you'll do it."

"You may dream of the occasion, Mister McCracken, for it shall happen only there."

"God, I love the way you deliver insults, darlin', all wrapped in velvet."

"What?" Sable twisted around. "Oh, dear," she gasped, breathless, eyes round. "Oh dear."

He was so broad and tall and whereas the bath water covered her, it exposed his chest, bent soapy legs, and as he rose up to reach for the pitcher, a great deal of naked hip and . . . *that* part of him. It lay flaccid, unthreatening, yet she knew from recent experience that it would grow and harden—a gauge of his desire.

Hunter glanced up and caught her gawking. He looked pointedly at his lap, then back to her, grinning hugely in the face of her cherry-red blush.

Her gaze was glued to his manhood and instantly he felt his thickening response. Her eyes widened. "See anything you want, Sable?" He chuckled, lowering himself into the tub.

Her gaze snapped to his face. "Oh! Oh! You—you—you—!" Why, the man was absolutely incorrigible, she thought, jerking the blanket tightly around her, aware that she hadn't yet averted her eyes.

"Hey, lady, you're the one grabbing an eye full." He sluiced water over his head.

"Your stitches!" she warned, hand up as if to stay the flow.

"Can't be helped," he shrugged, pushing hair out of his eyes. "Hand me that, will you?" He pointed to the shaving kit and when she looked like she'd refuse even that remote contact, Hunter started to climb out of the tub.

"No! No! I'll get it, for mercy's sake!" Afraid he might parade across the room in the altogether, Sable leaped to her feet and grabbed for the kit. In her haste she forgot the blanket and gave Hunter a delectable show of a naked woman shrouded in a shirt that had been washed too many times. He stared openly at the pale shapely calves exposed below the hem of his shirt.

"Now who is grabbing an eye full?" she said, dropping the kit on the stool.

His gaze snapped up to meet those chastising lavender eyes as she wrapped the quilt around her waist like a skirt. It served to yank his shirt tighter across her breasts, and hell, she might as well *be* naked for the alluring pear-shaped outline she offered him. The worn cotton clung, defining the tender points and darker surrounding circles. His palm itched, his mouth gone dry. She really was a beautiful creature, he thought, moistening his lips, then occupied his lusty imagination with laying the gear on the stool while she returned to the braided rug.

Sable dabbed at the perspiration on her brow and neck, feeling her heart beating in her throat. *The way he looked at me,* she thought, *as if his eyes had fingers.* She plucked at the shirt, her body tingling in private places. She squeezed her thighs tightly together, suppressing the ache. But this time he hadn't laid a hand on her. And this time she craved the solid feel of his touch, the friction of calloused palms on her body. *Oh, this is highly improper—delicious and wonderful . . . I cannot pursue this,* she reasoned, only half appalled at herself. *It will only gain me . . . what?*

Pleasure, a voice whispered through her brain.

Unspeakable pleasure.

She glanced over her shoulder, certain he'd spoken and found him scraping shave soap near the cut on his cheek while attempting to hold the mirror with wet hands.

"Let me help," she said and without a thought Sable scooted close, taking the mirror. He adjusted the position and continued, smiling his thanks. Sable noticed the gash at his temple, his hair covering where the bullet had grazed him, but before she realized the predicament in which she had put herself by being so close to a naked man, her attention shifted to his relentless scraping. "Careful. You'll rip open the stitches."

"Then take them out. They itch."

"Oh, very well," she said exasperatedly and took the razor from him, stropping it twice before coming up on her knees beside the tub. Grasping his chin in her palm, she gently plucked out the stitches, then shaved the tender area. "Stop smiling," she scolded.

"Can't help it."

"Don't talk either."

"Are you always so bossy?"

"It's random." She frowned. "I think."

"I like it."

Her brows shot up. "Really?" Why was she so flattered? "Most men insist that a woman be docile, quiet, to share the opinions of their men while suppressing their own—all of which I've discovered I can no longer tolerate."

"I'm not most men."

She met his gaze, pausing in the shave.

"Oh," she said on a laugh, "you have definitely proven that!"

"That good or bad?"

"That's twice you've asked that of me."

"And you didn't give me a straight answer before."

She held a razor at his throat, his chin in palm. He was such an unusual man, constantly leaving himself open to pain and rejection from her. He deserved an honest answer for a change. "It's good, Mr. McCracken," she said in a throaty voice, and his vulnerable smile pricked a hole in her heart.

She took the last of the bristle from his skin.

Hunter hoped to God she didn't look down and see the effect her closeness had on him. He couldn't remember when he'd been attracted to a woman like this, so obsessively. He burned for her. It was dangerous. She belonged to another, and at that moment he couldn't picture her with Black Wolf, didn't want to—not a man who thought of her as possession, like his horse or bow. She needed more than that from a man. *Like you know what a lady like her needs,* a pestering voice said. He allowed his eyes to roam over her porcelain delicate features, those supple curves shifting beneath the gauzy shirt, beckoning his attention. Remembering her mouth on his made him feel deranged. He floated the wash rag in the general vicinity of his distress, and decided, for her sake, he should have taken a five-cent bath in the stalls behind the barracks like he'd planned.

"That should do it," she murmured, smoothing her fingers over his jaw, checking for missed stubble. Hunter caught her

226

hand on the first pass, holding it there, and Sable was trapped in his stormy gaze. "Please don't, Mr. McCracken. We both know this isn't right."

"I keep telling myself that." Her pulse leaped in her throat and he saw it. "But you'd tempt a saint, woman." His words were rough, brimming with tension.

Beyond curiosity, it had never mattered to him if she was the daughter or the wife of an Indian or a senator or a sergeant, only that *he* had put her in this dangerous position when she'd begged him not to. Yet getting her out meant giving her up to him, her husband. Black Wolf. Why did it have to be him!

I am just playing on borrowed time. The thought disgusted him. He shouldn't be borrowing a damn thing, since he didn't want to return a moment spent with her.

"You don't love him," he said and she tried to pull away, but he lifted a hand from the water, pressing a finger to her lips. "Shh, I can feel it," he hushed, leaning closer. His finger slid across her lips, wetting them, then down her chin, drawing a damp mesmerizing line to the throbbing pulse at the base of her throat. Water merged from his fingertip onto her skin, the droplet disappearing between the swells of her breasts exposed at the opening of the shirt. She shivered deliciously and didn't draw back when he freed her captured palm. Instead she let it drop to the cool skin of his shoulder.

"So beautiful," he murmured and her eyes widened a fraction in disbelief. He liked that, that she didn't know of her effect. He'd be useless if she did.

His fingers toyed with the buttons of the shirt, his mouth hovering a breath above hers and she made a little sound of need and anticipation, and he knew she was as wanting as he, whether she admitted it or not. Hunter's forearm gazed the tip of her breast and her shocked breath tumbled into his mouth. His lips touched hers, barely, like the flutter of a wing.

God.

A warrior's woman.

"A Sioux wife has the right to choose a new husband." Jesus, what made him say that?

"Are you offering for the position?"

"No." Final, without hesitation. And the single word sliced him in half.

Sable jerked back, flushing with embarrassment. He wanted only a lover.

"Then my status with him is hardly your concern." With a smattering of dignity, she plucked at the shirt and scooted to the rug.

"Considering what the hell just happened—what happens every time we get close—I think it is."

"Don't think so often, Mister McCracken, you'll overtax that addled brain of yours," she snapped, throwing a towel in his face, then giving him her back.

Hunter sat in the tepid water, cursing himself and wondering why he opened his fat mouth when Black Wolf was going to kill him anyway. He left the tub and dried off, then quickly dressed in fresh clothes.

Jamming his shirt into his trousers, her quivering voice made him freeze.

"I fail to see the purpose in tormenting me the way you do."

She glanced back over her shoulder and he was there, grasping her arms, dragging her from the floor and into his strong embrace. He crushed her mouth with his, lips hot with uncapped sensuality, his hands diving beneath the shirt, wildly caressing her back, around her sides to mold her bare breasts. She whimpered against his mouth. Her legs buckled and instantly her back met the unyielding hardness of the wall. Her arms clung around his neck as his hands slid down to cup her buttocks, lift her, grind the tender core of her to the erection so prominent in his jeans. He nudged her legs apart. Moans and caught breaths filled the tiny room as Hunter took and mastered. Sable gave and relished. Suddenly he drew back, breathing heavily against her lips.

228

"Tormented enough, darlin'?" He jerked her leg up, fitting her tightly to his thickness and she answered with a restless squirm. "Or are you going to wait until I'm buried between those pretty white thighs," he drawled caustically, "before you act the least bit married?"

With that he released her, scooped up the soiled clothes, holster, coat, and hat, and headed for the door.

He ignored her choked sob and knew he would need more than a drink tonight.

Chapter Twenty-three

Hunter offered a smile to the scantily clad blonde perched on his lap as she wiggled playfully, her hand sliding down his bare stomach and over the bulge in his trousers. She squeezed and gave him a practiced hungry look as she licked her lips and squeezed again. Nothing but a twitch, he thought. Nothing like what Sable did to him with just a glance.

With a smothered curse, he grabbed his drink and dashed it down, then set the empty glass on the side table and shoved it away before he wrapped his arms around the woman, nuzzling her neck. Her hands moved deeper between his thighs, rubbing harder, and he heard her husky pleas to take what she offered. He wanted to, and closing his eyes against the thick scent of her perfume, he pushed the thin chemise strap off her shoulder, pulling it down to reveal a small tight breast. His hand covered the rounded flesh as she flipped open the first couple of buttons to his trousers with an expertise he recognized. Hunter tried to lose himself to the skill of her hands, her explicitly coaxing words. Another button came free, then another.

He tensed, then released a long tired sigh.

I can't.

This is useless.

They'd been at this for an hour now with no results, damn it. Every time he looked at her, his mind replaced her blonde hair and dark eyes with the sultry contrasts of Sable's.

But he couldn't have Sable either.

His last image of her flashed in his mind. Sable, hurt and confused, her lips bruised from his violent kiss. He'd pushed her too hard.

Abruptly he placed the woman aside, ignoring her pout and fastening his clothes as he stood.

"Sorry, Lettie."

"Nellie," she corrected sourly.

"Yeah, well." He flushed with embarrassment, swaying as he reached for his shirt. "Too much liquor, I guess." What a laugh. He was roaring drunk. At least it was a quiet roar, thank God. He'd made a spectacle of himself enough today.

"We got all night, sugar. I ain't busy." She rubbed herself against him as he pulled his shirt up over his shoulders, the scent of other men creeping from beneath her sickeningly sweet perfume. Ought to smell better for the fort's laundress, he thought, donning his jacket and hat but not bothering to button his shirt.

"You sure?" she asked, cupping him between his legs, smiling coyly as she stood on tiptoes for a kiss. He couldn't bring himself to oblige her and pressed a coin into her hand, then patted her rump, offering an apologetic smile before slipping out of the little shanty and into the night.

The blast of cold air made him feel the alcohol with a blinding force as he forged his way back to the hostelry on unsteady legs. For a moment he considered hunting for another bottle, then decided his senses were blunted enough. The hour was late. Sable would be asleep by now.

What a coward he was.

Lily-livered sap.

Hunter couldn't face her this drunk, not after being unmanned in the arms of an experienced whore because of his attraction to a married woman. If he'd left her alone, neither would be hurting like this. He had few values left and wanted to retain some small dignity—his honor, his word. It was all he had.

And he'd already twisted that until it was unrecognizable. He was being melancholy, definitely a bad sign.

After scaling the mountain of stairs, Hunter jammed the key in the lock and opened the door, stumbling over his own feet as the latch ran away from him. He caught himself, briefly swaying like a willow before he straightened. Too much Toas Lightning, he thought, tossing his hat toward the chair. He watched in hazy fascination as it sailed to the floor. His holster dropped to the rug with a thud and he shushed it as if it would listen, then battled with his coat, shaking the offending garment from his hand and leaving it in a pile. He paused to catch his breath and senses while toeing off his boots. His gaze swept the room. The tub was gone and the tray, but the wine bottle and chipped glass lay on the rug before the hearth, the bottle on its side. Empty? He swung around, focusing on the small bundle tucked in the farthest corner of the bed.

Sable—soft and silky and violet-eyed.

Sable with her fleshy hills and valleys and supple curves which he wanted to explore, slowly, deliberately.

Sable with her secrets and her baby and her God-damned husband.

Hunter hugged the bedpost, watching her shift and sigh. Her hair spilled across the white sheets in a chocolate river of curls. He didn't know it would curl, for she never wore it down. Not for him.

"Too damn pretty to be wasting away like you are," he slurred, shaking his head. "Can't understand why you want to go back to a man who wouldn't even come after you. You're too good for him." He snorted a laugh. "Too good for me, too, God dammit. I'm trouble." He thumped his chest. "Not clean enough to even be touching you, let alone wanting you like air. You," he snapped a hand in her direction, "with your innocent eyes and social graces and eloquent chatter. You with your sweet little rump and plump breasts, aching for me and holding back for him. Him! Damn me and my twisted

232

life," he muttered, rubbing his hand over his mouth, remembering the exquisite feel of her lips on his.

"Compare me to him, Sable? His kiss to mine?" There was a pause and then, "Why the hell should I bother? You're his." He lashed an arm in frustration. "I don't have the right to ask! Hell, you belong to him so much you're sacrificing everything to bring him his child!" He swallowed thickly, licking his dry lips. "But have you ever loved your warrior?" he asked, then leaned close and whispered, "Does he create a fire in you like I can? Are you wild and passionate in *his* arms? I thirst for it—that tenderness, that incredible heat." Briefly he squeezed his eyes shut, remembering. "God, what fire. Every time we touch. Do you feel me soak it up?" His voice hardened, his features sharpening. "But you deny it, for his sake. Damn Black Wolf."

He moved on shaky legs to the side of the bed, staring down at her for a long moment before he lifted a lock of her hair, watching in the faint lamplight as the silken strands sifted through his fingers. The ache to bury his face in the dark cloud tightened his throat.

"Wanting you is the purest thing I've known in years," he rasped.

Hunter craved to gather her in his arms, woman-soft and willing, to feel her body take his deep inside her. Accept him. Receive him. To see if he still had anything left that would merit his existence. See if he could love, just a little. Maybe then he'd like himself, maybe then he'd feel deserving of joining the real world again. He brushed a finger lightly across the curve of her cheek and whispered in a tight voice, "God curse you, Sable. Why did *he* have to find you first?"

No answer. But then, he never expected one.

This kind of talk is killing me, he thought, sinking down onto the opposite side of the bed and staring at her shadowed outline. He laid back and sighed heavily. "Are you escaping to the wild—like me, Violet Eyes?" He yawned hugely. "Or looking . . . for it."

233

A moment later his soft breathing filled the room.

Glowing embers in the fire broke and fell, sending a gush of sparks and ash into the air. Sable rolled onto her back and stared at his sleeping form. A tear slid down her cheek, staining the pillow.

Oh, Hunter. I'm sorry. So sorry.

The impact of her deception hit her dead in the heart, crushing her with guilt. He'd persecute himself until she could tell him the truth.

Merciful God, he was so torn up inside. She'd seen him mask those haunted looks often enough to know there was more to his pain than wanting a *married* woman, but if she pried, he'd shut her out, closing himself in that coarseness he wore like a cloak.

She caught the scent of cheap perfume and unwanted jealousy tapped her heart. This is my fault, she blamed, studying his relaxed features, black hair curling wildly about his forehead and jaw, the usually bitter twist of his mouth now soft and appealingly sensual. Was that simply drunken talk? Or did he merely want because he couldn't have? And if they did become lovers? How long would it last? Where would it lead? Shocked that she'd even consider the prospect, Sable didn't believe that giving herself to him was the solution to his torment. He was unpredictable. Cynical and unscrupulous. And he doesn't want to be your husband, she reminded. Only your lover. It all sounded so torrid.

Lovers.

Expelling a soft breath, she snuggled down into the warmth of the covers. She was living now, for the first time in her life, but what if they were arrested in the morning? Resigned to never having a family of her own once this adventure was made public, could she resist the temptation to grab this one chance? Would she grow old with just a memory of him?

Lovers.

The single word generated silken images of warm bodies entwined, coaxing whispers and the throbbing ache of discov-

234

ery. She squirmed, closed her eyes, and tempted sleep, knowing she was losing her heart to a man who lived on the fringes of life.

A short while later a cry snapped her awake and for a moment she thought she imagined it. Movement beside her made her twist around. Hunter thrashed on the bed. His shirt was gone and she could see the film of sweat on his skin and face. His muscles tensed and bulged. He's fighting demons again. *This always happens when he drinks.* No matter how cantankerous he acts, his secrets fester, she thought, watching him struggle with invisible bonds, battle foes within the haze of nightmares. Suddenly he arched his back, breath hissing through clenched teeth. The motion was repeated three, four, five times before he sank into the mattress. Still. Silent. He'd been whipped, she discerned, horrified.

Sable's heart clenched with pity, remembering he'd survived a Confederate prison. He cried out for his mother, his father, begged to be forgiven and refused to forgive in the same breath, his mumblings drifting across the small spanse to sink like tiny arrows into her heart. She squeezed her eyes shut, a tear sliding from the corner to dampen her hair as she tried to block out his agony.

Interfering could do more harm.

Then he screamed a denial, a tortured howl that shook the room and made her skin shift. Sable glanced at the door, fearing someone would hear and burst in and see him like this. She would spare him that humiliation.

Leaning over, she shook his arm.

"Mister McCracken," she whispered, then repeated his name when another scream bubbled in his throat. "Mister McCracken, wake up!" Nothing but a low growl.

On her knees now, she grasped his shoulders and jostled hard. "Hunter, you're dreaming. Wake up!"

His eyes opened, his brows drawing tight.

"Hunter?" She frowned. He looked queer. "It's Sable. You were dreaming." His searching gaze held her motionless as he slowly reached out. His hand trembled as it touched the side of her jaw, then slid into her hair. He was so cold! Instinctively she covered his cool flesh with her palm.

"You came back," he whispered in wonder, rising up to capture her mouth with his own, his kiss deep and piercingly sweet, both hands sinking into her hair. "You came back." It was such a crucifying sound, his voice, like he didn't deserve to say it and Sable gripped his shoulders.

His lips ground across her jaw, down her throat, wet, tingling, and she dropped her head back, sensations flaring. Pulsing. Turbulent. There was something so different about him.

"How did you know I needed you?" he rasped darkly, palming her spine, the flesh beneath her arms, then covering her breasts. She moaned, leaning into the pressure. I should call to him, shake him, she thought fleetingly, but when he gently lifted the plump swells, his tongue laving at her cloth-covered nipple, all doubt was banished and she sank into the luxury of his attention. His lips pulled, toyed. The material clung wetly to her breast.

Sable melted.

Hunter suckled.

And the nightmare vanished beneath his secret fantasy as he drew her across his lap, bending to take her mouth again. Sable knew he was caught somewhere between dreams and desire, but his lips were moist-hot and rolling. His tongue probing deeply into her. She quaked with sharp desire, curling close, soft in his arms as his calloused hands swept the length of her legs, gliding up across her buttocks, catching the shirt. Cool air delicately breezed her skin.

"Come into my dreams, Violet Eyes," he pleaded hoarsely, taking her down with him to the mattress. "Make them clean again."

236

A sob caught in her throat. She couldn't resist, not this needy cry for tenderness.

He cradled her, fragile, like a child, draping her legs over his thighs.

"You're mine now," he said as if she could not escape. His hand scorched over her body like a starving flame, memorizing the texture of her skin, the contour of her thigh. He shaped and stroked, cherished and whispered praise as he adored each slope and valley, coaxing her legs apart to caress the downy mound between.

She inhaled sharply, her hips jerking back. "Hunter," she pleaded, her body dampening with desire as he rubbed. He probed her delicate flesh, pushing a finger inside. Sable arched against the unfamiliar invasion, a liquid burn coating where he touched.

"Let me love you," he whispered, shifting his knee, spreading her legs wide, a second finger sinking deep, then rising, drawing her into the storm.

"Hunter, I don't—" Her untutored body controlled, grasped, slickening with every stroke. It frightened her, the power of it. So luxuriously wicked, this undefinable thrill tearing her between desire and conscience. Yet as her mind rebelled, she ached to conquer her virgin impulses and steal this secret interlude for herself.

She grasped his arm with the feeble intention of pushing him away but her hand to his skin ignited a blaze in him that was unquenchable. His mouth was suddenly devouring hers, sweeping and savage. She whimpered, her breath ragged, a strange dark fire bursting within her. He licked and nipped, then plundered her lips again and again, satisfying his furious hunger as he withdrew his fingers from her moist body and thrust again with fresh demand.

Her hand rode up his shoulder, his broad neck, fingers curling into his hair.

Her body spoke, drawing deeply.

"Yes, take it," he breathed, his hips rocking her thigh. He

was long and hard against her and she wanted to touch, to discover him. His fingertip circled the sensitive core of her and Sable jolted at the snap of hot pleasure, gasping for her next breath. "Touch the stars, love," he whispered into her fervor and Sable gathered close each new sensation he introduced. His tempo increased and he smiled when her hips swiftly joined his rhythm, rising to meet his thrusts. His breath warmed her ear, her throat. "Let me give you this."

Sable couldn't speak, unable to muster a thought beyond the roaring in her veins. Her body pulsed tight with excitement, desperate to know if there was an end to this sumptuous torment. Between her thighs burned. And she twisted, drawing up one leg, trying to ease the fire.

A sob escaped her. Tears blurred her vision. Muscles clenched, and she bit her lip, her buttocks digging into the mattress.

"Hun-ter!" she cried, throwing her head back, her body clamping to keep the sensations within. A frisson of heat spiraled, riding through her blood, her skin, her womanhood, and she pressed a hand over his, grinding him into her.

"So sweet," he murmured, his gaze thirstily absorbing her sparkling bliss as he stretched her out on the bed, his body fused to hers. Her excitement swelled and he whispered how beautiful she was in her passion, what joy it gave him to see it, feel her body climax in his arms, how she made him crazy to be thick and driving into her as he clutched her fiercely. Rubbing. Thrusting. Stroking. And Sable clung to him, trembling, the peak slow to fade as all movement stopped.

Seconds passed.

Her insides simmered.

Her chest rose and fell, her rasping breath the only sound in the room. Beyond the walls a dog howled mournfully, a door slammed. Sable squeezed her eyes shut, turning her face into his shoulder, fighting to regain her lost senses while her innocent body screamed for something more, something she couldn't name.

His embrace loosened. Her throat worked with stifled tears as Hunter slowly lifted his head, his features tense, his eyes shocked and confused.

His gaze moved down her half-naked form to where his hand lay, where he had her leg pinned, then back up to her glossy eyes.

"Oh, Jesus," he mumbled, then buried his face in the pillow aside her head. Like a deflating balloon his body went oddly slack. She jiggled him uselessly. Passed out, she realized, staring at the cracked ceiling, humiliation sweeping over her. He thought it was all a dream. He was so drunk he didn't realize—!

Without his strength to battle she easily shoved him away. He flopped on his back.

Sable sat up and drew her knees to her chest, yanking the covers around her, feeling rattled and confused. Her body still throbbed, satisfaction only half full and she didn't understand why. She stared at his silent features. An instant later her arm shot out, her fist smacking hard against his bare shoulder.

"Blast you, and your dreams, Hunter," she whispered. "They found you first."

Chapter Twenty-four

The scent of musty wet earth, frying bacon, and horse dung permeated the cold air. Real pleasant, Travis thought, watching Hunter slop through the mud to the pair of horses and secure the last of the packs and bed rolls. Leaning against the wood support, Travis warmed his hands on the mug of coffee. Ought to be dang peeved, he reasoned, burrowing into the fur of his coat. Gettin' woked up by that young cuss even before the mess cooks had a decent pot brewin'. Heck, if it weren't for his admiration for the little half-breed gal, he'd still be snug beneath a foot of buffalo hides. Must be goin' soft.

Despite the lazy sun bristling at her new day, the fort was alive with activity. Guards changed duty, freshly saddled horses nickered and stomped as their groggy riders emerged from the barracks, yanking up suspenders and donning hats and coats against the biting cold. Hunter returned to where Travis stood on the steps and grabbed the parcel he'd left at the shopkeeper's feet.

Travis gave him a speculative look over the rim of his mug. "Up two hours, Hunter, and you still look like someone spent the night stompin' on your face."

Hunter rubbed a hand over his jaw and chin, his head pounding so hard his ears throbbed. "Funny, that's just what it feels like."

"Drunk *all* night ag'in, were you now, lad?"

Hunter snapped a look over his shoulder. Dugal stood ankle deep in mud, hands on his hips, glaring like an angry parent. "And after trippin' a few wit' me?" He shook his head. " 'Tis me own fault, offerin' you the brew."

Hunter sent him a level look. "I'm a big boy, Dugal. I can handle it."

Travis snorted and Hunter pinned him with an icy glare.

Trav shrugged, looked away and sipped. "Best quit that shit. One day you're gonna wake up and find—"

"What? Find myself alone?" Hunter winced at the sound of his own bellow, then jammed the package beneath his arm. "Right now," he made a show of looking at each man, "it'd be a damn blessing," he mumbled sarcastically, then strode across the grounds toward the hostelry.

Dugal met his long strides, his expression scolding. " 'Tis a sad day when a mon willna bury 'is mistakes an' get on with thin's, lad."

"But damn if they don't keep slapping me around every now and then." Resentment tainted his tone as he lifted his gaze to the room. "Just so I don't forget."

Dugal opened his mouth to offer more advice when he caught sight of the colonel leaving his quarters. He siddled closer to Hunter.

"Where 's yer woman?"

Hunter's gaze snapped to the side. "She isn't—"

"What 'ere she is, lad, get her gone. Maitland's headin' tae ye," Dugal said in a rush, then veered off on his own.

Hunter didn't spare a glance, and quickened his pace to the hostelry, praying the call to formation would keep the commander away. He didn't breath a decent lungfull until his feet overtook the inn's stairs two at a time. Reaching for the latch, he hesitated, knowing his pre-dawn departure had nothing to do with getting an early start to avoid more question.

Coward.

No doubt about it.

How could he face her? After humiliating himself last night and using her to do it. Would she cry rape? She was well within her rights.

The trumpet sounded assembly, making his decision for him, and Hunter knew he had less than ten minutes before the gates opened.

He rapped gently on the door.

Sable flinched when the knock she'd been dreading finally came. Darting to the window, she cautiously drew back the worn curtain. Colonel Maitland took that moment to glance in her direction and she jumped back, looking at the sealed door. Had he sent a trooper for her?

The knock repeated, stronger, demanding entry.

"Yes." Hesitant and scared.

"It's me."

She wilted against the bed post. "For heaven's sake! You choose *now* to knock?"

Beyond the door, Hunter flushed and smiled a little. Least she was talking to him. "You decent?"

Dumbly, Sable looked down at herself. Decent? A quilt and his shirt? Her gaze swung unwillingly to the rumpled bed and she prayed that he didn't remember, that his drunken stupor blanked his mind. The door opened and one look at his face told her he did. She swerved around. I must be a despicable sort of woman, a hidden wanton, she decided, for she desperately wanted him to gather her in the circle of his arms and draw those exquisite sensations from her again.

Hell, she can't even bring herself to look at me, Hunter thought, slipping into the room and shutting the door.

The hollow click trembled between.

"Clothes," he finally said, tossing the parcel on the bed. Sable glanced to the side as the thick paper-wrapped package bounced on the mattress, her mind flooding with the images of how intimately he'd touched and manipulated her body, drawing that wild hunger to a glorious peak, then leaving her hanging on some invisible threshold. To die what felt like a slow merciless death, she thought, closing her eyes, trying to blot away the torrid memory. But it remained—as bold as an imprint on her skin.

Hunter passed her on his way to the window. He drew back the curtain. "We've got to be quick," he said. Sable suddenly peered around him, frowning. "Maitland looks ready to drag us to the stockade and repeat the Spanish Inquisition." He let the fabric drop and faced her, nearly knocking her over. Catching her before she tripped, Hunter noticed her kiss-swollen lips and wondered what other marks he'd left on that flawless skin.

Sable back-stepped out of his grasp.

"With all those soldiers, how will we ever get out?" she asked, worrying the edge of the quilt. "You said the commander suspects, and if they detain us what will happen to Little—"

"Listen." He shoved his hands in his pockets, effectively clipping the urge to hold her close. "I'm damn near committing treason for you, and you'd better not do something assinine like faint on me!"

"I shan't swoon." Her nose snubbed his insult. "But you could very well be arrested."

He slanted her a half smile. "So could you."

Once Maitland knew who she was, none would dare harm her, but him—she grasped his bicep. "I can't let you do this." Mahogany silk spilled over her shoulders as she shook her head. "Not anymore."

"Sorry, Violet Eyes," he said in a husky tone she recognized. "You're stuck with me." Her stiff carriage withered, and Hunter realized she'd offered him a way out. Gambled on him staying. Even after—God, he couldn't comprehend the emotions tumbling inside him just then and the urge to touch her overwhelmed him.

Recklessly, he took a step closer, lifting a thick shining lock from her breast and wrapping it around his fist.

Her gaze searched his, turbulent gray eyes communicating a darker struggle than she could fathom and tiny chip of her heart fell away. What part did she play? He tilted his head a hair's breadth nearer and for a wild moment she thought he'd kiss her, wished he would. She longed to ask him why last night left her empty and aching inside, why she felt a little cheated. And where were those stars he promised? But she couldn't utter the words, not now. Unseemly and improper were no longer her reasons for silence; no time, threats of arrest, and the sudden guarded look on his face pressed her to protect herself.

Briskly, he moved away. "I'll be waiting outside," he said, heading for the door. Sable tensed when he didn't immediately depart, yet remained with his back to her. "Ah, Sable? I—um—ah—" Hunter swallowed, gripped the latch, unsure of what would happen should he bring up the sensitive subject. "About last night." He forced himself to meet her gaze. "I'm sorry you saw . . . that."

Tortured embarrassment sharpened his features, and she sensed again the terror of his dreams, the hollow lonely cries. A proud man brought low by untouchable phantoms.

"You had a nightmare and weren't yourself last night." She shrugged, her pinkening skin betraying her. "It's as simple as that, is it not?"

Hunter couldn't hide his shock. Just like that, he was forgiven? He cleared his throat uncomfortably.

"It's not that simple." And she knew it.

"Perhaps I'd understand if you told me what gives you such awful nightmares."

"No." He turned toward the door and Sable knew he was going to shoulder the blame. It wasn't fair.

"Hunter?" Soft, pleading.

He tilted his head back and squeezed his eyes shut. She rarely called him by his first name and the sound of it on her lovely lips made him ache to hear it again. Then he felt her sudden presence, close at his side, and he filled his gaze with the sight of her. In that instance he relived everything: the feel of her naked and sultry in his arms, the musky scent of her passion, the silken glove of her womanhood beneath his touch, and most, her quaking gasp of ecstasy when she found paradise in his arms. God. How was he to survive the next weeks knowing that? Then he recognized her shame and knew he was the source.

"Don't, Sable," he rasped when she opened her mouth to speak. "Please don't say anything more." He couldn't bear her excusing his behavior. "I feel bad enough as it is."

Sable ached to soothe his dejected posture and gathered the courage to say, "You're not entirely to blame."

Bitterness carved his words. "Yes. I am."

"I allowed myself to be a part of it."

He snorted with disgust. "Like I gave you a choice."

"We all have choices."

Something burst in him. "Christ, don't you understand? I can't *control* those nightmares," he growled, shoving his fingers into his hair. "For God's sake, that could have easily been violent." He snapped a hand toward the bed. "I could have raped you!"

"But you didn't." She gripped his arm, her voice low and disarming. "So you aren't perfect. You drank, you needed someone, and I was . . . available."

"You know better than that!" he scoffed, pressing his forehead to the wall and closing his eyes to the forgiveness he saw in hers. "I want you, more than just in my bed, but I can't." He looked at her, miserable. "Even if you were free. I can't keep taking."

But he gave, she thought, as he depressed the latch and yanked open the door. She blocked his path.

"Sable," he warned.

"Forgive yourself, Hunter McCracken," she said, touching his jaw, her gaze locked with his. "I have." When he did nothing but stare, she became incensed. "Blast, but you've got

245

to be the most irritating, mule-headed man I've ever met!" She punched his shoulder to make her point.

He rubbed the spot, the corners of his mouth lifting slightly, rough waters gone smooth.

"And you've got three minutes to be ready." His eyes scanned her face impersonally. "The dye's faded since yesterday, so keep your head down, and for God's sake, don't talk to anyone."

"Go get some more coffee, Mister McCracken." She pushed him out the door. "You're *such* a grouch this morning."

He smiled as she shut the door in his face. He hastened down the stairs, feeling as if he'd been gifted with more than her pardon.

Exactly three minutes later she appeared and walked briskly down the boarded walk, head bowed, the tiny shells and blue beads adorning the buckskin dress clicking with every step. The butter-soft hides swished at her ankles and beneath it fringed moccasins wrapped her legs to just above her knees. She'd braided her hair into two plaits, weaving the thin hide strips into the locks, completing the picture with a simple head band, all to fool the inhabitants. He'd thought of everything, though no Indian woman would dare wear the abbreviated pantalettes and chemise he supplied. She was relieved when she caught sight of him.

Pulling the horses along, Hunter crossed the muddy grounds, meeting her before she stepped into the mire. His gaze caressed the costume and the delicate creature within, before he wordlessly swept a thick buffalo robe from the horse's back and ascended the walk to drape it around her shoulders. Sable slipped her hands through the cut slots and snuggled gratefully, smiling her thanks. He moved away, then paused, grasped her hand and slapped something into her palm.

Sable's gaze flew to his and he offered a lopsided grin.

"I hear you can handle that."

It was the knife she'd used on that nasty boy yesterday.

Pleased he thought her capable enough, she tucked it in the wrapped waist band, tested its accessibility, then adjusted it comfortably.

She looked up to find most everyone studying her, especially Travis Moffet.

"Get on the horse," Hunter said softly, handing her the reins.

"McCracken, me lad. A word wit' ye."

Hunter groaned. The burr was unmistakable.

Sable stepped to the mounting block.

"I'll make this quick," he said out of the side of his mouth and met his friend half-way to avoid giving him a close look at Sable. No use in forcing Dugal to commit treason, too.

Sable felt a tap on her shoulder and turned. Noah Kirkwood.

"May I help you?" he offered.

Sable shook her head, swiftly lowering her gaze.

"You certainly look different."

She tensed and grasped the pommel, slipping her foot into the stirrup.

"Especially from the woman I saw in Salvatore's in Washington two years ago."

Sable flashed a look over her shoulder. "You are mistaken," she managed on a whisper, resisting a telling look for eavesdroppers.

"I don't think so." He tipped his hat back. "No one mistakes eyes the color of yours."

The gates were opening, she noticed, carts slowly filing inside.

"I'm afraid duty dictates . . ." He reached for her arm.

Sable eluded his grasp, her eyes narrowing to slits. "You owe me your life, Lieutenant, and I'm collecting. Now!"

Noah tensed at the icy censure she aimed like a dagger. Again he saw the desperate woman who killed two Pawnee without batting a lash. Lowering his hand, he noticed her

247

eyes flare and followed her line of vision. Moffet moved steadily toward them, an expression of startled recognition on his weathered face. Noah's attention shifted quickly to Hunter, who was coming closer by the second, then beyond to Colonel Maitland, who had five armed troopers at his heels.

Sable's gaze darted nervously between the colonel, Moffet and the guards.

She swallowed tightly.

They'd been found out!

Or would be in a matter of seconds if the Colonel spoke with either Noah or Moffet.

Her terrified gaze pinned Hunter. His steps faltered for a second, then he bolted to his horse as Sable swung up onto the saddle, reining around. Orders to close the gate sounded as she kneed the animal. A small dray crossed her path, and before she could draw back Hunter shouted, "Go over!" and she ground her heels into horse flesh. The horse lurched, and Sable hung on, beast and rider sailing over the cart, startling the onlookers. Troopers blocked her escape, pistols drawn, but Sable rode hard, sending soldiers diving for safety as the colonel's cry not to fire sang in her head.

She cleared beyond the gates.

Chunks of wet earth kicked up, littering a trail behind her. Brisk winds made her eyes water and she blinked, glancing back. Hunter was right behind her, thank God.

Indians came out of teepees as they splashed through the river and up the embankment, weaving between citizens and animals and wagons. Horses bucked at the violent intrusion, children cheered, then scattered like chicken as they plowed through the crowds.

She rode, the blaring bugle call punching fear through her veins. The horse chugged up the incline like a locomotive, hooves digging, breath bursting in duel gusts of white steam. Lather splattered his neck, yet the instant he crested the rise the charger took his head, a beast possessed.

A demon ride.

Hoofbeats rumbled, close behind and rapid. She gripped the pommel, too terrified to look.

Suddenly Hunter was there, the closeness of his horse pushing hers to veer left. She glanced at him, frightened by the dangerous speed.

"A squad behind!" He gestured with his head. And that's too damn many to elude, he thought as they plowed into a strand of trees, branches lashing at their face and clothes. Hunter urged her to keep up, weaving them in a wild zigzag pattern, then bringing them out on the farthest side of the strand.

He slowed, yet waved Sable on. "Go! Go!" he shouted, then headed back the way they'd come—back into the nest of trees.

Sable obeyed.

Hooves thundered on the plains.

Hunter dredged up every trick he'd learned from the war and some from the Sioux, doing his damndest to disguise their trail. Scarcely into the thicket, he slid from the saddle, ground tethering his horse before grabbing his field glasses. He traveled on foot, an odd combination of grasping branches to swing over wide areas, climbing from tree to tree and stepping in the center of bushes and on thick roots to conceal his prints.

From his perch on a broad limb, he hugged the trunk and sighted through the magnifiers, scanning the horizon beyond the brush. Nothing. But that didn't mean squat. Wiping the sweat from his forehead with the back of his hand, Hunter knew he couldn't take any chances, even though the near frozen ground might hide their path out onto the plains. They had to keep moving. He sighted again, squinting, his smile was slow and tight. Troopers, young and new, so new their pristine hats and unmarred insignia gleamed from the distance. Greenhorns. Scrambling down, Hunter returned to his horse, careful to maintain an erratic trail unnoticeable to anyone but a seasoned scout. Hunter rode out of forest at yet another point. Now, to catch up with Sable.

Chapter Twenty-five

Hunter's palomino surged from the forest like Pegasus on a mission for Zeus. He rode hell bent for leather, dodging scrub brush and boulders, his mount agilely leaping over gullies, valiantly maintaining its sure footing down rock-scattered slopes, then rounding a thick cropping a trees on a sharp lean—very nearly colliding with Sable's horse.

Hers reared and briefly pawed the air as she fought to regain control.

"What the hell are you doing back here? Jesus, Sable!"

Hooves landed with a thump as she yelled back, "And where was I supposed to go? North? West?" Her horse sidestepped and with a sharp jerk she forced him to submit. "I don't have a pistol and it's far too open out there if troopers are still following!"

"They are, dammit!" Hunter glanced behind, field glasses poised at his eyes as he briefly swept the terrain. "Come on!"

Sable followed, packs slapping the horses flanks with the tremendous speed. Sable didn't think the animals could take much more when Hunter led them out to open country, the cover they needed gone sparse where the land melted flat and barren. She was breathless and perspiring when he finally slowed, slipping behind a sprinkling of boulders. He edged around the boulder just enough to search with the magnifiers.

"Shouldn't we keep moving?" Her horse sidled nervously.

He shot her an agitated glare, then looked through the sights again. "I'm trying to think of a diversion, since you blundered into the first." They had to get far enough from the fort's wood trains bringing materials for new forts and the railroad. Damn!

"I apologize."

"I swear—"

"Yes, you do—With exceeding regularity."

"—sometimes, Sable," his voice rose in volume, "You haven't got a damn thing in that pretty head but air!"

"I said I'm sorry!" she popped back. "You needn't continue with this barrage of insults." Unexpectedly he unstrapped his weapons and one bulging saddlebag. "What are you doing?"

"Be quiet, woman." He leaned over and slapped his gear on her already burdened horse. "I'm so angry right now I could toss you over my lap and fan your butt for coming back."

"Pardon me for being concerned for your safety."

Ignoring the pleasure that gave him, he snarled, "I'm capable of taking care of myself!" then pointed to a low slope beyond the rocks. "Go down there and wait." His hand clamped the fur robe and jerked her close. Gray eyes drilling her. "Do not, I mean, *do not* come up that rise until I say."

"As you wish, m'lord," she said with a haughty look he never expected, jerking the robe from his grasp. A muscle worked in his jaw as she rode away.

Before he disappeared from her sight Sable saw him dismount, smack his palomino's golden haunches, then drop to the ground. The animal bolted toward the left of their trail.

Surely they'd eluded the squad by now. They had to be at least five miles ahead of them, for mercy's sake! Like a burst from the horizon, Hunter came skidding down the slope and storming up to her. Without a word he grabbed her upper arms, hauled her from the horse and up to greet his fury.

"There's a squad of troopers spreading out and ready to kill me to get you back. Now out with it!" When she didn't answer he shook her so hard her neck threatened to snap from her shoulders. "Who are you, God damn it?"

"You—you already know!"

"The hell I do! That's a lot of men tracking one woman." Silence, and his grip tightened, his tone caustic and deadly. "The Army knows you don't have the boy." He backed her up against the horse, pinning her with his hard body, "And *I* know you don't have the experience of a woman held captive. Now, who are you!"

"His aunt!" she blurted.

His brows shot up. "What?" Fast fury and shock.

"I'm Little Hawk's aunt! Not his mother!" she shouted in his face.

For a breathless moment they stared and the memory of her mistakes flitted across his features, explaining themselves and dissolving his confusion.

Only one question remained.

And it came in a hostile command. "Your name." His fingers flexed as if bracing himself for the impact.

She swallowed, licked her dry lips. "Sable . . . Cavanaugh."

His features yanked taut, nostrils flaring as his blistering gaze flicked down her body like the crack of whip. "Richard's brat," he ground between clenched teeth. It didn't made a damn bit of difference to him now. "Did you kidnap that boy?"

"No!" Lord, he looked ready to beat her.

"Woman! I swear I'll leave you to them," he warned, his complexion molten with rage.

She gripped his arms. "My sister charged me to take him to his father. You must believe me!"

"Why the hell should I?" he sneered nastily. "You've lied to me all along."

"I had to. Papa was going to abandon Little Hawk to strangers without telling Lane. I couldn't risk that. Please, Hunter, don't you see I had to do it?"

He did and he didn't. Hunter was so angry he didn't dare

say another word, afraid of losing control and doing something stupid like physically hurting her.

Not his mother.

His heartbeat drummed painfully in his ears, his skin hot with his temper as thoughts careened with questions, seeking the logic of answers in his muddled brain.

Not his mother.

Releasing her with a sound of disgust, Hunter mounted her horse and looked down. Hesitantly she lifted her face, tears spilling down wind-chapped cheeks. Her trembling hand floated near his booted calf, the small gesture a plead for understanding.

"Hunter?"

His curse was clear and vulgar as he leaned down, clamped his arm around her waist and hoisted her off the ground, dropping her roughly on his lap.

"But we'll kill this animal!"

A raven-black brow arched menacingly. "What the hell do you care, woman," his savage tone tapped chills down her spine, "as long as you get what you want."

Hunter reined the mare around and headed north toward the badlands.

Jesus.

She's not his mother.

Spring crept across the plains in small bursts of lavender pasqueflower, yet even the warming air went unnoticed by the pair walking across the thawed ground.

Hunter's fury radiated with the strength of a beacon; in his hunched shoulders, in the digging strides he took along side the horse, opposite Sable.

He hadn't spoken to her in a week. A week! Not with anything more than a primal grunt, she though maliciously. Not even a swear. And he pushed her like a green cavalry trooper. When she walked, his stride was hurried, when she rode with

253

him, it was a brisk bone-jarring lope. If he wanted her to do something such as dismount to give the horse a rest, he did it first, then waited impatiently for her to wise up and do the same, turning his face away to avoid even the barest glimpse of her. And worse, he kept a wide berth to avoid touching her, and if he did, looked as if the contact would make him explode. That hurt the most. Each night he tossed the bedroll at her and a small pack filled with fresh clothes he'd obviously purchased at the fort, yet he never left her alone, not even to change or relieve herself! Standing three feet away and turning his back was the only privacy he'd conceded. Sable slept alone, cold, and afraid she'd waken to find him gone.

His pace was brisk, far too long for her short legs, which ached all the up to her buttocks, yet she managed to keep up. They'd been moving steadily since dawn. Her thirst was uppermost at the moment, but Sable didn't dare ask where he packed the canteens, afraid she'd unleash a tirade she wasn't yet prepared to defuse. Stumbling for the fifth time, Sable caught herself before landing in the dirt. Hunter never broke his stride, nor did he spare her a glance to see if she was injured.

Beastly man! Who did he think he was, anyway? He was being well-paid for his services. What did it matter that the Army was looking for her? No, not the Army. Papa and his influence. And surely whatever favor Colonel Maitland owed Papa hadn't included orders to shoot—not at her, at least. Staring at the ground Sable felt the depth of her hatred for her sire. This was his fault. She would never have been forced to bargain with the devil if Papa hadn't denied Little Hawk or her sister's marriage to Black Wolf.

She glanced at Hunter but could only see the crown of his battered, stained hat. He'd gone from a man seeking her forgiveness to the accuser. Sable wanted the other man back, the one who withstood her verbal tirades, who bought her rare scented soap and traveled through the night to rescue her, the one who'd teased and coaxed her desires. She wanted the man who promised heaven could be found within the circle of his strong arms. Sable realized she wasn't going to see that man again anytime soon.

Her stomach rumbled. "I'm hungry," she stated petulantly. "Can we at least stop to eat something?" He did stop, yet stared straight ahead and sighed.

The dry wind howled, swirling pebbles and dirt. Tall winter-weary grasses swayed and danced on the barren plains.

"Mister McCrac—" Words withered on her lips when he slanted her that half-lidded glare. Her dander rose. "I'm about out of patience with your sulking. We have walked, ridden, and run for over one hundred miles. One hundred! Obviously we've eluded the patrol. My feet hurt. I'm starving, thirsty, tired, and dirty. Blast you!" she added for spite.

He grunted, continued walking, veering off to the right, down into a gully where a stream fanned off to a broad finger river of the Cheyenne. Water, thank God.

Sable dogged his footsteps.

"Will you at least talk to me instead of chopping me into pieces with every look?"

No answer.

"You can't continue this silent vigil. We still have a long way to travel."

Still no response.

"Mister McCracken!"

"Leave it alone, lady."

"So, we're back to that again." She grabbed his arm, but he shook her off like an annoying insect and kept walking. Sable stopped, fuming. "Are you going to talk to me or remain the angry coward?" she tossed at his back, her hands on her hips. He froze, then turned slowly. She wished she'd kept her mouth shut. His darkening eyes promised retribution.

He threw the reins aside, balling his fists to keep from throttling her. Hunter looked away, his lips clamped to a bloodless white. His lungs worked, his nostrils flaring like a charged stallion's. All the restraint he'd mastered this entire journey left his emotions mutilated, shredded, and bloodied on the ground, and he wasn't certain he wanted to gather them up and piece them back together, wasn't sure he could. Damn her! Damn her lies!

"Think you got it all figured out, don't you?"

Her chin poked the air. She refused to wilt now. "I know if you don't let go of these phantoms, you're going to die old and friendless."

The stone wall he'd built around himself shifted at her reference. He shored it back up, his lips twisting cruelly. "You don't know me, lady. You have no idea what things have shaped me into what I am."

"Then tell me." He simply *had* to talk with her. They had to get past this and if this was the only way—instantly he was there, leaning down in her face, coal gray eyes blazing, hatred sculpting his features.

"Listen the first time, woman, 'cause I won't repeat myself." His acid tone spat and burned. "I don't want to be near you, talk to you, look at you, see your infantile tears, or even smell you." She flinched with every word. "You're a liar, a tease, and I'm well on my way to hating your pretty little guts. Which I'm damn good at, so get the hell away from me!"

Sable reared back as if he'd struck her, but he'd already turned away from her, moving further down the bank. "Stop trying to prove how crude you can be, Hunter D. McCracken! Because I know you better!" she called over the gushing water.

"Don't bet on it!" he shouted, still moving.

"Well, I'm through being your verbal whipping boy, McCracken!" she screamed. "Do you hear? McCracken!" He strode faster. "Blast you!"

Sable took off at a dead run and leaped onto his back, clinging like a monkey as she pounded his shoulders. Stunned by the impact, Hunter instantly lost his footing and slipped, tumbling down the embankment with Sable still stuck to him. Her cry of shock was lost as they rolled around, sliding in the thick mud to a hard stop at the water's edge. Sable immediately came to her knees.

"You're a beast, a tyrant!" she cried. He hadn't made it completely upright before she hurled a clump of sopping grass. "A nasty blackguard with a dead soul!" It hit him in the throat and sank beneath the folds of his shirt. His brows shot up, disbelief blanketing his face.

She didn't care. "You're a swine—"

Hunter barely deflected the ooze that skipped off his shoulder. "Stop it, Sable." He stood, advancing on her.

"—selfish and inconsiderate and mean. Mean. Mean! Mean!" Fistfuls of mud pelted him with every word, and Hunter threw up his arms to shield his face.

"Woman!" he warned, his chest heaving. Another clod hit him in the face, a stone lost inside stinging his wounded cheek.

Sable jumped up, knowing she'd ignited a dangerous fuse in him. Lifting her skirts, she took off in the opposite direction, running for safety. She couldn't out-distance him, but hoped he'd be too tired to follow. His boots thumped hollow on the bank close behind her. She slipped, grappled for footing and ran.

"Sable!"

She ignored him and kept on. The river widened, the rush of white foam drowning out his curses. Suddenly a stitch caught in her side and she folded over. Gasping for air, she rubbed the pained area, then straightened. Hunter was but a few feet away, motionless, threatening. Sucking in cold air, she scrambled around a boulder, one arm out as if to ward him off while she took cautious steps backwards.

"N-now, Hunter, wait." He advanced, slowly, like a stalking panther, his scarred cheek blaring white. "Try to calm down," she gulped, inching away. His rage was palpable. "Admit you were being unreasonable." No answer. "I was merely attempting to make you see we're not all perfect," she shouted unnecessarily. "To get a response from you!"

He took a step. "You did."

"All I'm asking is that you try to understand—to see beyond my lies!" she begged hoarsely. She'd sooner perish if he refused to see her side of this.

Silence.

His glacial stare moved past her, and Sable felt what little ground they'd built crumble beneath her feet. She bent with the startling pain of it.

"Damn you, Hunter!" A rough desperate wail and his head snapped up. "You did things to me in that room no man had a right to do! And I forgave you! I understood, and I forgave!"

In two strides he was on her, his arm shooting out, snapping around her waist and slamming her against him. Knocked breathless, Sable met his steely gaze, trembling, distrusting.

"I ought to beat you for keeping that from me," he growled savagely.

"But you won't." She squirmed and his arm clamped down on her rebellion.

"Would teach you a damn lesson if I left you stranded for the Army to find."

"You're too honorable."

A brow flared, black and intimidating. "You're so sure?"

"Always."

"Damn you!" he hissed at her confident presumptions. "You push too far!"

"Then you have nowhere else to go."

Wicked hunger darkened his gray eyes, seething and dangerous.

"And neither do you."

His mouth crushed hers, his lips rough and tormenting, his hands possessive and insistent as they swept furiously from her breasts to flaring hips. Flames licked and scorched. Swift passion raged between them. Even as she pushed at his chest, she pulled him back with her luscious mouth, her throaty moans, and Hunter knew he couldn't stop.

Not this time.

Not when Black Wolf no longer stood between them.

Chapter Twenty-six

Raw fury uncoiled through him like a serpent, reaching out to make her feel it, his mouth a hard slash, his head rolling round and round. Taking. Taking. Taking.

"Damn you, Sable. Damn your lies!" he hissed into her mouth, then hungrily took her again with a punishing force. He felt explosive, frantic to have her and tore at her buttons, yanking the coarse shirt off her shoulders, his lips devouring, licking, teeth scraping down over the exposed slopes of her breasts. "I've been torturing myself for weeks!" He jerked her. "Weeks! Over wanting another man's wife!"

"You feel betrayed," she said in a rush. "I know."

"You haven't a damn clue!"

He'd wanted *her* to break those vows, waiting, agonizing, praying for her to say *come to me*. But she didn't. He would have her—he would! He would make love to her. Here, now. Wildly, like she drove him. Desperately, like he needed. Hunter saw nothing beyond her response, his heavy ache to take her, fill her, ride her until he spent the lust suppressed for so long . . . so long. He cupped her bottom, fingers digging into the soft flesh, wickedly coaxing her legs apart and rubbing her feminine heat against his manhood even as he bent her back over his arm, his mouth seeking the tender pink centers of her breasts.

His tongue rasped over nipples, and she gasped for air,

259

clung, yielding to his rage, buffeting it with womanly softness. He had the right to be angry, just as she had the same to keep those secrets. She'd never have managed this far if anyone had known she was not Little Hawk's mother. Him especially, and he knew it.

"You've made me confused and damn crazy." He advanced, making her step back and back, forcing her to cling to him or fall. Yet he refused even a fraction of daylight to pass between them. She tripped; he caught her, wedging her tightly to his long muscular frame. He ran his hand down her arm, fingers curling around her wrist and dragging it across his lean hip. "You do this to me," he whispered savagely, pressing her palm to the bulge in his trousers.

Her breath caught, eyes fluttered closed, her lower lip briefly caught between white teeth. She moved restlessly against him, wickedly delicious sensations spiraling through her. He was so warm and swollen and hard and she wanted to put her hands all over him, explore this extremely male part of him that intrigued and aroused and frightened her. It was wanton, she knew, but she didn't care. Freedom spun through her, hot and wild as their surroundings. The sound of the rushing river roared in her ears. Her fingers flexed over him, shaped and outlined, and Hunter trembled, clutched tighter.

"God," he groaned, the dark masculine sound flooding her with exhilaration. "Sable, Sable, Sable," he chanted over and over, the sound of it defusing his anger. She rubbed, just the suggestion of her wanting him made him savage and reckless. He would touch her and kiss her and push his body inside hers, deep and slick and . . . oh God! He'd dreamed of this and scrounged for control before her hurt her.

He kissed her again—hard, staggered by the strength of his desire.

Her shoulder hit the horse's haunches and as it sidestepped, Hunter reached blindly past her for the buffalo robe, fanning it across the ground.

"Don't be angry. Please," she whispered against his mouth, brush fire excitement heating her bloodstream as the swollen shaft pushed against her hand. "There are no more secrets."

Hunter's legs buckled and he sank to his knees, taking her with him.

"Oh, but there are." His lips ground a moist path along her jaw, her throat. "Here." His fingertips whispered over her nipple and she shimmered like liquid glass. "And here." His hand trailed down her flat belly to rub the tender divide of her thighs. "I want to kiss you, everywhere." She met his smoldering gaze. "I want to put my fingers inside you again and feel your desire." Sable whimpered at the image, burning with anticipation.

And he felt it in her kiss, the push of her tongue between his lips, the movements that told him she wanted to be naked, wanted him to do everything he promised. He palmed the length of her arms to the shirt caught at her elbows, sweeping the fabric down, exposing her naked breast to his hungry eyes. His look was a steaming caress, making her feel beautiful, adored, possessed, and with a sultry moan, he cupped the plump globes, squeezing, molding, working her nipples into deliciously tight peaks. Voluptuous tremors shook her body and she leaned into the tantalizing pressure, groping for his waist, his skin, his warmth.

"Oh, Hunter." Anxious, urging, as she yanked at her shirt, destroying buttons and his control. "Please. I want to feel you."

Hunter didn't think he could stand her undressing him and tore off his shirt and kicked off his boots. His holster thumped to the ground. Instantly he caught her high against him and she grasped his shoulders as his tongue swirled over the plush cushion of her breasts, laving, heating her feverishly. Then his warm lips closed over her hard nipple and Sable thought she'd faint from with the luscious feel of his drawing it deeply into the hollow of his mouth. He hummed as if devouring a

261

sumptuous dessert and Sable twisted her hands in his hair, tilting her head back as he tasted and licked.

"Love me, Hunter, I want you to," she panted while she frantically toed off her boots, abandoning herself to her needs. He yanked at her skirt lacings. His knuckles brushed an incredible warmth over her skin and she couldn't be still, her palms absorbing the strength of his biceps, the carved definition of his chest.

He quaked, growled low, peeling her skirt down over her hips, a broad hand caressing every inch of satiny skin he revealed to the sun. A helpless sound escaped from deep in her throat. His lips were fierce and hungry on her breasts as the steel band circling her waist briefly lifted her off the ground. She threw her arms around his neck, cool air suddenly dancing across her bare buttocks and legs; pantalettes, petticoats, and skirt were swept away in one motion.

Hunter explored the exquisite curve of her naked spine, the roundness of her bottom, fingers seeking, pressing into the soft dip between. She squirmed against his touch, spreading her thighs wider, and Hunter thought he'd come apart at the seams with the sheer joy of her surrender.

His kiss was long and blistering, greedily absorbing every pant and gasp and plea for succor, until he was mindless to have her, be inside her. Love her, he thought, it's your one chance. Love her. His hand was between her thighs, fingers probing, manipulating pale silken skin, rubbing up and down and around, slipping in and out to wet and stroke and stroke, until she was twisting frantically, rocking, swell after swell of blissfully hot pleasure consuming her. She clawed, arched in wild abandon.

"Hunter. Oh, my God. Hunter," she cried. He tormented and encouraged, gave and took, flooding her with an ecstasy of scent and heavenly sensation, and an ache to release the pressure enslaving her. "Please, please," she whimpered, and groped at his strained trousers, flipping a button.

He caught her hands.

"Are you certain?"

She nodded shakily, flushing as his fingers dipped, lightly fanning the fire in her.

"I have nothing else to offer you, Sable. Nothing."

Sorrow flared past his desire and Sable smoothed a loving hand over his shoulder and into his black hair. He was her dark angel, solitary, wandering in his own hell, yet somewhere between skinning rabbits and his startling vulnerability in the hostelry, Sable had fallen in love with him. There would be no other man for her, no other time so precious. Her heart soared.

"Yes, you do, Hunter." She drew him close to meet her lips. "You just don't see it." He made a pained sound; sank into her lush kiss.

"Sable, Sable." He wrapped his arms tightly around her. "What you do to me."

"Give me those stars, Hunter."

He grinned.

Victory.

Total capitulation.

"I will. I promise."

"Don't promise." She thumbed another button of his pants and yanked open his trousers, her eyes glinting with eagerness. "Show me."

For an instant Hunter was stunned at her boldness. This was so unlike the prim woman he'd known. But then he saw it in her eyes—exhilaration, bright and free. No secrets, no lies, no proper rules, nothing between them but skin and desire. His arousal jolted and she smiled slyly, discovering her power over him. He loved it. It made his blood boil.

"Make a dream, Hunter, for us."

Her words thundered in his brain and he didn't hesitate. He wanted to experience as much as he could; enjoy the sensation of her body draped over him, her naked breast mashed to his chest, her delectable bottom on his naked thighs.

"Straddle me," he said hoarsely, falling back onto his

263

haunches, urging her onto his lap as he flipped the last buttons of his pants. His erection sprang free, iron hard, brushing her stomach.

Sable looked down, breath caught, her eyes wide in amazement and fear. He couldn't mean to put *all* of that in her! Surely she could never accommodate . . . oh, how different he was, she marveled, innocently reaching out to stroke up one side of him.

A bolt of hot lightning stabbed through his groin. "Oh, Jesus!" he rasped, clamping her hips and rocking her moist woman-flesh along his manhood. "I'll never make it, not if you keep that up."

But she did.

Sable's fingers smoothed the glistening tip of him, then curled around the marvelously rigid length nestled between her thighs. His breath hissed and she met his smoky gaze. He seemed suspended, and Sable reveled in the potency of her touch. He pulsed in her hand. So solid and warm.

She stroked and he exploded with, "You little witch," and crushed her to him, crushed her mouth beneath him as his hand closed over hers, guiding his arousal into her velvet crevice. He nudged, gently stretching her. Jesus, she was hot . . . and damn small, and Hunter wasn't certain this wouldn't kill her.

"Oh ohh, Lord," she keened softly, nails digging into his skin. It was glorious, the fullness, so thick and throbbing with life. He withdrew, then pushed deeper. Each time the exquisite pressure built. Her pleasure intensified. His movements quickened. Then he cupped her buttocks and surged up into her in one sharp thrust, filling her. She sucked in her breath, sinking her teeth into his shoulder.

Sable felt rent in half.

An absurd notion briefly flitted through Hunter's mind but he instantly dismissed it to the incredible fire circling him, the enchanting woman surrounding him like hot silk. He moved, impatient for her body to adjust. Then the silken glove clasped him and he thought he'd burst right then.

Sable didn't care for this part, not at first. It hurt. Then he kissed her, grindingly sensuous and primitive, touched where their bodies joined and the pain swiftly blended into a sweltering heat. Hidden instinct told her she was in control. She rocked. He answered. And she embraced the passionate tide rushing toward her. Nothing she'd felt earlier compared to this reckless splendor.

His name hovered on her lips as she held his face in her hands, kissing, nipping, stealing pleasure and fire. Scalding tremors raged inside her. He thrust, smooth and purposeful, and Sable's body jolted with sweet wet glory. Sable rode him, keenly aware he watched.

His strong hands possessed her, untamed and sinful.

Her blood simmered. Her heart thumped madly. Her body took over, taking him further inside, gripping, and she luxuriated in feel of him withdrawing and filling her, over and over. His hands closed over her breasts, squeezing, rotating, and she held him there.

"Ahh, yes, Sable, yes." Her ragged shudders tumbled into his mouth. Blood pounded through his groin. "Give it to me, love, to me. This once. Be wild."

Her breath wouldn't come fast enough. Her hips curled in swift jerks. "Hunter!" She clawed at him. "I—help me." The stars. She felt them, saw them. Just out of her reach. "Please, do something!"

She was near tears, her mouth rolling over his, hands molding his male breasts, then dribbling down his flat stomach to feel his manhood disappear into her body. She lifted and slammed down. Again and again.

Faster. Deeper. Hotter. The ground sizzled around them.

He felt her throbbing climax like a cyclone, swift and dangerous. His hands slid over her stockinged calves, pushing them around his waist as he toppled her to the fur. He stuffed the discarded garments beneath his hips, then locked his arms around her, his body pumping with hers, driving, hard and savage. He couldn't help it. She was so breathtakingly beautiful in the throes of her desire. And he watched it, felt the sweet agony of her release as if he owned it. She convulsed, a paralyzing arch that suspended her on the edge of rapture and in one blinding charge, he stamped his claim, plunging into her with a force that sent them across the fur. She cried out his name, holding him close as Hunter's entire world dangled helplessly for several exquisite moments, spinning from a tenuous thread before it snapped, his body raked with spasms of ecstasy.

"Mine. Mine. Mine," he murmured harshly, throwing his head back and spilling his seed, and Sable savored the sparkling downpour of sensations, the bright flash of voluptuous delight gushing through her limbs, coating her heart. And for a moment she was weightless, soulless . . . and then whole.

Like a leaf floating to the ground she went slack beneath him.

He hadn't caught his breath when he kissed her again and again, slow and tender, then buried his face in the cloud of her hair.

Sable turned her head, trying to see his face. His shoulders rose and fell raggedly and she sifted her fingers through his black hair. A breeze kissed her bare skin.

"You knew it would be like this?"

"God, no!" he whispered and happiness filled her. She smiled at the Dakota sky. Her hand rode over his damp back, grazing battle scars and sun-browned muscle to his taut buttocks.

He moaned, shifted his hips.

"Ohhh, Hunter," she said in a throat purr.

"God, I love it when you say my name like that." He dropped tormenting little kisses across her bare shoulder, pushing slowly into her, and the breath hissed through her teeth.

"I want you again. And again and again until I can't

move." He managed to drag himself to his elbows. "I suppose that's a bit selfish of me, huh?"

"Be selfish." Her fingers twisted in his hair, drawing him down so she could taste his lips at her leisure. "I am," she said after a moment. Her tongue snaked out to trace the line of his mouth, then down his chin.

He trembled. "You're incredible." It was a growling gush of emotion that made her insides flip and roll. No one had ever said anything like that to her but him. She met his gaze and she smiled, almost shyly. Sunlight dappled through the trees, gleaming off his black hair. Somewhere off to her right the horse nickered softly.

Everything in her world had changed the day she left home. Contentment filled a space in her heart she had thought would remain empty for a lifetime. She could never go back. And she had not a single regret. She had learned what was most important to her.

Survive and love. And live.

She wanted to stay here forever.

"What are you thinking?"

She sighed. "That I like it here."

He gave her a suspicious look. "No parties, carriage rides or fancy clothes on the frontier."

"I don't care anymore." She stretched beneath him and when he made to leave her, she clutched him tightly. He sought her cheek with an unstable hand, drew lacy patterns on the flesh below her collar bone.

In a shaky voice he asked, "What *do* you want, Sae?"

Sae. Private, intimate; she liked it, and after a thoughtful moment said, "A river at my back, land surrounding me for as far as I can see, and a place to watch it change, watch children grow and run free without rules and proper behavior to inhibit them."

His eyes were sympathetic. "You would have never known such a life existed if not for this journey."

"I would have never known *you*, Hunter." Her thumb

brushed his lip and he caught it in his teeth. "And that's what makes me want those things." His soul took flight, then smashed into reality. *I can't give you those things,* he thought, hiding his heartache and touching his lips to her cheek, her eyes, her temple.

"Guess what I want?" He wiggled his brows.

"I believe we've established that," she said with a laugh as he firmed inside her. That a lover was all he wanted—all he claimed he was able to be, didn't daunt Sable in the least. There was so much she needed to know about this wonderful man. And they had a long way to travel yet.

"We'll go slower—this time." He was grinning, she could feel it against her lips without looking.

Suddenly his head snapped up, his eyes scanning their surroundings as he instinctively reached for his gun. It would be justice, he thought, to get caught with his pants down by some Indian or a nosey trapper.

Briefly, he met her gaze. "We aren't alone."

Chapter Twenty-seven

Hunter's brows drew tight.

"What? What is it?" Sable whispered, mortified that someone should find them like this.

He cocked the pistol. "Something just nudged my leg."

Her eyes widened further. "Don't you think you should um—ah," her gaze dropped meaningfully to where he lay between her thighs. He started to move but stilled when he felt the nudge again, this time on his rear. He twisted to look just as something wet and scratchy slithered across his back.

"Damn."

"Your swearing is atrocious," she admonished, then peered cautiously around his shoulder. Her gaze flew back to his, a mischievous smile tugging at her lips. "Save me, Hunter," she crooned dramatically. "There's a ferocious beast prepared for attack."

He gave her a wry smile. "Don't laugh." She giggled behind her hand. "For God's sake, Sable, quit."

"I can't. Oh, dear!" His manhood slipped from the wet haven and she turned apple red, but couldn't stop her laughter.

He grinned. "I told you." He rose up slightly, dropping a light kiss to her naked breast before he rolled away and came to his feet, staring face to face with his horse. "Well, it's about time you showed up," he said, fastening his trousers. He glanced over the animal's coat, noting a couple of scratches, bits of dried lather, but no injuries. "Where the hell you been, you sorry sack of cavalry chow? Chasing mares, again?"

"Must run in the family," Sable said, her soft musical laughter peeling through the secluded bower. He tossed her an amused smile as she stood and wrapped herself in the buffalo robe. Their eyes met and his smile was one of contentment and she lowered her gaze shyly, a flush stealing into her cheeks. He chuckled. She had a great deal to blush about, the little hellcat. He adored the woman she became in his arms, wild and free with her passion. God, he wanted her again.

His horse playfully nudged his jaw, and Hunter patted him affectionately before he pulled his gaze from Sable and loosened the cinch, dragging off the saddle. He froze when he saw his hands. Blood? His gaze fell to his half-secured trousers and the smudged stains. The saddle dropped to the ground and he spun about. His vision darted between Sable poised at the river's edge and the garments he'd used to cushion her hips.

"Jesus!" He squeezed his eyes closed, fists clenched. Never did he imagine she was pure—untutored, maybe—but . . . "I've ruined the most gently reared debutante in Washington," he murmured guiltily, remembering the barrier breached.

Sable turned at the soft words. "Hunter?"

He scooped up the garments and went to her. "Why didn't you tell me it was your first time?" He shook them beneath her nose, furious that he hadn't even considered this before today.

Sable backed away from the soiled petticoat, flustered. "I didn't see where it mattered."

"Didn't see—" he exclaimed. "Christ, you're a virgin!"

"Was," she said with a slow seductive smile, moving closer. "And thank you very much, Hunter. I thoroughly enjoyed being ravished."

His features yanked taut, and he hesitated for a moment before he dropped the clothes and gathered her in his arms.

"Jesus, Sae. It's not something a woman gives away lightly."

"I didn't." Her embarrassment over discussing such an indelicate subject vanished as she stared intensely into his confused gray eyes. "Oh, Hunter, what happens between a man and a woman was always some awful dark secret no one but Lane dared discuss with me." She dropped her gaze to the pulse throbbing in his throat. "I wondered why, if it was so repulsive, any woman would willingly submit." She lifted her gaze to his. "But the moment you kissed me I knew feelings so glorious that couldn't be horrible, and that there was more, and that everyone but Lane had lied." She stroked his cheek, coaxing away his frown. "I wanted so very much to share it with you."

He swallowed, an incredible warmth filling his chest as he pressed his forehead to hers, overwhelmed. Whether or not he thought himself worthy of such husbandly gift, she did. And he needed to hear it.

"And of course, you were *rather* persistent," she added cheekily.

The smile started in his eyes, then melted across his face. "What am I going to do with you?" he asked gently.

Her skin held a perpetual blush as she hesitantly opened the robe and drew him inside, naked breasts rubbing enticingly against his chest. "You could teach me, love me."

She didn't mean it, not like he thought, not like he wanted. She was a virgin in the throes of her first crush, but he was caught, sinking into her luminescent eyes. God. She made it seem so easy. Hunter groaned, capturing her mouth in a soul-stripping kiss. He was her first.

He'd never been anyone's first anything.

And her father was going to kill him.

Abruptly, he drew back.

"What's the matter?"

"The colonel is going to have my hide on a flag pole."

Briefly, Sable lowered her gaze, breathless from his kiss. "I hardly think it's any of his business." She dug her toes into the cold squishy bank, hating the jolt back to reality.

"Believe me, Sae, he'll know we're lovers."

Lovers. Was that all he really wanted? Had she been so wrong? "Papa will say I deserve to have my reputation ruined, if that's what you're implying. Not that it wasn't the moment I left Washington unchaperoned. Besides," she shrugged carelessly, "you needn't worry. You were his prize soldier. Papa will forgive *you* anything."

Hunter nearly choked on that. He didn't think there was a father alive that would forgive a man for taking his daughter's virtue in the middle of the wilderness without first speaking vows.

She studied him. "You aren't worried Papa will actually demand you wed me, are you?"

That hit a nerve. Richard knew better than anyone that Hunter wasn't clean enough to marry his little girl, even with a rifle pointed at his back. And Hunter wasn't about to pull Sable further into his twisted life.

"He could, but I won't."

Her expression drooped, hurt springing into her eyes, and she stepped out of his embrace. "Is marrying me so horrifying?"

"God, no! But I can't."

He wanted her in every way a man wants woman, but didn't think he had the ability to love her like she wanted or needed. He could offer her no future. And a woman like Sable Cavanaugh deserved a man that was at least sane. Not a man who walked on the edges of sanity. Christ, he'd made a mess of things this time.

"It's not that you can't." she said carefully. "You won't even consider leaving this place,"——her eyes sparked with a knowing light—"because of those dreams."

He schooled his features and turned away. "Forget I mentioned it."

"Was it something to do with your incarceration?"

His shoulders stiffened. She made it sound like a hotel visit.

Sable grasped his arm and tugged, the robe slipped off her shoulder, chilled air pricking her bare skin. He wouldn't look at her.

"I know you were whipped."

Her soft whisper was a stinging talon of pain. Jesus, what else did she know? "Yeah, me and a hundred others."

"Talk to me, Hunter," she begged softly. "I've eavesdropped on enough of Papa's conversations to know you were a spy."

He gave her a measured look. "I said forget it." He shrugged off her touch. She didn't need to dip in the filthy well of his past. God, not now.

Desperate to penetrate the source of his pain, Sable realized she knew almost nothing about him. "Do you have any brothers or sisters?" He looked at her sharply. "Are your parents alive?"

"What the hell has that to do with anything?"

"I'm trying to understand why you won't talk to me." The silence stretched. "For heaven's sake, Hunter, let me in!"

"You are in."

"Liar! You throw up a wall every time I get close to what's hurting you!" There was a blankness in his eyes, and she'd seen the like often enough to know he'd willingly let his dark secrets keep them apart. Hot anger shot through her veins and when he made to touch her, she back-stepped, her heels sinking into the bank, rocks cutting into her arch. "Go ahead then! Hibernate. Stay in that pathetic hole you've made for yourself. Drag it over your head. See if I give a damn!" She turned toward the river.

"Your language gets worse by the minute."

"Must be the company I keep!"

"Sae. You'd never want to be near me, if you—"

She spun about, glaring. "How dare you assume anything about me, Hunter McCracken." He reached and she curled

273

away from his touch. "I don't want to be near you now. I was right before. You're a coward."

Another nerve sliced open. His entire being seemed to darken, the scar on his cheek gone white. She moved back, frightened. "But damn good enough to ride between those pretty white legs." The insult tumbled too easily from his lips and he despised himself for it. "You want everything to be perfect, your way!" He advanced on her. "Well, wake up, little girl, life is ugly and unfair and we take our licks like big boys. And if you're lucky, you find a scrap of pleasure." He looked her over, cold and calculated. "Well, I found it in your body." She flinched as if he'd slapped her and took a step back. "We're lovers, Sable. Nothing more."

Thick tears glossed her eyes and her lower lip quivered wretchedly.

She opened her mouth to speak when the ground suddenly gave way beneath her feet. Sable tumbled back into the Cheyenne river, the frigid temperature engulfing her, freezing the scream in her throat. She struggled for the surface, arms flailing, then her buttocks touched the soft sandy bottom and she sat up. Her head and shoulders popped through the icy liquid.

Hunter's deep laughter rang in her ears as Sable pushed sopping hair from her face and glared at him. His hands on hips, he stood on the bank, not lifting a finger to aid her.

"Serves you right for antagonizing me."

"I'm not done yet, you—you jackanape!" She shuddered, drifting. "and if you ever address me in that odious manner again, Hunter McCracken, so help me, I'll—I'll—shoot you!"

"You have to get a loaded gun first," he taunted. "And I ain't stupid."

"You are! But imagine yourself a gentleman and," her fists pummeled the water with each word, "get me out of here!"

"Get yourself out."

Sable tried, had been trying, but the heavy buffalo robe, her rapidly numbing limbs, and the shifting river bottom

274

made it difficult to get satisfactory footing or balance and she could do no more than tread.

"Let go of the robe and swim."

Annoyed that he wouldn't help, yet knowing he was simply getting back at her, she released the buffalo robe and dug her arms into the water, suddenly discovering she had to fight the current. The water rushed around her with more force than a moment ago, and she looked up at Hunter, panicked when she hadn't progressed an inch, but was further away.

"Stand up!" he shouted, his expression darkening as he waded in. The river widened slightly but not enough to accommodate the melting mountain snow and rain water of the past weeks.

"I can't!" Sable tried to touch her feet down but the comforting bottom had disappeared. The water swelled, pulling at her, bubbling white. "Hunter!" she screamed, reaching out. He was already in the water, chest deep, his arm extended. She stretched, treading frantically; her legs were cramped, her breathing labored. Almost there. Almost. He held onto a toppled scrub bush, giving them anchor. Sable mustered her strength past the pain in her legs and lurched. His fingers grazed hers and they both tried to firm the grip. He smiled with relief.

It was the last thing she saw as the swirling river yanked her violently from his grasp.

Hunter immediately dragged himself back onto the bank, ignoring the terror building in him, ignoring the fear he'd seen in her eyes and forcing his heavy legs to move. He ran along the bank, never taking his eyes from her. Her head bobbed, her small hands piercing the surface as she grappled for anything to stop her wild ride. She called his name. He couldn't believe a moment ago she was close enough to touch and now he couldn't find her. Then she appeared, like a piece of wood, her body rolling with the current, sliding on the surface, not able to stop it. His throat went tight, his bare feet digging into the ground as he accelerated to his limits. *She's not dead, not dead. Not after the hell I've put her through. Please, God. I couldn't handle it. I couldn't. I let her fall in. For spite, I allowed her to sit there, floating closer to the rapids.*

Scrambling down a slope and into the water, Hunter's gaze searched the river. Seconds passed. His heart slammed painfully against his ribs with each frantic beat.

Surface, damn you!

Then he saw a flash of white. Her naked skin. Swiftly working hand over hand on barren roots the water had exposed, Hunter wedged himself between rocks and caught debris before testing the strength of his life line, yanking hard, then again after earth gave way under the pressure. Water surged. His gaze lit on a jagged boulder barely parting the surface. He had to get to it before she passed. If he didn't, she'd never make it.

Freezing water flooded against his naked chest, weakening his grip as his gaze flicked across the white foam for the human buoy. She was coming fast, and he prayed the current would take her right to him. Choking on a mouthful of water, he worked to the thinning end of the root and extended his leg, missing, then bracing his foot on the boulder. His frozen toes gripped it. His new position lifted him out of the water to mid-thigh. Suspended from the branch, Hunter balanced precariously, a half straddle, one foot stable, the other floating free, waiting for the leap home.

Come on, darlin', come on. His hand plunged into the icy water. *Closer. Closer.*

Her body twisted, flopped back and Hunter lurched, grasping a handful of skin and hair before she passed beneath his leg. The root groaned, threatening to snap under the combined weights, dipping them deeper into the water.

"God almighty. Help me!"

His back and arm muscles flexed and bulged as the current dared to take her from him again, but he wouldn't let it. Maneuvering her against the boulder to better his grip on her arm, Hunter took two quick breaths, then pushed off. He flailed wildly for a second, wrenching his shoulder with the effort to swing their weight toward the bank. Pulling her into the wedge of rocks and debris before she floated back out into the swift current, he levered himself onto stable ground, then with a mighty jerk, hoisted her onto the soggy earth.

For a moment he could do no more.

She lay lifeless, sprawled like a rag doll. A knot twisted in his throat as he shoved her onto her stomach, dealing several sharp pumps to her back. Her skin was like ice. A voice in his head said he'd risked his life for a dead woman. An empty body. *Breathe.* Hunter blinked, his eyes warm and burning. *Breathe. Breathe!* He flipped her on her back. Her face was pale, her lips blue. So still. His heart cracked, pain flooding in. *No. No!* Desperate, he thought to give her his breath, his life, and covered her mouth with his, blowing hard. He thumped her chest when she didn't respond.

"Damn you, Sable." He blew into her mouth again. "Just like you to leave me."

A gurgle, a tiny sound he scarcely heard over his own laboring lungs. Then it came louder as her body suddenly convulsed, water streaming from her lips. Immediately Hunter pushed her on her side as she vomited half the Cheyenne river.

Sheer joy pumped his heart.

"Sable? Darlin'? Can you hear me?"

She retched again, then moaned. Her hand moved, and he grasped it firmly. She squeezed back and Hunter pressed it to her lips. Shivering violently, she struggled to sit up. Hunter didn't give her the chance and gathered her in his arms, crushing her to his chest. Her arms slipped weakly around his waist.

"God, oh, God, Sae. I'm sorry." He squeezed his eyes shut. "I thought I'd really lost you." His voice broke.

Sable swallowed thickly. Her throat burned and in a raspy voice she said, "S'alright . . . knew you weren't . . . ready to

get . . ." she swallowed again and winced. ". . . Rid of me . . .
yet."

Still so confident, he thought, his smile full of self-reproach
as he tilted her face to the sun. Her eyes were bloodshot and
her hair was a matted tangle plastered to her scalp. Her naked skin was scraped and covered with mud. She was beautiful. The muscles in his chest squeezed down on his heart,
threatening his air as he plucked a clump of sopping hair
from her cheek. He would remember the sight of her blue lips
and motionless body for the rest of his days.

I love her.

*Why do I keep fighting it? She's not going away, not even if she could.
She forgives and comforts and she believes in you, you bastard.*

His body shaking, he tenderly brushed his mouth across
hers and whispered, "You sure know how to get the upper
hand in an argument."

"Did I win?" she croaked. She quaked with a deep chill,
her muscles cramping and she looked up at him, cold and
helpless.

He smiled, eyes watery. "You don't want me to lie again,
do you?"

Chapter Twenty-eight

He had to do it.

She'd die if he didn't get her warm and dry.

Dragging his gaze from the cave he looked down at Sable snuggled in his arms. The shock of the icy river was bad enough, but the near drowning had stolen all her strength. Unconscious and limp, she was wrapped in his bed roll. She hadn't woken except for that one instance and he deemed it her personal revenge to get in the last word. He thanked God again she'd remained conscious long enough to relieve his darkest fear, while overhead the incessant roll of dark angry clouds rapidly reduced the temperature.

He looked again to the yawning mouth of the cave and rode closer. Sweat popped out on his upper lip and throat. Images—ugly, dark, and degrading—surfaced. A tightness crept up his spine, a slow clawing that rose from the base.

He couldn't go inside. He couldn't. It would kill him. He'd go mad. Sable drew her knees up, unconsciously easing her cramping muscles and the picture of her cold, blue lipped and motionless, taunted him. She was dead then, he knew. Dead. No soul. No life. The pain of the memory nearly knocked him out of the saddle.

This is my fault.

She needs shelter.

He looked toward the cave.

God.

I'm going to be sick.

Her body shuddered, hard, and he opened his jacket, snuggling her closer to his chest. He took a deep bracing breath, then nudged the horse up the small incline. She was still naked beneath the blankets. He hadn't dared waste anymore time than it took to gather their belongings and secure them to her horse before tethering it behind his own.

The rain came, falling fast and hard. The horse's legs dug into the slippery hill side, thick muscles bunching with his effort to pull the group higher. Hunter paused on a rocky plateau to slap the reins of her horse over a scrubby bush. He'd get it later, he decided, any reason to leave the cave. His hands flexed on the reins and he urged the mount on.

"That's it, boy, you can do it," he praised the steed. Cold seeped into his body, his jacket doing little to ward off the damp chill from his wet trousers. Hunter slid from the saddle, taking Sable down with him, and stepped inside the cave just enough to give her shelter from the rain, then gently laid her on the ground. He immediately went back outside, bracing his hand against the wall to catch his breath. Damn, he thought, glancing back over his shoulder once, then pushing away to gather wood before it was too wet to be of much use. He kept telling himself this was for her. He would do anything to keep her alive.

Anything?

He forced his concentration on what he had to do and within minutes, fear pushing him hard, he had a small smokeless fire going and had settled her close, wrapping her in his only dry blanket. He wished he had the buffalo robe. What kind of trapper was he not to have any furs?

She still shivered, her skin and hair soaked and cold, but Hunter had to leave her again to retrieve her horse. He returned moments later, dropping the packs and saddles near the entrance, rubbing down the horses, setting pots and tin mugs out to fill with rain water before he gathered the nerve to urge the horses to the rear of the cavern. He prodded them cautiously past Sable.

Each step echoed in his head, the crunch of stone vibrating up his boot heels. His stomach roared, and he swallowed the bitterness. Sweat beaded on his temples and dripped, making him itch. It took an unrealistically long time to complete the simple chore. The ceiling was barely low enough to accommodate the horses; they wouldn't be able to do more than shift. The stone roof grazed Hunter's Stetson, tipping it, and he cringed, angrily tossing it aside. His stride quickened, and he stopped at the entrance, inhaling deeply, swiftly, clamping his eyes shut and falling back against the rocks.

Damn.

Rain poured.

Tilting his face to the black heavens, he let the spattering mist cool his skin.

He'd been here before, yet never that far inside, least ways never long enough to more than bed his horse and toss in his furs. Hunter always slept beyond the mouth of the cave, regardless of the weather.

He couldn't take that luxury now. Sable would die.

Hunter commanded his feet to move back inside, then knelt before her, stroking her cheek, rubbing the pad of his thumb across her lips.

"Sable, darlin', can you hear me?"

No response.

Hunter shivered, then stripped off his clothes, except for his trousers, using his shirt to blot some of the moisture from her hair. His gazed darted to the ceiling as he spread the dark mass out on the blanket, hoping it would dry. He glanced around. The walls seemed to creep closer, darkening his surroundings. His lungs worked harder to draw in air. Water dripped, the soft sound magnified in the emptiness of the cave.

Jesus, help me.

Swiftly he added wood to fire, carelessly hooked clothes on

protruding rocks, then slapped a pot of coffee together. It nearly fell into the flames in his haste to leave, and he skidded to a halt at the entrance, sucking damp air through his nose, deep and loud. His heart thumped erratically against the wall of his chest. He couldn't calm it. He swallowed dryly.

He dumped dried meat into a tin of water and forced himself to re-enter and set it on the rocks surrounding the blaze. The meat floated like wood chips in the broth. It was disgusting, but he'd do better later. Later, when he knew she would survive.

He left the cave again, sinking to the ground in a pitiful heap.

Suddenly he shifted enough to flip open a pack and dig for a bottle of whiskey. His arm trembled as he uncorked it and tipped it to his lips. Hunter drank and drank, his Adam's apple bobbing, liquor dribbling from his mouth, down his throat as he drained the half-full bottle. He tossed the empty aside. The glass popped, the tinkling shatter sounding like brass wind chimes.

His fingertips gripped his thighs and he choked on the liquor fighting its way back up. Thunder roared; a silver streak of lightening rent the black sky. Rain splattered, the force tossing up pebbles and mud.

A faint scuffle drew him around and he raced inside. Sable was shaking so hard the blanket had fallen away. Her body glistened, her hands tucked between her knees, torso curled tight. Her teeth chattered and his eyes snapped to the stone walls around him, then back to her.

Do it. She needs you.

Yet he hesitated, cursing roundly before he angrily shucked his boots and trousers, then lay down beside her. Naked, he pulled her into his arms, forcing her stiff legs down and wrapping his arms and legs around her. She was like a block of ice. He turned her back to the fire and draped the blanket around them both, his hands vigorously rubbing her arms, back, and hips. Her soft breasts were pressed against his chest, her nipples, hardened to tight little nubs, bored into his skin. Her smooth thighs were nestled between his own. He tried to concentrate on the woman in his arms and not his surroundings.

Get control.

"Easy, love, easy," he murmured into her hair. He rubbed briskly, fitting her body more tightly to his own.

He wasn't aroused by the feel of her skin on his. It was the sounds, the darkness, the musty odors of the cave which captured his complete attention. His hands roamed unconsciously, his eyes darting warily to the shadowed corners. Somewhere, in the rear of the cave, water trickled, the sound tensing his shoulders with every drip. His respiration increased. Droplets of water slithered down the uneven quartz walls, glistening like crystal. Each rhythmic splat on dry ground rang like a slap. He squeezed his eyes shut, lips pressed to a thin stark slash.

God. It's coming again.

He swallowed, but there was no moisture in his mouth to get over the rock in his throat. The smell, dank and wet and gritty, crept into his bones. In his eyes the ceiling drooped, shaped itself square.

He didn't feel her hands shift on his chest, didn't notice her settle less stiffly against him. He knew only the suffocating heat of his mind, the rats scurrying across his bare feet, the foul-smelling slop bucket he imagined wedged in the corner of the cell. Within the confusion of his brain he heard the gravely pleas of his men, begging for escape, a doctor, a sip of water, a merciful death. Dysentery, foul and degrading, weakened his men in body and spirit. Bodies wedged tight, bare feet shifting listlessly. Disease swift and killing. Once strong soldiers, skeleton-thin and shrunken, reeked of death and lost hope. And their suffering ate at his soul until he'd do anything to see them live, anything for enough strength to escape.

Keys rattled. Iron scraped stone.

Wanna eat, bluebelly?

Anything for clear water or food not crawling with maggots. The whip snapped, hot talons curling around his waist. His chest heaved with great gulps of air. Bile rose in his throat. His hunger burned. No mercy for the spy, the spy.

I won't tell, Capt'n.

I know, son.

Honor the code, sir.

The code, Lieutenant.

"Hunter?" Soft, raspy. "You're holding me too tight. I can't breathe."

Not a muscle moved in response. Sable pushed her head between the tight circle of his arms to look at him.

Air hissed in and out between his clenched teeth. She smelled liquor. His eyes were squeezed so tightly closed the corners were creased and pale. He was like iron against her, immovable. His skin flowed with perspiration. She was lucid enough to know something was very wrong. He seemed paralyzed. She couldn't believe it.

When he drinks, he dreams.

Calling his name gained her nothing. She glanced around, realizing they were sheltered in a cave as she pushed against his locked arms. He didn't budge.

The fire popped and hissed softly. Rain drenched the earth beyond the entrance.

Hunter's mind twisted with memories, images brightened, then receded into the depths of his brain. Faces gouged with decay, every man he'd killed for God and honor and country. A shape, broad-shouldered and vague came into focus—his gray uniform, tattered and dirty.

Ready, Yankee? Laughter, harsh and cruel. Slotted light colored his face; square, smooth, pretty. The guard.

You talk, they eat.

Go to hell.

Thick hands fondled, groping at proud men too weak to

284

fight. *Refuse to speak.* Another of his men vanished, leaving a gut-ripping scream as epitaph.

She wedged her hands from between their bodies, then slid them around his waist, settling on his hips. She breathed a little easier.

"Hunter? Relax, please. It hurts." Stiltedly, because he held her upper arms and shoulders with such a crushing force, she stroked her hands up and down the base of his spine. The motion didn't ease his tension, but increased it.

"Hunter?" His breathing came faster, shifting her with the power of it. Her fingers drifted to his tight buttocks. He recoiled violently, shoving at her, a wild attempt to free himself from the tangle of arms and legs, his strength so driven she nearly rolled into the fire. A dark tortured howl erupted from him like an explosion as he scrambled out of the cave, then fell to his hands and knees, muscles ripping as he vomited uncontrollably. His fingers grasped the muddy earth. Rain pelted his back.

Sable lay motionless propped on her side, confused and stunned.

Water splashed against his naked skin, soaked his hair, and he coughed, drove his muddy fingers into his hair and finally sat up, tipping his face to the sky. His chest rose and fell with short, rapid breaths. He drove his fist into his thighs, rivulets of red mud streaking his skin. He cursed, bent over and retched again.

Hunter let the sheets of rain water bathe him, digging the heels of his palms into his eyes, then holding his head. A tight sound came from him, clipped and restrained. He flinched at some imaginary foe, jerking his body to the right.

"Don't touch me!" he screamed viciously. "I can't take it." He gripped handfuls of his hair, his voice going weak. "I'm begging, for the love of God! I need peace!" he ground out, pulling the dark locks. In his mind, he flailed and fought, iron wrist shackles yanking his arms back when he tried to reach too far. The guard slammed him up against the stone wall, a sticky slime covering Hunter's unclothed body. The cold chains beat against his skin.

Tell me the rendezvous points, bluebelly.

The soldier pushed himself against Hunter's back, naked hardness probing, and he rebelled violently. Hunter vomited and couldn't stop.

Talk, or I do your L.T.

Don't, Capt'n. The code.

Hunter held his silence. More would die. Many more would die.

The rendezvous! the guard demanded, unfastening his pants.

Have mercy! He's just a kid. A kid!

The torture cries came. And this time, they forced him to watch.

Rape. Of a young soldier whose only crime was idolizing his captain.

Guilt and horror and shame swept Hunter in heavy fluid swells, and he wanted to die.

If ever, he wanted it now.

Shoulda talked, spy.

His lieutenant whimpered like a dying animal.

Not your fault, sir.

No! No! come on, son, don't! We'll get out.

Hunter fought the chains, watching, helplessly bound to the wall, unable to stop his lieutenant from throwing the chain over the hook dangling from the warehouse ceiling.

Lieutenant, stop! That's an order!

Didn't break the code, Capt'n. I didn't.

He slipped it around his neck. The starved lieutenant's weight instantly sent the pulley up, his cracking neck echoing in Hunter's mind.

Squeak, swing, squeak.

Hunter heard the chuckle, triumphant and lusty, and he vomited.

I'm sorry. I let him die.

Then suddenly he wasn't restrained, his relief overwhelming. In his mind he saw his mother, his father, and brothers. His disgrace was theirs. He'd dishonored himself, his family. The damage was irreparable.

Sable's breath lay trapped in her throat. The torment, the agonizing pain in his expression, cut into her soul like a dull knife, yet she didn't dare interfere, terrified of the consequences.

Then Hunter reached for his gun.

Sable edged closer, her heart thundering in her chest as he calmly checked the load, sniffled, then with his thumb slowly drew back the hammer. A bullet moved into the chamber. He stared at the weapon. Then she watched in stunned horror as he slowly raised the revolver and pressed the barrel to his temple.

"Nooooo!" Sable screamed and lurched for him, knocking the pistol upward. It fired into the night.

"Get away," he snarled, shoving her off and she tumbled onto her back, hard.

He lifted the gun to his head again.

Sable scrambled to her feet and threw herself at him again, clamping both hands over his, calling up the last dregs of her strength to keep the barrel from his skull.

He fought her, jerking the weapon, his eyes, red and tortured, stared somewhere beyond her.

"Put the gun down, Hunter. Please." She couldn't maintain the hold for long, not when he wanted to keep it. Trapped in his private hell he was too strong. Her feet shifted in the muddy earth, thigh muscles begging for relief. "Give me the gun, Hunter!" Her arms trembled with her effort and her balance faltered. "Oh, please, give me the damn gun!" She kneed him in the stomach.

He didn't even flinch. His grip flexed on the wet pistol stock. And she covered the broad index finger curled around the trigger with her own.

Sable squeezed.

The gun fired above his head, and Sable pumped the trigger again and again, sending the five rounds in rapid succession safely into the blackened sky.

He flinched at the final blast. The echo faded quickly, white smoke poured from the bore, then vanished beneath the onslaught of rain.

She sagged against him, her breathing rushed, small hands still tightly closed over his. She cried with sadness and fatigue.

With a slowness that was recognizably unnatural, Hunter lowered his gaze to the bowed head pressed to his chest. It took a supreme effort to do that and even longer to feel the dead weight of the gun in his palm. The hot barrel burned against his skin. Light from the cave glowed into the darkness like a tired beacon.

Instantly Hunter knew what he'd done, and that she'd stopped him.

The muscles in his throat worked to a make sound.

"Sable." Dry, weary.

She twisted a look up at him, her watery gaze searching his taut features for the man still caged. "Welcome back." Her lips curved faintly.

The small gesture was like a reprieve from God.

He wouldn't make Him regret it.

Or her, either.

Chapter Twenty-nine

He couldn't move, not without an incredible strain, for every inch of muscle, bone, and sinew screamed with a tight agonized protest. His breathing wouldn't slow and his head reeled from the swift intakes of air. He forced himself to calm down.

He was alive. Alive.

Hunter stared at the rain-splashed contours of her face. *I love you,* he wanted to say. *I love you for being a tart-mouthed witch, for risking your life for me, for being impertinent and squeamish and growing up before my eyes, and for weeping over dead bunnies and for loving that little boy so much you lost everything.*

And for sticking by me. When I need someone most.

I love you. It was useless to tell her. She couldn't possibly return the feelings. Not after this.

It hurt so deep inside to know that.

God. It hurt.

The sudden notion that he might have harmed her made him burn with disgust. He wasn't in his right mind; after all these years he still wasn't sane.

"Did I—" he cleared his throat, licked dry lips. "Did I hurt you?"

"No, of course not."

So confident, no doubt in her tone. Christ, he didn't deserve such faith.

He shifted and she cautiously eased back off him, a fierce blush snapping over her naked skin. He didn't notice. His gaze immediately dropped to the spent pistol still clenched in his fist.

"Get out of the rain," he rasped, tossing it aside. Sable's gaze followed the tumbling path of the gun, then returned to Hunter, and she sensed he wasn't going to speak of his torment. He couldn't even look at her.

"You come, too." She reached for his hand, but he flinched.

"Get in the damn cave, Sable." Softly spoken yet with an underlying warning, telling her not to push. His gaze was riveted to the cavern and fear sparked his gray eyes.

Sable studied the utter despair creasing his features, confused as to how to help him, then she rose, gathered the blanket she'd lost earlier, covering herself as she went into the cave. Settling close to the fire, she poked it with a stick, then tossed on more wood, trying to ignore the wretched and lonely figure still sitting in the rain, naked. But she couldn't. Her eyes refused to leave him, afraid of what he might do.

So she watched and waited, taking pleasure in just looking at him and knowing he breathed. He climbed to his feet, corded muscle flexing, and her insides did a quick shift, her body dancing with the sweet memory of their loving as he walked to the mouth of the cave and slumped to the ground, folding his arms on his knees. He stared at the blackness, his face averted from her.

He's afraid to come inside the cave, she realized. Had that set off this dangerous nightmare?

She agonized, aching to go to him, to hold him, yet she didn't think he wanted her near, nor would he accept any words of comfort. Sable wrapped the damp blanket tightly around her and said nothing. He would tell her when he was ready, yet the depth of his pain was so great Sable wondered if he would ever recover enough to confide in her.

For what felt like hours Sable watched him, sipping the

coffee he'd obviously prepared earlier. He sat so still she thought he might be asleep, then he shuddered raggedly and mashed a hand over his face. He looked so incredibly drained. Rain drenched him. He would catch his death of a cold out there. He needed food and rest and warmth. Sable chewed her lower lip, trying to figure out how to accomplish all of that without him knowing. Men were really such willful creatures sometimes.

Her blanket was dry now, and so were their clothes and his bedroll. Her movements hadn't drawn his attention, and she worried further over his state of mind. Tucking the blanket beneath her arms, she used her heavy wool skirt to capture some rocks that surrounded the blaze. The heat penetrated the cloth quickly and Sable cushioned her hands with his bedroll, then carried the warm bundle over to Hunter.

He didn't move, didn't acknowledge her presence, but he was shaking violently. She placed the bundle close to his side and he melted a little.

"Come inside, Hunter," she whispered, tossing her blanket over him. "Just out of the rain, that's all."

Her tone was soft, a wind's caress, and Hunter thought it a dream.

"Come to me," she coaxed. Her voice, sweet and lovely, floated to him like a beckoning mist. Hunter turned his face to the sound of it. She was kneeling in the rain with him and it was warm. How could she do that? Half of him was so cold. He hadn't noticed it until now.

"Go back." A weak croak.

She shook her head, a curling waterfall of mahogany hair shimmering across her shoulders. His red-rimmed eyes roamed her naked body in a fractured pattern before returning to her face. His head was slow to bend as he stared at the blanket draped over him, then back to her. She held out a steaming tin mug of coffee. He worked his hands out from beneath and took it. He sipped once as she snuggled close, naked and brave, slick with rain, and Hunter's heart wrenched over her sacrifice.

But he said nothing, did nothing. She was stubborn and would stay. Her palm smoothed over the arm propped on his knee, and she placed a soft kiss there, then settled beside him as if they were in a room, in a four-poster bed beneath coverlets and goose down. The notion made Hunter relax a little. He edged closer to the heat she radiated. He knew she shouldn't be in the rain. She'd get sick and die. Die. With a raw moan he threw the mug aside and turned to her, and her arms engulfed him like wood smoke.

She held him against her breast and he was ashamed. He cried. He confessed his sins. But she said nothing, rubbing his back in gentle circles, stroking his hair. Hunter never wanted to leave her.

It was good, so good and clean and loving, and Jesus, how he needed her.

Hunter stirred to the scent of roasting meat. His muscles were stiff, the ground beneath him hard and rocky. He felt as if he'd been beaten and dragged behind a speeding horse. He frowned, not remembering anything, then remembering it all in one sharp flash.

He jerked upright. A hand came from somewhere behind him to touch his shoulder and press him back down.

"Rest," she murmured and he closed his eyes against the memories and absorbed the feel of her curled behind him, and a strange comforting sensation spread through him. He remembered now. She'd coaxed him inside, doing it little by little. First it was the coffee, then the promise of being dry, then the warmth, the blankets, the rest. How he needed to sleep. Hunter felt he could do it for a century. His eyes snapped open and he stared at the low ceiling. *I'm inside. Inside.* His breathing accelerated, his body trembled. And she sensed it, rubbed his back and shoulders, sifted her fingers through the hair at his nape, speaking inconsequential words, and Hunter found himself gradually relaxing despite his fears. This was different, he kept telling himself. No cell. No guard. No swollen-faced lieutenant swinging from his neck. Just Sable, soft loving Sable.

He couldn't look at her. Not yet, and he was glad she was tucked to his back. Grease from the spit hare splattered on the blaze, hissing gray streamers of smoke into the cave. Good fire, he thought ridiculously, and wondered how she managed to snare the rabbit. He noticed the charred remains of the fire he'd first built and realized they were not in their original spot. She'd moved the entire mess closer to the entrance. For him. There was extra wood drying by the fire, clothes neatly folded, coffee warming, and Sable—wedged close to him. So giving, so brave.

He reached behind and grasped her roaming hand, pulling it around and tucking it against his chest. She snuggled, squeezing his fingers. He squeezed back. For the first time in years Hunter sank into a dreamless sleep.

Hunter's eyes were gritty as he tried to open them. The sound of splashing water came to him and his gaze focused on the land beyond the cave. The rain had stopped and the sun scarcely broke the horizon. His eyes shifted to the sound and his breath stuck in his chest. In the far side of the cavern near the entrance, Sable knelt on the ground, her body naked and lathered with soap, her sudsy hair shifting wetly against her skin. She dragged a cloth over her shoulders, across her breasts and down between her legs. Hunter watched every movement. Her bare breasts swayed as she reached for the cook pot, steam rising in powdery swirls as she brought it close, tested it. She stood and lifted it over her head, pouring slowly and Hunter tamped down a groan as water slid over her hair and body, sheening her like molded glass. The sight was incredibly erotic and desire, fresh and aching, jolted to life. Water pooled and muddied her feet. She rinsed her hair again, splashing the remaining liquid over her skin once more, then set the pot aside, wrung out her hair and reached for a towel.

He remained still, watching as she dried herself, then moved to a blanket where her clothes lay neatly folded. She dressed, rolling stockings up her slender legs, slipping into lacy drawers, then dropping the chemise over her head. His gaze clung to her fingers tying the dainty pink ribbons at her breasts. The fabric molded damply to her skin, outlining the dusky tips. She slipped into a dark blouse and buttoned it, then stood, searching for her skirt. She found it, picked it up and groaned at the burn holes scattered throughout. The heated rocks, he thought, that she'd brought to warm him.

She fished in her pack and withdrew the buckskins, shook her head, then dug further. With a surprised frown, she withdrew the clothes he'd bought her, shaking them out.

"My word. What on earth was he thinking?" Her gaze swung to him and she snatched the trousers to her breast. Hunter rose up on his elbow and stared.

"Good morning," she said. He offered no smile, simply looked at her strangely, and an uncomfortable silence lengthened. She eyed him dubiously. "How long have you been awake?"

He smiled, roguish and soft and her insides felt it. "Long enough."

"I might have known." She flushed ten shades in two seconds. "Ah, Hunter?" She held up the pants. "I can't possibly wear these."

"Why not?" He sat up, the blanket pooling at his naked hips.

"It—it's indecent!"

"They're practical, Sable." He reached for the coffee and mug. "And do you have anything else? God, I hurt all over."

"Well, only the buckskins, but it really is too muddy out for—" His smile widened to a grin. "Oh, for heaven's sake!"

She stood, turned her back and jammed her leg into the trousers. Trousers. Denim ones at that! Oh, she was thankful no one but him would see her. A lady simply did *not* wear trousers.

Hunter choked on a mouthful of coffee as she pulled the trouser over her hips and stuffed in her shirt. It was a mistake, those things. A big one. Every ripe curve and crease was defined by the heavy tan fabric. It hugged her trim hips, showed the flatness of her stomach, the length of her legs. She bent to pull in her boots and Hunter thought he'd pass out. She turned fully, his gaze riveted to the cleanly molded valley between her thighs. Damn. The pants were snug, but how the hell was he supposed to judge her size. They were meant for boys!

"Well?" she asked.

"They'll do," he managed.

She dropped onto the blanket beside him and poured coffee for herself, then gingerly removed the cooked rabbit from the spit, setting it on a tin plate beside him.

He smiled his thanks and started eating, feeling embarrassed. He ought to be doing the hunting, not her.

She glanced at him, dragging the comb through her tangled hair. He had a drop of grease on his chin and unconsciously she reached out and dabbed it with her thumb. He flinched, scowled at her, then softened. She handed him the damp towel and he swallowed, then wiped his mouth and hands, his gaze never leaving her face.

"Where are the horses?" he asked, inclining his head to the rear of the cave.

"Down the slope—hobbled, grazing, and saddled."

A warmth burned in the vicinity of her stomach at the pride in his eyes, making all that heavy lugging worth it.

"You shouldn't be exerting yourself."

"I'm fine." *How are you,* she wanted to ask. He seemed to know what she was thinking and looked away. But not before she saw the humiliation in his eyes.

"I need a shave," he said, rubbing his hand over his bristled chin. She jumped to her feet and retrieved a tin pan of water from outside, then gathered his mug and shave kit, laying it beside him as she sat.

"Sable, stop it."

She stilled. "What?"

"Stop catering to me like this." He waved at the shaving kit. "I'm not a God-damned cripple!"

At his sharp tone, Sable looked at her hands folded on her lap. "I know you're not, but—but—" She bravely lifted her gaze, tears blurring her vision. "I want to. You did the same for me, didn't you?"

His angry glare faltered and Hunter reached for her, sliding his hand up her arm, her shoulder, cupping her neck and pulling her against him. Her arms slipped around his waist and she gripped him fiercely. Her tears cut him in half.

"I'm sorry, darlin'," he rasped. "I'd give anything to have spared you that."

"I was so scared last night . . . so unbelievably frightened." She punched him in the back. "Don't do that again—ever."

There was a strained moment before he said, "I can't promise anything, Sable, and I think you know that." She lifted her head and stared. Hunter wiped a tear with the pad of his thumb.

"Perhaps talking about it might help?"

"Sable, please." It was a tired request to give up.

Rubbing her hands up and down his bare back, Sable gathered the courage to say, "We've shared so much, Hunter. Why not this?" Silence and a closed expression answered her. "Might I at least know why?"

No resentment, no anger in her voice, as if she were asking for the time of day. It made him feel almost gentle inside.

"Because prison is ugly, degrading, too horrible—"

Tears immediately bloomed in her eyes. "What could be more horrifying than watching you put a gun to your head?" Her fractured voice ricocheted off the damp walls as she turned and gripped his arm. "Nothing could have prepared me for that, Hunter. Nothing!"

"I'm sorry, Sable. Jesus." His heart ached for all he'd put her through, the scars it would leave. "What do you want me to say?"

She shook him, once and hard. "Anything to make me believe you don't want to die!"

For what felt like an eternity he gazed into eyes the color of wild snapdragons and wished for the world. *I want to be alive so I can keep loving you,* he wanted to say, but didn't think she'd believe him capable. Not after trying to take his own life. Nightmare or not.

"I'm glad *you* pulled the trigger." The words ripped into the silence. "Grateful you braved an idiot with a loaded gun." His hands slid up her thighs and fanned her waist. "But I wish it had never happened, wish you had never seen me . . . like that." Disgust thickened his voice and his fingers tightened. "Wish to God I didn't have anything in me that needed fighting."

"It's only there if you make it stay." She grabbed him before he could turn away, fall away and hide. "You survived," she said, cupping his jaw in her palms, forcing him to look at her, face more than her. "You did the best you could when the world was falling apart around us all." He covered her hands with his own. "Oh, Hunter," her voice broke. "Do you think you're the only one who came away from the war with scars?" His heartbeat choked his breath as he stared up at her. "Forgive yourself for living."

He squeezed his eyes shut. Forgive. It sounded so easy. He couldn't seem to do it. "It was my fault. They suffered because of me."

She wanted to slap him. "Have they come for you?" she demanded, dropping her hands to his shoulders. "Have they laid the blame at your feet, asked for your life in return?" The answer both knew was left unsaid. "It was a *war*. Those men knew they could lose their lives, and you can't carry the burden for the rest of your days!" Her voice lost its edge. "And something inside you says you can't."

"What the hell do you know? The Confederates threatened my men to get to me, Sae. Healthy soldiers starved to death not because they were Union officers, but because *I* was a spy! And I still wouldn't break silence. Jesus." He raked his fingers through his hair. "I sent them to their death and didn't do a damn thing to stop it!"

"I believe you did," she murmured softly, refusing to fuel his temper. "You endured everything humanly possible for those men, to see they lived another day closer to freedom. Not even God can ask more of you." With a sigh, heavy and burdened, he bowed his head, pressing it against the softness of her breasts. Sable bit her lip, sifting gentle fingers into his hair as with an agonized slowness he wrapped his arms around her waist. His warm breath penetrated her rough shirt.

"If you hadn't been the honorable man you are, Hunter, more lives would have been lost."

His head snapped up, his gaze narrowing, sharp and defensive. His chaotic heartbeat vibrated against the wall of his chest. His breathing accelerated. There was a knowledge in her tone, sympathy in her eyes. It speared a bolt of raw pain straight to his gut.

"You told me last night, Hunter. All of it." Her voice drowned a string of curses. "The guard's vile threats to you, the lieutenant's suicide—" She swallowed and when his gaze fell from hers, her nails dug into the muscle of his shoulder, forcing it back. "And what pushed him to it."

"Jesus!" He couldn't believe he had spoken of it. Worse, he couldn't remember speaking the words to another soul before. And now she knew. She knew! "Oh, Jesus!" He twisted and pushed but she wouldn't release him. "I'm going to be sick!"

"No. You aren't!" She blinked and forced her voice not to wax. "You aren't." Her fingers curved around his ear, and

298

she felt him flinch, clench his teeth as they smoothed beneath his jaw and she tipped his head back. "And neither will I."

He stared.

The fire hissed, smoldering embers dying beneath white ash.

His throat worked suspiciously, his eyes glossy. "Sable." Harsh and low.

"Neither will I, Hunter." Suddenly he sank like a stone before her, pulling her down to his lap and curling her body around him, his arms crushing her to his chest. He buried his face in the soft curve of her throat, breathing her name, breathing in the fresh clean scent of her. Clean. So clean.

The breeze swirled dust, dirt, and pale ash, blending it before banishing it from the cavern. Neither spoke, finding no world beyond their little cave.

Slowly Hunter eased back, taking her with him and indigo eyes collided sharply with storm gray.

"I love—" she began.

Hunter didn't give her a chance to finish and kissed her, hard and deep and long, his hands roughly molding her back and hips, then sweeping up to cup her breasts. She moaned, went liquid against him, wrapping her arms around his neck and pressing her hips to his. It was delicious, it was heaven. He loved her, needed her to know it, but couldn't manage to get the words past the knot in his throat, so he deepened his kiss, his tongue plunging between her parted lips. Hastily he thumbed open the buttons of her shirt, his knuckles brushing the tips of her breasts. She drew back enough to draw air.

"Hunter." A weak protest even to her own ears. "But I've just bathed and dressed."

"I need you, Sable."

Her heart hammered in her chest. The desperate hunger in his eyes rocked her to her feet, his need for her so poignant she felt a chill grind up her spine. He looked as if he'd perish without her.

"Please, Sae." His lips hovered close and Sable melted into him like hot honey.

Hunter couldn't speak, couldn't tell her how much her acceptance meant to him, how much he needed it, needed her. So he showed her, with his hands and lips and his body. She'd become his only link to life, his tangible hope, and he would cherish her for as long as he could. With a reverence that left her breathless Hunter kindled the fires within her, impatient for her cleansing cries of rapture.

Chapter Thirty

Lane Cavanaugh shut the faded cloth-bound book and clutched it to her breast. She closed her eyes, plump tears seeping from the corners. She didn't bother to brush them away. They were tears of grief, for the mother she scarcely knew.

Mama had followed her husband west. A weak woman, pampered and vain, had performed the only selfless act in her life; she left her daughters in the care of relatives and nannies and traveled with her husband to the frontier, to further his career.

There she had died.

Cholera, Papa had told them. Another lie.

And now Little Hawk suffered for those secrets.

The tears came faster, crisp and laced with self-torture. *I should have taken him,* she agonized, despair burrowing deeper into her heart. She felt abandoned, forsaken, terrified of what had become of her precious son because of Papa's lies.

Doffing his hat, Hunter crouched, then lay flat on the sloping ground, elbows bent as he brought the field glasses to his eyes. Tall buffalo grass shifted on the breeze, hiding them from anyone but the birds.

"See anything?"

He smiled, casting a quick side glance at Sable. "I haven't had the chance yet."

She flushed and rolled on to her back. "Who else knows about this cabin?"

"Just about everyone's made themselves at home in my place." He let that speak.

"Fine time to mention that," she muttered, looking briefly up the lush green slope, then back to him. "Surely Swift Arrow must be there. Where else—?" His expression didn't change. "Oh Hunter, how will we find him and the baby, if he's not?"

He looked at her, magnifiers still poised, and spoke calmly. "If for some reason he had to go, he would leave a message or a sign for me. We'll find them, Sable. I promise."

The tension left her in a subtle wave and Hunter's chest tightened at the absolute confidence she placed in him.

She shifted to her side, head cradled in her palm. "Why doesn't being in a room or tiny cabin affect you like the cave?"

Her directness no longer made him defensive and he kept his tone casual as he surveyed the cabin.

"I guess it was the stone walls and the low ceiling. Libby was just a warehouse, but reeked of everything ever stored there, from slaughtered meat to manure." She wrinkled her nose yet her hand continued to smooth up and down his bicep in a light caress. He shrugged. "Because the charges against me were espionage, I was made an example." He inhaled and let it out in a quick rush. "I was caged in a livestock pen. The cave made me feel trapped again."

He looked at her, and she smiled tenderly, still rubbing his bicep and shoulder, and he felt an odd, almost draining sensation, an emptying that came each time he talked about it. She never interrupted, just let him go on. This woman was good for him, more of a partner, and sometimes too damn smart for her own britches. Tight britches, he reminded with a warm look, then sighted again on the cabin.

"Why did you let me come spying with you?" she said after a moment. "It really is so unlike you to *allow* me along."

He grinned at her petulant tone. "Would you have stayed back?"

"Certainly not!"

"Figured as much." He shrugged. "Just saving myself a headache, that's all."

She whacked him a good one on his back. "It's impolite to say such things to a lady."

He lowered the glasses and leaned close, his gaze sketching her body from head to booted toes, then back up. "Lady, huh? Was that a lady I made love to this morning?" he murmured throatily. "Could have sworn it was a cat I heard purring."

The crisp afternoon air did nothing to ease her fierce blush every time he looked at her like that. And he did it constantly. As if he could strip every scrap of clothing from her body with just that burning stare.

"You really are an incorrigible wretch, Hunter McCracken."

Suddenly his arm snaked out, wrapping around her waist and pulling her flush to his body. "Yeah, but you already knew that," he growled before he kissed her with a searing hunger that left her aching and thoroughly aroused before he leaned back, breathing hard.

"Behave yourself, sir," she scolded breathlessly, smoothing curls from his brow.

"Not a chance." He ducked his head and kissed her again, a wild play of lips and tongues, utterly possessive, erotic. "You don't know what you do to me wearing those tight britches."

But she did. She felt it in the hardness pressed solidly to her hip that sent a sharp tingling heat straight up her thighs to warm the sensitive space between. "You bought them," she tortured mercilessly.

"Guess that gives me the right to take them back?"

His fingers toyed with the button and she gasped, "But I don't have anything else to wear!"

"My point exactly."

His intimate touch brought back a rush of erotic sensations and gentle memories, of the hours he'd made painfully slow love to her in the cave, on the ground and every time since then.

And that crooked grin said he'd enjoy doing it again.

Hers said she'd let him.

"Quit looking at me like that, Sable," he groaned, his hand mapping curves and valleys in rough sweeps, "and I might be able to concentrate on something else besides how damn good it feels to be inside you."

Her cheeks ripened at his bold words. "You started it," she accused righteously. "And shouldn't you be off investigating?" She waved toward the slope.

"Yeah. Right." He hesitated another moment before scooting farther up the incline and sighting through the lens again. Ignoring the tightness in his trousers, it took a full minute for him to regain his concentration. His cabin. Nestled in a cluster of trees on a gentle rise, it bore no luxuries, and it was with respect that any one passing left it still standing. Whoever was in the damn place either knew it was his or was a desperate fool, for the pile of timber was perched smack on the border of the badlands.

"The suspense is killing me, McCracken."

"Ground's torn up more than it should be for one unfamiliar horse."

"You've had some callers. How civilized." He grinned at her dry tone. "What else?"

He shrugged, still squinting through the glasses. "It isn't Indians. They'd know who was in the area before anyone poked a toe over the border, even if that damn smoking chimney wasn't signal enough. And if it was soldiers, the Sioux would hightail it further north. Could be why we haven't seen unshod tracks."

304

"What's that mean to us?"

Us. He liked the sound of that. "Could be a scout. Army's still hot on our trail."

"That's Papa's doing." She sighed, her lips twisting sourly. "He's surpassed the realm of all logic with his actions thus far. It's doubtless anything else he might attempt would surprise me."

He didn't agree or deny it. "Different horses don't mean much either. Swift Arrow's mount might have gone lame, or he might have had to loose the pack animals. The cabin is defenseless, out in the open like it is."

"For an intelligent man, you constructed your cabin in an exceedingly poor location."

He didn't mention that at the time he hadn't cared if he was slaughtered in his sleep. He did now.

He turned to her. "Say you want me, Sable."

Her nose primly tipped the air. "Ladies do not say such words."

"You can to me, Sae." It was a gentle offering, a way into his heart and she wouldn't let it pass.

"Make love to me," she whispered, scooting close, the fragrance of crushed grass perfuming the air between them. "Make love," she repeated, her eyes locked with his, every inch of her face and body telling him how much she loved him, even if he never let her say the words. But she wouldn't give up. "Make *love,*" she said throatily before his mouth touched hers, the intruders in his cabin momentarily forgotten as sweet waves of desire washed over her. It was a tenuous kiss, infinitely gentle, a slow cherishing, lacking in passion, heat, and urgency. A bonding, she thought, her eyes tearing. They kissed as if there weren't soldiers searching for them, famed warriors in the area, trouble in the cabin. She touched her palm to his chest, felt the steady thud of his heart beneath. Strength. Survival. Hope, it beat. Hope, for she never wanted to lose this moment and cradled it carefully to her heart, precious and fragile.

Slowly he drew back, then pressed his forehead to hers, his broad shoulders trembling. Scents mingled, of tobacco and soil and the green carpet beneath them, newborn and fresh. He said nothing, yet there was a peaceful look in his eyes, in the set of his mouth. He shifted, studying her face as if to commit it to memory, then he shimmied up the slope, all business.

Her gaze lovingly toured the rough contours of his face, the crinkled corners at his eyes as he strained to see the enemy. The enemy. It had come down to just the two of them against the Army, her father, Maitland. And she considered that what was important to her a few weeks ago—gowns, bonnets, and socials—were inconsequential now. Killing a couple of human beings to save one's life had that effect on one's character. Seeing Hunter try to take his own brought the barest needs of life down to daily survival. We do as we must. Sable was proud of him, proud he'd survived. He did what was necessary. She ached to heal him, knew he was trying.

But he wanted his freedom.

She wanted a lifetime.

Lord, how could she feel so wonderful and hopeless all at once?

"Why so sad?"

She jolted at the sound of his voice, soft and close. He was lying on his side, staring at her intently. Sable forced her features to smooth out and asked, "What's up there?"

He frowned. It wasn't like Sable to keep her mouth shut if something bothered her, and her avoidance made him uneasy.

"Hell if I know."

Donning his hat, he gestured for her to follow him down the gully where the horse were hobbled and grazing.

"But what if there are others hiding beyond?" she said, dogging his heels. "Did you see any movement?"

"Nope." He tossed the reins over the horse's head, then

looked at her. "I'm going up, alone. No, don't argue with me this time."

Her dander rose. "If you think I'm going to let you ride out there alone you're crazy!" His brows shot up into his forehead. "I apologize, I didn't mean it like that. But I'm a decent shot and you know it. Another pair of eyes and another weapon covering your back isn't going to hurt. Or is your pride still so monstrous you can't let me help you?"

He grinned. "My pride's sufficiently squashed, thank you, ma'am."

She flushed. "Can we draw them out? Fire off a round, something?"

"I'd rather we not alert any more undesirables, Sable."

His tone said he wouldn't let her help and she sighed, resigned.

Her gaze fastened on his open shirt collar for so long he frowned. "Hey," he tipped her head back. "What's this?"

Her eyes glistened with unshed tears. "I'm frightened, Hunter. Little Hawk has been without a mother for so long and you said yourself Swift Arrow wasn't used to babies, and I miss my nephew so much my arms ache to hold him. She stomped her foot, scraping at her tears with the back of her hand. "I swore not to become a blathering ninny, but I worry what awful surprises are up there. What if someone attacked and Swift Arrow is hurt or dead? Little Hawk might be dead. What if someone's waiting just for this opportunity to hurt you?" Her eyes begged him. "Please. Can't we just wait it out?"

He shook his head. "The chance the Army will find this cabin and Swift Arrow first is too much to risk."

"But what if—"

Hunter captured her mouth, silencing her. She was frightened for him, he realized, and couldn't blame her, not after what he'd put her through. She was suddenly wild in his arms, driving her fingers into his hair, knocking off his hat,

307

her kiss hot and consuming, her lithe body grinding against his. He couldn't get enough of her.

"Be careful." She trembled against him, with fear and the power of her desire. Fiercely she gripped his arms. "Please, please, be careful."

"I'll be back, Sae. I swear it." A single tear fell and moved slowly down her cheek. He tried hard to ignore it. "Stick to the plan and don't move from here," he warned against her lips, then moved out of her embrace. Her hand slithered down his chest, reluctant to give into the separation, then she grasped her horse's bridle and nodded jerkily. "Wait here until I signal you," he said, scooping up his hat.

"I *have* learned *something* on this trip, Hunter."

Her spunk was back, and he felt better about leaving her alone. "I know, but it'll be dark soon. You have your gun and knife?" She brushed aside the blanket draped over her shoulders, then modeled her boot to prove it, though he'd asked her twice already today. "Good girl."

He checked his gun, slipped the strap of his field glasses over her head, then donned his battered hat. He was just swinging up into the saddle when he heard her voice, wet with tears.

"I love you, Hunter McCracken, whether you like it or not."

His heart did a quick slam to his stomach. His eyes met hers with the sharpness of a sabre cut, yet his expression spoke the tenderness of more than lovers.

"No accounting for taste, is there?" he murmured in a tone that sounded strained.

"I've widened my palette."

He leaned down and kissed her again, then wheeled around toward the cabin, clearing her image from his mind. He needed his wits.

The palamino took him the half mile closer in moments, but he still cautiously skirted the cabin, moving on foot to briefly check for horses stashed behind. Then he rode out in plain sight, dismounting before his scarcely-used home as if nothing was wrong. But there was. Swift Arrow would not be so careless as to allow smoke to give him away.

Withdrawing his pistol, he slowly thumbed back the hammer. Cautiously he stepped onto the porch and weathered boards creaked as he raised his leg to kick open the door.

He never got the chance. The shot splintered the wood door, penetrating his side like a streak of fire and knocking him off the porch. His head cracked against the hard ground and he heard a baby's shrill cry before everything went black.

Chapter Thirty-one

Gun cocked and ready, ignoring the foolishness that told her the danger inside was greater than even he expected, she kneed the beast harder, leaning over its neck as the charger took the head.

Don't be dead, please don't.

But she'd seen it; she'd seen her worst nightmare through the field glasses, heard the shot, then watched helplessly as he fell. It repeated continuously in her mind until she could scarcely breathe past her tears. Sawing back on the reins, she slid from the saddle, her heart dropping into her stomach as she ran to where he lay awkwardly across the step, dark crimson staining his green shirt. With an agonized cry she fell to her knees beside him, staunching the flow of blood with her palm and calling his name.

He didn't move. Tears blurring her vision, she glanced to the open cabin door and saw nothing. Her gaze jerked back to his wound, the chest that did not rise. His blood colored her hands, oozed between her fingers, dripping steadily onto the dirt. He couldn't be dead. He couldn't!

"Hunter?" Every cell in her body quaked fear as she pressed her ear to his chest, listening for a heartbeat. She couldn't hear it; hers was drumming too loudly. "Don't die, Hunter," she begged between sobs, trembling fingers frantically searching again at his throat, his wrist, her eyes straining to see his chest move. "I love you, damn it! Don't you dare die!"

The click of a pistol hammer rang in her ear, and she froze.

"Leave him." Her eyes shifted enough to see the gun barrel poised at her temple. "He's dead, and if he ain't—slow is fine with me. Get up."

Vaguely she realized the intruder must have circled around behind her for her not to have seen him. She didn't know who it was, didn't recognize the voice or a reason why he'd done this, yet knew in that moment she could actually kill him, and enjoy doing it.

When she didn't move immediately he pointed the pistol at Hunter's forehead, and Sable screamed, "Noooo!" knocking it away as she straightened. Her eyes remained fixes on Hunter. If there was a chance he breathed. A chance. But he was shot in the stomach. Droplets of his blood fell from her fingertips, splattering on her boots. He would die without a doctor, and there wasn't one for two hundred miles. Her head swam with dizziness, and her gaze shifted to the horse, Hunter, his pistol inches from his fingertips, hers cocked and lying near his knee, and in wild desperation she lunged for it. The man fired, the shot spinning Hunter's weapon off the wood step and releasing its charge into the dirt.

"Inside." He gestured sharply with the pistol, and when Sable turned her head she came face to face with Nate Barlow.

"You!"

"Fancy that, huh?" He smiled thinly, showing blackened teeth. His gun poked her chest. "Now, do as I say or there'll be three dead."

The minute he said it, fresh panic coated her.

A baby cried and her head snapped toward the pitiful sound.

"Little Hawk," she gasped and started past him, but he caught her arm, shoving the barrel under her chin.

"Slowly," he warned, forcing her to gingerly step over

Hunter and into the darkness of the cabin. Her foot hit something solid, and she looked down. Swift Arrow lay sprawled across the floor in a pool of his own blood. A low moan escaped her and she bent to help him, but Barlow jerked on her arm and dug the gun deeper. She swallowed, her gaze searching the cabin for the baby.

"Little Hawk," she whispered to where he lay on a rough wood bed. "Let me go to him," she pleaded, struggling, her arms aching to hold him. "Let me go!"

He seemed to mull over his options against it, then finally released her. She flew to the bed, gathering the boy in her arms, tearing his wrappings open as she examined his body for wounds. He was chubby and healthy and would die if she didn't get him away.

Her gaze shot to Barlow, who stared at her with a self-satisfied smirk. "Why are you doing this?" She clutched the child beneath her chin, her body shaking violently as she inched toward the door.

"Cause I can." His chuckle turned to a fit of coughing.

Swift Arrow moaned, shifting minutely, and Sable's hopes leaped. Nate cursed and aimed his gun.

"NO!" She put herself between the Cheyenne and the gun. "Please, no. I'll do anything you want. Don't shoot him!"

Bloodshot eyes briefly looked her over from head to toe. "Anything?" He pulled back the hammer, his tongue snaking out to lick his lips.

"Yes! Yes! Only don't shoot," she screamed, scaring the baby.

Barlow shrugged, swiping the back of his hand across his mouth. He didn't care anyhow; he wasn't bargaining.

Sable looked down at Little Hawk nestled in her arms and choked back a scream. He was covered with Hunter's blood. Her gaze shifted to her love, and her heart crumbled with utter hopelessness. She prayed and prayed, yet even if he wasn't dead, he couldn't help her or the baby. She inched toward the door. Barlow fired a round into the floor, and she flinched. The baby screamed, pitiful and piercing.

"Ain't a smart squaw, are yah?" he snarled, and Sable realized he still held the image of her when they'd first met. The dye was nearly gone!

Barlow moved around the cabin, his limp pronounced, yet he never took his glassy eyes off her, nor did his hold on the heavy pistol falter as he dug his hand into the packs.

"Where is it?"

"I don't know what you're talking about," she said as he jammed his hand into another pack, then dumped its contents onto the table. He searched the pile of supplies, scattering them to the floor. "Where is it, God damnit?" he bellowed, and the instant he took his eyes off her, she darted for the door. He fired, the bullet thunking into the wall near her shoulder. She froze, head bowed, baby protected.

"Next one is in your back. Now gimme the damn gold."

Sable whirled about, eyes wide. He did this for gold? "I don't have any."

He chambered another bullet, the click pinching her nerves. "Lying'll jest git ya killed."

"It—it must be in there." She nodded to one of the packs she recognized as her own.

Barlow dragged it to the table and overturned it, knocking items on to the floor until he found the small leather pouch. He hefted the sack and glared at her through thick lidded eyes. "Where's the rest?"

"Rest?"

He aimed the gun again at Swift Arrow and she hated him more for using his life to wield power over her. "Hunter must have some left. We spent it on provisions," she said in a rush.

Barlow gathered supplies from the other packs and stuffed them into one, deciding to get the rest of the gold when they were outside. He slung a pack onto his shoulder. "Lose the kid." She hesitated. "Do it," he shouted. "Or I put a hole in the Injun." His arm lengthened to accommodate the threat.

313

"I can't just leave him!" Sable knew if she relinquished Little Hawk, he would die without proper care. Her gaze jumped around the room for a solution; to Hunter scarcely visible through the doorway, Swift Arrow dying at her feet and back to Little Hawk. She lifted her gaze. "He stays with me."

"Get rid of the brat or I will." He dropped the pack and lurched forward to take the baby.

She twisted, shielding Little Hawk against the curve of her shoulders and chest.

Nate Barlow was out of patience. Someone was bound to hear those shots, he thought, as he dug his hand between her and the kid, grasped the boy's arm and buckskin shirt and yanked.

Little Hawk squealed, yet Sable held tight, kicking out, her booted foot connecting with Barlow's shin. He howled in agony, and she darted for the exit and tripped, falling to the floor, shifting her body in time to protect the baby. The impact knocked her breathless, and the air died in her throat when Barlow leaned down and pressed the barrel to the back of the infant's head.

"Wanna see how fast his teeny little brains splatter?"

It was an easy threat, composed and casual, like a call for dinner. It sent a fresh streak of terror up her spine. He would do it without compunction. He would do it for gold that didn't exist. Little Hawk was safer away from this greedy maniac. Shaking her head, Sable struggled to stand on weak legs and placed the baby in the center of the bed, cushioning him snugly with a tattered quilt. He was so small and helpless, she thought, her blood-stained hands trembling as she stroked his downy head. Suddenly Barlow's arm slapped around her waist, jerking her back from the bed. She went wild, screaming, kicking, and scratching at anything she could reach, her battle savage and relentless as if by her efforts alone she could make the child safe and Hunter alive.

The gun dug deeper into her ribs as he dragged her from

cabin. Stumbling backward, she tripped over Hunter's inert body before Barlow dumped her on the ground.

"Stupid ass bitch," he growled, "I'm 'bout tired of wastin' good bullets to keep you in line," then kicked her in the stomach. Sable curled into the pain, reaching out to Hunter who lay less than a foot from her, but Barlow ground his heel viciously onto her fingers. A putrid odor filled her nostrils as he grabbed her by the hair, forcing her to her feet. Agony shot up her side. The sour smell lingered.

She stomped on his injured leg. He screamed, firing a bullet into the ground and releasing her so hard she stumbled forward. Sable ran. He fired twice, missed, and her feet tore across the prairie, tall grass slapping her calves. He had to reload, she thought frantically and pressed to her limit, muscles screaming. Hoofbeats thundered, vibrating the ground. The horse hit her broadside, knocking her off her feet and she tumbled, rolled, flailing for purchase.

He reined up before her, nearly trampling her head.

"Get up," he said, aiming the pistol. She crawled to her hands and knees as he dismounted. Before she climbed to her feet, he hooked leather over her hand.

She twisted and jerked her hand, the other flailing to keep him from securing the leather. He caught her wrist, twisting sharply backward and jerking it up to her shoulder blades.

Sable arched, and his voice hissed in her ear.

"There's more, ain't there?" He gave her a yank. "Lots more, I figure."

If she said yes, he'd force her to show it to him. If she denied the existence of the gold, he'd kill them all in a rage. She nodded mutely.

"Yeah, thought so," he chuckled, securing her bonds to a length of rope, then tying it to his saddle. He mounted, his gravelly laughter peeling across the plains as he rode toward the badlands.

* * *

The painted warriors stood over the white man's sleeping mat and stared at the boy-child wiggling on the blanket. His heart smiled at the innocent sight yet his face revealed nothing as he bent and lifted the babe in his arms, immediately examining him for the source of his wounds. Finding him unharmed, he strode out of the shack, nodding to the two braves who waited patiently on their horses.

The other braves frowned at the child and the warrior shrugged at the silent question, then wrapped the bloodied infant snugly in the tattered quilt. He swung up onto the bare Appaloosa's back, his knees directing the steed as he cradled the young life close to his chest.

Chapter Thirty-two

Smoke burned his lungs and soft rhythmic chants filled his ears. He struggled to move and sharp needles of pain lacerated his head and ribs, hot and rippling. He couldn't muster the strength beyond breathing. Fetid odors filled his nostrils, familiar but not comforting. Warm hands bathed his naked skin, the water silky-cool.

"Sable," he called out and the hands stilled.

"Rest," a feminine voice murmured and he fought to open his eyes.

"Violet Eyes?" tumbled weakly from his dry lips as he battled the haze that kept him from reality.

Beads softly clicked, voices whispered, gentle hands restrained him as he twisted with memories, then helped him as a cool liquid dribbled between his lips. His weakened body absorbed it, a painless cloud covering him, taking him away from the agony—of his body and his heart. He had to get to her. He had to.

Brooding, his face deeply creased with worry, Swift Arrow sat cross legged with his back propped against a mound of furs. His head pounded unmercifully, and he fidgeted with the blanket, then plucked tiny stones from the floor, angrily tossing them into the small fire in the center of the teepee. He cursed himself for allowing a pitiful little weasel like Barlow to get the jump on him when he'd gone off to investigate the source of a foul odor. The dead animal he thought was outside the cabin was Barlow's gangrenous leg. The skinny bastard, he gnashed, never imagining he'd survive, let alone come back.

It was a warrior's failure alone when he underestimated his enemy, his father had warned him. He'd been too long in the white world. His father would be ashamed of his carelessness, his mind gone soft over his growing love for the boy. Agonizing over the babe he'd been trusted to care for and lost, he rubbed his face, leaned his aching head back and did battle with his emotions. He knew the unbelievable fear of a parent with a missing child, and it cut his heart open with pain. He could do nothing.

And what had become of the woman? Was she with Hunter? Had she been killed by the Pawnee weeks before or by Barlow? Had Hunter come alone to the cabin? Or was she here now, somewhere beyond the hide wall of the lodge? He hoped, but no one had come to tell him one way or the other. He snatched up another stone and threw it, impatient to stretch his muscles and seek out information, yet he forced restraint, knowing his body wouldn't allow such a luxury.

Abruptly, the flap to the lodge opened, light flooding in, making him flinch. A tall muscular man ducked inside, a child cradled in his arm.

Swift Arrow sat up straighter, ignoring the stab of pain in his head. "He's been here all this time?" Joy laced his voice. "No one told me." His eager gaze followed the warrior as he settled down across from him.

"He is fit." The warrior offered the boy. "Is he your son?"

Swift Arrow shook his head, regretting the painful motion as he accepted the child and cuddled him familiarly. "I don't know who his parents are," he said, seeing for himself he was fine. "Perhaps Standing Cougar can tell you. He traveled with a woman when I last saw him. Pawnee captured her and I have cared for this little warrior—"

"Warrior?" He peered close.

"Can you not see he is of the People?"

"I suspected, but his eyes—"

"Are the color of rain clouds," Swift Arrow interrupted with a smile and the warrior stiffened, his black gaze piercing the babe. "Standing Cougar?" the Cheyenne asked.

The other shrugged. "He still breathes. The wound on his head is worse than the one in his side."

Swift Arrow gingerly rubbed the stitched crown of his skull. "We are fortunate you found us."

The warrior made no comment to that, gazing intensely at the boy. "My brother's wife has recently given him a son. She offered to care for the boy until you are well, if that is your wish." Swift Arrow agreed. "He is hungry?" For the first time the warrior smiled as the baby sucked frantically on Swift Arrow's knuckle.

"He is *always* hungry." The Cheyenne smiled broadly, then glanced up. "You did not find a goat?"

The warrior nodded. "That is how I discovered you. The animals are familiar and pack together."

"And the woman?"

"We found no woman." Swift Arrow scowled at this news.

"Damn it to hell!" Swift Arrow mashed a hand over his face.

"You sound like the white man," the warrior muttered disgustedly, coming to his feet.

"Half of me is," Swift Arrow countered on a grin.

The warrior's lips moved to keep back a smile. "This I have learned to forgive in you, my friend," he said, then headed toward the open flap.

"Does he know she's not here?"

Beads and flowing black hair shifted over bare shoulders as he shook his head.

"Don't tell him until he's well enough to travel." Swift Ar-

319

row eased back onto the furs. "He'll go mad when he finds out."

"This woman," the warrior asked hesitantly, "she is of the People?"

"No. And I don't think this boy is hers, either."

"A white woman!" He said it like a demand, his expression fierce as Swift Arrow confessed his own suspicions about the woman and her background. "I understand the twisted ways of the white eyes, Swift Arrow." There was impatience in his voice, speaking of the damaged reputations and unjust prejudices. "Why would such a woman travel here," his hand sliced the air, indicating the Nation, "with a babe not of her blood?" Silently he considered the danger this reckless female would bring to his tribe and cursed her. "Has she stolen this child from its mother?"

Swift Arrow stared down at the baby on his lap. "Only she can answer that, and we'll never know the truth if we don't find her."

"We?" He scoffed caustically. "Do not give your problems to me, Cheyenne. I have enough of my own," he murmured, his dark gaze touching on the child before he ducked out of the lodge.

"That was Black Wolf, in case you were wondering," Swift Arrow said to the boy. The infant punched the air, gurgling a puff of bubbles. "I know. Not a happy man."

The column of uniformed troopers surged across the grassy plains, immediately surrounding the small cabin. The leader dismounted and strode into the shack, gun ready. His gaze fanned the interior, halting on the blood-stained floor and bed linens. He shuddered, anger boiling in his veins as he withdrew a paper and tossed it on the rough-hewn table. He started to leave, then turned back and with a growl of rage, withdrew his knife and stabbed the parchment to the wood. The thin blade vibrated as he strode from the cabin and

320

swung up onto his horse. Pale blue eyes pierced the wood walls as if trying to understand what had happened. He raised his arm and wheeled about, his troops following obediently, in perfect military order.

Nate Barlow glanced back over his shoulder and smiled thinly. Ought to cut up her leg up a bit, he thought, so she really knows how hard walking can get, then decided he had better ideas for her. Tied to his saddle with a length of hemp around her wrists, she intermittently stumbled and ran as he mercilessly switched from trot to walk to canter. Once he'd galloped outright, but it dragged her across the ground too much. He didn't want her dead, just too tired to fight him.

He didn't like women who fought.

Chapter Thirty-three

Eyes—dark and wet-black as pebbles in the bottom of a clear pool watched the visitors depart. Standing Cougar's avoidance of him made him suspicious, yet he could not blame his white brother for wanting to leave so soon before he was healed. His woman was missing, perhaps dead.

Yet, he worried as much for his friends as he did for the boy. *Eyes the color of rain clouds,* Swift Arrow had said. How many times had he spoken the same words to his wife? He had to know of this woman, he thought anxiously. He had to see her.

He'd sent scouts out when Swift Arrow first mentioned her, but they had not returned. None were to interfere, for vengeance was Standing Cougar's, just as his own was against the bluecoats.

"You're a God-damn white woman!" he shouted, round eyes gawking at the pale flesh surrounding his palm. "A white woman!"

Sable winced as his grip on her breast tightened. Pinned beneath him, her hands tied behind, she could do nothing as he tore her shirt from her trousers and with a starving eagerness, inspected further the shade of her skin. Humiliation swept over Sable, and she struggled against his groping.

322

Suddenly he landed hard on top of her, his hands fumbling between them. "I ain't never had me a white woman," he panted, his breath sour in her face, his skin and clothes reeking of sweat and dirt, of months without washing.

"Rape me and I'll never tell you," she rasped in a deadly voice. A bargain with the devil, she thought, yet she would say anything to keep him at bay. She refused to die with this man's touch on her body.

Barlow stilled, brows furrowed as he considered whether a white woman would even know the location of the gold mine.

"Never," she repeated, watching his eyes and seeing greed battle with his lust.

Nate climbed off her and fastened his pants. "Where's it at?"

Weakly Sable rolled to her side and struggled to kneel. With her hands tied, wrists raw and bleeding, it was difficult, but she managed.

"North."

"Yer lyin'!" He backhanded her across the face and Sable scarcely felt it beyond the blood wetting her lips. She was grateful for the moisture in her mouth after two days without food or water. The knees of her denim pants were torn, the exposed skin beneath scraped raw and ground with dirt. Blood trickled down her calves and into her boots. She didn't care really, not for herself, but she wanted to stay alive long enough to draw him deep into Indian territory, where someone was bound to kill him for merely trespassing. It was all she had left.

Hunter had died for her.

Hunter. His name echoed a hollow ache in her chest and she closed gritty eyes, her body so parched she couldn't even shed a tear for him. Hunter. Grief pierced her soul, stirring an anger so cold it made her tremble. At that moment, she cared less if she survived this, except long enough to avenge his death.

"You best tell me——" Barlow made to belt her a good one.

"I don't believe that's the wisest of moves, do you?" she said, shaking her hair from her face and glaring up at him. "Do you?" Her voice cut with a razor's edge.

Barlow's arm hovered in the air for a moment before he lowered it to his side. Them purple eyes of hers had a way of stopping a body in his tracks, telling him if he smacked her again she'd gladly take the location to her grave.

Jerking her to her feet, he shoved her toward the horse.

"How far north?"

"I'll tell you when you get there."

"I will search for more signs," Swift Arrow said and Hunter looked up from where he sat on the ground, the baby nestled in his arms. He nodded, squeezing his eyes shut and rubbing at the pain dancing in his skull as Swift Arrow disappeared into the thicket. He held the child gently despite his discomfort and drew from the peace of innocence Little Hawk gave him. He fed the infant with the milk bladder, his body unwillingly relaxing as he watched the boy suckle. He was a good little fella, never fussed or cried, though he knew Sable and Swift Arrow's teachings were now ingrained within the child not to cry unless hurt, for it would alert the enemy.

The scruffy goat grazed near his feet, tethered tight and close. Swift Arrow strapped the animal across the rump of his mount when the pace was too rapid. It was the only hindrance in finding Sable, aside the pain of their wounds. He had but to imagine what Sable was suffering, and his own comfort became inconsequential.

She thinks I'm dead, his stomach twisted in knots, tormenting him. Jesus, how it must have torn her apart to leave Little Hawk behind with two "dead" men. Images terrorized his sanity, stealing his hope that she still lived. Had the bastard shot her, too? Was she dying now? Did he rape her while I lay bleeding? Was she hungry? Was she thirsty? Warm? Cold? Was she lying somewhere out here, left for dead, picked by vultures or taken by another tribe? *She'll fight.* She'll try to escape, Hunter told himself. Sable wouldn't give up, not easily. She'd proven that to him already. But what odds did a woman have against a lunatic with a loaded gun?

The boy cooed and Hunter looked down. Wide eyed, the hint of a smile on his tiny bow-shaped mouth, the infant gazed up expectantly.

"Hi," Hunter said conversationally. "Dinner all right?" The babe cooed and gurgled, and Hunter freed him from the snugly wrapped blanket and let him wriggle. His calloused hands rubbed the soft flawless skin of the babe's legs and Hunter's smile widened.

Setting the milk bladder aside, he lifted the boy in front of him, teasing his exposed tummy with his bristled chin. Plump legs kicked the air and a giggle escaped the child, melting with Hunter's deep chuckle. Little Hawk grabbed the brim of his hat and tried to stuff it in his mouth and Hunter settled him on his lap, prying the tiny fingers loose, marveling at the small perfection of the baby's hand.

That was how Swift Arrow found him, playing with the boy, jiggling and tossing him, making ridiculous chatter. He smiled. He'd never seen Hunter relax and escape even for the slightest moment and the subtle changes in his friend suddenly became more pronounced.

"Now you see why I will hunt for a wife."

Hunter glanced up, a flush creeping to his pale face. "How's that?"

"I want lots of those." He nodded to the boy.

"I never thought someone so puny could make me feel—I don't know—good."

"Surprised me, too."

"I can't get over how soft and small they are," he murmured, studying the miniature eyes and nose.

"And that the road from stomach to bottom seems endless."

Hunter smirked. "They have to grow somehow."

"You are an authority now?" Swift Arrow grinned.

"Jesus, no." He positioned the boy on his lap and gave him his dinner as Swift Arrow sat down across from them.

"Can you imagine how her sister must feel? Wondering what has become of your Sable and her boy?"

"She's going mad," Hunter murmured quietly, his expression sharply creased, brows drawn tight. The feeling was familiar.

"I still cannot believe your Violet Eyes is Richard Cavanaugh's daughter."

Hunter's gaze flew to Swift Arrow's. "Or his attitude toward his grandson?"

"That's what troubles me. He has always known of my heritage, and it's never seemed to bother him."

"I think it has something to do with his dead wife." Hunter put the boy to his shoulder and gently patted his back, his broad hand covering him. "I remember playing poker with Richard once and he mentioned Caroline." Hunter drew in air and let it out slowly. "We'd been drinking all night and his tongue got away from him. I don't think he ever wanted anyone to know about Caroline."

"Is Sable aware of this?" Swift Arrow asked after he relayed a sketchy story of Caroline Cavanaugh's kidnapping, the severe starvation and beating she suffered at the hands of the Crow. And the bastard babe she bore.

"I don't know," Hunter shrugged. "Maybe. But I think that's why he doesn't want this little guy around. Perhaps he saw it happening again, with Lane. It's a shame. The circumstances of his birth aren't his fault."

Swift Arrow nodded. His Indian heritage was lost in his mother's features shaping his face. The only mark of his father's people was the shade of his hair and his dark skin. But it went deeper than what the eyes could hold: the Cheyenne gave him an inner power; the English side had given him nothing. His mother's people tolerated him because he was

326

an heir, a link of lineage—nothing more. All the education and refinement in the world hadn't changed that.

"When are you going to get the nerve to tell me what you found?"

Swift Arrow looked up from where he'd been drawing in the dirt and recognized the restraint Hunter showed.

Hunter leaned forward a bit. "Out with it, pal."

"We're at least two days behind them—if it's them we're following."

Swift Arrow's doubts showed in his expression, but Hunter ignored it. He had to. He had nothing else to hope on, if it wasn't. "We already knew that. What else?" he said impatiently.

Swift Arrow mentally tallied what he'd found: uniform tracks of several shod horses, fresh dung, the remains of poorly disguised camp fires.

"We aren't the only people searching this way. There's a squad in the area."

Hunter secured the boy in his cradle board and stood, slipping it into place on his back.

"Those soldiers might be looking for her or they could be after Black Wolf. We saw enough burned wagons and dead settlers to know the Army's out for blood payment."

Swift Arrow came to his feet. "I think he's pulling her behind his horse." Hunter's head snapped up, his skin paling to near white as his features went slack.

Walking.

Across the badlands!

Dear God.

All those miles! He gripped the saddle horn, and the tighter he clasped the harder his expression grew, masking his turmoil.

Swift Arrow did the same, ignoring the little voice in his head telling him Hunter had the right to know—now. But he didn't have the heart to say it, for the Cheyenne believed Nate Barlow dragged a dead woman behind him.

327

Chapter Thirty-four

Behind the men seated around the fire, the painted hides of the teepee depicted tales of great bravery, coup counted on the enemy, battles won with skill and cunning. Masculine voices murmured softly, drifting up to mingle with the *parafleches* and ceremonial weapons hanging from the central pole.

"Leave this white man to his own fate," a brave said after the scout had delivered the location of the woman and her captor.

Black Wolf's glare sharpened on the young Sioux across from him. The youth considered only the shade of skin—not the blood of the People running in the child's veins or the helpless woman.

"Standing Cougar has proven his loyalty in the past," Crooked Hand said, his voice gravely with age, stone gray hair shifting across his stooped shoulders as he studied the council members. "We are wrong if we leave him with only a wounded Cheyenne to take back what is his. They carry a child of the blood, a young warrior." He directed the comment to the outspoken youth. "Can we turn our backs to this and sleep peacefully?" Crooked Hand relaxed, fading back. "These are my thoughts."

"What of the soldiers? Perhaps it is a trap. Perhaps they know we would help because of the child," Long Knife pointed out. "Standing Cougar and Swift Arrow both have worn the blue coats," he spat the words as if they left a foul taste in his mouth. "Do we accept that risk?"

Men argued among themselves, and as voices rose to a fevered pitch, Black Wolf's deep calm tone cut through the conversations. "Long Knife speaks the truth." The noise died swiftly. "Yet when Standing Cougar no longer walked among us, he did not betray Lakota." Black Wolf paused, waiting for this to be accepted for its worth. "The blue coats steal from Lakota what cannot be owned. Mother Earth, Father Sky, our freedom, our homes. Some we will take back, others we will never hold again." His voice tightened with a mix of anger and resignation. "But do we let them take our children as well?"

In the silence of thought, Black Wolf stood, his gaze glancing over the others as each man nodded. The boy, whether Sioux or Cheyenne, Comanche, Ute or Blackfoot, it did not matter. The life of a young warrior, the future of their race, was at risk. Nothing else need be considered.

Black Wolf slipped out of the hide lodge. No voice rose to dispute his right to see to the matter himself. Standing Cougar was part of his family. His pace never faltered as he strode to his own lodge to inform his sister of the scout's news and the council's decision.

"It is Lane." Black Wolf scoffed at yet another of his sister's predictions, and Morning Sun's lips curved, her gaze on her work. "I knew she would return."

"So you have been telling me."

The maiden transferred the ground meal to a pouch, ignoring her brother's impatient sigh. "And for seven moons you have made war on the white man with a vengeance. They have felt your rage, my brother, as have I felt the sting of your tongue."

A muscle flexed in his jaw. "Are you saying it has been difficult to live in my lodge?"

"Yes," she answered, boldly meeting his gaze. "Lane did not leave willingly, as you believe."

"You cannot know! No one but she can say this."

Morning Sun bit the inside of her mouth to keep her voice even. They had traveled this path many times before. That he had not taken another woman to his sleeping mat was proof enough that his heart was still taken.

"You were not always here, my brother—you did not see how hard she worked to please you, to shed the white ways and become Sioux."

"My wife was not Sioux," he shot back.

"Here she was." Morning Sun touched her fist to the spot over her heart.

He sent her a disgruntled look. "White Eyes cannot be trusted. For *if* this woman Red Bow saw is Lane," his tone said he didn't believe it was, "why did Standing Cougar not tell me of her?"

"Perhaps he has made a promise of silence with her? Or maybe she is frightened of you." His expression clearly spoke he did not like that idea, for he'd taken great patience to prove to Lane he would not harm her. "Or perhaps we are all mistaken, and it is not the *fire of your heart* wandering the land unprotected."

At the mention of his private name for his wife, Black Wolf glared at his sister, but she was unaffected by the menacing stare. She had grown up with it, and though frightening, she knew it to be harmless.

"Swift Arrow does not believe she is the mother of the boy."

"But you will see this for yourself." It was a statement and even as she spoke she slipped provisions into a parafleche. She pulled the string tight then held it out to him. He did not accept it. "Will you not help Standing Cougar?" He stared at her, his brow, black and smooth as a raven's wing shot up. "There is a chance that the Great Spirits have smiled upon you again, Black Wolf," she reasoned quietly, dropping the

330

parafleche at his feet. When he did not respond she twisted away, searching beneath a pile of buffalo hides. "And perhaps with a child," she added, producing the worn blanket she herself had made.

Black Wolf snatched the blanket, turning it over in his grasp, a chill spreading over his skin. The markings were too distinct and familiar to ignore. It was the only item Lane had taken with her when she left him.

"The boy was wrapped in it."

His gaze flew to hers. His fist clenched the butter-soft fabric, sudden anticipation sweeping through him, the same glorious sensation he experienced in the happier days before Lane vanished, knowing she was there, waiting, eager for his company, his touch. In a small corner of his mind he saw the boy nestled in Lane's arms, himself lying beneath a tree beside them. The peaceful image shattered the instant he recalled the woman's vague description and the strength of Swift Arrow's suspicions. He smashed the pleasure down, twisted it to anger.

"This means nothing," he growled, tossing the blanket aside. "Lane has the right to choose another mate." That it could be Standing Cougar made him boil with outrage.

"Ahh, I see you have not made up your mind whether your wife is white or of the People," she said knowingly, then boldly put up a hand to stay his next retort. "Will you listen to your wife's words? Hear more than your pride? I warn you, brother, do not bring her back to be another reason to bleed. For I am weary of it."

"You have no say in the matter, woman," he snarled.

Morning Sun came to her feet gracefully, her small body tense with her own frustration as she stared up at him. "I think you should remember, *war chief,* how miserable an unhappy woman can make your lodge." With that she ducked out the opening of the teepee. An instant later she heard the clank of kettle and utensils colliding, then a white man's curse. Picking up a water skin, she walked sedately toward the stream, her smile hidden in the frame of straight black hair. Morning Sun's heart lifted with expectation. Black Wolf still loved his wife, no matter how deep he had buried his heart.

He kept his eyes on the woman lying curled on her side in the dirt. Nate Barlow tipped the flask to his lips and slugged back more whiskey. He glanced at the mountain a few miles off and grinned, swiping the back of his hand across his mouth. He'd see gold in his pockets by the end of the week. He'd swear it. Rubbing his leg, he gingerly pushed off his boot, pain shooting up to his thigh. He stared at the blackened skin of his toes and foot to beyond the ankle. If he didn't know better, he'd swear that shit was climbing. Shoulda had it doctored, he thought, wiggling his toes and finding they moved only in his mind.

Bleary eyed darted again to the woman when she groaned and he cursed himself for flinching. Dang if she didn't make him nervous. She'd already stuck him in the arm once with a knife. How the fool bitch kept it hidden in her boot all this time he didn't know, but he didn't trust her unless she was tied up. She was wily and stared at him a lot when she should be balling her eyes out, begging for food and water.

Instead she told him the Army would be searching, the Indians would track him, and she'd laughed at his undisguised fear when she'd told him whose kid he left behind: Black Wolf's.

An anxious prickle danced up his spine when he imagined what that savage would do to him, and Barlow cautiously glanced back over his shoulder, searching the forest. Feeling stupid, he shook off the sensation and took another swig of liquor. They'd made it through the badlands with no sign of anyone tracking them. Yeah. The Injun and Hunt were dead. Ain't nobody gonna find him. Just the same, he'd hightail it to Mexico, soon as he had enough gold.

She climbed to her feet, stumbling clumsily, and Barlow

sent her a suspicious glare. Her gaze dropped to his bare foot, then slowly returned to his face. She smiled thinly and Barlow felt her pleasure like a damp chill. No food and walking for the last fifty miles hadn't taken the starch out of her attitude.

"Untie me . . . so I might . . . relieve myself." Her raspy voice grated his jangled nerves.

After a moment's consideration he gingerly eased the boot back on, picked up his gun and limped to her, dragging his leg behind him. Weren't no fun watching her piss all over herself anyhow. "Stay where ah kin see you," he warned, loosening the bonds, then stepped back when those purple eyes glared pure hatred in his direction. She's ill now, he thought, weak enough with starvation. He smiled, his lust growing. Hell, a good screw never killed anybody. He'd have himself a white woman before night.

Straining not to rub her bloody wrists, Sable walked slowly into the woods. Her step was cautious, each press and lift of her feet sending pain throbbing to every point of her tortured body. She smelled foul, her skin was hot, raw where even her stiff trousers rubbed her hips and thighs. Sable hadn't the strength to stand for as long as it took to relieve herself and leaned against a tree. Several moments passed before she mustered the energy to straighten and right her filthy clothing. She no longer cared that he watched. Pushing dusty matted hair from her face, tangled strands caught on the cuts and callouses covering her palm. She blinked dryly at the mess, plucked hair and a stone from the torn flesh, then staggered to the water's edge. The nose of the gun barrel followed her steps. She could feel it, almost sense the bullet—waiting for the pressure and charge to send it streaking out the metal cylinder and into her body. With nothing else to grasp that didn't threaten her sanity, her mind drew on it, making her keenly aware of that gun, how he wore it, held it, how often he checked the load. And he knew it.

He hungered for the gold.

He was weak, dying from gangrene.

333

And she didn't have much time before he'd find out she was lying, and kill her, too.

Grief struck her, the blow swift and nearly unexpected, choking her breath. A bitter hardness lodged in her throat. Hunter. Hunter. His death tortured her. A dry barren space lay where her heart had once beaten. Was Swift Arrow dead? Little Hawk? What chance did a baby have? Uncertainty taunted her.

I failed, Laney. I'm sorry.

She swallowed, focused on the river, shoving her pain into the emptiness of her soul as she numbly sloshed into the water. The cold stung her blistered feet as it seeped into her thin-soled boots. She moved deeper, her parched skin screaming to be completely submerged. Bending to cup her first drink in two days made her world tilt wildly.

Her arms flailed frantically for balance before she staggered forward on surer feet. He cackled at her helplessness, but Sable kept moving, seeing her final chance to escape. She sloshed across the water, heard him scream for her to stop. Liquid churned in her wake, dragging at her. Barlow gave chase, his dead leg slowing him down. She sensed the gun aimed at her back, imagined his finger flexing on the trigger as she met the opposite shore.

But she didn't have a child to protect this time, no others who might die if she didn't do as he demanded. Sable ran, her weakness slowing her. She grabbed stubby bushes and tree limbs to pull herself along. Blood throbbed in her temples. Her lungs labored. Each lift of her legs drained her strength. Water splashed, his staccato tred thundering on the bank. He called her ugly names, his voice harsh with angry panic.

Then she heard the gunshot.

Chapter Thirty-five

The bullet whined past her, chipping off a branch somewhere to her left. Her chest heaved, a stitch caught in her side, and she staggered at the barbed thorn of pain, tripping over her own feet. Reaching out, she clutched a thin tree trunk to keep balance, then shoved away.

His blow impacted with the back of her thighs, knocking her off her feet and catapulting her forward before she landed hard on her stomach. She hadn't drawn a breath before Barlow climbed on top of her. Spitting dust and dry grass, she twisted violently, marshalling the dregs of her energy and ramming her boot heel into his gangrenous leg. He howled in agony, and she scrambled for freedom, but anger made him fast, and he clapped a hand on her hair, coiling a fistful as he viciously yanked her head back.

"I'm gonna do yah now, bitch," he sneered in her ear just before his fist smashed into the side of her skull. Pain detonated in her temple, her vision darkening. "Ain't nobody gonna know who you was."

A blade scraped her skin, fabric tugged and ripped, and she screamed hoarsely, groping at vines and thick grasses in a desperate attempt to drag herself from beneath him. Air touched her bare flesh of her buttocks and thighs as he shredded her trousers. Then he shoved her legs apart, mashing his naked groin against her, and Sable wished to God he'd shot her.

At the sound of gunfire Hunter's entire body went still as granite as he attempted to judge from where it had come. Then a scream pierced the air and he kneed the horse to the tree line. *That has to be her.*

Swift Arrow was beside him, calling warnings as they cut into the thicket, ducking branches and weaving through the brush. Hunter's heart pounded so loud in his ears he scarcely heard Swift Arrow's plea to give him the baby.

Sable. She was alive.

He'd almost given up.

Swift Arrow grabbed his arm as Hunter slid from the saddle and yanked the cradleboard straps. Hunter handed the boy over then took off, thrashing through the woods. She screamed again and he felt it like a stab to his heart.

He paused just for an instant before the river's edge, then splashed through the cold liquid. Terror clawed hot in his gut. His chest labored, his side burned. His head throbbed and he ran, his anger escalating with every breath he drew into his tired lungs.

Then he saw them. He froze for a split second. Barlow was raping her, trying to—from behind. Years of rage exploded and Hunter lunged, knocking Barlow from her back and sending his broad-knuckled fist into his startled face. Bone separated from cartilage under the first blow, the second shattered it, the third turned it to powder, and he kept pounding until Barlow no longer moved. It wasn't enough.

A sound called him and he immediately twisted toward Sable, swiping a bloody hand beneath his nose as he cautiously staggered toward her. She crawled, her pale bruised body vulgarly exposed.

336

His hand shook as he reached. "Sable?" With infinite care he grasped her shoulder.

"Nooo!" she screamed, scrambling away. "Nooooo!"

"Sable, Sable, Sae." Hunter half crawled, half stumbled to her. "Sable. It's me, darlin'." She kept going, grabbing at vegetation to pull herself along. Yanking up her torn trousers, she hadn't made it completely to her feet when Hunter shouted, "It's me. Hunter!"

She turned sharply, lost her balance, and he was there, sinking to his knees before her.

She fought him.

He held her tightly, saying her name, telling her his, waiting for recognition. As she calmed, he murmured, "It's over, darlin'. It's over," his hands frantically skimming her body, his mind accounting for every cut and bruise, every drop of blood spilled before he pushed her hair from her face to look at her. His insides wrenched at the sight of her numb expression.

Blood trickled from the side of her head as she lifted a hand to his face. "H—Hunter?" There was as much shock as question in her voice while her trembling fingers traced his brow, the shape of his nose, the smoothness of his lips, her movements rough and quick. "You're alive." Her hand scrubbed through his hair, over his shoulders and chest. "But I saw you . . . die," she choked on a panicked sob, as if she still didn't believe he was the living, breathing man before her. "I saw—!" Her hand went to his side, searching for his wound.

"I'm all right." He covered her fingers, brought them to his chest, and Sable clutched his shirt, twisting the fabric in her fists as she stared into his eyes.

Tears fell, one by one.

"Ooohhh God . . ." Her body jerked with hard sobs, her anguish peeking to shatter the last of her control as he cupped her jaw and tremulously pressed his lips to hers. She clung, with mouth and body, sobbing against his lips, her arms clutching his shoulders, his holding her gently when she wished to be crushed. *I grieved for you. I died without you,* she wanted to tell him, but refused to spare the separation.

"I love you," he murmured against the sweetness of her lips, and she cupped his jaw and took his mouth with a blazing need, then buried her face in the curve of his throat, crying harder. "I love you and I'm sorry this happened, Sae. Jesus, I'm sorry." Hunter blinked, his eyes unusually wide as he rubbed her back.

Suddenly she sank bonelessly against him and he frowned. "Sable?" he whispered, but got no response and his heartbeat accelerated as he tilted her head back; it lolled loosely and he flinched, supported her nape, then quickly gathered her in his arms.

Pain tore his side as he climbed to his feet. "Sable, honey? Sable!" Panic cloaked his voice. Staggering under her weight, he adjusted his hold. A distinct click chilled his blood, and he turned. Barlow, his face smeared with blood, crimson oozing from his nose and mouth, leveled a pistol at him. Before Hunter could react beyond stepping out of the line of fire, an arrow whistled through the air, piercing Barlow's shoulder. He screamed, the gun tilted in his grasp, the shaft still quivering as a second arrow whined past Hunter's leg, skewering Barlow's hand. He cried out shortly, coughed as the gun slithered slowly from his fingers. Hunter spun about, though he had no weapon drawn, no free hand to fire. Relief swept him as Black Wolf strode from the woods and briefly, he closed his eyes.

"Thank you," he murmured in Sioux.

Black Wolf tore his gaze from the woman, nodded once, then dragged Barlow from sight.

Hunter's eyes drifted down to Sable's lax features, her loose-limbed body, the wounds so fresh and brutal. A savage ache coiled deep in his chest. It was worse than the Pawnee had done. Her head dangled over his forearm and with his first step, Hunter winced, cradling it gently to his chest as he strode into the river, wading out to his hips. At the touch of the icy water she arched, her shrill cry echoing in his heart as she squirmed in his grasp.

"Easy, love. Easy," he murmured, his voice cracking with tears. Jesus, there wasn't an inch of her left unmarked!

Swift Arrow appeared on the bank and Hunter met his gaze, his expression tortured.

"Look what he did to her!" he agonized, clutching her close. "Look at her!"

Swift Arrow's gaze shifted to Sable and he forced any reaction from his features. Her clothing hung in tatters, exposing patches of white skin scraped, blackened, and rubbed raw; an angry thin red stripe marked her from hip to thigh. Blood trickled over her discolored cheek and jaw. Her torn shirt revealed a greenish bruise on her ribs. Delicate wrists bore rope burns so deep they'd never completely vanish, and even from the distance, he could see debris embedded in her palms and knees. Barlow will suffer for this, the Cheyenne vowed, tightening his grip on the empty bow.

"I will build a shelter," he said flatly, then put action to his words.

Hunter floated her in the water, his knee bent to support her. His hand trembled as he trickled water over her cracked and blistered lips, and Swift Arrow appeared with a fistful of thick bruised leaves of Bouncing Bet, instructing Hunter to use it like soap. Hunter stripped off her clothes, the herb lathering easily as he cautiously cleansed and rinsed her hair and body, his voice a gentle murmur as she cried. Her wrenching sobs never stopped, her eyes never opened, and Hunter firmly ignored her pitiful pleas until her wounds were completely clean. She slipped into unconsciousness by the time he carried her from the river. On the shore Swift Arrow held out a blanket, his face impassive as he draped it over her naked form, then gestured toward the shelter he'd prepared.

"We will leave you."

Hunter's gaze darted to Black Wolf standing a few yards behind. "No, the boy. Bring the boy—in a moment."

"But Hunter—?"

"Bring him, Chris. She has to know he's alive."

Swift Arrow nodded and Hunter moved to the shelter and laid her on the buffalo fur. He wrapped her tightly in the blanket and fur, then lit the wood neatly peaked beside them. Hunter watched her, keenly aware that this was his fault, aware she would forgive him, and knowing selfishly that he would let her. Air shuddered past his lips, and he ground the heels of his palms into his eyes, swallowing repeatedly. Then with a ragged sigh, he slowly lowered his hands.

Swift Arrow had brought all the supplies and packs. There wasn't much in them, Hunter thought, searching for something to bandage her wounds. He had nothing to soothe her raw skin, yet found her last petticoat in the stack of her garments. She'll forgive me for this, too, he thought, tearing it into strips. His mind on his task he never realized that his wound had re-opened and fresh blood stained his shirt.

Newly promoted Noah Kirkwood's head snapped toward the west, his gaze searching the horizon. His eyes saw nothing but green rolling hills lifting to lush mountains in the west. Yet his ears did not mistake the echo of gunfire. He would find her. Discovering exactly who he'd allowed to escape the confines of the fort left him with the burning need to rectify his failure to do his duty, no matter the consequences or the obligation. Holding himself accountable for the incident and anything she suffered as a result, Captain Kirkwood raised his arm and wielded his mount around toward the valley shadowed by the Black Hills, determined no woman would keep him from his duties again.

Sable opened her eyes to see Hunter sitting cross-legged beside her and her heart brimmed with joy. He was alive, breathing, living, and Sable knew sweet rapture. She quietly studied his face, the heavy growth of beard, letting her gaze drift over his body, then to the child in his arms. Tears burned her eyes, sharp and sweet, and she let them fall, watching, absorbing the gentle sight of him feeding the baby, murmuring funny little sounds and grinning when Little Hawk cooed in response. As exhaustion stole them from her sight, Sable didn't wonder how they all survived. She didn't care. All she knew is they had, and she was alive to know it.

Chapter Thirty-six

A warmth brushed across Hunter's cheek and his lids snapped open. He stared into eyes the shade of wild pasque-flower.

"I love you, Hunter McCracken."

His vision blurred. Every time she said it, always with a little defiance, he wanted to crush her to him, meld them together so they'd never be parted.

"God, Sae," he said, his gaze burning over her features as he took in the beauty hidden beneath the cuts and bruises. "I love you, too."

"Oh, Hunter," she whispered and slipped her fingers along his jaw.

"Don't cry, love, please don't." Her tears made him feel so damn useless.

"Kiss me so I'll know you're real."

He propped up on his elbow, leaning close. His body trembled with anticipation, his hand hovered at her waist. He never thought to hear her voice again, see those bright violet eyes looking back. Tenuously he pressed his mouth to hers and her fingers slid into his hair and tightened, holding him. He let her kiss him, let her do anything she damn well pleased. Her pressure was firm and demanding—the pressure of a woman who knew exactly what she wanted.

"Touch me, Hunter, please. I need you to." The words

came from deep within, to know she wasn't tainted by Barlow's attack. And Hunter heard it, thank God, but she was too weak for this, and if she didn't have enough sense to know it, he sure as hell did.

"Sable?"

She ignored him, nipping his lips, and he didn't have the will to push her away just yet. "As much as I'd love to ravish your sweet little body—oh God—" he moaned when his hand encountered the lush cushion of her breast and Hunter gave up, his mouth opening wide on hers, his tongue sweeping eagerly as he filled his palm with soft woman-flesh. She leaned into him, teasing him with cracked lips and liquid curves and Hunter absorbed it like a dry sponge.

"This is ridiculous," he mumbled into her mouth, dragging air into his lungs. "You'll wear yourself out." He could almost feel her draining energy.

She pressed her forehead to his, fingers fanning his jaw, her thumb smoothing over his lower lip. "I'm just glad to *wear* at anything."

His glance swept meaningfully down at her naked body. "What you have on is my idea of high fashion."

"Contrary to appearances, Hunter McCracken, I am still a lady." She attempted to scold, but her tone lacked conviction when she made no move to cover herself.

His gaze darted again over her naked curves, air hissing past his teeth. "Ain't the lady part of you I like."

"I'm delighted to hear it," she said, for her body bore the unmistakable mark of Barlow's hands. She pushed herself upright, wincing when she bent her wrist too far. His hands were there, gentle aid and firm.

"How do you feel?" he asked, wrapping the fur against more than just the cold.

"Hungry—for food," she clarified primly when he wiggled his brows.

"Thrown over for cooked meat," he muttered dryly. His

gentle gaze hardened when it lit again on her bandaged wrists and feet.

"What have you done with Little Hawk?" she asked, sensing his growing rage. She tucked her hands beneath the robe. "I saw him with you before."

"Swift Arrow has him, down by the creek," he answered distractedly, studying the fingerprint bruises on her shoulder and chest.

"Swift Arrow!"

Her shock drew his attention and he assured her the Cheyenne was fine, playing the dutiful mother without protest.

"Bring my nephew to me, please," she begged, eager for the sight of him. "I need to hold him. Please."

"All right, all right," he said calmingly when he thought she'd burst into tears.

Sable watched him slowly rise to his feet, noticing he favored his wounded side, and she cursed her selfishness. "Hunter?" He looked back at her. "Your wound—is it healing well?"

He glanced down to where his hand covered his thickly padded side. He didn't want to lie to her and say Black Wolf had stitched him back into his skin that morning. She wasn't ready to meet her brother-in-law, for it meant giving up the boy and after what she'd been through, it was just too damn soon.

He knelt, grasping her hands. "The bullet went straight through, Sable. It didn't cut anything vital. Least I don't think. Cracking my head on the ground did more harm."

"Don't you dare hide anything from me, Hunter," she warned in a watery voice. "Swear to me."

With a tender smile, he drew a broad cross over his heart, swearing to get her out of here, away from the dangers that threatened to take her from him. *But what can you offer her?* he thought as he disappeared into the dark to find Swift Arrow. *More hurt?*

When Hunter returned with the infant and his foster uncle,

they found Sable fast asleep. Nestling the boy close to her and tucking them into the furs, Hunter turned abruptly away, leaving the Cheyenne to guard her.

Swift Arrow squatted close, offering cooked meat bedded on a scrap of cloth.

Sable grabbed it with a hungry moan and tore into it.

"Slowly, little one," he said and she complied, noticing his chest and arms were wet from a recent bath but that there was blood on his trousers. From dressing the hare, she assumed.

"You'll catch cold," she said, chewing, then gave the meat a dubious look and tossed it aside, already full. "I dare say when I leave here I will never eat another of those tiny creatures again." That was her first solid food since the day Hunter was shot. It seemed so long ago. The pain of their separation, the horror they'd lived with, believing the other dead, rinsed away every time their eyes met. He'd come for her. Wounded and feverish he'd struck out with her nephew to find her.

"Where's Hunter?"

"Standing watch," he said, avoiding her gaze. "His incessant hovering over you had become most annoying."

A howl came, distant and low and Sable frowned while licking grease from her fingertip. "What in heaven's name was that?"

"Owls," he said, then offered a cup of water. She wanted coffee, but he didn't think her stomach could take it.

Sable sipped, aware he studied her.

"You should rest."

"I'm not in such bad shape . . ." she touched her cheek. "Am I?"

"You would not wish to see a mirror, Sable."

"My, aren't we gallant this evening," she muttered, rueful.

345

"Sleep," he said, taking the cup and pushing her down onto the furs next to her nephew. "You are safe."

The cry came again and she recognized it for what it was. "That's not owls," she said. A pause, then "Swift Arrow." His lips pressed tight he refused to answer. "Christopher Waythorne Swift!" He grimaced at his true name. "You answer me this minute!"

"What happened to the reserved maid who screamed at the very sight of me?"

"She grew up. Now answer me."

He met her gaze. She was prepared for the worst and deserved to know it. "It is Nate Barlow." Her eyes widened a fraction and she swallowed. "And he is paying for his crimes," he uttered coldly, then straightened.

"I see." Sable shivered, snuggling into the furs and drawing her nephew into the warmth. Staring down at the innocent babe tucked to her breast, Sable remembered the unquenchable terror when Barlow put the gun to his tiny head, and nothing could soften the fear she knew when he forced her to leave him unprotected. And the grief. Lord, the grief.

Swift Arrow stood over her, watching her emotions skitter across her face. She has grown much, he thought as her lids drifted down, sealing out out the night.

A while later Hunter appeared at his side, his voice seeping into her dreams. "Barlow's dead."

Daylight was just scarcely breaking when Hunter caught her leaving the thatched shelter, dressed in the doeskin and moccasins.

"What the hell are you doing? You should be resting," he growled.

"Honestly, Hunter, I'm much better, really." She clutched the baby tightly, muffling a moan of pain as she took a step away from the shelter. It didn't hurt much. The blisters were

346

lanced and drained and cushioned in the buckskin. "I was truly more thirsty and hungry."

"And damn near dying from it!"

"Hunter, please. I know you—" Then she gasped, "Merciful heavens!" her eyes widening until they absorbed her face as in one smooth motion Hunter twisted, drawing his gun and taking aim.

"Jesus. Don't do that!" he snapped at her, pointing the barrel at the sky and easing the hammer down.

"Who-who is he?" Sable breathed, clutching Hunter's sleeve, her eyes on the man hovering on the fringes of darkness like wood smoke.

Tall and slim, his gleaming straight hair fell like a black waterfall over muscled shoulders nearly to his waist, shifting in the light as the visitor strode closer. Like a graceful cat, she thought, noting the beads and grouped feathers dangling from his crown. His face was painted, black across his eyes like a mask, white beneath, flowing over the bridge of his nose and cheeks. It was frightening. He was scarcely clothed; moccasins caught below his knees, bare-chested but for a breast plate of ribbed bone; feathers and beads on a hammered silver disk centered his armor. A yellowish stone hung from his left ear lobe. She licked her lips, utterly spellbound. This Indian was not at all like Swift Arrow. This man was fierce and wildly savage and wore his power like a titled lord.

"Hunter?" she prodded as the warrior advanced, and Sable realized his earbob was a gold nugget. She couldn't take her gaze from the Indian. He was magnificent. "Hunter?"

Hunter pulled her forward, slipping an arm around her waist as he holstered his gun. "That's Black Wolf," he whispered.

She inhaled sharply. Her sister's husband, the Sioux war chief, a legend. And Little Hawk's father.

Her gaze dropped abruptly to the baby in her arms. "Why didn't you do it, Hunter?" There was only curiosity in her voice.

Hunter covertly glanced at the warrior, then whispered, "I, ahh—I thought you deserved that privilege, after all you've been through for the little fella."

Squeezing her eyes shut, she briefly touched her lips to the boy's head. "Thank you, Hunter," she murmured, reaching up to stroke his stubbled cheek.

Praise God, I finally did something right, he thought as she bravely faced her brother-in-law.

Suddenly the warrior was within inches of them, grasping Sable's jaw and tilting her face to the sun. Her hand on Hunter's arm restrained him from interfering, and she held her breath as shrewd raven-black eyes moved possessively over her face. She recognized the shock, then the disappointment on his coppery features.

"You thought I was Lane," she murmured, a little stunned.

Slowly, his hand lowered. "But you are Say-bell," he said as if testing the feel of her name on his lips. "Sister to my wife." This woman explained the presence of his blanket and his spirits crumbled as he glanced at the sleeping boy. Had his feelings been so wrong?

At the mention of her sister's status Sable experienced again Lane's unconsolable loneliness, the tormenting hours she'd spent watching the Nebraska horizon, hoping he'd take her from Papa's ridicule, and the heart-wrenching sobs that lasted deep into the night when he didn't.

"If she is your wife, why didn't you take her back?"

He folded his arms over his chest, his gaze raking her. "Your sister chose to leave Lakota."

"That's a lie!"

He reared back, his face darkening with quick rage. "Your woman dares much, Standing Cougar."

"Yeah, I know," Hunter muttered in a dry tone as she stepped away from him.

"*You* have your gall," she spat. Black Wolf transferred his insolent gaze to his sister-in-law and Sable had the irresistible urge to kick him. "You, sir, have bestowed nothing but heartache on my sister, and Lord knows why she was ever happy with you, but when the Army stole her back, when she needed you, you abandoned her!"

"Sable, honey, don't you think you're being a bit hard?"

She rounded on Hunter, defiance and anger churning, the horrible day Lane gave up her son repeating in her mind. "I don't honestly care," she said righteously, tears glossing her eyes. "Lane's life is empty, empty! But for the small hope that we are alive and her husband has not completely forsaken her!"

"Silence!" Black Wolf barked, and Sable glared at him through a curtain of hair. That he would allow this female to accuse him of such dishonorable behavior tore at Black Wolf. "I searched for her and found only her tracks and the markings of the soldiers. That spoke the truth. She wants nothing of me."

"You're a fool, Black Wolf." Her voice held more pity than malice. "She was berry-hunting when they stole her. Most of the men were with you—raiding," she stressed. "They threatened to attack the village if she didn't come quietly."

His only reaction was a flaring black brow but he could not ignore the echo of Morning Sun's words. Unwillingly his gaze sought the sleeping boy.

"But when she discovered only a handful of men, she fought!" Tears made her vision swim. Weeks of worry, harboring doubts and fears boiled to a head. "Three times she attempted to return," she said, her shoulders drooping dejectedly when he remained coldly impassive. All this way and he offered her nothing to take back to Lane. "But Father took us both to Washington," her voice dropped to a tired whisper. "Quickly and under heavy guard."

They stared, black eyes boring into pale blue-violet, and Sable held her breath as a wild play of doubt, reason, then regret, raced across his chiseled features, briefly visible, then discarded like rubbish. He was hurting, too, and her anger softened.

349

'For your sister you walk to the land of my People to tell me this?" He waved, the gesture indicating the long dangerous trek and Sable nodded. "She has asked too much of your love, Say-bell."

"And what will I tell her of yours, Black Wolf?"

He broke eye contact, his face impassive, yet he could not stop the image of Lane's sorrow, believing he had discarded her. For months his own heart lay bleeding and to know this grueling pain was unnecessary was a guilt he alone must bear. Abruptly he brought his gaze back to Sable's. "Why did she not journey herself?"

"Haste was crucial and Lane wasn't well at the time." She stepped within a hair's breadth of him, boldly meeting eyes black as midnight. "My sister loves you, Black Wolf. She lives only to be with you again. But I'm not the one who must be convinced." Sable lifted the child up between them. "Perhaps your son will be enough."

Black Wolf's gaze shot between the woman to the boy with eyes the color of rain clouds. *His son.* He swallowed tightly, his emotions battling for supremacy as he studied the boy-child he never dared consider was his own blood. Lane had carried his child, born him a son, alone, in a land where people despised her for merely touching him.

"He was not safe with her." He scowled and Sable decided to let Lane tell him of their father's misdeeds. "The Army wanted to use him to lure you from the hills."

"For my son—they would have succeeded," he said, his arms out to take him.

The sound of rapid hoofbeats made them all turn, Hunter's weapon already drawn as Black Wolf vanished like mist.

Clutching the baby, Sable twisted and turned, searching for the warrior as Swift Arrow drew up short, sliding from the animal's back. "Troopers," he said breathlessly. "They found Barlow's tracks. Headed this way."

Black Wolf dropped from a tree, so close to Sable she stumbled back with a startled shriek. As if she wasn't there, the three men went about striking the camp. "Black Wolf? Hunter?" she asked, but no answer came. "Hunter," she cried, and he looked up from loading the packs.

"I can't do it. I can't leave him. Not like this."

He came to her, grasping her shoulders, looking deep into her eyes. "This is it, Sae, what your sister wanted, why you deceived and disguised and even killed—to put this boy in his father's arms. Well, darlin'," he nodded to the warrior, "there he is."

"But it's too soon," she wailed, clutching the baby to her breast. "I wanted to be certain he loved him."

Tossing the blanket over his horse's back, Black Wolf came to her, grasping her trembling hand, his touch warm and reassuring. "He is the child of my heart. I will love him."

Her eyes shifted between Hunter, Black Wolf, and her nephew. Little Hawk cooed up at her, the innocent sound stabbing through her heart. "Remember the talks we had?" she whispered. The baby gurgled, tiny fists punching the air. "Well, this is your papa," she whispered on a sob, shakily pressing a kiss to the boy's cheek.

Sable looked up, exhaled a ragged breath, then placed the child in the safety of his father's arms.

"It is a great thing you have done, my sister," he said, awe in his voice.

Tears dripped off her chin and she stared at the baby, reaching out to caress his tiny arm, then cover it from the cold. Then her gaze flew to Black Wolf's, her tone suddenly defensive. "Who will care for him? Some squaw?"

Black Wolf recognized the pain in her eyes. It was much to give up the child to a stranger. "This is my son," he said proudly. "He will be raised by his father and . . . his mother." Distrust darkened her features. "This I promise, Say-bell." He touched the spot over his heart. "And my wife? Where is she?"

"I don't know." His eager expression faltered. "I'm sorry. I haven't seen her since I left."

Scowling Black Wolf leaped to the painted gray's back with practiced ease, cradling his son between his thighs.

"Wait!" Her call kept him still. "Papa must be searching for me and he wouldn't leave Lane behind." Black Wolf understood. Lane was close. "There's a chance they are at Fort Kearney." Doubt tainted her voice. "Or McPherson."

Rumbling hoofbeats grew louder, vibrating the ground as Black Wolf leaned down, unaffected by the encroaching danger, and cupped her cheek. Covering his hand, she stared up at him, crying for his son and his safety, and Sable felt a bond with his strength and his love for her sister.

"With the rise of the new moon, I will come for my wife, Brave Heart." His thumb brushed a tear from her cheek. "I will send *you* a message."

"But—"

"Sable, put a fire under it!"

"I will come for her!" His tone left no room for dispute and she nodded as Hunter urged her to a horse. Instantly the Sioux warrior spun around and sped off across the plains. The bugle call sounded and Swift Arrow's horse charged from the cover of the forest, veering in the opposite direction.

"My God! We have to do something," she cried. Troops raced toward Black Wolf, weapons drawing a bead on his back. "They'll never get away."

"Sable! No!" He mounted as she dug her heels into horseflesh. "Shit!" he cried as he surged forward, leaning out to catch the reins, nearly unseating her as he yanked. "Damn it, Sable, haven't you learned anything?"

"But they'll shoot."

"They're on Indian lands with only a couple of squads, Sae. If they shoot, they break a treaty."

"When has that mattered!"

"Now seems convenient. Look."

Like a ripple in the water, the soldiers slowed their breakneck speed, their faces going slack, weapon aim faltering, and Sable's gaze shot to Black Wolf. As his stallion charged up the slope, nearly a hundred Sioux warriors painted for battle crested the rise behind their leader, like a line drawn in the sand.

Pausing on the hill, Black Wolf shook his fist at the sky in defiance, his shrill war cry raising the hackles on her nape. He'd taken back the white man's power over him once more —he'd taken back his son. Across the expanse of whispering grass he looked in her direction, nodded once, then wheeled about, vanishing over the horizon.

Vastly outnumbered, the soldiers retreated.

"You did it, Sae."

We did." She turned soulful eyes on him. "Take me home, Hunter. Please."

He tried to smile. "That was the deal, wasn't it?"

Chapter Thirty-seven

Sable pressed her naked back to the solid wall of his chest, and grasped his hands, drawing them around in front of her.

"Come on, Sae, not like this."

She could feel his body stiffen, curved to her spine. She tilted her head back, looking into his troubled eyes. "It's not the same, Hunter. Feel *me*," she coaxed as she brought his hands to her breasts, filling his palms, hers covering his. She held him there, allowing him to adjust to the position he'd refused. "Touch me. I'm here, Hunter, not them. Prove it to yourself and touch me." Resting her head back on his shoulder, she captured his mouth, wet honey sliding between his lips, her arms rising up like wisps of smoke to envelope his head and hold him there. Her mouth opened wide on his, primitive and erotic. She licked and nipped, sucked his tongue deep into her mouth, and Hunter sensed the tide of his past was going out to sea for the last time as he closed his eyes and sank into the carnal pleasure of her mouth.

He'd tutored her too well.

Blood pulsed thickly in his loins, burning him as he fondled and stroked her breasts, rolling her nipples between his fingers. He wanted them in his mouth, wanted to suckle and savor the taste and feel of them, hear her feminine sighs of pleasure. The image sent streams of yearning crashing over him as his calloused palms scrubbed down over her tight ribs, her flat belly to dip between her thighs. Her kiss swelled to ravenous, as savage as their surroundings while she spread her knees and pushed his questing fingers into the dark treasure between.

"It's not the same, never will it be." Her bottom nestled snugly, his manhood felt like an iron bar behind her, nudging her. "Feel," she murmured into his mouth, guiding his fingers into the lush mound of femininity. Hunter moaned, low and hoarse, grinding kisses across the back of her neck, her shoulders, as he stroked and manipulated wet silky flesh. Her hand covered his, feeling him as he felt her. It heightened senses already achingly raw with desire. "I'm not them, I am?"

She didn't expect an answer, and wouldn't get one; he was lost to the petal soft skin beneath his touch as he pushed two fingers deep inside. A shudder raked her slender form like summer steam as she invaded his mouth, hot wet ferocity driving her, a caged cat unleashed, her hips matching the cadence of his thrusts as she reached between them and clasped his manhood, stroking.

"Jesus!" he groaned, snapping an arm around her waist and burying his face in the curve of her neck. His hard arousal jumped to life, elongated further in her hand as she lifted a fraction, pressing the stiffness down until it rested between the dip of her woman-flesh. He tensed.

"No." Warning and fear and memories crowded the single word.

"I won't let you leave me, Hunter," she whispered defiantly, meeting his gaze. "I won't," she repeated, sliding her hand torturously across his manhood and he moaned at the erotic entrapment. When his mind rebelled she used her body to free him, squirming and rubbing, rocking him into a luxurious madness. There was no use denying her this lesson. She was doing her damndest to make him forget the past and know there was a future. A future.

Hot creamy wetness scorched him as she slid back and forth along his length. Her hand came down between her legs to meet him, and Hunter trembled as she leaned out and pressed the moist tip of him into her. "Oh, Hunn-terr," she said in a long, throaty moan and he knew he'd climax the second he drove home.

"Inside me, hurry." Her fingertips stroked the root of his shaft, guiding, impatient. She abruptly widened her stance, angled herself and jammed back against him, burying his erection inside her. Her heavy guttural moan of satisfaction accompanied the sharp toss of her head, a curtain of mahogany hair shimmering over her arched spine. Exotic, feline, secret, Hunter thought as she glanced back over her shoulder to look at him, her thighs spread wide over his. Never breaking eye contact she pulled away, then pushed back against him. Again and again—slowly away, then crashing back. She was untamed and hungry, and she sucked his strength, met him, matched him, dared him.

"Yes, yes," she moaned, rolling her hips, reaching back to urge him faster. He dove into her softness, slick and solid steel, his body pumping with sensations and scents and pleasure, thick and hot. "Love me, Hunter. Watch."

And he did. He wanted to and he did. He watched his body disappear into her glistening womanhood, liquid heat slickening his path, and he thought his chest would explode if he dared breathe. Suddenly she drew her legs together, her soft pink petals turning to iron, crushing him, squeezing, urging him to join her. It was happening; he felt the pin-pricking spiral of ecstasy, in this way, the way he never dared touch a woman. Dark thoughts and images vanished as sweet fire exploded, and he drove into her, pulling her tightly against the curve of his body. He squeezed his eyes shut; his body sang, nerves yanked and snapped and his manhood pushed and pushed and pushed. She jerked and bounced fretfully, her mouth greedy on his as luminous rapture throbbed through her blood, ravishing her with a luxurious gush of heat and love.

He moved his hands down to her center, touching her

lightly and she cried out, mashing his fingers to the sensitive core.

"I love you, I love you, I love you," she murmured and Hunter heard the tears in her voice.

"I love you, too, Sae. God, I do."

Please don't take this away, he prayed, his body still drawing on hers.

In the secluded bower beneath the dappled shade of a spreading cottonwood tree, Hunter found home.

It had been there all along; he just never imagined he was worthy of stepping over the threshold. He felt as if he'd broken above the surface of cold back waters after floundering in the icy depths for nearly five years and her love was the lifeline drawing him back. She'd always pulled on it; from the moment he'd met her, she yanked and tugged him back to the living side of his existence.

Sable would love him, regardless of his past, his numerous failings.

Sable had loved him back home.

"I think I've been patient enough, Hunter. Why did we stop there?" Sable glanced back at the slim, auburn-haired man still standing on the porch, waving. She nodded, her gaze touring over the handsome log home, cattle pens, horse corrals, pausing on the hundreds of teepee's occupying the surrounding lands. Serfs to the robber baron, she thought distastefully.

"Don't like him, do you?" Hunter asked.

Her gaze sharpened on his. "Jack Morrow is a thief!"

"And you were very polite, thank you." With the dignity of the lady she was, she'd declined the invitation to dine even though the half-mile journey across the Platte in hip deep water left the last of their supplies as saturated as their clothes.

"He sells those Indians liquor!" She gestured to the empty bottles of Drake's Plantation Bitters littering their trail. "And steals livestock from the wagon trains, then has the gall to offer to *find* them! For a price, of course."

"Of course." He grinned at her indignation.

"You have no remorse over dealing with such a man?"

"Nope." He fished in his saddle bags. "Jack owes me." He tossed her a peach and she caught it, sinking her teeth into succulent fruit with a hungry moan.

"I think we need to discuss the caliber of the people with whom you associate, Hunter McCracken."

Drawing up his knee and resting it on the saddle horn, he broke open a round of crusty bread. "Before or after you finish eating his food?" He smiled, popping a chunk into his mouth.

"After, definitely after," she said, her hand out for a sample.

They felt it, as tangible as the warm summer air surrounding them, the raw landscape that spread for miles. They were headed back to the fort. To civilization. Their happiness would be shattered and she wasn't certain it could resist close scrutiny, repel her father's manipulations.

Sable reined up sharply, staring at the rise which covered a view of the fort. Leather creaked as Hunter twisted in the saddle. He frowned.

She shifted her frightened gaze to him, and still saw nothing good coming from this. "We don't have to go there, Hunter. Please. We can bypass it. The train is close enough. Let's just leave and never look back."

Nothing would please him more. "Those soldiers will keep hunting us, Sable. And you know it." Hunter wanted to do it; hide, seclude themselves in their happiness. Indecision showed in his face and she pressed her suit.

"We haven't done anything wrong, really. It wasn't any of their business."

Sable waited for him to ask her to run away and make a life with him, but he didn't.

"We have to finish this." It wasn't the first time Hunter cursed the duty and blasted sense of honor pulling him toward the fort.

"But they'll separate us."

He flashed her an easy grin, smoldering gray eyes sweeping her lush body with deliberate slowness. " 'Fraid you'll not get your daily pleasures?"

She blushed bright red and he laughed, sidling over to her.

"You're incorrigible, Hunter McCracken," she said as he pulled her from the saddle and onto his lap. Her arms immediately looped around his neck, her mouth hot and starving on his, as if they hadn't made love just hours before.

"True, isn't it?" he said moments later, pulling air into his lungs, his groin thick with warm blood.

She snubbed the air, violet eyes sparking with sensual mischief. "A lady refuses to answer to such ribald accusations."

He mashed her to him. "Forget the lady—I want the wild-cat."

His chuckle was dark and lusty as he palmed her breast, the trim curve of her waist, the flare of her hip, dragging his hand roughly between her denimed legs. She curled to him, and he took her mouth again, his tongue invading deeply, probing the pleasurable haven he knew better than any man. Her bottom ground against the bulge rising beneath her and Hunter growled, clutching her tightly to his chest. She leaned back to look at him, her breathing heavy, her eyes crying her love and fear. "I love you, Hunter McCracken," she whispered, always with a little challenge, and his muscles clamped down on his heart.

"I know you do, darlin'," he said, brushing her hair from her face and cradling the curve of her jaw in his palms. "I was dead before you stumbled into my sorry excuse for a life, Sable Cavanaugh," he said with every sharp edged emotion hammering in his chest. "I have loved *only* you. And if there is a forever, that's when I'll love you still."

Tears glossed her eyes. "Oh, Hunter," she choked as he

slowly pressed his lips to hers, tender, brief, his body trembling with the startling force of his love. Gone was the scared little kitten who withered under his stare, a fire breathing she-cat emerging with the strength to best his ridicule, battle his nightmares, and face down a legendary warrior, bringing him to his knees with her quiet strength.

The warm summer wind whispered around them, stirring the tall grass like a stroke across velvet green as he held her, kissed her. The horse sidestepped impatiently and he drew back, pressing his forehead to hers and whispering his love and aching to show her. Reluctantly he set her back on her horse, smiling at her playful pout as she swung her leg over the horse's neck. She immediately checked her appearance with a smoothing hand.

"Properly presentable, ma'am?" he teased, his eyed riveted to the thighs stretched wide over the horse. Damn trousers.

"Certainly. But how in heaven's name will you hide that?"

Hunter didn't need to look where she indicated; the heavy throbbing was bad enough. "Got any suggestions?" he asked, kneeing the horse forward.

"Yes." He glanced at her and she grinned, very smug. "But you lost your chance." She was off like a shot, and Hunter kicked his mount into a gallop.

Don't bet on it, he thought slyly.

No bugle sounded when they were sighted at midday. Sable slowed her horse, glancing fearfully at Hunter, but his eyes were scrutinizing their surroundings, darting to the sentries, inside the fort, then to the Indians and traders milling outside the gates. All appeared normal, yet it was oddly quiet, the air fraught with an undercurrent she couldn't name. They'd sent a squad after them, so why wasn't there a sentry here to take them inside?

"I don't care for this at all, Hunter. It scares me. Where are all the people?"

"Turn back," he ordered sharply before they passed completely through the yawning gate of Fort McPherson. Without hesitation they wheeled about in unison and came to an abrupt halt as the gates swung together. Sable's horse reared and Hunter leaned out to grasp the bridle, controlling her mount as nearly a dozen soldiers materialized from behind the closing gates.

His eyes met hers, instantly reading her desperate panic. "Don't fight it," he warned in a low voice as sliding carbines and clicking revolvers echoed in the quiet fortress.

She nodded shakily and slid from the animal's back as Hunter put up his hands.

His acquiescence didn't matter.

Soldiers yanked him roughly from the saddle, quickly disarming him. Hunter ignored their search for hidden weapons and kept his eyes on Sable.

"I'm not going anywhere," he growled over his shoulder at the sergeant, shaking off the restraining hands, then pinning his gaze on the soldier imprisoning Sable. "Take your hands off her," he said, deadly and dangerous. The trooper smirked insolently, and Hunter took a threatening step, his words snapping with the stinging force of a whip. "Do it or I'll kill you."

"Behind you!" Her warning scream matched the hot explosion high on his back as a trooper rammed the stock of his rifle between Hunter's shoulder blades. "Hunter!" she cried as he dropped hard to his knees, yet remained upright as Sable wrenched away from her jailer, sliding to the ground before him.

"Oh, Hunter, don't. They won't hurt me. Papa won't allow it. Fighting will only make it worse."

"Should have taken my own advice, huh?" he muttered, breathing deeply as the pain subsided in his spine.

"When do you ever?" She smoothed his hair from his damp brow. "We'll get out of this."

"Sable! Come here!"

She twisted at the familiar voice. "Papa!" He towered above her, blocking the sun, his eyes traveling over her home-spun shirt and tight canvas trousers. She read his distaste and didn't care, meeting her father's censure with cold eyes brimming with outrage. "I knew you'd be behind this treachery," she hissed as she and Hunter climbed to their feet. Her eyes narrowed on Maitland, who flanked her father like a haughty earl.

"Come here, girl," Richard commanded, hardly recognizing his youngest daughter.

Defiantly, Sable stepped closer to Hunter. Cavanaugh reached out and grabbed her arm. She winced beneath his painful grip. Hunter took a step toward her, but Maitland moved between them.

"You, McCracken, are a traitor." Hunter stiffened, his eyes flat gray and wrathful. "The charge is treason."

"No!" she gasped.

"You self-righteous bastard," Hunter growled, advancing. "You have no grounds!"

Instantly troopers restrained him and Hunter fought the human bonds, itching to throttle the fool.

"Don't I?" he sneered and a sergeant clapped his wrists in irons.

Sable's panic accelerated. "This is absurd." Her gaze shot to Hunter, Maitland, and her father. "Take those horrid things off him!" Her voice rose to an arrogant summons. "Tell them to release him. Now, Papa."

Richard Cavanaugh stiffened, glaring harshly at his daughter, the change in her almost frightening. "Do not demand of me, child," he hissed lowly, yanking her tightly to his side. "You have made enough of a spectacle of yourself."

She shoved at his chest, sending him a look meant to maim, her lips twisting bitterly. "And I will continue to do so, Papa, until Hunter is free."

"You seem to forget, Miss Cavanaugh, that you also are

under house arrest," he finished in a tone just shy of a sneer. He gestured sharply to the guards. "Take him away."

"Nooo!" she screamed.

His shackles chinked, marking the air with dread and their eyes locked as they dragged him from her.

Don't humiliate yourself for me, his expression said. *We'll get out of this.*

I won't let them do this, her eyes replied, chin lifting.

His lips twitched at her defiance. *I've been through worse.*

I won't abandon you.

Nor I you.

But they were taking him away from her to the stockade. A cell. His nightmares could find him in there. And she could lose him.

All brashness fled as Sable whirled on her father, clutching his lapels, her eyes pleading, her voice desperate.

"Hunter will die in there, Papa," she said for his ears alone. "You must get him released. Put him in a barracks, under guard, but please, not there!"

Her father stared back with compassionless eyes and she jerked on his coat.

"I'm begging you, Papa."

Richard pried her fingers from his uniform. "Control yourself, young lady," he murmured. "People are watching."

She wrenched away as if he'd slapped her. "Do you honestly think I care," she returned hotly. "That's all you have ever cared about, Papa. Not me or Lane or even Mama. Only what appearances will do to your career."

Something inside Richard crumbled, and his broad chest rose and fell with hidden sorrow. She would never understand that he had to take care of her, protect her and her sister, for he'd failed so with their mother. He would not allow it to happen again.

A river of emotions flooded across his haggard features but Sable was too angry to see the pain hidden there. He motioned and two soldiers flanked Sable. "Escort my daughter to my quarters and see that she doesn't leave." His gaze roamed her clothing with obvious disgust. Belligerently Sable hooked her thumbs in the belt loops, hips slanted. "You will clean yourself up as befits a lady and present yourself in the commander's office in one hour." He leaned down in her face. "Is that clear?"

Sable refused to answer, her eyes narrow and harsh as she ignored the guard who gestured for her to precede and took a step closer to her father. Her voice was low, her jailers backing discreetly out of earshot.

"My life is no longer yours to manipulate, for all that I have suffered lies before your polished boots, *Colonel*." Thick heartache surfaced in her throat and she swallowed it back. "And I am ashamed to admit you're my father."

She heard his sharp intake of breath as she spun away, her pace brisk, scarcely noticing the escort striding beside her. Her eyes never left Hunter. As if he could feel the intensity of her gaze, Hunter lifted his head, staring at her from across the compound. *I love you,* she mouthed. A guard jerked his arm and his expression evaporated into sullen resignation as he was stolen from her sight.

Chapter Thirty-eight

Lane peered out the window, watching Sable's rapid approach. "Melanie! Hurry! You must come see this! Land sakes! I never imagined to see her in pants, of all things!"

"Bath's right full. Gots more water to boilin' already," the slim housekeeper said as she shuffled across the parlor, wiping her hands on her apron before she peeked around Lane's shoulder. "Lor-dee! Can't say I've ever seen her in such a fit."

"Neither have I."

Lane's heart pounded furiously, anticipation channelling through her. Flanked by two armed guards, Sable looked as if she'd spit fire the instant anyone crossed her path. Her stride was long and determined, her hair bouncing wildly around her shoulders to her hips, arms swinging in a most unladylike fashion.

She had done it.

Little Hawk was safe with Black Wolf. The Army wouldn't be in such a snit if he wasn't. Ignoring Melanie's chiding that ladies didn't run, Lane raced to yank open the door. The women stared for a second, then Lane swallowed Sable in her embrace.

"Lane." Her name was a breath of relief. "I wasn't sure if you were here."

"And you didn't dare ask the Brass Bear?" she said on a shaky laugh, then stepped back.

"Heavens, no," she groaned, battling tears. "Did you see what he did this time?"

"Who didn't?" Lane urged her inside.

Footsteps sounded behind and Sable rounded sharply, glaring her jailers back when it appeared they would enter the house.

"We have orders to keep an eye on you, Miss Sable."

Sable drew herself up regally. "Do your orders include following me to my bath?"

Lane smothered a laugh and the trooper stiffened, withdrew his pocket watch, flipped the spring catch and gauged the time.

"One hour, Miss Cavanaugh." He closed the watch with a snap.

"And if I'm not ready, corporal?"

"Well, then I reckon I'll have to come git you," he said, his gaze prowling over her body, lingering at the divide of her denimed thighs before returning to her face.

Sable wanted to retch. "The prospect of being in your company is so revolting, corporal," she said in a voice saturated with contempt, "that I guarantee I'll be available at the appointed time!" His face went red as she turned her back to him, entered the house and slammed the door. "The nerve of that insolent little snot-faced—!"

"Lor-dee my," Melanie tisked, her hands on her hips. "If britches ain't nuff, she's done takin' to swearin', too!"

"Melanie!" Sable forgot her irritation and hugged the old woman.

"Ahz so glad you's safe, Miss Sable," she whispered. "So glad."

Sable's heart swelled with affection for her former nanny, yet before she could comment, Melanie gave her a hard squeeze, then pushed out of her arms. Straightening her shoulders, she tugged at her apron strings. "You two go on back to de rooms." She waved commandingly. "And I'll fetch water fer your hair rinsin', Miss Sable. Go on now, git 'fore de bath grows cold!" Then she trotted off toward the kitchen.

"She prayed for you every night," Lane said.

"It worked," said Sable, and the sisters exchanged a gentle smile before Lane wrapped an arm around Sable's shoulder and urged her down the hall. Sable gave her sister a squeeze.

"Was that really Hunter McCracken out there?"

"Yes," Sable replied as they entered the rooms.

"Maitland told Papa you were with him, but I thought he was dead."

"So did he." Sable crossed the room to the windows, trying to see the stockade.

"What?" Surely she misunderstood?

"It's a long story." Sable waved away the question as she drew the drapes and turned. Briefly surveying the bedroom, Sable recognized her trunks and several of her personal possessions. *So blasted sure of yourself, aren't you, Papa?* she thought with fresh anger. Those items meant nothing to her. All that was anything in her life sat in a dark cell, and Sable shivered at what this incarceration might do to Hunter. Immediately she searched out a fresh gown, undergarments, slippers, and hair pins, while her mind worked on a way to get Hunter out of the cell.

"I could shoot Papa for perpetuating this," she muttered, tossing the gown over a chair with a snap of her wrist. Melanie swept into the room, deftly setting a tray of cold meats, bread, and a pot of honey on the bed, then emptied a kettle of hot water into the tub.

"Sable?" A pause, then very softly, "How is my baby?"

Sable spun about. Melanie stilled by the door. Her sister stood in the center of the room beside the tub, her hands clenched in the fold of her shirts, her face cloaked in sorrow. And Sable just now recognized her ghastly thinness, the smallness of her waist. How she must have suffered here, under Papa's ridicule, where every soul in this place was desperate to see her husband dead and her son used as a hostage.

Ashamed that she hadn't taken a moment to assure the young mother, she first checked the open windows for lurking eavesdroppers, then went to her sister.

"Chubby, happy, and safe." *With his father.* She didn't have to say it. Lane knew. And behind her Melanie beamed approvingly, her eyes suspiciously glossy as she closed the door after her. "Pack your things, Lane," she whispered, grasping her hands. "He's coming for you."

Shocked joy soared across Lane's features and Sable realized Lane hadn't expected Black Wolf to want her enough to come for her. Dear God. All along she'd been prepared to give up her son to his father and never see him again! Sable was still wrapped in awe when Lane suddenly twisted away, her pleasure replaced by fear.

"We must get a message to him." She paced several steps, then halted. "As much as I want him to, he can't come here. He'll be killed."

"He knows that, Lane," Sable said patiently, working off her boots, then flipping open the buttons of her shirt. "Even if we got a message out, it would do little good. He seemed very determined to me." She swished the water as she kicked off her trousers.

Lane smiled despite her misgivings. Black Wolf and Sable—this new Sable. She would have loved to have seen *that* confrontation.

"Frankly, I don't know exactly how he's going to make himself known." Naked, she stepped into the tub. "But he swore he'd be here the night of the new moon."

"But that's in two days!" Lane said, dropping into a wing back chair.

She glanced up, thoughtful. "Is it really?" It didn't seem like it'd been that long ago. Shaking her head, Sable sank into the hot scented water. "I'm sure we'll think of something," she assured her sister before dunking fully, letting the hot water seep into her pores. Hunter, Lane, Black Wolf, and the baby were in as much trouble as when they started, she realized. She burst through the surface with, "Blast Papa!" then shoved sopping wet hair from her face and snatched up the soap. "I'd like to pound him a good one for his interference." She sponged and soaped with a vengeance. "He's thinking only of the marks left on his career!"

"You mustn't be so hard on your skin, little sister—or of Papa."

Sable blinked through the watery haze. "Why not? All this is his fault. How can you be so—so—?"

"Forgiving?" Lane supplied, rising from the chair and moving to a trunk. "I think you should see something." She rummaged in the bottom, then straightened, holding out a cloth-covered book. "It's Mother's. Read the last page."

Sable looked at her sister's solemn face, then to the book. She dried her hands, flipped pages and read.

I cannot bear to meet his eyes any longer. He stares at me, putting no voice to his thoughts, but I can read them. The very sight of me is a constant reminder of his failure to protect me, of the shame I carry. A man other than my husband has bedded me. Regardless that it was unwilling, Richard can neither forget nor forgive. My Lord, but I am too weak to endure my beloved's sorrow another hour. The savage's babe did not survive and I am glad, for Richard's hatred would surely have killed him. My only regret is that I will never see my precious daughters again.

Sable looked up, tears spilling, her voice a tormented whisper. "He's lied to us."

"Shielded us." Lane knelt beside the tub. "All these years he's protected us so much it brought about what he feared the most. Mama took her life, Sable, and Papa blames himself."

"But Lane," Sable cried, "he tried to give away your son!"

"I know, I know. But I honestly think he was reliving it again." She nodded toward the diary. "Imagine what he was feeling then ... and now. Papa did what he thought was right."

Swiping at her tears, Sable read the passage again. She was trying to understand, really she was, but his recent actions had made it difficult to believe Mama's death had anything to do with locking Hunter in cell.

"It's pure selfishness," Sable snapped, closing the book and handing it back.

Lane sighed, guilt masking her lovely features. "Then I was equally as selfish."

Sable's brows shot up. "How can you say that! Your life is destroyed—"

Lane put up a hand, silencing her sister. "And you gave up your entire world *and* your spotless reputation—for my son."

"Oh pooh!" she waved airily, not liking the pedestal she sister tried to build beneath her. "Besides," her eyes twinkled devilishly, "a few interesting specks on one's pristine reputation are worth a little sacrifice."

"Well, my, my," Lane gasped at such a comment coming from her straitlaced sister and studied her more closely. "Any of those specks include a legendary spy?"

"Certainly," she admitted unabashedly, lathering her hair.

"You're lovers." It wasn't a question. "Papa knows you spent the night in the hostelry. Colonel Maitland didn't spare a detail."

Her hand buried in the soapy hair, she looked at Lane. "Maitland just feels like a fool because Hunter outsmarted him, that's all."

"Has he proposed, Sable?"

"Well, no, but I know he loves me." Sable shooed, flicking soap foam. "I can't think about that now. He's in a cell under weak charges and I have to get him out."

Lord, Lane thought, *where did she get all this confidence?* "This is the Army you're trying to fight, little sister."

370

Sable arched a sudsy brow. "I've been sparring with Hunter for the past months, Lane. Nothing could have prepared me better."

The door burst open and Melanie, all business, hustled in to assist Sable in rinsing her hair.

Over the rush of pouring water she heard, "I knew you could save my son."

Sable twisted water from her hair, her gazed darting between Melanie and Lane.

"Well, hell. *I* didn't."

"Lor-dee, my," Melanie clucked, shaking her head as she trotted to the door. "I hope that Mister McCracken fella done learned you some'fin else sides swearin'."

Lane smothered a bubble of laughter as Sable cast her a sly glance, her face cherry red. "Yes, and he said I was an excellent student."

Lane let loose a soft chuckle as Melanie sent them both a reproving glare, wagging a boney finger in Sable's direction. "Dat girl done got a sassy mouth on her now, Missy Lane, and it be your fault, and dat man's, and yer Papa's, and . . ."

Melanie's lamenting faded as Sable left the tub, toweled dry, then slipped into a dark blue day gown, forgoing the corset and extra petticoats, yet savoring the thin soft batiste against her skin. She stared at her reflection in the silver glass as she brushed out her hair, uncomfortable in the heavy garments. Outwardly, the iodine dye had faded, leaving her complexion warmly kissed by the sun, though her skin still bore the stroke of Barlow's cruelty. Her hair was streaked lighter, her hands calloused, and her violet eyes held the gleam of experience and knowledge, the past weeks shaping her into a woman she admired. Warning her sister not to do anything rash, Sable swept from the room, her step quick and smooth as she realized looking and acting like a lady had nothing to do with being a woman.

Chapter Thirty-nine

Ankle chains chinked and dragged.

Loose stone crunched beneath his boots as Hunter counted the steps, turned, and counted again. Memories fluttered through his mind and he pushed them aside and thought about Sable, the delicate contours of her face, the sprinkle of freckles she tried to rub off when he mentioned liking them. He shoved his hands deep into his pockets, felt strange without his guns, and paced. A thin beam of sunlight flicked apart and became whole as he moved back and forth across its path, and he imagined the mischievous sparkle in her eyes when she was about to say something provocative. His lips curved and he could almost feel the softness of her skin, her lips, her body—naked and warm and willing, pressed to him.

He halted, swiped the back of his hand across his brow and cursed. This wasn't Libby Prison. There wasn't a sodomite guard threatening him through his lieutenant. No shamed young man swinging from a meat hook. No one was begging for help he couldn't give. So why was he breathing so damn hard? Dropping to the ground, he leaned his back against the wood wall, drew up one knee and propped his forearm.

It wasn't Libby Prison and Hunter knew it. Nothing was the same any more. He would never think of that time with the burdens of his mind. He'd grown too much, had dealt with it for weeks. She'd done everything in her power to help him smash the lasts of his demons. A few lingered—but not in here.

He dropped his head back and blew out his breath. For several minutes Hunter didn't move, didn't see, yet waited for the crush of guilt, the humiliation to sweep over him. He waited for the need for several ounces of whiskey to pull at his gut. It didn't come, and he waited some more.

Instead, the faces of his parents filled his mind, his younger twin brothers, his little sister, Camy. Had Pa's ranch survived the war? Did Ian and Luke follow him into battle? The scrawny boys had always looked up to him; it would be just like them to lie about their age and go searching for him. They'd be about twenty-one now, and Camille, at least seventeen.

He was ashamed that he didn't know what happened to them, hadn't seen them in all this time; not one letter, not one visit. They didn't know he was alive but for the time or two that Dugal had relayed, and the magnitude of the heartache he'd caused his family hit him with the force of a smithy's mallet.

He'd done that, left obligations and family and himself, behind. It wasn't the cure and he refused to make the same mistake this time. Not if he wanted Sable.

He wanted her forever.

But he couldn't take her into a life he didn't have. Part of him wasn't ready to be with people, yet he loathed the thought of existing alone again. He knew he had to go back where he started and make amends.

Hunter wanted out; he wanted to get on with his life. Now. Restless with anticipation, he climbed to his feet, the constricting shackles making his movement clumsy and angry. He glared at the iron bonds, his muscles clenching. This wasn't Libby Prison, God damn it, and they weren't at war. Incarcerated without valid charges, Sable out there suffering God knew what, with two demented colonels manipulating the situation for private gain, Hunter pitied the fool who encountered him first.

Sable stepped out onto the porch, ignoring the guards as she headed toward the stockade. She hadn't made it half way across the compound when a squad of mounted troopers rode into the fortress.

Despite the fringed buckskins and layers of dirt, she instantly recognized Noah Kirkwood. He reined up beside her, yet Sable continued on her destination.

"Miss Cavanaugh?"

Sable didn't stop, using the time to form a suitable reply before encountering the lieutenant. He hadn't seen her with the baby, nor with Black Wolf, so she really had nothing to hide. Right?

"Miss Cavanaugh?"

She halted and turned fully. He strode close. "You have put me in a most unacceptable position, Madam."

"And you ought to reconsider what you say to me, Noah. I saved your life."

"You nearly got me court-martialed!"

"It would serve us both if you'd imagine what would have happened to you if I hadn't come along."

"Been captured, you mean."

She snubbed the air. "Either way, you are alive because of me and Hunter."

She was right, damn it. But that didn't excuse her reckless behavior at the fort. "My patrol searched for weeks for you."

"What for? It was obvious I didn't want to be found."

He scoffed. "A white woman, an unmarried attractive white woman, on reservation lands."

"I didn't need your help, Noah, nor the Army's. I was more than safe."

"Really?" He folded his arms over his chest, the move

374

sending a cloud of dust around them. "What happened in McCracken's cabin? There was blood all over the place!"

Sable's eyes bloomed with tears, the grief of believing Hunter and Swift Arrow were dead coming back like a blade through her breast. When she caught her breath she said, very softly, "Why don't you ask him yourself?"

She didn't wait for a response and whirled about, rounded the corner of a barn and froze.

Hunter was at the cell's only window, his arms through the bars, forearms braced on the sill, and cards—cards of all things—in his hands. Here she was worried about him and he was indulging in gambling! A red-haired man, with arms the size of tree trunks straddled a bench resting beneath the window. Hunter tossed down a card and laughed. Her heart lifted.

"Gambling, Mister McCracken?"

Hunter looked up. "Uh-oh. When she calls me mister I'm in for it."

The burly man lumbered to his feet, smiling broadly as she approached. "I'm Dugal Fraser," he said, moving the bench aside. "An' 'tis me own fault, lassie, I talked him intae the game." *This wee bit is the reason the lad's sae bleedin' chipper.*

Sable felt Hunter's gaze like a hot caress as he introduced her to his former sergeant-major.

"How is your sister?" Hunter asked softly, holding out his hand to her.

She grasped it tightly, sweeping closer. "Rather thin and pale, but she's fine." She kept the news of her father's lies to herself. He had enough problems. "Lieutenant. Kirkwood is back." She glanced over her shoulder but he was no where in sight. "And I'm to present myself before Papa in a few minutes." His chains rattled. "This is ridiculous! You'd think you were Red Cloud or something!"

"I'm alright, love. Not as bad as Libby, but I'll manage." She searched his pewter gray eyes, their calm reassuring her worried heart.

Dugal blinked, looking between the two. "She knows?"

Hunter cast a side glance at the blacksmith. "Yeah, she beat it out of me."

"Oh, you wretched liar."

"Tart."

"Beast."

"I love you, Sae."

"I know." She gripped the bars, lost in his loving gaze. "I know you do."

Dugal felt like an intruder and slipped away quietly, not that they'd ever notice.

"Oh, why did we come back here, Hunter?"

"Because running away and hiding doesn't solve a damn thing."

"Fine time for you to realize that," she snipped.

"Your fault. You taught me." He touched her cheek. Immediately she covered his hand, turning her face into it and pressing a kiss to the palm. That she would do that before spectators gave him the strength to endure the prison a little longer.

"So," she whispered faintly, then glanced to the side to be certain the guard was out of ear shot. "How do we get you out?"

"Tell them I'm ready to chat."

She arched a tapered brow. "You aren't thinking of escaping, are you?"

"With you dressed like that, hell no. You'd never forgive me for ruining that little confection. Nice dress, Sae. A bit too much cleavage for these starved animals, though." His eyes hadn't left her bosom since he mentioned the gown.

"The only animal I see is you, Hunter McCracken."

He met her gaze. "Maybe you ought to put on some more clothing, then?"

Pushing back from him, her arms akimbo, Sable's eyes dared him to tell her what she *ought* to do. "This is more than

376

I've worn in months, Hunter McCracken, and if you hadn't been such a hermit, you'd know this is a very modest dress."

"Like hell," he said sourly. "And isn't there some rule of etiquette that a woman shouldn't show her bosom before three o'clock?"

Jealous, possessive, and Sable adored it. "My my, you've turned into *such* a prude." She lowered her voice. "Most times you're trying to talk me out of my clothes."

"Go get your Papa, Violet Eyes," he growled, "so I can do just that."

Sable smiled, her body warming beneath the layers of navy blue cotton.

He kept her guessing.

"Put a fire under it, woman."

"Yes, m'lord," she said, moving away, then hesitated, glancing curiously over her shoulder. "What are you going to tell them?"

He stroked his bristled jaw, casting her a sly grin. "Haven't decided."

She threw her hands up. "Wonderful."

Richard Cavanaugh paced the carpeted floor outside the commander's office, pausing once in his steps to stare at Sable. By God, she was a different woman! A woman, no longer the child, but mature, defiant, and in love. He'd witnessed the looks exchanged between his little girl and Hunter, and experience reminded him the emotion could force a person to do the impossible. What ever else had transpired between them, Richard didn't want to know. He'd interfered enough this year.

His daughter sat rigidly on the edge of a weatherbeaten chair, acknowledging no one. Up until a moment ago Lieutenant Noah Kirkwood stood off to the side at parade rest, glaring holes in the back of Sable's expensive gown. He'd heard the words passed between them. Kirkwood owed Sable his life. The circumstances were laid out for Richard the moment he'd arrived on the post, but he found it hard to swallow such a story. He just couldn't imagine his *Pumpkin* killing another human being.

She hadn't spoken to him since that first moment, refusing to even look in his direction. It hurt. Nothing would ever be the same, true, but would she or her sister forgive him for what he'd done?

He sighed raggedly, focusing his attention on the infrequent words he could hear coming from the commander's office.

"Surely . . . something?" Maitland's voice, prodding, coaxing.

Sable tried not to appear as if she was listening. She stole a glance at her father. He was, intently.

"Why didn't you attack?" Maitland's voice grew louder, clearer. "You had reason to believe she and the child were with them, or are you a damn coward?"

Sable inhaled sharply, Richard ceased his pacing, and they both stared at the sealed door, aghast at the accusation.

"There would have been a massacre, sir—their numbers tripled ours." His tone was patient, precise. "An assault would have broken a treaty."

"You yourself have experienced how well those damn savages obey treaties! You have a loyalty to the Army, Lieutenant!"

Neither could decipher the remaining conversation for their voices softened before the door opened abruptly. Noah strode out, hat tucked close to his side, his handsome face creased with a scowl. He froze when he saw Sable, his lips working as if to say something, then thought better of it as he met Colonel Cavanaugh's gaze above her head. He straightened, saluted, and left.

Sable looked at her hands clenched tightly on her lap. She felt awful that Noah was taking the brunt of this from his commander and wondered continuously what Hunter had in mind to get them all out of this mess.

Maitland's voice bellowed for their presence like a king to his subjects. It set Sable on edge as she rose and preceded her father, studying the familiar office, noting the rearranged furniture before she saw the table set for tea.

Her lips twisted wryly at the thought that he would ply her with crumpets and scones.

"Miss Cavanaugh," Colonel Maitland said, indicating the stuffed leather chair beside the service.

Sable sat, defiance in every cell of her body.

"Would you care to pour?"

Arching a tapered brow, she relaxed into the chair, chipped nails tapping the arm. Maitland flushed, hurrying to serve tea. Sable didn't touch the china cup he set before her.

"What do you want Colonel Maitland? I need to be with my sister."

Regardless of what he asked, Sable wasn't going to be the catalyst for bringing the entire Army down on the Sioux, not at the risk of her precious nephew and brother-in-law.

"I want to know why you thought it necessary to disguise yourself."

"The lady has a right to her privacy," Hunter said from the doorway. "And if she didn't want to be noticed, that's her choice. Considering the way you spoke of her and how the people here mistreated her, she was well within her rights to protect herself."

"What's this?" Richard demanded, taking a step forward, his gaze shooting to Maitland, then to Hunter and back.

"Not now, Papa, hush!" Sable waved as Hunter strode inside, alone and unshackled. His hair was damp and curling, his jaw clean shaven, and though she didn't recognize the crisp blue shirt and black canvas trousers he wore, she knew the knowing flicker in his eyes.

"A month ago you insisted it was Sioux who attacked the patrol and kidnapped Miss Cavanaugh."

"Wasn't it?" Richard interrupted, glancing between Maitland, Sable, and Hunter.

Hunter shook his head. "Pawnee, Richard."

"You aren't mistaken?" His hot gaze pinned Maitland. Richard didn't doubt Hunter's ability to tell one tribe from another. Maitland had used his request to help locate Sable as an excuse to ride after the Sioux, any Sioux. Richard hated Black Wolf for what he'd done to Lane, wanted to see his head on a staff, but to falsify an official report? Even he had *some* ethics left.

Maitland avoided eye contact and shuffled a stack of papers, then waved airily, dismissing the line of conversation and said, "You failed to supply information necessary for the capture of Black Wolf, McCracken."

"How do you figure that?"

"Do not be flip. You know very well—"

"Pretend I don't.

"Miss Cavanaugh hired you to take her to Black Wolf. You had to know where he was to do that."

"Even Red Cloud doesn't know that. And why would I take her there?"

"To give him the baby, of course."

Hunter's brow shot up, a look of innocent questioning. "Did you see us with a child?" He included Sable with the flip of his hand.

"You know I did not."

"Did Kirkwood?"

"He insists you two were alone."

The comment was snide and Hunter went in for the kill.

"Enough! You have no grounds for charges. And I'm certain the newspapers would be very interested in how you two," he looked at each man, "have manipulated innocent lives, sacrificing soldiers, supplies and government treaties, all for your *personal* vendetta against the Sioux."

Maitland came to his feet, outraged. "She'll never betray her father." He lashed a hand toward Sable, the threat to his military career terrifying him. "You'll ruin her!"

Sable's gaze clashed with her father's as she said, "My reputation has nothing to lose, Colonel. Does yours?" It was a plea to end it now before she and Hunter were forced to drastic measures.

Hunter braced his hands on the deck, leaning into Maitland's face. "If you press this I'll see the matter reaches a military tribunal."

"You have nothing to base this on, McCracken."

Hunter straightened. "Jack Morrow already has my report, Maitland. It will take one word to send it on to Washington." The colonel's eyes widened. "And I think we both know Noah Kirkwood well enough that he isn't a coward, nor has he a dishonorable bone in his body. Can you count on your story about his slaughtered patrol, the Pawnee, and the search for Miss Cavanaugh standing up against all three testimonies? *Sir?*"

Maitland stared at McCracken, absently moving papers around his desk. He picked up a pen, tapped it twice, then tossed it aside as he broke his gaze.

The silence stretched and Sable's heart pounded. He was the commander and his word still held power in this isolated fort.

She rose, slow and graceful, rounding the curve of the desk to stand before him. He wouldn't meet her eyes.

"Your wife is gone, Colonel Maitland," Sable said very softly and he sagged. "So is my mother," her gaze collided with her father's over Maitland's shoulder, and she recognized the deepening wrinkles in his face, haggard with old pain and new worry. "And I'm sorry, but not one drop of spilled Sioux blood will bring either back."

Her heart suddenly went out to both men, recalling the agonizing grief she experienced when she thought Hunter was dead; the unquenchable need for revenge.

The silence lengthened.

G.T. Maitland stared out the window, winding and unwinding a stained ribbon around his finger. He'd failed and now he must salvage what he could of his career. G.T. met Richard's gaze from across the room. The latter nodded ever so slightly. Tossing a faded strip of yellow on the desk, Maitland murmured dejectedly, "You win, McCracken." He tore the charges in half. "Dismissed."

Chapter Forty

In the small foyer outside the office door Hunter took Sable into his arms and kissed her, long and deep and thoroughly.

"I've wanted to do that since I saw you in that damn dress," he whispered into her hair.

She smiled, running her fingers across his lips then into his hair, stealing another kiss before she whispered, "You were magnificent in there. Somehow I knew you would get it over with as painlessly as possible."

The door handle rattled and they pulled apart an instant before Colonel Cavanaugh stepped out. Sable stared at her father.

"Sable, go to the quarters."

She started to defy him, but his beaten expression changed her mind. She opened the outer door when she heard her father ask to speak with Hunter.

"I don't think that's wise right now, Richard."

"You've won, Hunter. Give me this."

With a backward glance, Sable stepped out onto the wood walk.

Hunter watched her recede from his sight, then faced Richard.

"I wanted to thank you." Hunter's brows rose a fraction. "For keeping her alive. And Colonel Maitland and I thought it best that we let it be known we misunderstood your situation." Hunter's gaze narrowed. "I'm certain Kirkwood will have no problem with that. We'll shoulder the responsibility."

"I'll keep my promise," Hunter said, half threatening as he made to leave.

"Hunter?"

He stilled, his back to Sable's father.

"I would die for her, Richard."

Sable stared into the darkness of her bedroom, the breeze fluttering the sheer drapes, molding pale moonlight across the carpet. She tossed and fretted on the feather mattress and considered dragging the coverlet to the floor. Rolling to her side, she stared at the blackened ashes of the note passed to her just prior to the closing of the gates. As she was walking to the quarters a small Indian woman with an armload of baskets had blocked her path, insisting, quietly vehement, that Sable purchase one. She did and even as the woman disappeared out the closing gates Sable discovered a yellow stone and a small scrap of beaten wood fiber inside—Black Wolf's message. She didn't consider how he managed, just that he had. He was coming for his wife.

At least Lane knew her future.

Tucking her hands beneath her cheek, sleep eluded Sable. Hunter was sharing quarters in the livery with his friend Dugal and she missed him, missed having his arms around her while she slept, missed the warmth of his body, the sound of his breathing. She missed his loving.

She was just drifting off when a shadow passed across her face and her eyes flashed open, her frightened cry smothered by a heavy hand. Sable kicked and screamed and clawed.

"Shhhh! It's me, darlin'. Ouch, will you quit that."

Sable relaxed and Hunter released her, his weight dipping the bed as he slid in beside her.

"Are you crazy?" she hissed.

"Reckon so," he murmured, pulling her into his arms. "Jeez, those nails are dangerous, Sae."

"Serves you right for—" His lips found hers in the dark and she clung to him, her body molding to his, responding, her mouth opening wide for him, and Hunter thought he'd be shattered with his need for her. Damn, it was a mistake to get this close to her again.

And he knew why. For the sake of her tattered reputation, he'd done everything in his power not to come near her. But his memory was spitefully vivid, reminding him how responsive she was, how good and clean and happy he felt inside her, loving her.

"You took my breath away at dinner tonight, and I wanted to kill every man that came near you."

"That was Papa's doing. He's still trying to save my reputation."

"Hell, he succeeded tonight."

He couldn't get within five feet of her all evening, forced to watch men fawn over her from across the hall. How different she'd looked in the elegant green gown, her hair swept high onto her crown, jeweled earbobs flickering in the lamplight. It made his heart ache to see her like that. Sable—with grace and style and wanting for nothing.

"I need to see you."

The bed creaked as he suddenly left her and she heard the swish of drapes, then the scrape of a match. The glow softened as he lit the lamp, adjusting the flame low and shook out the dying match. She tilted her head back, staring up at him.

He'd never seen her like this, in a real nightgown, her hair a wild riot of curls about her. This was the woman only he knew, feminine, forbidden, exuding sensuality like perfume. She robbed him of his thoughts. The transparent white fabric slipped off her shoulder as she sat up and he reached for her, pulling her to her knees at the edge of the bed.

"We could be caught," he murmured, his lips teasing the neckline, nudging it lower.

"Then maybe you should leave." She yanked his shirt from his trousers, curling her arms beneath his and pulling him close. Her touch was smooth, a whisper of cool in the growing heat of the room. His heart quickened, sweet and tight. His hands memorized the shape of her spine, the swell of her buttocks, gathering the gauzy nighttrail. His knuckles grazed her skin and his gaze shot to hers, his fist bunching the material at her hip, bringing her sharply against him. Bare. She was naked beneath the white fabric. After seeing her in pounds of clothing today, he hadn't really considered that. His breathing accelerated, his groin growing harder than it had been in weeks.

Christ, it was dangerous to touch her when he felt like this, wild, impatient. He couldn't give her any more than his desire and in a flash of anger he damned the world. He wanted all the time with her, didn't want to share her with another living soul for as long as he could.

Suddenly Hunter's arm snapped around her waist as his lips crashed down onto hers. His kiss was hard and greedy and passionate. She gasped, startled at first, then clung to him as he lifted her against his body and sank to the floor. He didn't stop until he pressed back to the carpet.

He deepened his kiss.

Sable burned, swift and hot.

His fist still held her nighttrail, his knuckles rubbing her bare hip, inching higher. His tongue pushed between her lips and swept deeply, searing her desires to a flushed peak. His hand spread, sliding down her thigh, fingers curling beneath her knee. In a sharp motion that startled her, he jerked it upward, fitting her tightly to his arousal. She moaned, a husky sound that split him in two, and his body answered, thrusting and rubbing, chest to chest, hip to hip.

His lips streaked across her cheek, down her throat, impatient and damp, and Sable tilted her head back, wishing she was naked and then she was, his fingers tearing the delicate fabric to her waist, exposing her to his smoldering gaze.

385

Her bosom swelled, ached, begging for him to taste.

"Beautiful," he murmured, filling his palms, staring before he bent his head, taking her nipple into his mouth and rolling the tight nub with his tongue.

Sable cupped his head, fingers driving into his hair as he drew the pink crest fully between his lips. This was wicked and dangerous, she thought, loving him with so many people so close. It excited her. Her breathing quickened, sweat beading on her neck and between her breasts, and when she didn't think she could take another moment of the luxurious torture, he devoted his attention to its mate.

His tongue slid around the sensitive tip, then dragged across the skin beneath her breasts, wetting it, heating it, his hands impatiently kneading her bare buttocks. She was exposed to him, his face nuzzling greedily at moist skin and white batiste. His hands scrubbed up and down her thighs, taunting her as much as himself before his fingers found her core, liquid and hot, sliding smoothly inside. She arched to his touch, inviting each demanding caress, and Hunter drank in the look of pleasure on her face. But he wanted more. Of everything. Just once—everything.

Hunter slid down her body, his teeth scraping provocatively over her flesh, his naked chest mashing her plump bosom, absorbing every soft inch of her as he moved lower. She was so ready, so hot.

"Hunter, what—?"

"I want to taste you, Sae, all of you."

Sable was delirious, unable to understand his meaning. Yet even as his broad shoulders wedged her legs open, she didn't care, didn't know what he was about until, with her clothing, he pinned her hips against the floor and his mouth covered the apex of her thighs.

A startled gasp poured from her throat. Her fingernails dug into his shoulders. She whimpered. She was dying. That was all there was to it. Nothing could feel this glorious, this wicked.

His tongue flicked across the womanly core of her and she squirmed, the bud hardening beneath his touch. He laved and suckled, drove and nipped, bringing her closer, into him, and her legs trembled. Boldly he drew one over his shoulder, and Sable melted like hot sap onto the wood floor.

His tongue dipped deeper.

"Hunter, Hunter, oh God, please," she panted. "I can't . . . you must stop . . . I want you." Abruptly he covered her with his body, took her mouth with his own, and Sable tasted sweetness, a tang, herself. Anxious hands tore at the buttons of his trousers, her fingers molding his rigid shaft.

"Now. Now!" She jerked open the fabric, releasing, freeing him into her palm.

Hunter shuddered raggedly. "Oh, God!"

Her fingers curled around him, pressing him down to meet her softness.

"Hurry, Hunter."

"I am," he groaned, lifting her up, pulling her pale legs around his waist as Sable guided him into her liquid depths. He growled, low and harsh, but Hunter couldn't take it, not slow, not now, and surged forth, slamming her against the carpet. She gasped at the invading heat, the scrapes to her back, but he didn't stop, withdrawing and thrusting into her hard, plunging over and over. He gripped her buttocks, fingertips digging, stilling her as he took her, frantic and consuming. He chanted her name, his love, what she did to him. Her blood sang. He was vulgar and sexy and it was powerful, more than raw passion, more than his sexual desire for her. It was a loving demand, that she see what he was really like, what he would always be. Barbaric and uncontrolled.

Sable didn't care. She loved him. She loved him any way he was. If only he could see that.

He pounded into her until it was painful, yet Sable accepted him, drawing on his power, clamping him to her soul. Her lips trailed over his face, his throat, tasting sweat and

387

man. Her insides coiled and coiled, a sparkling in her veins, in every pore of her skin, then each separate sensation seemed to gather up in a snug strand, then snap, bursting in a wet explosion. She savored the tight clamping shudder, sinking her teeth into his shoulder as he plunged once more, hard and solid, sending them across the floor. He held her suspended there, his body buried deep inside hers, his hot breath fanning her throat, his seed spilling.

"Ohhh Hunter," she said in a husky moan, holding him, stroking his damp skin, soothing where she'd marred him.

Wrapping his arms around her, he kissed her, thick and deep. Somewhere an owl hooted, a horse stomped. A sudden cool breeze swept their flushed skin, and his grip tightened as he lifted his head to look at her.

"I acted like an animal."

Her lips curved, feline pleased and sexy. "Yes, you most certainly did."

Her smile sent an arrow straight through his heart.

He kissed her, gently this time, savoring the taste of her, cherishing her response. For a long time Hunter simply worried her lips, holding her, and when she succumbed to sleep he carried her to her bed. Tucking her beneath the coverlet, he watched her sink into her dreams, then pressed a last kiss to her cool lips.

She whispered his name, but he was gone.

Chapter Forty-one

Sable stirred from sleep, reaching out to the space beside her, already knowing it would be empty. Curling on her side, his love lingering in the tenderness of her body, she closed her eyes, reliving it—the primitive desperation in his kiss, the harsh declaration of raw passion as if he'd never get enough of her, burning the image of him into her mind and body so she'd never forget. Not that she ever would.

She sighed, snuggled deeper.

Suddenly her eyes snapped open and she sat up. Her heart pounding furiously as she reached for a fresh nighttrail and dressing gown.

He'd come to say goodbye.

A knot swelled in her throat as she cautiously slipped from her room and padded quickly through the silent house. *Oh, Hunter, don't do this, not now.* At the front door she briefly inspected the grounds for guards before slipping outside. Gathering her gown above her knees, she raced across the compound to the stables. *Please be there, please.* Bracing her palm on the wide open door frame and favoring the catch in her side, she stepped into the barn.

His back was to her. He was saddling his horse.

She couldn't move. Every inch of her heart screamed that this wasn't happening. But he was checking the cinch and girth, his packs, the load of his weapons, in the same sequence she'd witnessed a hundred times before. She knew she shouldn't, for less than an hour ago she was certain of his love for her, but now the misgivings—the torturous doubts of her useless life, her ability to be worth more than a parlor ornament—surfaced.

Then he grasped the reins and led the horse from the stall.

Hunter froze when he saw her, silhouetted by the lantern burning behind. The nighttrail and gown hung like a white shroud, yet the firm line of her body shone through the transparent fabric. She looked out of place in the dark musty stable, so delicate, ethereal, the blush of his loving still clinging to her skin. Something jagged and raw moved in his chest.

"How can you make love to me like that and then just abandon me?" Her words whispered on the air, frightened, hurt.

"Jesus, don't look at me like that, Sae." Gravely, strained. "I'm not abandoning you."

"But you have." She rushed to him. "You've already left me," she said in choked voice, flicking a hand to the horse. "Why, Hunter?"

"I have to go home and make a clean slate."

"With who?"

"Me. You. My family. I have to like the man I see in the mirror, Sae."

"I love that man."

"Well, I don't! Look at me." He flung his arms wide. "This is all I am. A pair of colts, a saddlebag, and a broken-down nag."

He didn't have anything to offer her.

No home.

No land.

No start.

But she would take it. She would come to him naked and penniless and if he was a coward, he'd accept it.

"You need a man that can at least give you a roof over your head and a decent meal on the table." He grasped her shoulders, his dark stare holding her motionless. "Darlin', you deserve a life like I saw today, with gowns and jewels—and pride."

"Don't insult me." She wrenched away from him. "What a person has isn't a measure of who he is, Hunter." That he thought her so shallow infuriated her. "And I've never asked you to be anything you're not."

"I know, darlin'." He took a step and she retreated, clearly armed for a battle he wasn't prepared to fight. "But I need to be more than I am." He had to make her understand or he'd crush any hope for a future. "Until you came into my life, I ate, I slept, I talked. I drank. But I wasn't here, Sae—I was just a machine without working parts. No better than dead. And my family believed it. I let them suffer. And I have nothing to show for those years."

"But you don't have to do this alone." Did he not want her to meet them?

"I can't take you with me." Her crestfallen face nailed a hole in his heart and he looked away, the pain telling him he was a fool, that he should steal her away now and never look back, but then he'd never know. It would eat at him, grind him down until it twisted him inside. He'd gone too close to the edge to turn back now. "The debts and obligations, they're mine. It was my responsibility as the eldest son. I could have returned home after the war and help rebuild, but I didn't." He met her teary gaze and his jaw grew tight with anguish. "I have to finish this."

Sable didn't want to risk it. But what could they have if he didn't deal with the last of his demons? The image of a life without him was desolate, lonely. A prison. And he was leaving. Shutting her out. She saw it in his eyes. Nothing she could say would sway him and she refused to use that she might be carrying his child to keep him. Lord. He hadn't even asked her to marry him. He had never spoken of it or indicated he wanted a life with her. Was this his way out of her life?

"What about me?" she said softly, fighting her composure. "What about us?"

A stretch of chilled silence. She had the power to make or break his world, and Hunter struggled with what he was about to do. He knew he was asking a lot, he knew it. She loved him, that he would never doubt, but this need to scrape the past clean for their future was like a disease gnawing at him. Inside he was a mess and didn't think he could get the words out. But they came.

"We have to . . . wait."

Her spirits sank, another thread of her life unraveled. And Sable grasped one more time. "Until when?"

He looked away. "I don't know."

Indefinite. He wouldn't commit to anything, not to her, not to even the vagueness of time. What was she supposed to do while he was on this honor quest, seeking his damn fortune? And why couldn't she go with him? To exclude her now, after all they'd shared, with no promise to hold, was a cut so deep anger surged ahead of her hurt.

"And what if I'm not here?"

His head snapped up, his features yanking taught. The breeze swirled into the adobe barn swirling hay at her feet and the gown against her legs and Hunter thought he'd died again.

"If you can't include me in your life," she said furiously, "then don't expect me to stitch samplers until you feel good enough to come love me again." She strode up to him. "The man I love I met in the mountains, not the one you used to be, Hunter." She grasped the reins and jammed them into his hand. "Go. Find out if they still want their son. They will, you know. The way home is easier than you think, Hunter. Let your life hinge on someone else's acceptance. I won't."

She felt herself crumbling into a thousand crazy pieces as she turned and strode out the door.

Hunter thought he saw a breath of hesitation when she

reached the horse pen, but she kept going, taking off into a dead run.

She was gone.

Her parting words pulled the hay dusted floor out from beneath him.

She wouldn't wait.

His gaze shifted wood box next to the tack and Hunter knew Dugal kept a bottle there.

He wanted a drink.

If ever in his life he wanted one, it was now.

He didn't know how long he stared at the empty space of the livery doors before he mustered the nerve to lead his horse outside. He couldn't bring himself to watch her run from him, away from him and kept his head down as he crossed the parade grounds, fighting the emotion swelling in his chest.

Taking a deep breath, he signalled the guard. He'd received special permission to leave the fort. Maitland was likely glad he was out of his sight, glad to be no longer haunted by the evidence of his mistakes. The gate swung open, so slow it sounded like wood breaking. It was open, waiting for him to go through.

God, this hurts.

He took a step. A sound drew him around. She stood several few away, one trembling hand covering her mouth, the other clutching her gowns out of the dirt. And in that instant he saw her greatest fear: that she'd never see him again. In three strides he was there, grasping her shoulders and hauling her against him.

"You're mine," he growled fiercely. "And I'll find you. No matter where you are, how far you go, I will find you!" Suddenly he crushed her in his embrace, kissing her once, hard and savage and thick with his love. "I love you. Believe in me a little longer, Sae." His desperate words brushed her lips, gray eyes clouded. "Trust me."

Do you love him enough to allow him his dignity, a voice asked her, *to forgive him this opportunity to make peace with himself and come to you clean of his past?*

"I do, I do," she sobbed into his mouth, her hands scrubbing over his shoulders, his chest, up his throat to cup his jaw. Her body jerked, moans of her heart's crushing pain filling the air around them. "I love you," she whispered and he pulled her hands from his face and set her from him. Without a word, he strode to his horse, swung up into his saddle, then slipped around the half-open gate.

Sable remained there, her feet sinking into the mud, her breath caught in her chest until the sound of hoofbeats faded. She forced herself to turn away, yet as the doors shut, sealing him from her, Sable's heart shattered again, a thousand razor sharp wedges floating within her breast, jabbing her, reminder of what she'd lost, lest she ever forget. She covered her face with her hands and wept. She swore it would be for the last time.

It wasn't.

Chapter Forty-two

In the dark, the coins falling from her hands sounded like chimes as Sable paid the horse trader, then promptly grabbed the reins and swung up onto the roan's back. Holding out her hand, Lane followed suit, wedging her satchel between them. Sable knew that inside the worn carpetbag were clothes Lane had painstakingly made for her infant son, to keep her sanity. Kneeing the beast, the pair charged off into the night, leaving the fort behind.

The purple-gray haze of dawn scarcely broke the horizon when Sable dismounted beneath a cottonwood tree. Lane, not used to the hours in the saddle, was slower, yet her anxiety couldn't be contained and she paced, stretching sore muscles as they waited. And waited.

"Are you certain he'll be here?"

"As certain as I can after three weeks." Sable scanned the are for encroaching troopers, praying their departure hadn't alerted anyone. Dugal, bless him, had sneaked them out in the back of a trader's wagon and she hoped the kindly Scot didn't pay for his aid. Sable picked up a stone and threw it. He'd done it because of his friendship with Hunter. Her eyes burned hot, a hard pain grinding in her chest. Hunter. She kept her teary gaze on the horizon, pushing the hurt down and concentrating.

Her sister passed before her again.

"Sit down, Laney, you're making me nervous."

"I can't help it. I miss him so much."

"I also have missed your presence, fire of my heart."

Lane spun about. "Black Wolf," she gasped, her eyes brimming with tears.

Sable rose slowly, dusting her hands on the seat of her pants.

They stood close, yet not touching. Black Wolf's dark eyes searched Lane's features with such intensity, Sable felt it.

"Is this how you greet your husband?" he said softly, and Lane launched herself into his arms. He crushed her to him, raining kisses over her face and throat, proclaiming his love as he fitted her body to his. When the welcome became too amourous, Sable cleared her throat.

"Little Hawk?" Lane asked breathlessly.

"He cries for his mother." Black Wolf left her to pull his mount forward from the shadows. Lane squealed, yanking the cradle board free and clutching her son. She dropped to the ground, sobbing, rocking, and it took her husband to pull her to her feet. She leaned into him, dividing kisses between her man and her boy. Sable silently cried for their happiness.

"My thanks, Violet Eyes," Black Wolf said, his arms around his family.

"Violet Eyes?" Lane said, a little jealously.

Black Wolf sent her a patient smile. "It is what Standing Cougar called her."

Sable's heart leapt, and she stepped closer. "Have you seen him?" She was terrified he'd gone to the cabin.

Black Wolf frowned, confused. "He is not in the hills, little one." He looked down at Lane, his gaze caressing her upturned face. "And he's a fool to let you out of his arms."

Sable nodded mutely, staring at her boots, envy clawing at her. She felt empty and cheated and alone. It was unfair that Lane—no, she wouldn't resent her sister's happiness because her own had vanished. Yet hourly she warred between going after him or swearing to turn him away for hurting her like

396

this, but dignity and her love for him forbade either. All she had left was hope, and it wasn't much to live on.

Her head jerked up at the sound of hoofbeats, and when she made to warn her sister, Black Wolf had already mounted his gray stallion, his wife and son nestled before him.

"Go. It's Papa! Go quickly!"

Black Wolf didn't hesitate and wheeled around. Lane's hand reached out, stretched in thanks to her sister. Sable smiled as they rode to safety.

"Lane!" Richard shouted as he met their hiding place. He drew his weapon. "Lane!"

"Papa! Don't!" Sable screamed, throwing herself at his horse and grabbing his arm before he could take aim. Richard turned tortured eyes on his youngest. "They're *married*," she said in panicked rush. "They are a family, Papa, a *family.*"

Boldly Black Wolf halted his mount and turned, facing Richard's gun.

"I can't let her—" Richard struggled in her grasp, but she held tight.

"Don't destroy her last chance at happiness. Look at her, Papa. Lane *isn't* Mama." Richard's eyes narrowed sharply. "She loves him." Her voice thickened, her nails digging into his arm. "He would die for her, Papa. Isn't that what you wanted for us? The deepest love. Don't do this. Please."

Slowly Richard relaxed and holstered the gun. Only then did Sable let go. He dismounted. Hesitating beside his horse, he gripped the pommel, then pushed away and walked out into the sunlight. The morning air was moist and warming. Sable clenched her fists at her sides as the men did no more than stare at each other from across the flat ground.

Then Richard lifted his arm. Sable inhaled sharply, taking a step, thinking he'd drawn his weapon again, but instead he raised it high above his head and simply waved.

Black Wolf raised his arm in salute. Lane clutched her baby and waved before the Sioux warrior whirled about and rode off.

"I'll never see her again, will I?" Richard said, lowering his arm, his gaze refusing to let go.

"Don't be too certain. Lane won't allow Little Hawk to forget he's a Cavanaugh."

"Perhaps," he said with a grim smile, then met her gaze. "At least I still have you, Pumpkin."

Sable's heart cracked again, hopelessness flooding in. "Yes, Papa," she said with a searching glance at the open terrain. "I guess you do."

Andrew McCracken frowned as the dust cloud moved toward him with increasing speed. Leaving his chair, he tossed aside the bridle he'd been repairing and squinted against the sun, straining to identify the rider. The visitor neared and Andrew's face rapidly drained of color, his features lax with shock.

"Charlotte! Charlotte! Come quick!" he shouted, then called for his wife again as he strode off the porch and out into the yard.

A woman, still shapely for her fifty-odd years, tucked strands of gray and blonde hair back into a bun as she hurried down the steps to her husband's side, yet half way she froze and watched as the rider stopped and dismounted.

"Hunter?" Andrew exchanged a look with his wife as the man walked closer.

"Hunter, honey—is that you?" Charlotte asked in a scared whisper.

The man doffed his hat and swiped sweat with the back of his arm, nervously turning the Stetson over in his hands before he lifted his head. His gaze locked with his father's and his breath caught. He'd caused them so much heartache, been away so long, he didn't know what to expect.

"Hello, Momma, Pa."

With a shriek, Charlotte ran to him and Hunter opened his arms to her, clutching her tightly. She babbled about loving him and being afraid and how come he never wrote and what changed his mind, all in one breathless rush. An instant later he felt his father's arms clench around them both, then the shout of his name, an second later the near toppling impact of his brothers.

Hunter squeezed his eyes shut, touching them, feeling their love and tears and anger with him all at once.

"Is there room for a peanut in there?"

Hunter looked up to see his kid sister shyly standing by and the family made space for one more. Hunter's heart filled swiftly, pushing out the regret and apprehension.

"Welcome home, lad. God love you, welcome home.

With his hand on his father's shoulder, his arm around his mother, Hunter let them lead him up to the house.

"Welcome back, Mister Hunter," a ranch hand said, waving a coiled rope.

"Good to see you fit, sir," another said, tipping his hat, then riding out on to McCracken lands.

"Knew those stories weren't true," another added, then went back to his duties. Hunter was stunned. Sable was right: the way home was easier than he imagined.

"You look thin," his mother scolded.

"Aw, Momma," he said, smiling. No one mentioned his tears.

"Her name is Sable, you know."

Andrew frowned at his wife. "What?"

She didn't look up and continued stitching the shirt as the constant crack of hammer to nail rang across the flat land to where she sat beneath the tree.

"I heard him call her name in his sleep."

"You were watching him sleep, Charlotte?" Pipe halfway to his mouth, he sent her a chiding look. "He's a grown man. It isn't right."

"I know, but I keep thinking I'll wake up and it will all be a dream and he won't be here," her voice broke yet her stitches were smooth and rhythmic. "And I'll worry over him again, imagining the danger of being up in those mountain, alone, so guilty and angry and—" Tears failed her voice and Andrew leaned over, pulling his wife into his arms. She sighed, resting her head on his chest.

"I know. Me, too, Char."

"I hate to see him suffer."

"Who is she? Did you ask?"

"I don't dare. Sometimes, when he thinks no one is looking, I see such regret in his eyes, and I want to hold him like he was a little boy and not a grown man." She toyed with the button of his shirt, pushing back the tears. "What can we do, Andy?"

"Love him, Char, just love him."

"Who is she, lad?" Andrew asked, and Hunter paused in hammering a nail.

"Sable Cavanaugh." He slammed the hammer down, the crack ringing like a pistol shot.

"You just going to let her be? Is that the way of it?"

"Yes. No. Hell, I don't know."

Hunter sighed, tossed the hammer aside, then dropped down beside his father. Pulling a rag from his back pocket, he wiped at the sweat on his face and neck.

"I left her. She told me she loved me, healed me, and then I left her."

"And you have the gall to think she'll to wait for you?" Andrew snorted. "Did you think you may have left her with your child?" Hunter flushed, the truth spreading across his face. "Here I thought all those years in the mountains had given you some brains."

Hunter cast his father a side glance. "Evidently not."

"She love you?"

"Yes."

Andrew was satisfied with his son's confidence.

"Sable showed me what I was, what I'd become and

what'd I'd be if I remained in the past. I would have never come down from the hills if it wasn't for her."

"And now?"

Hunter hung his head and whispered, "I'm dying down here without her." He snatched up a nail, tossed it once, then clutched it tight. "I've made so many mistakes, Pa. I had to clear the air with my family before I could ask her to marry me."

Andrew groaned. He hadn't even managed to propose before he left this woman!

"I had to know I could do it without her, be back here, with people. I'd been in the mountains so long I forgot how to even hold a civil conversation."

Andrew nodded sagely. "Do you remember that wolf cub you found? You were about six or seven." Hunter nodded, lips curving with memory. "You raised him and he was a gentle, loving pup."

"Damn beast used to drag me out of bed to feed him."

Andrew chuckled.

"Then you made me let him go."

"He was a creature of nature, needed to be with his own kind."

"Still, it hurt. It took me along time to forget about him."

"But he didn't forget about you. He came back with his kin, wild, a meat-eater and a leader of his pack, but when he caught your scent, he knew where he was raised."

Hunter smiled faintly, remembering the silver furred beast, how his long scratchy tongue lapped at his face.

"That hairy creature rolled around in the dirt with you and played and ate from your dish and obeyed your commands."

Hunter frowned. "If there's a lesson in this tale, I'm not getting it."

Andrew scowled. "By God but you're still the stubbornest, most hard-headed Scot I've ever known! He didn't forget how he was raised. Even though he lived in the wild, killed to survive, when he wanted to come home, needed to, it was the

401

same. And he knew it would be. That animal never doubted he'd be loved. And accepted."

Like they had him, easily, freely. "But this wasn't his home."

"No, that's with his mate."

"And he left *with* her," Hunter mused.

Andrew clapped a hand on his son's back, rubbing roughly. "Ahh, I see you're smartin' up on me already."

Hunter tossed the nail aside with a snap of his wrist, and stared at the vast stretch of golden land before him. This was the home of his childhood, of innocent memories, before his past had shaped him into the man he was. But now his life was with Sable.

"It's been a while, months. I know she loved me once, but wanting me back in her life after all the pain and grief I've caused her is another matter entirely."

"She will."

Hunter's lips twisted in a wry smile as his father stood and stretched. "You're certain."

"Smart woman, your Sable. She brought you back to us. I love her already."

"God, so do I."

"Then get off your butt, Hunter Delmahoy McCracken, and finish this house." He leaned down in Hunter's face, shoving the hammer in his son's hand. "That is why you're building it, aren't you—for her?"

Hunter glanced over his shoulder at the partially constructed home. It faced the sunset, had a river to its back and land for miles around. It's what she wanted, and he had never told her, never remembered that he owned such a perfect place to love and grow old with her.

He stood and tossed the hammer aside.

"Aren't you going to finish?" Andrew asked with raised brows as his son strode determinedly to the supply wagon.

"Nope," he said climbing onto the seat and taking up the reins. "I've waited long enough to start living." He snapped the leather, praying she'd forgive him for being such a fool.

Chapter Forty-three

Sable smiled so hard she thought her face would crack and excused herself from the fawning presence of a young, very green and eager lieutenant. Mercy, their intentions were so blatantly obvious and demeaning. She threatened to slap the next man that kept his gaze on her bosom instead of her face when he spoke to her.

She hadn't expected this night to be any different, the people to be any different, but as a favor to her father she'd arranged this party.

That didn't mean she had to stay.

Nodding to the guests, she wove her way between senators and their elegantly clad wives and daughters, young officers and aged troopers. More brass shining than in a bell factory, she thought with a small smile.

"I heard she slept in the wild like those savages, with some awful mountain man," a woman whispered as she passed.

Sable paused, then backed up a step. Without looking at the gossipper, she said, "I daresay we didn't sleep much." She snatched a canape from a passing waiter's silver tray. "Ought to try it some time, Louella—might take some starch out of that bustle," then she popped the morsel in her mouth and continued across the polished dance floor, her burgundy velvet skirts whispering quiet elegance.

She had to give them something to sink their teeth into, she thought, stopping before her father. "Your guests seem well entertained, Papa." Her short laugh was brittle. "And I need to return to the restaurant."

General Cavanaugh frowned with concern. He'd hoped arranging this gala celebrating his promotion and appointment to the War Department would have brought her out for some socializing, but she didn't appear to be enjoying herself. She'd rather be working! Working! Richard knew she hadn't allowed herself a moment's pleasure since returning from the Lakotas. She drove herself, never speaking of that time, nor of Hunter. Ought to seek the man out and demand answers, he thought, having an idea of what went on between them, but he knew it wouldn't gain him what he truly wanted: Sable's happiness. *Ah, Caroline, I'd give anything to erase the haunted look on our daughter's face. This is my fault—again. If I hadn't turned our grandbaby away she wouldn't be this unhappy.*

"Do you really have to leave, Pumpkin?" he asked, grasping her hand. "All your friends are here, wanting a visit with you."

Her gaze swept the crowd of party goers, unwillingly searching for the tall dark figure that never appeared. "They aren't my friends, Papa. Not any longer." She craved the open country, to wear pants and ride a horse hell bent for leather, to sleep under a blanket of stars and fill her lungs with fresh air—clean, sweet, green-smelling air.

And she ached for Hunter. A tight lump formed in her throat at the mere thought of him and she clung to his promise to find her. "I don't belong here anymore."

A captain appeared to her right, asking for a dance and for a brief moment Sable's heart skipped a beat, his coloring so like Hunter's her legs wobbled.

No, he was Captain Alexander Masters.

Her grip tightened on her father's hand and she whispered, "This is the last dance. Then I'm leaving, Papa," in a firm voice before allowing the captain to lead her to the center of the floor.

Sable didn't feel anything, not the strong touch of the man holding her, nor the soft lilting music. Some nights, alone in her bed, she could kick herself for letting Hunter leave. But he had to come back free of his past. It had been more than four months with no word, and her hopes were nearly gone, without even his child growing within her. So lonely. *Believe in me a little longer,* he said, *trust me.* And she would. She would!

The captain murmured something to her, and she looked up into his handsome face.

"I understand this celebration is all your doing, Miss Cavanaugh?"

"Yes," she said with a sigh. "Are you enjoying yourself, sir?"

"I am now." The comment was lost on her, and his interest increased. "I've dined in your restaurant. Very nice, excellent fare."

She smiled, warming to her favorite subject. "It isn't mine. I simply manage it for now. Signore Vaccarello owns it."

"But the elegant changes I've seen could only be your touch."

"Guilty as charged, sir." She looked away, concentrating on the swift steps of the waltz.

"You aren't happy, are you, Miss Cavanaugh?"

Her gaze snapped to the captain and she was about to reprimand him for being so presumptuous, then sighed wearily. "Not entirely," she admitted.

"I'll assume only a man could make you disinterested in parties? Ahh, don't look at me like that, I meant no offense." She could kill a man with those purple eyes. After a long moment he added in a low husky voice, "He was a fool to let you out of his sight."

Sable laughed, short and without pleasure. "So I've been told. Perhaps someone should remind him?"

He whirled her across the floor with practiced grace. "What? And ruin my chances?"

She smiled at his flirting. "You've already ruined your reputation by dancing with me—or was it a reputation you were hoping to gain?"

His grin said he was amused at her attempt to put him off and drew her a bit closer. "There isn't a man in this room that wouldn't give his right arm to be in my shoes." She was mysterious, beautiful, and no man had the power to affect her.

"You're a horrible liar, Captain."

The ringing clash of hoofbeats on marble startled the guests, stirring curiosity and escalating noisy speculation as everyone looked toward the open doors. The music faltered. Dancers stilled. The clatter ceased, instantly replaced by the thump of angry footsteps. Sable glanced at her scowling dancing partner, then to the foyer.

"Sable!" came the bellow.

Her heart slammed against the wall of her ribs with such impact she gasped, "Hunter!", her gaze absorbing every detail as he passed through the archway and moved across the wide ballroom like a panther, lithe and masculine, his body covered in fringed buckskins, sweat, and grime. Knee boots thumped, tracking mud, the wicked knife strapped to his thigh winking with each flex of corded muscle. The pair of Colts rocked low on lean hips as he barreled back into her life the way he'd first arrived—hard-bitten, trail dirty and determined.

She pressed her palm to her chest to be certain she still breathed as he stopped before her and tipped his battered Stetson back a fraction.

"I told you I'd find you."

A day's worth of beard darkened his features, and he looked tired and worried, a savagery lingering in his eyes, just beneath the surface.

"I never doubted it."

Alex's gaze shot between the couple and he smiled, gesturing to the orchestra to continue as he walked away, resigning himself to never having had a chance with Sable Cavanaugh, much as he wanted one.

Hunter didn't say another word and swept her into his embrace and into the steps of the dance. His entire body came alive the moment he set eyes on her and the days of non-stop riding without sleep, living on jerky and trail dust and the hope that she still loved him, was worth just one moment to be close to her. Yet seeing her in the arms of another man sent jealousy raging through him. He clamped it down and reminded himself that a vibrant woman like Sable couldn't be expected to crawl in a hole and wait. She said she wouldn't. Hell, she had a job, owned a home, and answered to no one, disproving any fanciful notions he might have had.

"Aren't you going to tell me I stink?"

"I've grown accustomed to the aroma," she murmured, her gaze moving over his features with loving familiarity. He's cut his hair, she thought stupidly, her eyes misting.

"How have you been, Violet Eyes?" he whispered, close to her ear.

She closed her eyes and let his deep husky voice coat her. "Fine, Hunter," she managed. "And you?"

"God damn miserable." Her eyes flashed open. "Rotten, lonely, sick of my own lousy company." Her lips curved and his hopes soared at the small gesture. "Now, how did I know that would please you."

Her smile fell with his heart. "Your pain never pleased me, Hunter, never."

"Aw, darlin', I always knew that." This was his one chance to get her back and if he failed, he'd die. They stared, not hearing the music, not seeing the guests, only each other, only the slim thread between happiness and utter desolation. "I love you, Sable."

"Please, don't say that."

His heart screamed to a halt. "Why?"

"Because I couldn't bear it if you aren't willing to share with me, Hunter, *really share* and not dismiss me from your life." Her gaze dropped to his chest and she struggled with her emotions.

"I didn't want to leave you, Sae."

"But you did, and it hurt." She looked up, her voice breaking. "It still hurts."

"I'm sorry." It sounded pathetic and he wished she would slap him or scream, do anything to make him feel like he wasn't a total idiot. But she didn't and he admitted, "I was a fool. You were right—going home was easy. But it didn't make one wit of difference, because it wasn't enough."

"Really?"

That was an *I told you so*, if he ever heard one. "Yeah, well, you know how God damn hard-headed I am."

"Yes, you are, and you swear far too often."

"Will you keep reminding me?" She stopped, held tightly in his gaze. Dancers whirled around them, music swelled, and Hunter said, "I know after all this time I don't have the right to ask—"

"Ask." She wasn't going to chance a thing by hiding in past hurts. "Ask, Hunter."

"Do you still love me?"

"Yes." Breathless with conviction.

Hunter's eyes burned. The lump in his throat swelled to near strangling. He swallowed it down and didn't care if he sounded pleading.

"Marry me, Sae?"

"Yes." She stepped closer, closer than was proper. She didn't care, her heart was light and bursting. "Kiss me, Hunter, please."

He grinned, the corners of his eyes crinkling, and he came dangerously close to disgracing himself with tears. "This is my Sable asking me to molest her, here in front of everyone?"

"If you don't hurry," she gripped his lapels, "I'll molest *you*."

"Jesus," he groaned, wrapping both arms around her waist

408

and molding her to his body. "Get a woman in the wild a few weeks and she loses all inhibitions."

"Damn shameful, isn't it?" she murmured before his mouth crashed down on hers. Several older women gasped in outrage, men looked discreetly away, hiding a smile, and young girls sighed with feminine envy; for the kiss was smooth and deep and wildly heart-wrenching. And in it Hunter and Sable experienced a fresh awakening, a cleansing as their love fountained and poured, soothing tired lonely souls.

General Cavanaugh strode across the room, trying to look displeased.

"I hope you realize what this open display with my daughter means?" he said when he came to them.

Hunter slowly drew back, not taking his eyes from Sable's as he brushed his thumb across her kiss-swollen lips.

"It means I love her," he said, his deep resonant voice rolling around the quiet room. "I love her," he repeated, sweeping her up in his arms. "And you'd better find a preacher, General," he tossed the order as he walked to the doors. "Tonight."

Over Hunter's shoulder Richard met his daughter's teary gaze. "Well, Papa," she waved to get him going, "put a fire under it!"

Hunter threw his head back and laughed, the rich joyous sound vibrating throughout the mansion, mingling between the shocked guests and making a romantic traitor out of the coldest of hearts.

Epilogue

"Oh, Papa, how could you let him get into that?" Sable scolded, wiping her hands on a dishtowel then slapping it over her shoulder as she hurried down the steps toward her son. "Oh, honestly. One would think a man of your caliber would have enough sense!"

Hunter stepped around the edge of the porch at the sound of her voice, then leaned against the rail support, smothering a laugh at the reproachful look she sent her father. Chastised again.

In the bright sunlight, Sable bent to lift little Jamie from the oozing mud puddle.

"Aw, let him alone, Pumpkin," Richard pleaded, stopping her. "He's having such fun."

"But I wanted him to look nice, at least until dinner."

"He will, I promise." General Cavanaugh hefted his grandson onto his lap, mud and all. The fifteen-month-old baby smeared black muck across his grandpa's chin and giggled. "We'll both be ready for inspection before you ring the dinner bell, ma'am." He dropped a kiss to the boy's dark head, and her father and her son gave her such pitiful pleading looks, Sable threw her hands up in resignation and turned back toward the house. Hunter grabbed her arm as she passed.

A wordless message crackled between them and she moved closer.

"How can I have you this near, all day, and still miss you?" he asked lowly, ducking his head.

Before his lips met their target a feminine voice called from the house.

"Sable, dear, the turkey is about done. Would you care to check?"

Hunter groaned. Sable sighed, disappointed. "Coming, Charlotte." She gave her husband an apologetic smile. "It appears I'm needed."

"Yeah, you sure the hell are," he growled, looking her up and down, pausing to feast on the lush sight of her bosom nearly spilling from the blue gown.

"Why Hunter McCracken, that look is positively indecent."

"I know." He sent her a lecherous grin. "Is it getting me anywhere?" The call came again and she reluctantly stepped back and hurried into the house. Damn his mother, Hunter thought.

"Be patient, son, we'll all be gone soon."

Hunter snapped around from where he'd been studying the sway of Sable's hips as she moved up the stairs and into the house, to Richard.

"Sorry." His skin brightened faintly. "Shows, huh?" Hunter knelt down to mix mud with his dirty little boy.

"Yes, and I'm damn glad."

"I second that." Hunter's silver-haired father strode across the dry lawn from the corral. "You've got a fine herd, son," Andrew gestured back over his shoulder, "and those wild mustangs are prize winners too! Damn handsome stock. Did you snare them yourself, or—"

"Sable and I did." Hunter glanced up, grinning at their stunned looks. "Guess who broke the big gray?"

"Papa! Papa!" Arms outstretched, his baby boy puckered his lips for kiss and his father obliged instantly, his heart blooming with love.

Richard blinked, his gaze shooting to the horse pen and back to Hunter. "And you *let* her climb on a wild horse?"

411

Hunter snorted, sending a skeptical look to his father-in-law as he straightened. "When did I ever have a choice? She did it the middle of the night, anyway. I woke to that monster," he nodded to the gray beast prancing the dirt, "bellowing his lungs out in protest."

"You sound displeased, Hunter," Andrew said. "Male pride a bit wounded?"

"Nah," he answered easily. "Sable's gouged my masculinity enough in the past—I could care less now." His sly look said he enjoyed her bluntness. "I was afraid she'd get hurt, that's all."

"Well, I'd never climb one of those filthy beasts," Camille said airily as she met the group relaxing in the warm sun. The blonde woman was flanked by her twin brothers, looking like a sparkling diamond between dark chunks of coal.

Hunter tweeked his baby sister on the nose. "God save us all if anyone let you loose on one, peanut. You're dangerous enough with that prissy little buggy."

Camille stuck her tongue out at her oldest brother. "Fat lot you know about anything, Hunter. It's a *Jenny Lind*. And the very thing for a lady to drive," she said, sweeping past as male laughter erupted.

"Oh God! She isn't going to help in the kitchen, is she?" Lucas said, looking aghast at his twin.

"Should we check?" Ian wondered.

"Hell, yeah! Remember what happened the last time she tried cooking?"

Ian groaned, unconsciously rubbing his stomach. He'd been sick for days after that fiasco.

"Leave her be, you two," Andrew warned, his stern look turning devilish, "or I'll tell her all about the time the pair of you got caught playing doctor with—"

"I give. Come on, little brother," Lucas said, throwing his arm over his twin's shoulder. "Let's see if our sister-in-law's talents will rub off on Camy. God knows she needs the help."

Hunter met Richard's soft smile.

"She's grown in so many ways," Richard said needlessly.

412

"We both have." Hunter looked down at his son, who was busy slapping mud on his boots in neat piles, then on his father's. Happiness beamed from every fiber of Hunter's tall form and he knew he'd never tire of the peaceful sensation. He laughed easily, his temper was tampered, his lust not, and the nightmares came less frequently, stretching to months apart. He hadn't taken a drink in over two years. But to have his family here, in his home, with his son—his son!—playing at his feet and a woman like Sable holding his heart was a dream he never dared imagine.

A lump formed in his throat and he turned sharply toward the house when Sable's laughter spilled from the open doors. He smiled wide, ridiculously pleased to hear it, and the elders exchanged grins brimming with parental satisfaction.

Hunter gave his son a kiss on his muddy cheek, then headed off toward the back of the house, determined to seduce his wife when it appeared no one would let him.

In the warm kitchen Sable dusted the flour from her fingertips. "I'll get the stewed peaches," she said, heading for the pantry, then paused to scold, "Gently, Camille, roll gently. Think of biscuit dough as—um, as delicate Chinese silk, very fragile. Hold the iron too long, it will burn, roll the dough too hard and it will be tough as saddle leather."

Camille nodded, trying valiantly to adhere to the lessons but she truly wasn't interested. Christopher Swift had arrived a moment ago and she wanted a chance to flirt with the handsome lawyer, show him she'd grown up since they'd last seen each other.

"She's never ironed a day in her life," Lucas said, leaning against the door jam, munching on an apple.

"I don't think she even knows what one looks like, to be honest," Ian put in.

"Lucas, Ian, outside, please," Charlotte said in a nononsense tone, "and take your sister with you." Camille was

413

through the kitchen doorway before her mother could finish the sentence.

Sable laughed. "That was me a few years ago."

"It isn't polite to lie, Sable," Ian said, following his brother out.

She blinked owlishly. "But I'm not!"

Charlotte waved, telling her to forget trying to convince men of anything. "You aren't upset, are you?"

Sable laughed. "About Camille wanting to be in the company of a handsome bachelor instead of flour and dirty dishes?"

Charlotte laughed lightly as Sable turned to the pantry. Stepping into the darkness, she found herself wrapped in a pair of strong familiar arms.

"Hunter," she breathed, sinking into his embrace.

"Seems to be the only way I can get you alone. And now that I have you . . ."

"Yes." Anticipating, greedy.

His mouth found hers in the dark, his kiss deep and heavy with suppressed need. He loved his family, was glad they were here, but a man could take only so much togetherness. Next house will have thicker walls, he thought, filling his palms with the satin-clad flesh of her breasts. She moaned the way that drove him mad, leaned into him and kissed him wildly. It was always good and fresh with Sable. Pleasures of the flesh were new and exciting—love did that. It was as if no one had come before her, and in his heart, no one ever had.

"I want you badly, Sae," he whispered into her ear before he kissed her there.

"Do tell," she purred, dropping her head back, letting him nibble and lick anything he desired for she wished more than he to be alone and naked with him. Her hands slipped between them, cupping bulge in his trousers. "Oh, Hunter, is that for me?" Her husky growl nearly undid him, and when she rubbed him with increasing pressure, Hunter wanted to toss up her skirts and have her right there—in front of the apple butter and corn meal.

414

"Damn. I can't wait." He buried his face between the deep swells of her breasts. "I'm taking you out for a ride right after supper." His chuckle was a dark and lusty promise against the skin of her breasts as he tugged her bodice lower.

"If you're finished molesting your wife, Hunter dear," Sable gasped and Hunter lifted his head from her bosom. "Would you pass me the peaches?"

His expression was sheepish as he reached behind his wife and handed his mother a mason jar.

"Thank you, son. Carry on," Charlotte waved cheerily.

"I'll try, Momma. I promise."

"Hunter!" Sable punched him in the side.

"You're about as red as those pickled beets, woman." He nodded toward the jars.

"As well I should be. Imagine what your mother must think!"

"She thinks I love you."

Sable melted every time he said it. And he said it often. Looping her arms around his neck, she kissed him, slowly, a sensual answer to his declaration. They remained in the pantry, lips molding, bodies pressing breast to chest, hip to hip, when the sudden silence of the ranch hit them.

Hunter frowned. "Something's up."

They left the kitchen and headed for the front door, Sable checking her appearance as she followed her husband.

Outside on the grass Hunter's family stood staring out onto the McCracken lands. Christopher Swift sat beside Camille on the porch swing, an odd look on his face as he gaged the young blonde's reaction. Sable's eyes shifted from her father's shocked expression to follow the direction of his gaze.

Two figures on horseback rode gradually close, their pace slow, apprehensive.

"Indians," Camille said, fear brightening her eyes.

"My daughter," Richard said, coming to his feet.

Richard walked slowly toward the riders.

"Lane," Sable said breathlessly, stepping off the porch to join him.

Hunter caught her arm. "Let him greet them alone, darlin'. This is a big step."

Sable nodded and Hunter wrapped an arm around her waist, watching as Richard approached the couple.

Lane dismounted and stood before her father. They stared at each other for a brief moment before Richard gathered her in his arms. It was then they saw the baby strapped to her back. Lane removed the cradle board, then freed the child, handing him to her father. He must have mentioned Jamie for she looked directly at her sister and smiled.

Richard handed the infant back to his mother, then turned toward Black Wolf.

The warrior remained in the saddle, staring down at his wife's father. Richard held his hand out and Black Wolf accepted it. He didn't smile but reached behind himself and pulled Little Hawk from the horse's back, settling the boy on his lap. Black Wolf spoke to his son, gesturing to Richard and then Lane.

Even across the open land all could hear in clear English, the glad cry of, "Grandpa!" as the boy launched himself into Richard's arms. Lane looked up at Black Wolf and the warrior sent her an approving smile.

Richard held the boy tightly, kissing him, talking to him, stroking his hair until he squirmed to be let down. Black Wolf slid from the stallion's back, clasping his wife's hand as the toddler ran unabashedly toward the ranch.

Richard discreetly wiped at his eyes and followed Lane and her husband.

"Oh, Hunter," Sable said, leaning against him. "Do you really think he can forget the past?"

"It's not as hard as you think, darlin'." He looked down at his wife, brushing his thumb over her lips, his eyes shouting his love for her. "When you know there's a future."